Depraved Indifference

Depraved
Indifference

Robert K. Tanenbaum

NAL BOOKS

NEW AMERICAN LIBRARY

A DIVISION OF PENGUIN BOOKS USA INC., NEW YORK
PUBLISHED IN CANADA BY
PENGUIN BOOKS CANADA LIMITED, MARKHAM, ONTARIO

Copyright © 1989 by Robert K. Tanenbaum

All rights reserved. For information address New American Library.

Published simultaneously in Canada by Penguin Books Canada Limited.

NAL BOOKS TRADEMARK REG. U.S. PAT. OFF. AND FOREIGN COUNTRIES
REGISTERED TRADEMARK—MARCA REGISTRADA
HECHO EN DRESDEN, TN

SIGNET, SIGNET CLASSIC, MENTOR, ONYX, PLUME, MERIDIAN
and NAL BOOKS are published *in the United States* by New American Library,
a division of Penguin Books USA Inc.,
1633 Broadway, New York, New York 10019,
in Canada by Penguin Books Canada Limited,
2801 John Street, Markham, Ontario L3R 1B4

Library of Congress Cataloging-in-Publication Data

Tanenbaum, Robert.
  Depraved indifference / Robert K. Tanenbaum.
    p.   cm.
  ISBN 0-453-00679-5
  I. Title.
PS3570.A52D47   1989
813'.54—dc20   89–9259
                                                                   CIP

First Printing, September, 1989

1 2 3 4 5 6 7 8 9

PRINTED IN THE UNITED STATES OF AMERICA

For the memory and exemplary life of courage and compassion of Ruth Hitzig Tanenbaum, my mother, and as always for Patty.

ACKNOWLEDGMENTS

Special thanks to my friend, confidant, soulmate, scribe, and cousin, Michael Gruber, without whom this manuscript could not have been completed.

1

THEY DIDN'T FIT the profiles. That's why they breezed through security at LaGuardia, past the two guards, the X-ray machines, and the metal detectors. The guards were looking for Arabs or Cubans, single, nervous men, or groups of nervous young people. Fanatics. Not an old guy who had to be over sixty-five. Not a couple of averages, both middle-aged and medium height. The fourth guy was young but an obvious lunkhead, muscles all over, with a big goofy smile. And not the woman, either: pale skin, blue eyes, blond, a straight little nose. A toothpaste ad.

Besides, it was a flight to Milwaukee, not one of your usual terrorist destinations, and not watched like the Miami flights and the internationals. The five of them were clean on the electronics, too; well, maybe not squeaky clean, because they could have had anything in that gift box they were carrying in the Macy's bag. But it was the end of the shift (they thought of that too, it turned out) and the guards were bleary from deciphering dim shapes on the scope.

The five sat together in the rearmost row of the 727, the old man and the woman sitting together and the three other men across the aisle. The group had stowed their packages in the overhead compartments or under their seats, as required by federal law.

The flight attendant doing her seatbelt and oxygen mask routine in the rear section noticed nothing remarkable about the group, except that the three men sitting together were looking at her with unusual interest. Maybe they were on their first flight, she thought. Or maybe they were the kind of passenger who regarded stews as high-altitude geishas. As the plane began to roll toward its runway, the flight attendant finished her demo and walked crisply up the aisle. As she did, the old man said something in a foreign language—Russian?—to the three other men. Whatever it was, it cracked them up. Rough laughter joined the sound of the accelerating engines. Flight 501 took off on schedule and headed west. It was 10:05 on September 10, 1976.

Milo Rukovina had laughed along with the others, as he always did, although the joke was on him. "Milo," Djordje had said, "if you want to pee, use the little bag behind the seat, not your pants." Yes, he had wet his pants when they planted the bomb in the train station locker, but he had told Macek that he had to go before they left the shop. He was dying by the time they got to the station. When they were leaving and he saw the two cops trotting toward them from the subway entrance, he thought they had been betrayed and he had disgraced himself.

But the police had rushed right by, en route to some other emergency, and for the next few months Djordje Karavitch had added Milo's wet pants to his store of needling remarks, along with swipes at Vlatko Raditch's slowness of wit and Pavle Macek's parade of women. Which Milo did not really mind, because it showed that the leader had noticed him, that he was part of the group, of the Party.

The plane was leveling off. Milo Rukovina pushed his seat all the way back, sighed, removed his thick glasses, and rubbed his face. It was a rabbity face with thin blond hair and myopic gray eyes. He replaced his glasses and glanced around at his companions. To his left, Vlatko Raditch was staring out the window, fascinated, like a child. He turned and smiled at Milo. "Ah, Milo, look, we're high up," he said inanely. He was a beautiful man, with glossy chestnut curls and a panther's tight body. The noble young head was as empty as a kettle, except for soccer. Milo could not help liking the fellow, but could not see why Djordje had made him a part of the Party's inner circle, since he was quite useless as a conspirator. Perhaps it was his name.

On the other hand, there was no question why his companion on the right was a member. Pavle Macek seemed hardly contained inside his skin. He had the look of the wolf—intense, deep-set yellowish eyes, hunter eyes that darted in all directions, and a vulpine face with a strong nose curving above a black mustache and thin red lips. His long, powerful fingers were always flexing, tapping his legs, clenching into fists. Although Milo worked with Macek every day at the electrician's shop Macek owned, he was still not comfortable in the other man's presence. Every political movement needed a Macek, Milo knew, at least in its early days, but when power was theirs and their nation was free again, men such as Milo Rukovina—calm, judicious, well organized—would be needed more than wolves like Macek.

A chime sounded and the seatbelt light went off. A voice came over the speaker, welcoming them to the flight and telling them that they were free to move around the cabin. Macek looked over at the old man, who nodded. Slipping out of his seatbelt, Macek

2

rose and removed the Macy's shopping bag from the overhead compartment. He carried it to the rear lavatory and locked himself in.

In the pantry at the center of the plane, Daphne West and Alice Springer were preparing to serve juice, coffee, and sweet rolls to the forty-four people in coach. The third flight attendant, Jerry Silver, was already pampering the first class. West had been a flight attendant for ten years, Springer for two. West's smiling muscles were wearing out. She had just about decided to chuck the job for something with more of a future. Also, she was having trouble keeping her weight under the airline's strict limits. She regarded Alice Springer with amusement, mixed with a little envy. Springer was born to stewardess. Petite, golden-haired, with a naturally sunny disposition shining from her pretty blue eyes, she believed devoutly that being a waitress in an aluminum tube thirty thousand feet in the air was a nobler calling than the same job in a restaurant back home in Hibbing, Minnesota. And she ate like a horse and never gained an ounce.

Alice pulled the cart into the aisle. First row left was occupied by a mother and two children under five, a party only slightly less grueling for flight attendants than a clutch of drunken Elks. Alice beamed at them and distributed sweet rolls and juice, napkins, and Handi-wipes. She looked back at Daphne. "Aren't they precious?" Another sunlamp grin. Later Daphne would reflect that it was the last time she saw that smile on Alice Springer's face.

The two men were waiting for her, the old one and the one with the yellow eyes, standing in the aisle as she dragged her cart to the last row. The old man touched her shoulder and spoke in a soft, slightly accented voice. "Miss, if you would, we have an emergency."

"Emergency?"

"Yes. Listen carefully to what I am saying and do not make a disturbance. There is a bomb on this plane—"

Alice gasped. "A bomb! That's impossible. There are children . . ." She turned toward the front of the plane, toward the captain, but she was blocked by her cart. The old man moved closer to her, and she caught his odor, like old leather. His blue eyes were remarkably clear, young-seeming despite the dark bags beneath them. Once caught in their gaze she found she could not pull away.

"Listen, I said! Now. There is a bomb on this plane. It is our bomb. Pavle! Show her!"

The other man held up a six-quart white enameled cooking pot by its lid handle. The top was held on with many turns of black electrician's tape. From a square six-volt dry cell taped to its side rose red wires that passed through a red-buttoned switch taped near the handle and then disappeared into the pot.

Djordje Karavitch observed the effect this had on the young woman. He liked what he saw; she would give them no trouble.

"You see, we are serious men," he continued, "and we wish to strike a blow for freedom in our country. And so we must borrow your plane for a little while."

Alice gaped like a fish and trembled. "B-b-borrow . . . ?" She was struggling to remember what she had been taught in flight-attendant school about such emergencies, but her brain was frozen, not so much by the thought of what a bomb could do to an aircraft full of people, but by the eyes of the two men who confronted her. The older man had a gaze as cold and pitiless as the thin air outside the jet. The other man's yellow stare was a nasty parody of the lecherous glances she encountered every day in her job. The look said, I not only want you, I want to consume you and make you nothing.

The older man gripped her arm, hard. He had been talking and Alice had not been paying attention.

"Listen to me! Are you listening now?" She nodded meekly. "Good. We do not wish to hurt you or anyone on this plane. So you and I will take a walk up to the cockpit. You will push your wagon and do as you do always. My friend will sit back here with his finger on the detonator. If things do not go precisely as we wish, he will destroy the plane. Do you believe me?"

Alice tore her gaze away from his, struggling to control herself. She wanted the bathroom. She wanted to cry. She looked around at the other people in the last row. The handsome one was smiling meaninglessly, like a dog watching his master play checkers. The little man with the glasses was watching with neutral interest, a student at a biology demonstration. Alice looked at the woman in the aisle seat. Her face was a blank, the eyes hidden by large sunglasses.

In a small voice Alice replied, "Yes. I believe you."

Daphne West was about to ask Alice to take over the coffee service when she saw the look on her face and took in the big man looming over her. "What's wrong, Alice? Uh-oh—"

"Daph, this man needs to, uh, see Captain Gunn, on the flight deck," she explained the situation in a tight whisper.

Daphne West had never been hijacked, but in ten years as air crew she had known a number of people who had. She pulled Alice's cart into its slot and patted the younger woman on the shoulder. "OK, kid, just do what you have to do and stay cool. I'll take care of things out here." She looked at the big man as they advanced past her. A monster for sure, she thought, and calmly gave him her best phony smile.

The third flight attendant, Jerry Silver, was serving drinks to the first-class passengers when Alice and Karavitch strode past. He looked on in amazement as they entered the flight deck. The prosperous first-class passenger to whom he was serving a bourbon and water caught his expression. "Any trouble?" he asked calmly. Jerry cranked up his reassuring grin. "No sir. Not so far as I know." He turned away and quickly slipped inside the curtain of the forward galley.

"Daphneee! What the hell . . . !" Daphne regarded her crewmate with an appraising eye. Jerry was a gorgeous blonde, like Alice. He was delighted to be a stewardess (for so he regarded himself, "flight attendant" being a term he never used), the realization of his life's ambition, and did what he could to compensate for nature not having made him like Alice in every single particular.

"Keep it down, Jerry," said Daphne in a low, controlled voice. "We're being hijacked."

"You're putting me on. Uh-oh, I guess you're not. Who, the big bozo with Springer?"

"Yes, and he's no bozo."

"What, guns, knives?"

"A bomb, they say. The party in the back row. Don't look. We're supposed to keep it close until they make an announcement. Look, how are you on CPR? There's a couple of old biddies and a guy in 20C looks like a corpse already."

"Oh, God, the kiss of life?" he asked, glancing out. "Anything for the airline, but keep the barf bag handy if I have to do 20 fucking C. My God, hijacked, and I've only just begun to live. Well, how do you like that! You think we'll be on TV?"

Daphne giggled in spite of herself. Jerry would do fine, even if, as she expected, Alice Springer went to pieces. "Sure, prime time. If we survive."

"Oh, we'll survive, Daphne. I just had a sixty-dollar razor cut. Life couldn't be that cruel."

Flying a commercial jet doesn't take much when things are going well, although from time to time a pilot will earn twelve years of pay in twelve seconds. Flight 501 was on autopilot at 28,000 feet over western Pennsylvania. The pilot, Arthur Gunn, was explaining to Bill Connelly, his copilot, how a real estate mutual fund worked when the flight deck door opened and Alice Springer appeared in the doorway.

"Hey, Alice, what's happening?" Gunn said cheerfully. "The plane still flying back there?"

Alice took a deep breath. "Uh, Captain, there's a man here who says he has a bomb on board."

Gunn scowled. "Damn, Alice, that's not funny. I thought they taught you jokes like that were off limits."

"It's not a joke, pilot," said Djordje Karavitch, pushing forward. The cockpit of a 727 is not designed to hold four people, and Alice Springer was jammed up against the copilot seat as Karavitch leaned over Gunn's upturned, startled face.

"Who the hell are *you*, buddy?"

Karavitch kicked the cockpit door closed with his heel.

"My name is Karavitch. What the girl says is true. My friend is holding a powerful bomb, and we will explode it if our demands are not met."

Gunn looked over at Alice, who nodded. The pilot took in the stewardess's face for the first time. The bright, American-girl look had collapsed into something like the pinched worry of a mother whose children are still trapped in the burning tenement. Gunn looked at Karavitch: was this the kind of man who would kill himself and sixty people to make a point? Yeah, he sure was. Gunn cleared his throat.

"OK, you're in charge. As long as nobody gets hurt, right?"

"Very good, Captain," said Karavitch, smiling thinly. "I require two things at once. First, I wish to make an announcement over your radio to the New York City police and the FBI. You will make sure I am connected properly. Next, you will immediately change your course. This plane is going to Montreal. There you will refuel."

"And then . . . ?"

"Then we will go to Gander in Newfoundland. And then we are going to Croatia."

Connelly, the copilot, spoke up. "Croatia? The Middle East. You're some kind of Arabs, right?"

"No, not Arabs. Croatia is in the Balkans."

"Yeah, Bill," said Gunn, "it's up by Lithuania, near Russia."

Even after thirty years in the United States, Karavitch continued to wonder at the profound ignorance and innocence of Americans. Croatians had ten centuries of history etched into their bones with the strong acid of massacre and betrayal. To him, Americans were gaudy, cheap shadows, like the images on television. He smiled again.

"I think we will have a geography lesson soon, but for now you need only to find Gander, Newfoundland. And do what is necessary for the radio, so that I can speak."

He gestured to Alice Springer. "You. Out! Make yourself useful. Tell the man with the bomb that all is well. And bring me a scotch whiskey and ice."

Gunn was about to object that alcohol was not permitted on the flight deck before he realized that it wasn't his flight deck anymore. That more than anything else started the cold chill moving up from his belly and out along his arms. "Bill, you might as well plot us up a course for Montreal," he said to the copilot, struggling to retain the insouciant down-home twang used by all professional pilots. "I'll get this guy patched in on the radio."

Back in the galley Alice Springer closed her eyes, leaned against the wall, and tried to stop shuddering. Daphne West stood with her arm around the younger woman and made meaningless "there there" noises, trying to exhibit a confidence she did not in the least feel.

"Daphne, I've got to go back there and tell the man with the, you know, with the . . ."

"The bomb? Yes, what do you have to tell him?"

"That the plane, is, is hijacked, and we're going to Montreal, so he won't . . . But I can't! There's three of them in the last row right. Oh, and they've got a woman with them too. The guy on the aisle has the, b-bomb. Daphne, he *scares* me." She was clearly about to burst into tears. Daphne clutched Alice's shoulder harder and guided her firmly into the forward lavatory.

"Listen. I need you in one piece on this. Lock yourself in, have a good yell, throw up, whatever. Then get your face back on and come to work. We start meal service in ten minutes."

That done, she marched down the aisle to where Pavle Macek sat. For an instant she had to suppress a giddy impulse to laugh. Sitting with his legs primly together and the thing on his lap, he looked like one of those cartoons of men on a bench outside the patent office clutching weird devices. He tensed and glared at her. She wondered again why men of a certain type made that ridiculous jaw-clenching, eye-popping grimace to show that they were tough guys who wouldn't take any shit off a woman.

The four terrorists leaned forward slightly, like the family of a miser about to hear the lawyer read the will. Daphne thought madly, what if I said, "Captain Gunn says, go fuck yourselves and we'll be landing in Milwaukee at 11:50 Central"? What she did say, coolly, was, "I'm supposed to tell you that we're going to do what you want."

The three men broke into grins, and the little one let loose a high giggle. They began chattering in their foreign language. Daphne West turned and went forward. She was angry and trying to keep it off her face. Daphne knew men, having been around the block a few times, as she put it. Although she had never met Pavle Macek, she knew him; she had twisted away from that type over millions of air miles. A shitheel like that, thought Daphne, might beat up a woman, might rape, might kill. But she doubted very much if he would detonate a bomb that was resting on his crotch.

2

"**O**K, LET'S HEAR it again," Elmer Pillman said. He was a special agent in the FBI's New York office, with responsibility for skyjacks and counterterrorism. The two other FBI agents in his office were his deputy and a junior agent named Joseph Stepanovic. The senior man was grave and solemn; Stepanovic was mainly scared.

The switch was hit on the tape recorder. Once again the voice of Djordje Karavitch filled the corner office, clear and powerful through the radio static:

"Today the Croatian people have struck the first blow in their crusade for freedom and independence. Shock troops of the Croatian National Freedom Party under the command of General Djordje Karavitch have seized control of an American airliner by means of a powerful bomb, which we have on the plane. The United States has deserved this from the support and money it has given to the terrorist communist regime in Belgrade, whose troops are even now crushing the Croatian people in their bloody grip. The worldwide offensive by the Croatian National Freedom Party will not spare any nation that supports the usurper Belgrade regime in its suppression of the legitimate national aspirations of the great Croatian people: democracy, independence and freedom to worship in their historic faith.

"We do not fear death. The freedom fighters of Croatia have never feared death, not against the Romans, the Serbs, the Turks, the Hungarians, or the communists. If our demands are not met, I warn you seriously, we will not hesitate one instant to destroy this airplane and everyone aboard it. And there are other bombs, many other bombs. There is one in locker number 139 in Grand Central Station.

"As our demands are met, we will reveal the location of the other bombs, perhaps before they explode, perhaps not. It will be unfortunate if innocent people are harmed, but this is a war we are fighting. Tens of thousands of innocent Croatians have been butchered by the communists and their jackals, and the world has

9

ignored their cries. No longer! With this offensive we move Croatia once again into her rightful place among the nations. The world will pay attention, or blood will run in every city, in every country.

"I have given orders that this airplane fly to Montreal for refueling. It would be foolish of anyone to try to stop this. At that time, we will issue further demands.

"Long live Croatia. Victory to the Croatian National Freedom Party!"

Then there was the sound of static, followed by the hiss of blank tape. One of the agents thumbed the machine off. Pillman rolled his eyes and scowled. He was a squat, frog-faced man with a gray crew cut, and his expression made it seem as if the frog had just missed a fat bug. He said, "Ah, crap! Croatia, my ass! OK, let's get a copy of this tape over to NYPD, or the assholes'll claim we're not cooperating on a matter of grave danger to the public. Offer them our bomb people, whatever, not that they'll accept. And make sure we're covered on the Canadian side too." The deputy got on the phone and spoke softly, relaying the orders.

Pillman spoke in a loud voice to no one in particular, "Who the hell are these jokers?"

Joe Stepanovic coughed nervously, fiddling with the folder on his lap. He was responsible for keeping watch on the dozens of Eastern European emigré political groups active in New York, a shadowy activity that the FBI did not advertise. These groups, after all, considered themselves to be part of the great anticommunist crusade. More important, any number of conservative American political figures agreed with that assessment. Or pretended to. Thus the FBI had to exercise a certain caution in watching them. It fed them money—not enough to invade Hungary, but enough to keep them solvent—and attended (in the person of Joe Stepanovic) their numerous meetings, rallies, and parades. Stepanovic took pictures with his miniature camera and took down names in his notebook. The point of this was ostensibly to spot the occasional ringer or provocateur, or better yet, uncover some ringer with connections to the CIA. But the Bureau did not consider these groups a threat. Their members were aging, their numbers were thinning with the years, and they were, of course, safely on the right side of the political spectrum.

So ordinarily Stepanovic had an easy, low-profile task. With his fluency in several Slavic languages, farmboy looks, and ready purse, he had no difficulty in gaining entry to even clandestine councils of East European emigrés.

Now he was high-profile and not liking it.

"Joe," said Pillman, remembering why Stepanovic was in the room, "you know this guy, Kara-whatsis?"

"Yes sir, Karavitch. Yes sir, umm . . ." He opened his file, shuffling the papers. "Djordje Karavitch, born 1907, Zagreb, now Yugoslavia, father a minor Austrian official, mother from a small land-owning family, Jesuit education, dropped out of University of Zagreb after two years, member of Eagles, a Catholic youth organization, political involvement with Croatian Peasants Party. After the German invasion he—"

Pillman broke in, "Could you put it on fast-forward, Joe? What's he been doing recently?"

"Oh, sure," Stepanovic said, shuffling papers again. "Recently? I would say, recently, he's been doing . . . well, nothing."

"Nothing? What do you mean? What about this organization, this Croatian National Freedom bullshit? Where are they coming from? Are you inside there, or what?"

Stepanovic's prominent Adam's apple rippled as he swallowed hard. "Ah, what I mean is, sir, that as far as I can tell, there is no such organization. That tape was the first time I ever heard of it. Karavitch is not what you would call a leader in the Croatian community here. He's not on the politically active list, I mean, so how could I . . ." His voice trailed off as he gestured with his sheaf of papers.

"OK, Joe, just fill us in, whatever you know," said the deputy.

"Well, it's not much. Entered the country in '48, from Trieste, under the Displaced Person's Act, got a job as a building superintendent in Brooklyn, which he still does, and also manages some buildings in Brooklyn and the Lower East Side. U.S. citizenship, 1955. In 1956, sponsored immigration of a Pavle Macek, also from Trieste. In 1962, married Cindy Wilson, American, age 25. Member of the usual Croat fraternal organizations, active in St. Gregory Catholic church. Nothing much else. Oh, yeah, last year, 1975, sponsored immigration of Milovan Rukovina and Vlatko Raditch, Yugoslav nationals. That's it."

Pillman lit a Tiparillo and leaned back in his leather swivel chair, regarding Stepanovic through the acrid smoke. "So tell us, Joe, this guy is such a good citizen, how come the taxpayers want you to watch him at all? What's his angle?"

Stepanovic essayed a slight smile. "He doesn't need an angle, sir. He was on a watch list when he came over, which is standard for people who were political on the other side."

"Yeah, in '48 maybe. But, hell, you know damn well we can't keep tabs on every Eastern European who gets into the country. What I want to know is how come he's on a watch list *now*?"

11

"Um, that I don't know, sir."

"You don't know?"

"No, sir. Anyway, it's not like he's under surveillance. We just sort of keep tabs, where he's living, who he hangs out with, political activity, contacts with known agents. Like that."

Pillman brought forth a particularly hideous scowl. "Like that, huh? Well, since this son of a bitch has just hijacked an airplane and planted Christ knows how many bombs, maybe you should make it your business to find out why the FBI has been interested in him for almost thirty years. How about that? And how about getting a look at his place before the cops arrive and screw things around?"

Stepanovic sprang to his feet and made for the door. He was almost out of the room when Pillman called, "Hey, Stepanovic! Are you a Croatian?"

"No, sir. I'm a Serb," replied the startled Stepanovic.

"Same goddamn thing, isn't it?" growled his leader.

"You could say that," said Stepanovic, and shut the door.

Twenty-five minutes later Elmer Pillman received a call from his boss, the assistant director in charge of the New York office, which was hardly ever a pleasant experience for Pillman. Since the FBI office in New York, which accounts for a quarter of all FBI personnel, is the only regional office that rates an assistant director on top, he resented that he even had a local boss. As far as he was concerned, the assistant director was there for public relations—giving awards to Boy Scouts and sitting on the innumerable criminal-justice coordinating committees erected to keep crime and subversion out of the New York metropolitan area. The assistant director had, however, another function, one less innocuous from Pillman's standpoint, which was passing the word from Washington.

The conversation was a short one. The word, to Pillman's surprise, involved the current skyjacking. This was how he learned why the FBI had remained interested in Djordje Karavitch for thirty uneventful years. It was enough to frighten him badly. And he did not frighten easily. And it was not even the real reason.

Later the same afternoon, a New York City police officer armored like a knight in thick Kevlar and a helmet was about to insert a key into locker number 139 in Grand Central Station. Terry Doyle had been out drinking until two the previous morning at a saloon on East Tremont in Throg's Neck. There had been a retirement party for one of the officers in his division, and most of the guys had drunk a lot more than Doyle's couple of beers. That was why the youngest member of the section of the NYPD Arson and Explosion Division, known as the bomb squad, was sweating like a pig under the bright lights trained on the locker.

Doyle was not particularly frightened. Although this was only the second time he had done a job like this, he considered himself well trained and was proud to be part of one of the best bomb-disposal organizations in the world. And the odds were right: the NYPD bomb squad had not lost a single man in over forty years.

"I'm putting the key in the lock," Doyle said over the telephone built into his helmet. He shook his head to knock off a drop of sweat dangling from his nose. "When you dispose of a bomb," his class instructor had said, "you tell someone else at the end of the phone line everything you're doing before you do it." If the thing went up, such information was useful to colleagues in dealing with similar devices. Or so it had proved in World War II, when this doctrine had been developed.

"Key in the lock, check," Sergeant John Doheny said at the other end of the line, in the bomb squad van. Doheny had been at the same party last night and had all he could do to keep both his stomach and his brain under control. "I'm turning the key," the voice reported. "I'm opening the door."

"Sarge, there's a pot in the locker. Looks like a pressure cooker. There's a six-volt taped to the side with black friction tape, a red and a black wire going from the battery terminals to a—it looks like a black plastic box about three by two, taped to the top of the pot. There's a blue wire and a yellow wire running from that into a hole in the lid of the pot. There's also a manila envelope leaning against the pot."

"Check, Terry," Doheny said. "You going to move it out now?"

"Right. OK, I'm moving the envelope away from the pot."

Doyle backed off from the locker and used a pole to move the envelope away from the pot. Then he carefully ran a canvas belt clamp around the middle of the pot, snugged it down, and clipped it to a pole.

"I'm moving it, Sarge."

"Check."

He backed away to the length of the pole and jiggled the pot. Then he lifted it clear off the floor of the locker and let it drop about two inches. It made a discordant rumble, like stage thunder.

"Looks good, Sarge. Let's get it in the bomb carrier."

"Check, Terry. Why don't you wait ten? I'll send D'Amato up."

Doheny rubbed his eyes and staggered slightly as he walked out of the van. This was not the right day for this to have happened. He blinked in the watery autumn sunlight and looked out on a

13

scene of near chaos. The threat of explosion had excised one of Manhattan's principal ganglia. Vanderbilt Avenue and the side streets bordering Grand Central Terminal had been sealed off and were full of police cars, fire engines, and their associated personnel. Park Avenue, where it ran on top of the Terminal, had of course been closed, and the Pan Am Building, perched atop Grand Central, had been evacuated. Doheny could hear the honks and rumbles of stalled traffic blocks away and the mutter of displaced office workers by the thousands across the gray police barriers. In a sense, an unexploded bomb, with its burden of the catastrophic unknown, caused more disruption than a bomb that had already done its worst.

The sergeant gestured to a dark young man in bomb armor who was hanging around outside the van. "Luke, go help the kid with the carrier. I want to get out of this whorehouse before my head falls off. I'm dying!"

"Yeah, you look it, Sarge," laughed D'Amato, though he knew he looked just as haggard. He picked up his helmet and checked his phone line, then headed through the polished brass doors and into the echoing, deserted station.

Working efficiently in the wordless cooperation of good technicians, Doyle and D'Amato placed the pot and the envelope in a large steel and Kevlar bucket. This they closed with a heavy lid and hoisted between them on a pole, like Chinese coolies carrying a water jar.

Once out in the street, they carried the bucket over to the bomb transporter, a heavy flatbed truck mounted with what looked like a diving bell. As Doheny supervised the securing of the bucket within the huge safety vessel, he reflected for the hundredth time on what would happen if a major bomb ever did explode in the glass-lined canyons of midtown Manhattan.

With the bomb thus enclosed, Doyle and D'Amato removed their helmets and had a smoke. They were both dripping sweat, and Doyle's damp blond curls were nearly as dark as D'Amato's thin black hair. Kevlar, despite its many virtues, such as the ability to stop bullets and flying shrapnel, does not breathe like your natural fibers.

D'Amato was a round-faced man of about thirty-five. He was puffing hard, coughing around his Kent, and his face was flushed and blotchy. "Too many damned beers last night," he grumbled. As he began removing his armor, Doheny spotted him from the doorway of his van, where he had been making arrangements to clear the route for the bomb-transport convoy. "Hey, Luke! You gonna get out and back in again when we get to the range?"

Somebody had to take the bomb out to the bunker and handle the deactivation. This would have been D'Amato's job today.

Doyle spoke up. "I'll do it, Sarge. Luke don't look so hot."

Doheny could appreciate that. "Oh, yeah? The kid's right, D'Amato. You look like I feel. Hell of a party, hey?"

Everybody agreed that it had been a hell of a party. The phone in the van buzzed, and Doheny received word that the route clearance had been set up. He turned back to his squad. "Whaddya say, Luke? You really crapped out?"

"Yeah, well, I could still do it, but you know, I think the heat's getting to me, or something—"

"I'll do it, Sarge," Doyle said cheerfully.

"Yeah?"

"Sure, let old Luke fuck the dog for a while. Old fart like him's about worn out anyway."

D'Amato had peeled off the armor, which lay about him in sections on the pavement like the shed carapace of an immense beetle. The air blowing against his sodden sweatsuit felt delightful, and he was not inclined to argue with Doyle for the privilege of crouching for perhaps hours in the armor.

"OK for you, Doyle," he said with a smile. "Just wait. You'll be old and tired someday."

Doyle laughed. "I'll never be as old as you, baby."

Doheny winced at another pang from his stomach. He wanted this day to be over. "OK, people. Let's clear up our shit and get rolling."

The sirens screamed. Two patrol cars, lights flashing, pulled past the barriers up Vanderbilt, followed by the bomb squad van and the bomb transporter and an ambulance. At 42nd Street one of the patrol cars pulled aside and slid back in behind the ambulance. The convoy, now complete, sped toward FDR Drive, the Triboro Bridge, the Bruckner, Pelham Bay Park, and the police weapons and bomb ranges on Rodman Neck.

On Flight 501 lunch had been served. Macek and Rukovina took turns holding the bomb while they ate. Macek, Rukovina, and Raditch each had a beer, which they paid for, although if they had refused to pay, Alice Springer was not sure what she would have done.

The young one smiled at her when she brought the beers. Instinctively she smiled back. "*Najlepshe hvala*," he said. The other two said, "*Hvala, hvala*."

"Pardon?" she said.

15

"Is mean, 'thank you' " the young one replied. "Now you must say, '*Nema na cemu*.' This mean, 'you welcome.' "

Alice smiled and said the phrase. They all chuckled and the young one clapped his hands and said "*Fantastichno!*"

There were introductions. The young one said, in phrasebook English, "Allow me to present . . ." and gave the names of his two companions and himself. The woman was not introduced. She had declined the meal. Instead she drank black coffee and chain-smoked Salems.

Alice gave her own name, surprised to hear it on her lips. It sounded like the name of a stranger. They drank their beers and chatted in Croatian. Alice smiled harder and concentrated on not looking at the bomb. She kept smiling and didn't move away, even when the one on the aisle, Macek, ran his hand up between her legs and squeezed her inner thigh gently, possessively, in the manner of an old lover.

Karavitch had moved to an empty seat in first class, which he had demanded so that he could be near the flight deck. He got first-class service too, including unlimited free drinks. He pushed his tray away and contemplated the line of Haig pinch-bottle miniatures lined up on the tray table of the empty seat to his right. There were seven of them. He arranged them in two rows of three, with one out in front, like a military parade.

He had a good head for liquor. In the war he had been famous for being able to drink anyone under the table, and the *ustashi* brigades had boasted some powerful drinkers. He had once drunk an entire bottle of plum brandy standing up on the hood of a truck climbing a mountain road near Bihac, while the men cheered him on. Pavle had been on that ride as well, he recalled. He also remembered that later that day Pavle had tried to imitate the trick, and had fallen off and nearly cracked his skull. Pavle had no head for drinking, which was why Karavitch had ordered him to lay off for the duration of the hijack. Karavitch stretched his cramped body and smiled. He could still drink. Even after seven scotches his head was clear.

He looked at his watch, then pressed the button for the stewardess. In a few moments Daphne West was by his side.

"We should be landing very soon. I wish the pilot to make the announcement we agreed on."

West murmured assent and went forward to relay the message to Captain Gunn. Karavitch watched her go. Power was better than scotch, even this good scotch. Idly he flicked over the leading bottle. It tumbled against the others and all but one fell over.

Karavitch watched as it wobbled in circles and then stood upright again. Always one survives, he thought.

Daphne ducked and entered the flight deck. "How're things back there?" Gunn asked. He was flying the aircraft while his copilot exchanged cryptic bursts of letters and numerals with Montreal air-traffic control.

"All right," she said. "A lot better than they're going to be after you tell the folks where we're landing. I bring orders from the chief bastard. You're supposed to make your speech." Her voice was tight.

Gunn caught her tone and swiveled around to look at her. "How about you? You holding up?"

Daphne shrugged and threw up her hands, the gesture of futility. "Oh, sure. You know me, the old pro. I'm just pissed off is all. If that's a real bomb, I'm a chimpanzee."

"Come on, Daphne, it doesn't do any good to think like that. You know the rules. Guy flashes a teddy bear and says there's a grenade in it and he wants to go to Cuba, it's next stop Havana, no questions asked."

Daphne sighed. "Yeah, I know."

"What about the others?"

"Oh, Jerry's fine. Alice, not so good."

"Oh? What's happening with her?"

"Concrete smile, but watch the eyes. This is scaring the piss out of her, poor kid. Good thing it's not a bunch of Ay-rabs with machine guns. Getting chummy with the boys in the back, too. Hand and foot service."

"Stockholm syndrome."

"Looks like it."

"You can handle it, Daphne," said Gunn, hoping it were so.

Daphne laughed, a low throaty sound. "Hell, yes. Count on that tough nut Daphne!" She left the flight deck, closing the door behind her.

Connelly finished his conversation and turned to Gunn. "Montreal has us cleared to land. They've diverted traffic and have emergency and tankers standing by on D-19."

Rodman Neck, the southernmost extension of Hunter Island, looks from the air like the head of a retriever emerging from the Bronx to sniff the waters of Eastchester Bay. Where the dog's nose would be, the New York City Police Department has fenced off a large chunk of real estate to serve as its outdoor shooting range. Besides the half dozen firing ranges there is a mock city street where cops are taught to shoot cardboard silhouettes of armed

17

criminals and not silhouettes of moms pushing strollers, as well as the kennels for the department's dope- and explosive-sniffing dogs. In the approximate center of this compound is the bomb range.

It was nearly three o'clock before Terry Doyle began to work on the pot bomb. X rays of it showed a shadowy pressure cooker with what looked like a half brick at the bottom. Wires descended from the lid of the pot and disappeared under the brick. They had X-rayed the envelope too. It contained only paper: a demand by the Croatians that a manifesto listing their complaints be published in the *Times*, the *News*, and the international *Herald Tribune*. The manifesto was included, neatly typed.

Doyle was working now in the bottom of a well made of packed earth. A dogleg vestibule was built into the well, from which a ladder led to the surface. The vestibule was in case you were deactivating a device and it gave you some warning that it was going to blow up. Then you could run into the vestibule, or throw the device into the vestibule if it was small enough, so that you had some buffer from the blast. There was a deep sump around the floor of the well for the same purpose. Of course, you had to have lightning-fast reflexes. Or a slow fuse.

Doyle had the pot on a heavy plywood table in front of him. He was still dressed in his armor, with the helmet in place. Only his hands were bare. You can't deactivate bombs if you're worried about losing your hands.

"I'm going to snip the external wires," Doyle said over his telephone. Its cable led to the bomb-range command bunker, forty yards away, and Sergeant John Doheny. Doheny said, "Cutting wires. Go ahead."

Doyle cut the blue and yellow wires and bent them carefully out of the way. Then he cut the red and black wires, telling Doheny what he was doing before and after each cut.

"OK, I'm turning the center handle counterclockwise. The clamp is loose. I'm rotating the lid counterclockwise. The lugs are clear. I'm lifting the lid. I'm shining the flash into the pot. I see a—it looks like a regular construction brick. I'm putting the lid down on the table. I'm pulling the yellow wire out from under the brick. It's free. I'm pulling the blue wire—it won't come loose. OK, I see that the brick is glued to the bottom of the pot. There's gray epoxy all over the bottom. That's it, Sarge. It's a pot with a brick glued into it. The city can sleep safe tonight."

"A fake?"

"No question, Sarge. Come see for yourself."

"You sure about this, Doyle? You want me to get Luke or somebody to suit up and take a look?"

18

"Hell yes, I'm sure. It's a phony. No soup, no detonator, no batteries, no primer, zilch. It's a pot with a brick in it."

"OK, hold on, we're coming over."

In a minute or so, Doheny and D'Amato were climbing down the ladder. When they came around the vestibule wall, they found Doyle leaning against the wall, helmet off, cigarette in his mouth. "Don't smoke on the range, Doyle" was the first thing Doheny said when he came in.

"Shit, Sarge, it's a fuckin' brick," Doyle complained.

"Don't 'shit, Sarge' me, sonny. You want to live a long time in this game, you follow the rules. And it's not a brick until I say it's a brick."

Doheny went over to the table and looked into the pot. He picked up a pair of pliers and rapped the brick sharply. It gave out the solid, metallic clunk of metal hitting brick.

"Well, is it a brick, Sarge?"

Doheny looked at the younger man sourly. "Yeah, Doyle, it is a goddamn brick. Jesus, what a fucking waste of time! OK, you bring that thing along, Doyle. It's evidence. Luke, help him clean up all his crap. I gotta get a handful of aspirin. What a pain in the ass!"

Doyle picked up the pot and put the lid back on loosely as Doheny started to enter the vestibule. Luke knelt down and began to close up the tool kit.

Doyle said, "Well, there's one thing you don't have to worry about, Sarge—"

But Sergeant Doheny never found out what that one thing was. At that instant he felt a terrible heat and a crushing force. Luke D'Amato felt it too. Terry Doyle did not, in all probability, feel anything, since his head had disintegrated in the first instant of the blast.

3

THE SEATBELT LIGHT shone its little cartoon and the people on Flight 501 heard the whisper of static. It was nearly one o'clock; the plane should have landed in Milwaukee by now and the passengers were glancing at their watches and buzzing for the flight attendants.

"This is Captain Gunn here on the flight deck," said the voice in the static. "We have a—a little difficulty here, folks. We will not be landing in Milwaukee at this time. I have been ordered to read the following message to you. 'This plane has been appropriated by the forces of Croatian national liberation. The plane is being diverted to Canada for refueling, after which it will continue to European points to continue the mission of the Croatian national forces. No one aboard the plane will be harmed in any way, but all passengers are warned that efforts to interfere with the mission of the Croatian national forces will be severely punished. There is a powerful bomb aboard this airplane. The Croatian national forces will not fear to detonate this bomb should their mission be opposed in any way.' "

There was a moment of stunned silence into which a woman's voice said clearly, "Oh my God." Then screams, babies crying, shouts of outrage and fear, the familiar chorale of the late twentieth century. Hearing it in the cockpit, Gunn went on, trying to keep the edge of desperation out of his folksy drawl.

"Folks, we, ah, have obtained clearance from Montreal to land the aircraft, and we will be landing shortly. We'll have to see what happens then, but these people have told us that they don't want to hurt anyone on the plane, so let's all try to stay calm and cooperate." He snapped off the cabin intercom switch and said sourly to his copilot, "And next time your plans include flying, we hope you'll think of us." Then he switched his headset to Montreal tower as much to drown out the sounds coming from behind him as to hear directions from the airport.

Daphne West took a deep breath and waded into the chaos. Her pockets were stuffed with tissues. A middle-aged woman was weep-

20

ing hysterically in 14B, and the two small children in row 12 had burst into sympathetic tears. A man was shouting about suing the airlines. Hands clutched at her jacket.

"Miss, does this mean we get our money back?"

"Please, can I call my brother? He's waiting at the airport . . ."

"I'm sorry, I absolutely *have* to be in Milwaukee for a three o'clock meeting."

Daphne shook these off and made a beeline for a heavyset man who was thrashing and writhing in an aisle seat, his face turning the purple-red of fresh hamburger. He was struggling to get something out of his pocket.

People were out of their seats now, pressing in on her from all sides. A hard finger poked her shoulder. She turned her head and found Pavle Macek's eyes four inches from hers.

"Stop this!" he commanded. "Get these people back in their seats!"

Daphne ignored him and bent over the struggling man. She searched his pockets and pulled out a brown plastic vial. As she wrenched at the child-proof cap, she heard Macek shouting:

"I will blow you up! I will blow up the plane. I will blow you all up *now! Shut up!*" More people began to shriek and moan.

A woman's voice carried through the cabin, "I don't want to die-e-e-e-e . . ." A man answered, "Aw, honey, honey, now . . ."

Daphne felt as though she was moving in slow motion. Push down the white cap and turn in the direction of the arrow. The stricken man was slipping to the floor and making noises like a tenement toilet. Push the cap *down* and turn. Macek was pulling her arm. The vial opened and Daphne extracted a pill and slipped it into the man's open mouth, under his tongue.

She yanked off her shoes and jumped up on an armrest. Half the passengers were in the aisle, the instincts that told them to flee the place of danger having momentarily won out over the knowledge that there was no place to go. She took a deep breath. "Ladies and gentlemen, *please*, you must return to your seats. We will be landing shortly. You are in *no* danger at the present time. *Please* return to your seats, fasten your seatbelts, and return your seats and tray tables to the full upright and locked position." There was an instant of silence at this, and then the woman in 14B took another lungful and resumed her aria.

Looking forward, Daphne saw Karavitch emerge from behind the first-class curtain. He strode purposefully to 14B, leaned over, and whacked the woman across the jaw with his open hand. Once. Twice. The sound carried through the cabin like gunshots, and the hubbub slowly died.

"Listen to me," said Karavitch in his deep, strong voice. "The stewardess is right. We mean you no harm, if you cooperate. We are freedom fighters, not savages. All passengers will stay seated, with seat belts fastened. No one will leave their seat without permission. Those who do not obey us will be strictly disciplined. Now, do as I say! Move!"

Thoroughly cowed, the passengers shuffled to their seats. Daphne checked her heart patient. He was breathing more easily and his color was better. She spoke a few words of encouragement, then loosened his collar and belt. Next she distributed tissues and wiped noses, made faces, rocked, tickled, and otherwise helped to calm the two children.

Jerry Silver came up to her and whispered, "What a horror show! Just like the movies. First class is calmed down, but they're yapping about lawsuits. Anything I can do here?"

"Yeah, check the lady he slugged. I want to see about our Alice."

Jerry went over to the woman, a plump New York matron with false golden locks and a kewpie-doll mouth. She was trembling in a stupor of fear. Jerry wiped her face and brought her some ice to put on her swelling jaw. He also slipped the woman a cup with two slugs of brandy, on the airline, and added a yellow Valium tablet, on Jerry Silver. She gulped these down. Within five minutes she had rolled her eyes back into her heavily blued eyelids and passed out.

Karavitch was still standing at the head of the cabin. As Daphne went past him, their eyes met and he nodded slightly, a pro acknowledging the performance of another pro. Daphne felt herself return the nod. The others might be loonies, but this son of a bitch was the real goods, she thought. As she reached the pantry, Alice Springer emerged from the forward lavatory.

"Well, you missed quite a scene," Daphne said with some asperity. "Are you feeling all right now?"

"Oh, yes, and I'm sorry, Daph. I mean, I just absolutely lost it. I mean, my whole insides, from both ends. I peeked out, though. You were marvelous! And Mr. Karavitch too. I mean, we could have had a riot if he hadn't kind of taken charge."

"True. Of course, if *Mr.* Karavitch had not taken this flight, we probably wouldn't have had a riot at all, huh?"

"Oh, right," said Alice, looking blank.

The plane banked and the engines changed pitch. "OK, kid," Daphne said, "let's get *Mr.* Karavitch and the rest of the passengers all comfy for landing."

As Daphne strode up and down the aisles, she was thinking

about Karavitch's speech. The man knew how to take control, you had to give him that. But it seemed too practiced in a way, as if he had given the same speech dozens of times. She thought about that off and on as they flew from Montreal to Gander, and again at Gander, when they separated the men from the women, the children, and the sick. The men would stay as hostages on the flight across the Atlantic. As she observed Karavitch standing in the aisle at the head of the gangway, arms folded, watching the tearful good-byes, Daphne thought to herself, he likes this. This is his favorite part.

Roger Karp, Butch to his friends, entered his apartment to a ringing phone. It was late Friday afternoon and he was returning, sweaty and dusty, from an after-work softball game in Central Park. For the past seven years he had played first base for the team that represented the New York District Attorney's Office.

He was in no hurry to answer the phone. He couldn't think of anyone he wanted to talk to, except possibly his girlfriend, and he doubted that she was calling. He strolled over to the refrigerator in the apartment's tiny kitchenette, removed a two-quart container filled with instant iced tea and drank about half of it. He returned it to the otherwise vacant fridge.

The living room of the apartment was as empty, except for the dust bunnies lurking in the corners. Karp owned no furniture except his bed. His only other domestic possessions were an old rowing machine and a small black-and-white portable TV resting at the foot of his bed. He had lived in this minimal fashion since his ex-wife had walked out on him six years before.

Karp tossed his mitt in the general direction of the hall closet and went into the bedroom. He flung himself down on the bed full-length and grabbed the phone off the floor. He still had his old-fashioned wool Yankee baseball cap on his head.

"Yeah?"

"Butch? This is Bill Denton. Where have you been? I sent a car up to the park."

"You sent a car? What, you heard I went oh-for-three and you figured I needed a police escort? I walked home."

Karp heard a short, hard laugh over the phone. "You walked from the Park to the Village?"

"Yeah, it helps me keep my girlish figure. What can I do for you, Bill?"

William F. Denton was the Chief of Detectives of the New York City Police Department. Karp knew him, of course, from his own work as an assistant district attorney. He liked and admired the man, but they were by no means close. New York City has five district attorney's offices, one for each of its five counties, but only one police department. A Chief of Detectives, one of the three NYPD "superchiefs" under the Commissioner of Police, draws enormously more water than any assistant DA, who are as common as parking meters. Denton had never called Karp at home before.

"Have you heard the news? On that hijack out of LaGuardia?"

"Just in general. A guy had a radio at the game. What's happening?"

"They left a bomb in a locker at Grand Central. It went off about an hour ago and killed a cop."

"Shit!"

"Right. I need to talk to you about the case, outside the office and not on the phone. Can I come over to your place in, say, an hour?"

"Sure, but I don't understand. Assuming they catch the hijackers and bring them back here for trial, it doesn't look anything special in terms of nailing them. From your point of view it's a grounder. Or am I missing something?"

"A lot. And it ain't no grounder. See you later."

Karp dropped the phone back in its cradle. He stood up and took off his sleeveless University of California sweatshirt and gray sweatpants and kicked off his socks and sneakers. Then he sat on the bed and unbuckled a massive contraption of canvas and steel that kept his left knee from collapsing when he played ball.

He walked to the bathroom. Karp had the body of a basketball guard—tall, hard torso, long arms, muscular wrists. Karp had, in fact, been an all-state guard as a schoolboy in New York and then a star at Berkeley in the early Sixties. In his junior year, however, a pileup under the boards had produced what the California Board of Orthopedics had voted the worst non-fatal sports injury in the history of the Pacific Conference. After a brief conversation with his doctor and a glance at the X rays, Karp had decided that he probably would never start for the Knicks. He sulked briefly, switched to pre-law, and ended up as a DA in New York. It was much the same thing. If you play basketball, you want to start in the NBA; if you want to prosecute criminals, you want to work for the New York DA's office.

Karp's bathroom was the best thing about his apartment. It was a relic of the Twenties, when each apartment had taken up an entire floor. The renovators had left it alone: the huge ball-and-claw bathtub, the marble-topped washstand, the heavy porcelain and chrome fixtures. Adjusting the shower to the Venusian temperatures he craved, Karp mulled over the strange phone call. The

Chief of Detectives was coming directly to an assistant DA, in private, with what could be a major case, heavy with publicity. Why hadn't he gone to Sandy Bloom, the New York County DA, with this prize? The DA had, of course, the pick of any case in his jurisdiction, and it was certain that Bloom would give any case with the slightest aura of potential professional benefit to Count Dracula before he would give it to Butch Karp. Denton would have to spend many chips to control the case in this way. Why? Because he thought that Bloom would not prosecute this case? Why again? Stepping under the shower, Karp laughed out loud. Singleminded is often absentminded: he was still wearing his Yankee hat.

Twenty minutes later, Karp opened his door to Bill Denton. Denton looked like what he was, a very smart Irish detective. He was impeccably dressed in a tan suit and had pointed, gleaming Italian shoes on his curiously un-cop-like small feet. Coming in, he looked around quizzically.

"You just move in?"

"No, I've been here six years. I'm not into furniture."

Denton nodded. "I can see that. You could have a dance."

"Right. Anyway, Chief, what can I do for you?"

Denton walked over to the window, which had a dusty set of old-fashioned wooden venetian blinds pulled all the way up. He looked out at Sixth Avenue for a moment and then turned and leaned against the window sill.

"This case. We have one cop dead and two others seriously injured up in Jacobi. The hijacked plane has apparently taken off from Gander and is on its way to Paris. They let the women and kids and a couple of sick people off. They have forty-two men on board, plus the flight crew of five. They don't seem to have any weapons but the bomb. And we know that they know how to make a bomb.

"After they took the plane, they contacted the FBI and told them that there was a bomb in a locker at Grand Central and that there were other bombs hidden around the city, but they didn't say where. They've demanded that the papers print a manifesto on the front page tomorrow, and then they'll tell us where the others are. In the locker with the bomb was an envelope that had the manifesto. The papers have agreed. Meanwhile, we're opening every public locker in New York."

"Find anything yet?"

"Plenty. We found heroin. We found cocaine. We found stolen goods up the kazoo. Ah, let's see, we found a dead baby, couple of dogs, also dead. A machine gun—"

"But no bombs."

"But no bombs. We're still looking, though. Now, let's look at this case. First of all, we have the homicide, potentially murder one, killing a cop in the line of duty. Two, we know approximately who did it."

"One of the hijackers."

"Right. OK, the bomb was placed in Grand Central, which is in New York County. The killing was done in Rodman Neck, which is in Bronx County. The killing was done in the course of the crime of kidnapping, which was initiated at LaGuardia Airport, which is in Queens County. And, of course, skyjacking and kidnapping are also federal crimes. So we have a case in which three district attorney's offices and two U.S. attorney's offices have an interest. You like it?"

Karp rolled his eyes. "I love it. Holy shit!"

"Yeah. We're looking at a jurisdictional and procedural mess that could take years to figure out, and that's with goodwill all around, which we might not have in some quarters." Denton raised an eyebrow and shot Karp a curious look. "I want to see these guys nailed before I retire in eight years."

"OK, so what's the deal?"

"The deal is, as far as the detectives and the PD are concerned, this is your case. You get the troops and the support; nobody else gets any, not Bronx, not Queens, not the Feds. Just you."

"And Bloom . . . ?"

Denton shook his head vigorously. "Believe me, Sandy Bloom is not going to go up against us on this one. A cop is dead. You've got one of the best conviction records in the DA's office. Everybody knows that you're a nailer and he's not. So what's he gonna do? Complain to the commissioner? To the mayor? He's the wrong party, one, and given his attitude, Mr. Bloom is out of favors in both places. No, he'll play along. He'll hate it, but I guarantee, in public at least, he'll roll."

"OK, that makes sense. But you understand, it's not beyond him to try to screw me on this. He hates my guts."

Denton smiled. "Yeah, I know. That's another reason we picked you."

Karp smiled back. "So now what? Where's the plane?"

"It looks like the hijackers are taking it to Paris. We're not sure why, but the French are holding a couple of Croatians who whacked out the Yugoslav consul-general in Marseilles a couple of months ago. The hijackers may want to deal for their release."

"Will they roll on that?"

"Who knows? The French could do anything."

"But obviously I work with the Feds to get the hijackers back here."

"Right. You know Pillman down at the FBI? He gives you any trouble, call me. I'll arrest him for impersonating a police officer. Oh yeah, Pete Hanlon up at Arson and Explosion is expecting you—that's all set up. You want any help, any extra bodies, let me know direct. I'm catching this one personally." Denton stood up and stretched. "My poor ass. You got a real comfy place, Karp. OK, anything else you need to know?"

"Yeah. Why?"

Denton frowned. "Why what?"

"Why everything. Why is the chief of detectives handling this one personally? Why are you using chips, fuck Bloom, fuck the FBI, anything you want, steal bodies from other cases? That why."

Denton looked uncomfortable and color started to rise on his neck. "I told you, it's a cop. You know what that means."

"Sure, I do, but cops have died before. Couple of years ago we had cops *assassinated* by radicals, and the cases didn't get this kind of heat. So all this is—what can I say—unexpected."

Denton was silent for a moment. Once again he looked out the window. The light was shading into nightfall, and when he turned, Karp could hardly make out his features.

"Unexpected, eh? Let me sum up thirty years of police work for you in one phrase. 'Expect the unexpected.' Want to hear a story? You ever hear of Kenny Moran? No? Yeah, he was way before your time. Kenny Moran. Helluva guy. From one of those old cop families, cops back to Cork. Father, grandfather, uncles, all on the job.

"We went to Academy together. I didn't know him real well then, but we were the same age; we made detective third about the same time. Then we were partners out of the one-seven, both of us hotshots. But Kenny was rare. Big, good-looking guy, black Irish, you know? Looked like a goddamn poster in blues. And he had a . . . a presence, never had to raise his voice. He could walk into a bunch of assholes making trouble and all of a sudden they were dancing his tune. Nobody ever saw anything like it.

"And religious. Pillar of the church: Sodality, Holy Name, whatever they were selling he was buying. Not preachy, he just had the faith. Went to confession couple of times a week, though God knows what he had to say. Guy was straight as a ruler."

"Sounds like he should have been a priest," Karp said, not knowing where this was going, but content to listen to the quiet voice in the darkening room.

"Yeah, I thought that, too. But what a cop! I was the bad guy, naturally, and when he did the good guy, shit, hardass slimeballs would be snitching on their mothers.

"Anyway, he had this sister, Kathleen her name was. He lived with her in this apartment off Flatlands Avenue. Of course, she married a cop. About three weeks on the job he decides to dive into Sheepshead Bay to pull out a drunk and cracks his head on a piling, bang, lights out. Leaving her with one on the way, also of course. So Kenny has an instant family to take care of, not that he minded. The sun rose and set on Kathleen.

"So one fine day in June, it's gotta be eighteen years ago—I remember every detail—we're in the car, and this squeal comes in, homicide, and they give the address, and Kenny goes white. We tear ass all across Brooklyn, hitting ninety on Atlantic Avenue, and we get to his apartment on Flatlands. The neighbors called in because they heard the kid crying.

"We go in and you guessed it. Groceries all over the floor, place ripped up. There's Kathleen, naked in the bedroom, cut to pieces, blood over everything, and there's the kid, must have been three, in his stroller, screaming. He's got her blood all over him."

Denton took a deep breath. Now he was just a silhouette against the fading day.

"Did they ever catch the guy?"

"Shit, yes, we caught him. That day, as a matter of fact. He'd of gone to Russia, we would have caught him. Mutt named Hector Sales, your basic Brooklyn punk mugger, in and out of the joint for robbery, assault—the usual. We put the word out on the street and by that evening somebody snitched Hector out; he was showing off Kenny's spare gun in a bar over in Canarsie.

"We went over and picked him up. The Lieutenant was antsy about Kenny making the collar, because of the personal involvement and all, but Kenny just looked him in the eye and told him that he was a cop and that it would be an honest collar, with no rough stuff, and the Loot believed him. And me too. You understand, Kenny was that kind of guy.

"I'm running on, but there's not much more. We grab Hector in his room. The gun is there. The bloody clothes. Even the goddamn knife. Down to the precinct. Kenny is treating this guy like a brother, I couldn't believe it. I do my bit, I yell, I threaten, Kenny sends me out. Twenty minutes later Kenny sticks his head out, Hector wants to make a statement.

"So there's four of us in the room with him—me, Kenny, the Loot, and the stenographer. This is before Miranda, of course. Hector says his piece. He raped her, by the way. Then Kenny says in a quiet voice, 'Why did you kill her?' Just like that, like he was

28

asking why he bought a Pontiac. And Hector just shrugs, and says, 'I don't know, man, she pissed me off. I mean, yelling and carrying on. What's a piece of ass, right? I mean, she wasn't no virgin or anything.' Then he smiled at Kenny. He *smiled*, can you believe it?

"And Kenny kind of nods and reaches out to take Hector's arm, I figure he's going to lead him down to the cells, right? I mean, Kenny's face is like stone. Then he pulls his gun and puts the barrel in Hector's ear and blows his brains out."

Denton sighed again. "That's the story. Expect the unexpected."

Karp's throat was dry; his knee was aching from standing. "What happened then?" he asked the voice in the dark.

"To Kenny? Not much, except of course he was through with the cops. Walked for the homicide on a temporary insanity. Spent some time in a hospital and got a job as a bartender in Paramus. Raised his sister's kid. Never married. Passed on two years ago, cancer."

"Yeah. I never heard that story. But, umm, the connection with what we were talking about . . ."

"The connection? Oh, yeah, you wouldn't know. The kid."

"What kid?"

"Kenny Moran's sister's kid. Kathleen Doyle's kid, Terry Doyle. He was the cop who just got his head blown off. You get the picture?"

"I got it," Karp said. "OK, I'll do what I can."

"Yeah, I know," Denton said. "One thing you ought to know, though. After the FBI got through to the Department about the bomb and the hijack, the PC called the DA's to tell them what happened. Bloom said, 'What have you got on this Karavitch?' That's the name of the leader of the hijackers."

"So? Did you have anything?"

Denton smiled an unpleasant smile. "That's not the point. Bloom knew the bastard's name before we told him. How about that?"

"How about that."

A mile to the south, Marlene Ciampi, Assistant District Attorney, beloved of Butch Karp, sat on the fire escape of her loft on Crosby Street, stroking Prudence, one of her two cats, and dabbing her one eye with a tissue. She had been crying ever since she had learned from the six o'clock news about the explosion at Rodman Neck. Marlene knew the three men fairly well, having become something of a bomb squad buff over the past two years. This had started as part of her job, prosecuting a case against a group of political bombers. Then she had been blown up by a letter bomb. Only the bomb had been meant for Karp, sent by a mass murderer up for a murder one rap. She had opened a package because Karp was married and she was having an affair with him and by some evil chance the letter had been postmarked from the city where his wife lived. The bomb had taken two fingers and an eye, and scarred the left side of her face.

She put the cat down. Lighting a cigarette, she blew a ragged cloud over Crosby Street. Now she thought about her new life, as it spread out from the bomb. The pain. The recovery. Throwing herself back into work. Getting used to the startled looks, the embarrassed, averted glances. Loving Karp.

Yes, that was the good part, or was it? Did Karp really love her, or was it guilt? She used to be suspicious of men who loved her because she was gorgeous; now she was suspicious because they might be guilty or pitying.

And of course, she felt guilty too, because underneath the sharp Barnard and Yale Law grad and tough-talking lawyer still lived the Sacred Heart girl from Queens, whose grandparents had come over from Sicily, and who wanted to get married in white in a church. Wheels within wheels. Marlene had been periodically depressed since the explosion, trying to work it out herself while slaving twelve hours a day at what arguably was the most depressing job in the greater New York area.

"I'm cracking up, folks," Marlene said out loud to the sympathetic silence of Crosby Street. She flicked her cigarette butt out into the street, watched it explode into sparks, and went back inside.

She poured herself a glass of white wine from the jug in the refrigerator. It tasted like air conditioning. She downed it and poured another. The phone rang.

"Hi. It's me."

"Butch? Hi, baby."

"What're you up to, Champ?"

"Going crazy. Drinking. Crying. Did you hear about Terry Doyle?"

"Yeah. All about it. Denton was here earlier."

"Denton? The Chief? At *your* place? Holy shit! What'd he want?"

"He gave me the case." Karp described his conversation with his recent visitor. When he had finished Marlene said, "Butch, that's cosmic. I'm in, right?"

"If you want."

"If I want? I'm the best you got on bombs, baby. Besides, I know all the guys on the squad. And they'll spill their guts to me, which could count heavy if somebody fucked up on the squad.

Otherwise it'd be the blue wall. Shit, I'm jumping up and down, Karp."

"Great, besides, I might get to see you more. For the past two weeks you've been avoiding me."

"Ah, Butch, come on, cut me some slack here. You know how I—"

"Yeah, I know how you feel, you don't like to see me when you're depressed. But I miss you, Marlene. When are you going to hear about the compensation?"

Marlene had been trying in vain to get the state to pay compensation for her injury and the colossal hospitalization costs. She had given Karp this as the cause of her depression, a plausible fib. Karp was not one for deep psychological probing.

"Oh, who the fuck knows. A couple of weeks. When do we start this case?"

"Tomorrow morning, if you want. We could go out to the hospital and then over to Rodman. Say ten?"

Marlene agreed and they hung up. Once again love was left unsaid between them.

4

"THE PLANE'S IN Paris," said the voice on the phone. "It landed about midnight, our time."

Karp sat up in bed and groped for his watch. Six-forty, Saturday morning. Denton was off to an early start. Karp knuckled the sleep from his eyes and said, "What's the situation?"

"Unclear. I got this from Pillman and he wasn't exactly forthcoming. You going to see him today?"

"I plan to. We were going to see Hanlon first and find out what happened at the bomb range."

"We?"

"I've got Marlene Ciampi working with me on this."

"The one who got blown up a couple of years back?"

"Yeah, what about her?" Karp had picked up on the dubious note in Denton's voice.

"Ahhh . . . well. Are you sure she's, ah, right for this particular job?"

"It's my case, Bill. My players."

"So it is. Who are you going to steal from our end?"

"I'll work with the regular DA squad for now and keep it small to begin with. I'll let you know if I need hands."

"You do that," Denton said.

Karp got up, put in his usual half hour on the rowing machine, and dressed in a tan poplin suit and cordovan loafers: his summer uniform. He had two of the tan and two navy pinstripes for the winter, bought from a Chinatown tailor he had helped out after a robbery.

Dressed, Karp called Lieutenant Fred Spicer's office. Spicer headed the squad of NYPD detectives assigned to help the DA's office with investigations. Spicer had a regular day off, but the duty sergeant agreed to send around a car and driver. After calling Marlene to say he'd be over in fifteen minutes, he called Chief Inspector Peter Hanlon and set up an eight-thirty appointment at police headquarters. Karp thought it unremarkable that the man

32

who ran the Arson and Explosion Division was in his office at seven-thirty on a Saturday. Not this Saturday.

Finally, Karp called Vinson Talcott Newbury, another assistant district attorney, at home.

"Hey, Butch! Make it snappy, kid. I'm out the door."

"Going to Annabelle's?"

"Where else? What's happening?"

"I need one of your well-placed cousins, V.T."

"Butch, your belief that my family controls the Western world is flattering, but I have to be in Great Barrington by eleven. Can't it wait?"

"Not really." Karp gave Newbury a brief outline of the bomb and hijack case. "What I need," he continued, "is a line into Paris, the embassy, or whatever—whoever's handling the U.S. interest in getting these guys back."

"Why don't you work through the Feds here?"

"I will, but I want an edge. Denton has a feeling that the Feds are not being their usual forthcoming selves. What do you say?"

"I say it's going to put a dent in my emotional life, such as it is. Annabelle believes there's a time for work and a time for play. However, between my fabled charm and my monstrously overdeveloped sexual apparatus—surprising in one of such diminutive stature—I believe I can repair any resultant damage. Besides, no favor is too great for the man who bought me my first knish. Let me make some calls."

"You have somebody?"

"Well, we have a first cousin at State: Andrew. He's in economic affairs, probably not directly connected, but he's pretty senior. I'm sure we have somebody in Paris, a second by marriage or a once removed. I'll find out. I tell you what—give me a buzz at Annabelle's around noon, I should have something."

The black Ford pulled up two minutes later. Doug Brenner, a large, jowly detective, was at the wheel. Karp got in the front seat and Brenner pulled away.

"We're going to the ranges, right?" asked Brenner.

"Yeah, but first we got to pick somebody up. Stop by 49 Crosby and honk."

Marlene was wearing a yellow shirtwaist dress set off by a white sweater knotted around her shoulders and white canvas shoulder bag. As she skipped lightly down the iron stairway from her door, she looked to Karp like a college girl meeting her date for the big game. Her black hair had grown out since the explosion, and she wore it shoulder-length, parted on the right so that it fell like a pall across the bad part of her face and her left eye. She had her glassie in place this morning, Karp noticed; this was her habit during official business. Among friends she wore a pirate patch and her hair pulled back.

Marlene climbed into the back seat, greeted both men, and lit a cigarette. Brenner lit the stump of a cigar he fished out of the ashtray. Karp opened his window. He caught Marlene's glance in the rearview mirror and winked. She smiled and stuck out the tip of her tongue for an instant. Thus their relationship proceeded in public, at Marlene's insistence, although the DA's office was wasting its money on any detective who did not know about it at this point. The same for their friends among the attorneys. Karp thought it childish and had said so many times, but lately he had left off arguing, resigned to playing things Marlene's way.

Karp had never met Peter Hanlon before, but he had known many people with something to hide, and Hanlon looked like one of them. He sat behind his glass-topped oak desk and regarded the two ADAs with a carefully neutral expression. He was a medium-sized man with a black pompadour and a small, sharp nose on which perched heavy, dark-rimmed glasses. The dark rings under his eyes indicated that he hadn't slept well.

"Mr. Karp," he began, "you seem to have friends in all the right places. Bill Denton speaks very highly of you. What can we do to help?"

"Well, Inspector, we're obviously going for a murder one on this for the terrorist group. Bill's notion is that we would put together a team of detectives from across the Department to gather all the relevant evidence—one investigation, one case."

"I see. And you would be in charge of all of it?"

"That's right."

"What about the Department's own internal investigation?"

"The Department can do what it likes, naturally. But we would expect you to give us any physical evidence you turned up, and access to any reports. The usual. I know it's early, but have you come up with anything yet?"

Hanlon shook his head and flapped his hand. "Oh, no, it's far too early for that. It hasn't been twenty-four hours since—since the accident."

Karp perked up at this. "Accident? Is that what you're calling it?"

Hanlon cleared his throat. "No, not at all. I mean the explosion, the event."

34

"But you said 'accident.' That implies that there was some kind of error that led to the explosion. Was there?"

Hanlon's face darkened and his jaw got tight. Karp thought, he's going to say he doesn't like being cross-examined. I just got started and I'm screwing this up.

"I don't like being cross-examined, Mr. Karp."

"Sorry," said Karp, forcing a grin. "Habit, I guess. Look, Inspector, I think maybe we're getting off on the wrong foot—"

"I knew Terry Doyle. He was a friend of mine," Marlene said.

Both men stared at her. She went on. "I met him back in '74 when I was on the Brownstone Bomb Factory case. He was new and I was new, so I guess we just gravitated toward each other. He was a funny guy. Cocky. He had this thing about booby traps. He loved to rig these little devices and leave them around. You'd go to sit down at the typewriter or pick up a phone and kablooie! White smoke, red smoke, whistles.

"But I'll tell you one thing, he loved the Job. Loved it. And the bomb squad, too. So I want you to know that I want to nail the motherfuckers who did this as much as anyone on the Job. But I want to do it the way Terry would have wanted it. If there's any shit flying around I'll do my best to see it doesn't stick to the Department."

For a moment the only sound was the hum of the ventilation system. Then Hanlon said, "I see. Naturally, I feel the same way, Miss, ah, Ciampi, is it? A real tragedy, a great loss. The inspector's funeral is Monday."

In the elevator going down, Marlene leaned against Karp's flank and sighed. He put his arm around her and squeezed gently.

"Thanks for jumping in with Hanlon," he said.

"I had to. Jesus, Butch, you can't get into pissing contests with police brass. In another minute you'd of had your shlongs out on his desk looking to see who's got the biggest."

"Mine is."

"Of course, but the point is we can't roll into these guys just because Denton is fronting for us. I don't care how corrupt some cop is, if they think the Department's going to get slimed, it's stonewall, period. Even Denton won't do you any good then. He's a cop too."

The elevator stopped and, demurely separated, they walked out onto Police Plaza.

"You're going too fast, Marlene. Why would anybody think the Department screwed up on this one? A cop tried to defuse a bomb and it blew up. We know who did it. What's the problem?"

"I don't know, but Hanlon was weirded out. You saw that too, right? So what else could it be except something that might reflect on the job? He's a secret Croatian? He doesn't want to catch a bunch of cop killers?"

"No, but I'll tell you something else wacky. He asked about whether we were going to get the hijackers back for trial. I told him we were sure that we would and that we had something working already?"

"Which was bullshit, of course."

"Of course. But he believed it. And he didn't look happy about it. Not at all."

They got to Rodman Neck at mid-morning. Captain Frank Marino, the bomb squad detective in charge of the investigation, was expecting them. Marlene knew him from her previous work and liked him. This guy didn't pull any punches.

Like his boss, Marino wasn't happy either, but for more obvious reasons. And he was willing to talk about them.

"I still can't believe it," he said as he walked with Karp and Ciampi toward the fatal bunker. "Jack Doheny has been taking bombs apart for twenty years. He was like my best guy. Now this. You know we haven't lost a cop since 1933?"

"I know," Marlene said. "You got a line on what happened?"

Marino didn't seem to hear. "The goddamnedest thing! A brick, he said, it's just a brick. I listened to the tapes about fifty times. They pulled it perfect at Grand Central, set it up, clipped it, all by the book. Then they go and pull a damn bonehead . . . OK, here we are."

They had arrived at the lip of the bunker. Several vans were parked in the area, and men were carrying equipment and bundles of plastic evidence bags to and fro, vanishing down the ladder and reappearing, like delving dwarves. A stiff wind was blowing off the bay, flipping Marlene's dress around. Somebody whistled appreciatively.

"Can we go down?" she asked.

"Yeah, sure," Marino answered distractedly. "Follow me."

The bunker was as active as a stirred-up anthill; the ants were PD technicians in blue jumpsuits with a couple of white coats thrown in. Most of them appeared to be involved in an impossible task—placing every scrap of wood, metal, wire, every crumb of interestingly foreign substance into a plastic evidence bag and neatly labeling it. By the light of powerful lamps set up on poles, two men were taking photographs like they owned stock in Kodak.

Marino swung his hand to encompass the crowd and said, "Marlene, you know what we're doing here, right?"

"Yeah, you're trying to reconstruct the bomb from the debris."

"Uh-huh. And we'll probably do OK on it. It wasn't much of a bomb, power-wise. We didn't get much scatter, you know? I figure from what this looks like, plus what we got on the tape, that we're talking no more than five, six ounces of high explosives, probably military."

Marlene said, "What do you mean, 'what we got on the tape'?"

"Oh, just Terry's description of what he saw when he opened the pot. It was empty, he said, except for a brick. They all thought it was a dud, a hoax. Brick was probably hollowed-out, the dumb bastards."

"I thought you X-rayed the bombs you get in here. Wouldn't they have seen the hollowed-out part in the films?"

Marino shook his head. "Some bricks don't X-ray worth a damn. Bricks have a lot of lead in them, and radioactives. You know that just living in a brick house could give you cancer? It's a fact."

Karp pointed to a group of men pouring sand through wire-mesh screens. "What are those guys doing?"

"Oh, they're looking to see if anything's embedded in the sand-bags. We take apart and sift through the ones that got punctured by the debris."

"Pretty thorough," said Karp.

"Yeah," Marino said bitterly. "I wish they'd been that thorough yesterday."

Marlene put her hand on Marino's arm. "Frank, we got to talk."

Marino looked at the hand sideways. "So talk."

"No, privately. It's important."

Marino smiled. "Come on, Marlene, I'm married, four kids."

"Damn, Marlene, I can't take you anywhere," Karp said.

Marlene stuck out her tongue at both of them and flounced away to the ladder. As if by a signal, every man in the pit stopped work for several seconds to look up her dress, then returned to their grim dredging.

In Marino's small office, Butch and Marlene sat in hard chairs while Marino poured three black coffees from a thermos into china mugs.

"Mmm, this is Medaglia D'Oro," Marlene sighed.

Marino grinned at her. "Close," he said. "I got an uncle runs a gourmet place, he sends me these beans. They cost about as much as cocaine. I got one of those little espresso pots, works pretty good." The three of them sipped their coffee in silence. Karp thought the coffee tasted like medicine and wished he had a quart of milk and a bag of Oreos. His mug had fake Chinese characters printed on it, which when closely examined turned out to say,

37

"Fuck you very much." He pretended to sip from it and waited for Marlene to make her play.

At length Marino spoke. "So? What'd you want to talk about?"

Marlene leaned forward. "OK, Frank, this is strictly off the record, so no bullshit, all right? We just got started on this thing, and already we're getting weird vibes. We don't know if the brass is covering their ass or what. So we have to know: *is* there something to cover up? Or are we imagining things?"

The detective drank some more coffee and fumbled in the pockets of his coverall. He extracted a crumpled pack of Winstons and lit one with a steel Zippo. "Off the record for real?" he asked through blue smoke.

Marlene gave him her flashlight grin. "C'mon, Frank, would I lie to you except to advance my career? Is something going on?"

"OK, here it is. Yesterday was a zoo around here after the blast. Around ten last night I noticed that Hanlon showed up, along with some of his people from downtown. OK, not unusual, a cop gets aced, the chief inspector shows up to view the ashes, et cetera. But I see his people asking questions of the guys around here. They got Jim Hammer in the office there, and they're doing a regular grill job."

"Who's Hammer?' Karp asked.

"Doheny's driver. He was at Grand Central. Anyway, I start getting a little pissed at this and I go to Hanlon. I get him alone and I ask him, you know, what the fuck is going on? He says the investigation has attracted interest at the highest level, and he will be personally involved and all that bullshit. Which is fine with me. Then he asks, was Doheny drunk?

"OK, I say, Jack Doheny has been known to take a drink, and he was at this big retirement racket the night before, so maybe there was a little hair of the dog that morning, but nobody who knew him for five minutes would believe that he was ever drunk on the job.

"So Hanlon says we have evidence that suggests that he might have been drunk and screwed up the deactivation, and that's why Terry got killed. I couldn't fucking believe it! Jack's in the hospital with a fractured skull and busted ribs, and this guy is trying to get him to carry the can for it. What could I say? He's a chief and I'm a captain, right? I always thought he was a pretty good guy—"

Karp broke in. "But Doheny did screw up, in a way. I mean, you said it was a dumb move, buying that the bomb was a hoax."

Marino glowered at him. "Fuck yeah, I said it! But I'm saying it *after*. I *know* it was a real bomb. All right, maybe they didn't exactly follow procedures. They should have waited longer. But I could have made the same mistake, anybody could. That's no reason for Hanlon talking like he was going to bring charges.

"Look, I'll be honest with you. Terry's dead, and Jack and Luke are probably off the job permanent on three-quarters. The important thing is getting the guys that did this. I mean, they did it once, they could do it again. So what I can't figure is where Hanlon gets off being a hardass about Jack."

"Yeah, that's the question," Marlene said.

"It doesn't make sense," Karp added. "You would think the brass would be doing the opposite. If the explosion was due to incompetence by cops, they would be covering it up, not selling it."

"Unless they're covering up something worse," Marlene said quietly.

Karp shook himself and stood up. "Or unless this is our imagination. Look, Frank, when you start getting a picture of what happened here, I'd appreciate it if you let Marlene or me know first. And be extra careful with any physical evidence. Just call one of us and we'll send somebody over to get it."

Marino gave a short, sharp laugh. "Great. That's just what Hanlon said."

"Oh, yeah? You might tell Chief Inspector Hanlon to call his boss about that. Or maybe I will."

Marlene stood up, too, and she and Karp made to leave. At the door she turned and said, "Thanks for the help. And Frank, for sure now, it wasn't a fuck-up, was it?"

Marino regarded her bleakly. "Marlene, whatever Jack Doheny did or didn't do, some bastard wired that pot for one reason and one reason only—to kill whoever tried to take it apart. And it worked, the son of a bitch."

Twenty minutes later, Brenner, Marlene, and Karp were eating lunch in a clam bar on City Island, an unlikely community more reminiscent of Nantucket than of the Bronx, of which it is a peninsula. Only a few minutes from Rodman Neck, City Island's bars and seafood joints are usually populated with odd mixes of off-duty cops, Saturday boaters from the nearby marina, and local moms and kids in for a weekend treat. This clam bar showed the bill of fare in black stick-in letters on a white board supplied by Coca-Cola, and most of the customers were eating fried clams served in red plastic mesh baskets.

They talked for a while about the developing case, and when the waitress came over they each ordered a dozen cherrystones. Mar-

39

lene and Brenner had bottles of Schaefer; Karp ordered a black-and-white malted.

"What're you, nutso? Nobody has a malted with clams," Marlene said indignantly.

"Yeah," Brenner said, "it's like pickles and milk. You get a bellyache."

"Beer gives me a bellyache," Karp said placidly. "You should have a malted, Champ. Or two, you're still a rail." It was true. Marlene had never regained the weight she had lost after her injury. Everything she ate—and she ate enormously—was turned to hot vapor by her torchlike metabolism, a biological freak for which ninety per cent of the women in New York would have committed any number of class-A felonies. Perversely, Karp had liked her better when she was curvy, and said so often, producing pouts or snarls, depending on her mood.

This time she ignored the remark and said, "Brenner, what do you think? Why is Hanlon acting like he wants to pin something on his own guys?"

Brenner looked sideways at Marlene. With his heavy-lidded eyes he appeared to be half asleep most of the time, but Marlene knew he didn't miss much. "Somebody's leaning on him. From the top."

"Come on, Doug, Denton's running this," Karp said. "You saying somebody's bucking Denton?"

"Don't have to buck Denton. There's channels and channels, my lad. There's other superchiefs. There's the politicals. The hell I know. But if something's moving funny, there's got to be a mover, no?"

"But Hanlon would have to be crazy to screw with Denton on this."

"Why? What are you going to do? Go to Denton and say that Pete Hanlon isn't cooperating? He is. Tell him you didn't like the expression on his face? Give me a break. Besides, you do everything Bloom tells you?"

"He rests his case," Marlene said after slurping her last clam. "And now gents, since this line of inquiry must await further developments, as we say in police work, I am off to the ladies' for a whiz, after which I'd like to go to Jacobi to see if Doheny or D'Amato can talk yet. Then I think it would be a good idea for me to go back to Rodman and watch the boys poke through the ruins. How about you, Butch?"

"I guess I'll hit the FBI after we drop you off. I got to make a phone call first."

There was a pay phone under a canopy outside the restaurant.

Karp bought a roll of quarters from the cashier and called V.T. Newbury in Great Barrington.

"V.T.? Butch. Have you got anything?"

"I made some calls, yeah. An interesting situation. Do you know anything about France?"

"Umm . . . they eat frogs and stinky cheese and the people talk funny."

"You got it. I meant the way they handle things like this hijacking. Authority in France is incredibly centralized. Nobody makes a decision about something like this without an OK from the Minister of the Interior. But underneath there's all kinds of rivalries. For a crime at an airport, you have the local prefectural cops, who everybody shits on; the gendarmerie, who are sort of a national police force; plus the *police judiciaire*, who investigate crimes and develop cases. Also, within the regular gendarmerie there's a specialized anti-terrorist unit. Nobody gets along with anybody, so in the typically French way they also have this committee, CNSAC, in which all the various police groups are represented, plus the airport managers and the political types."

"Great lecture, V.T. So what's the bottom line? What's happening now?"

"OK, I'm getting to the good part. According to Leland Wilkes, a second cousin at the Paris embassy, this group has been meeting continuously since they first learned the plane was heading for Paris. The hijackers are demanding the release of two Croats the French arrested in June. Apparently they aced the Yugoslav consul-general in Marseilles. Then they want the plane fueled and reprovisioned for a flight over Yugoslavia so they can drop leaflets. Then they want to land in Bulgaria. The Yugoslavs are going batshit. They're demanding that the French arrest the Croats and return them to Yugoslavia.

"The committee seems to be deadlocked. The gendarmerie wants to storm the plane. The local cops and pols want the plane out of France, period. The thought of an airliner loaded with explosives winging around over Paris freaks them out. The Interior people, and we can assume the senior government people, don't want to piss off the Yugos too badly. After all, they owe them one for letting the consul get wasted. Mostly they don't want a bloodbath involving Americans. The bomb that blew up in New York seems to have impressed them that these assholes mean business."

"What's doing down at the airport?"

"Waiting is all, according to Leland. He's been there, and tells me they've got the plane parked on a side runway. There's a tanker and a flight crew van out there, and a friend of his in civil

41

aviation says the crew in the van is suspiciously tough-looking and muscular for French airport workers."

"Sounds like their SWAT team's in place. Will they try something?"

"Hard to tell. The French have never stormed an aircraft, and they've got a shitty record in dealing with terrorists."

"So what are our guys doing?"

"Ah, that's *really* interesting. The Paris chargé, a guy by the name of Oscar Raiford, is getting very mixed signals from Washington. The FBI also has a guy on the spot, Jim Toomey, flew over this morning. Out of the New York office. You know him?"

"Never heard of him, but he must work for Pillman. What's with the mixed signals?"

"Well, SOP in cases like this—hijack originating on U.S. soil, American flag carrier—is to pressure the holding nation for return of the hijackers to U.S. jurisdiction and also to resist concessions to hijackers. The drill is to talk, talk, talk, figuring time is on the side of the negotiators.

"OK, that's the direction Raiford is getting from State, or was, through this morning. But Toomey was pushing in the opposite direction—give in, let them go, let the Bulgarians have them. Leland says Raiford seems confused, keeps cabling Washington for written orders. Also this guy Dettrick seems to be a big player, which is odd too."

"Who's Dettrick?"

"According to the cuz, a Deputy Public Information Officer at the embassy, but really the CIA station chief. Dettrick wants the plane stormed with no damn nonsense about saving lives."

Karp whistled. "What does Leland think of all this?"

"Leland isn't actually paid to think. He's paid to speak good French and act snotty. But between cousins he vouchsafed to me that it's a remarkable departure from normal policy-making. His view is that somebody would like these Croats either in Bulgaria or in the next world, but in any case not on trial in New York. And that's about it, Butch."

"Thanks, V.T. I hope it didn't screw up your weekend."

"Substantially. However, we WASPs are used to sexual deprivation. We had planned to perch on a settee and read aloud from *The Wings of the Dove*, thus whipping our etiolated libidos into white heat, but now—"

"Bye, V.T. Call me if you hear anything else."

5

THE FBI'S NEW YORK office was lodged in the old telephone company building on 69th and Third Avenue. The lobby still bore in mural and relief medallions some of the communication symbology dear to Ma Bell's frozen heart—wire-girdled continents, hands across the sea, the long progress from the African drum to the self-dial telephone of 1938. Karp noticed especially the engraving on the bronze elevator doors: the thin, naked kid standing tiptoe on the globe, with electric hair under his World War I helmet, looking hopeful as he held aloft a snaky tangle of cables. This same icon had appeared on the cover of the old green New York phone books and had fascinated Karp as a child, filling his mind with maddening questions: why was the soldier playing with spaghetti? How did he stay on top of the basketball? Why did he have a leaf instead of a wee-wee? It was his first big case.

Karp soon discovered that the spirit of communication did not enliven the offices of the FBI. Pillman's secretary, a squat and tough-faced federal-issue blonde, informed him that Mr. Pillman was in emergency meetings all day and couldn't be disturbed.

"I'm here about the hijacking. Mr. Pillman is expecting me. Karp, DA's office."

She looked dubious. "The DA's office is in with him now."

"What! Who?"

She consulted her desk calendar. "A Mr. Lucca, it says here."

Karp placed his large knuckles on her desk and leaned over her. "OK, Mrs. ah . . . Finelli," he said, picking her name off the black plastic plate on her desk, "as far as I know, I'm representing the DA's office in this case. You got somebody else in there says the same thing, it means I got to call my boss and involve Mr. Pillman's boss and maybe the assistant AG, too. It could have to go to Washington, I don't know. So maybe we could clear up the whole thing in about ten minutes and avoid all that. What d'you say?" He smiled brightly.

Washington was the magic word. A minute later Karp was standing in Elmer Pillman's bright corner office, looking at Pillman's

43

froggy scowl. There was another man in the room, who stood and shook hands with Karp. He was thin and wore a rumpled brownish suit and one of those polyester ties that sports two unrelated patches of plaid. He nervously introduced himself as Jerry Lucca, from the Bronx DA's office.

Pillman leaned back in his government swivel chair and said magisterially, "Mr. Karp, Jerry and I were just saying that since the hijacking was a federal case and your policeman was actually killed in the Bronx, we would coordinate the investigation, with the Bronx DA picking up the local charges. I assume that's agreeable to you?"

"No, it isn't," Karp replied, pleasantly enough. "Obviously, we'd like to work as closely as we can with the Bureau. But we intend to bring the murder case against the hijackers in New York County. Moreover, we've made arrangements with the police department to coordinate all investigations and evidence through my office. And no other," he concluded with a sharp glance at Lucca.

"Wait a minute," Lucca said, flushing and attempting a conciliatory grin, "we can work this out. First of all, we have the murder site in our jurisdiction. That counts for something. And two—"

"That don't count for shit, Jerry," Karp interrupted. "And we don't have anything to work out because it's already been worked out. It's my case. You don't believe me, ask Moroni. He doesn't believe it, tell him to call the C. of D."

This casual mention of two godlike beings, the Bronx DA and the chief of detectives, took the wind out of the young man's sails. Something was going on that he didn't understand. He understood he was here on Moroni's orders. Pillman had seemed willing to work with him. He was excited by the possibility of handling the action on a potentially big murder case. Now this guy Karp comes and makes him look like a jerk. Unless he was bluffing . . . He looked at Pillman, who was examining the way the smoke from his cigar curled against the ceiling. Karp continued to regard Lucca with bland indulgence. He did not look like a bluffer.

"I guess I better check with uptown and straighten all this out," he mumbled, standing.

Karp smiled benignly. "You do that, Jerry." Lucca shook hands sincerely all around and scooted out.

Pillman did not like this development at all. He would have loved a green kid tying up the local end while he himself controlled the case. Also, wrangles among local jurisdictions made the Bureau look good by comparison. He decided, as he always did, that the best defense was an attack.

"What the fuck was that all about, Karp? Like I told Jerry, this is a federal case; I run it. What I don't need is a bunch of local pols screwing around with it. We'll coordinate like we always do. I got stuff in your yard, I'll let you know. Am I clear?"

Karp smiled. "Yup. It's your show, Elmer, skyjacking, kidnapping, the works. Us political types are just interested in murder one, killing a cop in L.O.D. Any little crumbs off your table we'd be glad to get. And, of course, if any evidence from our extensive investigation of the homes and businesses of the suspects bears on your case, or on any little conspiracies they might have been planning, or any other little exploding surprises they might have planted, or any connections they have with other terrorist groups, why then, we'll be sure to do the same. Sound good? Now, what's the situation in Paris? How are we going to get these guys back here?"

Pillman blew smoke and grinned nastily. "You're a bullshitter, Karp, you know that? You can take your evidence and stick it up your ass. I'll handle the situation in Paris, and if I think of any way you can help, I'll let you know. Meanwhile, it's been a pleasure, but now I got to make some calls, so—" He waved toward the door and reached for his phone.

Karp stood up. "Good idea, Elmer," he said, "and by the way since this interagency cooperation is going so great, could I borrow a phone?"

Pillman paused, then pointed to one of the doors leading out of the office. "My deputy's out. You can use his."

Karp smiled his thanks and walked into a smaller but similarly furnished office next door. He sat down at the desk and dialed the district attorney's private number.

Sanford Bloom had recently adopted a tone of hurt avuncularity toward Karp, as if he were the bad boy of the office, bright but unreliable, who could not grasp that Bloom truly had his best interests at heart. Like everything else about the man, it was as phony as a lead slug.

Karp wasted no time on pleasantries. "This is Karp. I'm down at the FBI. I'm dealing with Pillman on the hijack, and I think we're getting shafted on this murder. I need an irate call to the assistant director and maybe poke somebody in Washington. The sooner the better." Bloom had been United States Attorney for New York's Southern District before becoming DA, and was well-known to have important Washington contacts. Indeed, he rarely stopped talking about them.

After a pregnant silence Bloom replied, "Hold on a second, Butch. I can't go making calls just like that. Can't you work something out with this Pillman?"

"Yeah, sure, I could, but I haven't got time. There's no way I can be in on what's going on in Paris without the FBI's cooperation, and I've got to be in on it or somebody will make a deal with them that could queer our case on the Doyle killing. Look, I'll hang around here while you make the calls. Tell whoever that a police officer has been killed, and the FBI is being uncooperative about bringing the killers to justice."

"Butch, I can't do that. It would set interagency cooperation back twenty years."

Karp said, "If you want my advice, the cooperation you got to worry about is with the New York PD. It gets out that you are not vigorous in the extreme in pursuit of a gang of cop killers . . ." Karp left the thought unfinished.

"OK, Butch, you made your point," Bloom said peevishly. "I'll ring some people up right now." Karp heard the phone slam down.

During this conversation Karp had picked up the phone and sidled over to the door, which he had left open a crack. He had observed Pillman listening closely to his own phone. After Bloom hung up, Pillman did too, and Karp heard the click on the line. He replaced the phone and went back into Pillman's office. With a jaunty wave he started towards the outer door.

"Uh, Karp?"

"Yes?"

"Have a seat."

Lucky for me you're a sneak, Karp thought.

For the next half hour Elmer Pillman gave as good an imitation of interagency cooperation as he could contrive. The scene in Paris was much as V.T. had described it (although Pillman significantly left out the mysterious Dettrick, and the mixed signals) with one important exception: about an hour ago, the gendarmes had shot out the tires of the airplane, immobilizing it.

"So they're not going anywhere," Karp said, feeling considerable relief. "What happened then? Did the hijackers do anything?"

"Yeah, they want a new plane by sundown or they'll set off the bomb. The same shit they've been handing out all along."

"What's the French position?"

"Who the hell knows? Facedown with their ass in the air, as usual, probably. Their main worry was keeping the plane from taking off again and flying over Paris with a bomb in it, which they've settled. Now we think they're willing to let the other guys make the next move."

"But what's our move?"

Pillman looked away, his face suddenly tense. "How do you mean?"

46

"I mean we want them back here. They killed a cop. The last thing we want is for the French to screw around with them for a couple of years and then maybe trade them back to Yugoslavia for a tractor contract. I want to offer the hijackers a deal that'll break them loose now, today."

"Like what?"

Karp's brain spun for about two seconds. He had not, in fact, given the problem any thought. However, he was in his natural element. One thing he knew how to do was make deals with crooks.

"Three choices. They can surrender to the French authorities for trial under French law. They can go back to Yugoslavia. Or they can come back here for trial."

Pillman frowned. "What makes you think they'll choose the one you want?"

"Because the Yugoslavs will put them up against a wall and shoot them. The French are pissed off at Croatians already, and they've got no leverage in France. But on the other hand, some of these guys have been in New York for a while. They've got support here, friends, lawyers. Plus they read the papers. They know how easy it is to beat a rap in New York. But I doubt they're familiar enough with the New York State penal code to know how seriously we take killing an officer in the line of duty. Or about the felony murder rule. They should roll our way on this."

"There's a fourth option," Pillman said, chewing the plastic tip of his cigar. "They could blow up the plane."

"Not a chance. These guys aren't maniacs. They haven't hurt anybody on the plane. They let off the women and kids. They're some kind of big patriotic front. They want positive publicity, which is exactly what they'll get from a big New York trial. I'm telling you, they'll go for it."

Pillman considered this for a long moment, his face reflecting a frantic search for some element in this scheme that he could turn to his personal advantage. At last he saw a glimmer of one and allowed himself a thin smile.

"OK, Karp. I got to make some calls, but I'll buy it for now. I'll keep in touch, hey?"

When Karp had left, Pillman lit another cigar and called the assistant director, his boss. After listening to a lecture about how upset Mr. Bloom was, and about how important good interagency cooperation was, Pillman said "Harry, don't worry about it. The whole thing's fixed. I just had a great idea about how to get those people back."

Back in the lobby again, Karp felt that he had done pretty well in Pillman's office, although he was by no means sure that the deal he had struck would hold. Pillman was obviously running his own game. Karp was dying to find out what it was, but had no levers to pry it out of the FBI as long as the Bureau kept up the appearance of cooperation. Which they were doing, for now, but it remained an open flank.

The other source of worry was the cops. He called Denton from a phone booth and brought him up to date on the case.

Denton asked, "You getting good cooperation from my guys?"

"Yeah, sure, the best. Only, ah . . ."

"What?"

"I'm getting funny feelings about Arson and Explosion. Are you sure everybody's playing on the same team?"

"What do you mean? Pete Hanlon's solid."

"Right. But I hear he's casting aspersions that the bomb blast might be the result of incompetence on the part of his own men."

There was a long pause on the line. Then Denton said, "That's bullshit. Anything else?"

Karp sighed. The Blue Wall ran long and high. "Nothing. Except I'd like it made clear that my people collect all the evidence in this case directly from the source. Just in case."

"You got it. By the way, you still think this case is a grounder?"

Karp didn't think so. It was more like one of those deceptive sinking fly balls behind second base that make backpedaling infielders and onrushing outfielders collide as it drops just out of reach.

At high noon in Paris, although it was not a particularly hot day, the heat within the cabin of what had been Flight 501 had reached the debilitation zone. An airliner is a thermos bottle; without the cooling provided by its own or ground-based power a couple of dozen human bodies can boil themselves in their own heat within a surprisingly short time. The plane was also nearly out of water and food, and its toilets had stopped working. The cabin stank like a sewer pipe.

Daphne West was by this time the only one of the cabin crew remaining fully functional. Alice had designated herself as the personal servant of the hijacker group, while Jerry was collapsed in an aisle seat, his face white and clammy with heat prostration.

Most of the passengers were in the same state. Daphne had scrounged salt packets from the trash and had tried to force tepid salted water down several throats. She had tried to talk Karavitch into at least opening the doors, but he was adamant: security. He was afraid the police would rush the plane. For the same reason he was keeping all ground crew at a distance until a deal had been struck with the authorities, which meant no resupply of food and water. It occurred to her that the suffering of the passengers was another bargaining chip to him.

She heard a crackling noise outside the plane. A few seconds later, the plane lurched and sank.

She heard a cry of rage. "Blow them up! Blow them up, the bastards!" Macek was dancing around in the aisle, trying to wrench the pot bomb away from the little guy with glasses, who had it clutched to his bosom. More shouts in that foreign language followed. Daphne heard Alice's shrill scream over the shouts, and the agonized mooing of the passengers.

Once again Karavitch restored calm. He waded into the scuffle between his compatriots, shoved them back in their seats, and restored control of the pot to Rukovina. Then he hurried to the flight deck.

When the tires were shot out, Karavitch understood that a certain portion of the initial plan would have to be abandoned. This did not upset him. He had never expected the reds to allow him to fly over their country. Still, it was well to open the bidding high; if you never gambled for high stakes, you never got rich. Also, the drama of it had made recruiting easier, and would make excellent propaganda in the Croatian community.

The question was, what to do now. The important thing was to keep out of the clutches of the Yugoslavs. Also, the French were not to be trusted; with their volatile politics, they could have a red-loving regime in power at any time that might listen too sympathetically to the demands of the communists. And the French loved the Serbs in any case and always had. No, he had to get back to the United States, to New York, where he had friends. Or at least people in high places who owed him favors. He began to think of how he might contrive to bring this about. He thought well under pressure and did not especially mind the heat. In an hour he had come up with several plans, none of which was entirely satisfactory, but none of which was, in the event, required. To his great delight, they soon dropped the thing in his lap.

Marlene Ciampi puffed her first cigarette in two hours on the sidewalk outside Bronx Municipal Hospital Center. She had talked to both Doheny and D'Amato. Doheny was in bad shape and could barely mumble, but D'Amato had been lively and voluble. Doheny swore he was not drunk. The blast that had killed Doyle seemed to have sent chunks of shrapnel into his soul; he blamed himself entirely.

Marlene did not think he was lying to save his job, and D'Amato confirmed this. The sergeant may have been feeling the results of the previous night's drinking, but D'Amato swore that Jack Doheny never took a drink on the job. Nobody in a bomb disposal gang would have worked with him if he had.

This made sense to Marlene, even if nothing else did. She stamped out her cigarette and looked idly across the street. The great massif of the Bronx Psychiatric Center loomed over Eastchester Road and the railroad tracks. It was half empty, she had heard, since they had let the crazy people out onto the streets. Marlene watched an elderly black woman in a long purple coat, pink trousers, and a brown turban, pushing a rickety baby stroller. It was loaded with greasy brown paper bags that appeared to be full of garbage. Naturally, the woman was talking to the city at large, announcing to its citizenry seen and unseen, temporal and spiritual: "My cherry, my chicken, they got me all right, all right. May the Lord bless and keep you forever."

Marlene was jumpy by the time she got to Rodman. She wanted to get to work, to move. With little difficulty she talked Captain Marino into lending her a set of blue coveralls and letting her help out in the pit. For the rest of the afternoon she sifted sand and picked and bagged odd bits of matter. The sky went yellow, then purple as the sun sank into The Bronx. A salty breeze drove in from the bay. The gang completed its work and went home.

Marlene went back to Marino's office. He wasn't there, but she found him in a larger room down the hall fitted out with black-topped lab tables. On them had been placed large enamel trays and piles of plastic bags. Several men were examining things through magnifiers and binocular microscopes.

Marino greeted her and waved her over to where he stood next to a balding man at one of the microscopes. "Long day, huh Marlene?" he said cheerfully. For a man who had been going for more than twenty-four hours, he looked remarkably fresh.

"Yeah. You look bright, though. How do you do it?"

He chuckled. "Eat right and stay regular. And lots of black pepper—it washes the blood. Hey, you want to see something? Here, I think we might have got lucky."

He led her over to an enamel tray that contained some small blackened metal bits. "Look at that. Neat, huh?"

"What is it?"

"It's how they set it off. We still got samples being analyzed at the lab. We're doing GC-mass spec workups plus the usual chemistry, but we think we got basically a disassembled hand grenade. The lab's got formulations for just about every conventional explo-

50

sive in the world, civilian and military. It'll help a lot to know where it came from."

"How do you know it's a grenade?" Marlene asked. "What *is* this stuff?"

Marino grinned and picked up a stainless steel forceps. "You know the general principle, right? You pull the pin on a grenade, release the lever, and a spring drives a pin into a percussion cap. This sets off a five-second or so fuse, which detonates the primer charge, which sets off the main charge. This here, we think, is the mounting for the percussion cap, and this little twisted bit coming off it was where the fuse was inserted." Marino picked up and rotated the tiny blackened bits of metal as he spoke. They all looked remarkably alike to Marlene, but Marino sounded confident.

"Now, they got to fire it at the right time. They're working in a real tight space, so instead of the normal lever-and-spring firing mechanism, they use this." Marino pointed to a blackened tube bent almost double.

"What is it?"

"It's a solenoid. A little electromagnet with a shaft riding in it. You got them in automobile starters. When the juice hits the magnet, it tries to shove the magnetized shaft out of the tube. They rigged it to strike the grenade's cap."

"But where did they get the juice? I thought Doyle cut the wires."

Marino's jaw tightened. "Yeah, he did. He cut the wires leading from the battery to the timer and the wires leading into the pot. That's the fiendish part. Over here. Hey, Barney, let's have a look at that gizmo."

The balding man got up from his stool and made room for them in front of the binocular microscope. It had two sets of eyepieces so that two people could examine the specimen simultaneously.

"This I've never seen before," Marino said, manipulating the object on the microscope stage with his forceps. Marlene peered into the scope and saw what appeared to be a split tube about four inches long, broken in three places.

"See that shiny glob at the top? It's glass."

"An acid timer?"

"Probably. That big, fused mass above it's got to be a relay of some kind. As long as there's juice in the circuit, the relay stays open against the force of a spring. When the juice stops, the relay snaps shut and drives a pin into the acid reservoir and cracks it, starting the timer. Now, if you look inside the tube, see that fragment—black stuff, sandwiched with metal layers?"

"Yeah?"

"A capacitor. It stores current and lets it out in a burst. That's where they got the juice for the solenoid. Fucking fiendish, right?"

"Yeah," Marlene said thoughtfully, "also wacky."

"Wacky? Well yeah, you gotta be wacky, put a fucking thing like this in a—"

"No, I mean the *bomb* doesn't make sense. Look, they've got two independent sources of juice, one the taped-on six-volt, the other this weird gizmo for the booby trap."

"It makes a lot of sense if you wanted to blow somebody up. Poor sap cuts the outside wires thinking he's cut the juice when in fact he's just activated the bomb."

They were silent for a minute, staring at the evidence. Then Marlene pointed to the microscope stage and said, "Frank, could they have made this out of, like, spare parts?"

"It's possible, but not likely. I think what we got here is a serious piece of military hardware. Look, it's even got a serial number."

It was true. Marlene could make out figures inscribed in the metal of the tube: D 144 Z.

"And you don't know what it is?"

"Nope. We could check with the Alcohol, Tobacco and Firearms unit. Or the military at Aberdeen. I was planning to do it anyway with the grenade mechanism."

"Could you just send them photographs without telling them where it was from?"

"I guess so. Why?"

Marlene straightened from the microscope and rubbed her eyes. "Just caution. This case is getting weirder by the minute. I'm not exactly sure who's on our team. Look, Frank, when you get all this together, the physical evidence, the reports and all, could you seal it in a big box and hand carry it to my office? I need this all kept in the family for a while. When do you think you'll be done?"

Marino glanced at his watch. "Seven-thirty now. I expect the lab reports in about ten. I could wire the photographs with an emergency priority. They're usually pretty good about that. If they recognize the stuff, I should be able to get back to you late tonight or tomorrow morning."

"Great. Look, I'm going now. If I give you my number, will you call me at home?"

"Sure thing, Marlene. Hey, Marlene, what do you think?" He waved his hand to encompass the scientifically arranged debris. "What's going on here? We gonna nail these guys?"

"Or die trying. But I'd give a lot to know where they got all these toys."

"Not in Woolworth's."

52

*   *   *

Marlene hitched a ride with a couple of cops who were going home to Staten Island and didn't mind dropping her in lower Manhattan. She sat in the back of the car, smoking and watching the reflection of her glowing cigarette move against the lights of the traffic on the Major Deegan and against the fairyland lights festooning the Triboro Bridge. The cops talked about the Jets, about PBA politics and the contract up for renegotiation this year, about good deals on washing machines.

No shop talk. A good idea, Marlene thought: put in your shift, do your eight and turn it off. She couldn't do it herself, and Karp couldn't either, for sure. They were both workaholics.

Heading south on the FDR, the driver said, "Where are you, Marlene, Canal? Houston?"

"Houston, hang a right on Lafayette."

They soon pulled up in front of her loft. She slid across the seat and was starting to get out when the driver said, "Hold it, there's a guy in the doorway. You know him?"

"What is it, a bum?" the other cop asked.

Marlene peered into the shadows and saw a figure in light trousers and sneakers drinking from a bottle.

"Yeah, I know him," Marlene said, getting out. She crossed the sidewalk and reached into her purse for her key. "I knew it was you when I saw the orange soda. No piss bum would ruin his stomach with that shit."

"Whimper, whimper, cringe," Karp said.

She opened the door and looked down at him. "Jesus, Karp, you look like Greyfriar's Bobby. How long've you been waiting for me?"

"My whole life."

"Well, you better come in, then." She entered the building and began to climb the worn wooden stairs to the top floor, four flights up. As she opened the police lock on her loft door, she felt Karp come up close behind her and palm her butt. She looked at him over her shoulder. "What are you doing back there, sonny?"

"Rubbing your ass, in a crude effort to get you interested in me."

"Oh, yeah? Well, first things first. This kid has been grubbing in the sandbox for three hours and every tiny crevice in my body is packed with abrasive grains. First, a bath."

She opened the door and flicked on the lights. She lived in what was essentially a single immense room, a hundred feet long by thirty-five wide. It had windows on either end and a skylight in the center. The walls and sheet-tin ceiling were painted white and indirectly lit by aluminum clip-on reflector lamps that only partially dispelled the gloom.

"Sure you wouldn't rather have a tongue bath from a close personal friend?" Karp said, following her in and locking the door.

Marlene laughed. "Uh-uh, baby, this is a job for Keystone Plate-E-Z." She disappeared behind a row of folding screens in the center of the room. Many lofts in SoHo have bathtubs in the middle of the living room or in the kitchen, depending on the distribution of the piping when they were converted by artists with little patience or money. Marlene's bathtub was black, four feet high, and the size of a queen-sized bed. The loft's previous tenant had been an electroplating firm, and when Marlene had first seen the place, it had been a tangle of ruined machinery, including four huge tubs used in the electroplating process. Marlene had saved one of these out of the general toss-out, scrubbed it, resealed it, installed a filter and a heater, painted it, and picked out its name and origin—Keystone Plate-E-Z, Scranton, Pa.—in sequins.

Karp sat himself down on a decrepit couch as Marlene flung various articles of clothing over the screens. A pair of filmy underpants floated through the air and landed at his feet. He heard Marlene lower herself into the tub with a long, gasping sigh. Then she said, "Butch, what're you doing?"

"I'm chewing on your panties and dreaming of times gone by."

A giggle from behind the mysterious screens. "Don't do that. They're from Bonwit's. OK, you can come in, but just for the bath. You can do my back and I'll bring you up to date on the case. And turn down the lights; I'm going to do the candles."

Ten seconds later, Karp was out of his clothes and behind the screens. Marlene had lit four tall, thick candles stuck to the four corners of the tub. Karp knelt behind her, worked up a lather with the scented soap, and rubbed her back with his hands. She stretched her arms out, her hands gripping the edge of the tub, and told him what she had learned.

Karp tried to remain professional. He shared with her what had happened at the FBI. Meanwhile his hand unprofessionally snaked farther forward, soaping her flank and straying lightly over her small, pointed breasts. He became increasingly aware of something growing beneath the candle-flickering surface of the water, where his groin squashed up against Marlene's warm flesh. This is crazy, he thought, we're sitting here in this wet dream, talking calmly about work. Our goddamn relationship in a nutshell.

"Anyway," Marlene was saying, perhaps a trifle too slowly and languorously (did he imagine?), "there are mysterious tendrils here. This is not just a gang of assholes who killed a cop halfway by accident. The connections—the cop brass acting weird, the FBI acting weird, the complexity and sophistication of the bomb. There's got to be something bigger involved, Butch, I know it. Butch? Are you listening to me?"

"Yes, Marlene, something bigger involved."

She spun around on her knees, sloshing water, and fixed him with a steely glance. "No, you're not. You're just rubbing me up and squeezing your dong against my back, hoping I'll get sexy."

"No, I really was listening, but come on, Marlene, you got to admit we're in a pretty romantic situation. I mean it's distracting—"

"Fuck the distracting! What about my idea?"

Karp felt his lust being replaced by annoyance and slid away to the opposite wall of the tub. "OK, let's talk about your idea," he said harshly. "First of all, things often *are* what they seem. Some assholes left a booby-trapped bomb that killed a cop. That's the fact of the case. Why did they do it? Who gives a shit! They're assholes, right? The cop brass is acting weird because they haven't had a bomb squad cop killed in forty years. Again, who gives a shit? The FBI? Business as usual, close to the vest and just feed the locals what's good for them. Now the grenade, or whatever it was—"

"It was a grenade, I saw it."

"You saw a couple of pieces of burnt shit on a plate. When we have a sworn statement by an armaments expert that it's a grenade, *then* it's a grenade. And even if it does turn out to be a grenade, the case doesn't need any goddamn 'tendrils.' You got any idea how many guys brought souvenirs home from Vietnam? Not to mention stuff ripped off from the National Guard?"

"What about the timer? You got an explanation for that too?" Marlene shouted furiously.

"No, but I guarantee you I could go down to Canal Street tomorrow and buy twenty pieces of military hardware that somebody like that hijacker who repairs electronics for a living could rig up as a bomb timer."

Marlene glared at him. "You're such a bastard, you know that? I trot out my pissy little theory and you get this big kick out of squashing it flat. You know, you've got a sadistic streak in you I can't stand."

"Fuck this. I'm going." Karp rose abruptly from the water, scattering droplets and making the candles gutter.

Marlene lunged forward like a striking trout and grasped his leg. "No, don't go! This is all fucked up. Don't go. Come on, sit down in the bath."

When he had done so, Marlene sat in his lap. "Ah, Butch, I

didn't mean to blow up that way. Honestly, I was so happy when I saw you sitting on my stoop tonight, drinking your little orange soda."

"That's OK, Marlene, I'm sorry—"

"And it was so dreamy in the bath, you rubbing me. I guess I was expecting a big hand for my brilliant deductive logic and then a glorious descent into fleshly pleasures, I don't know." Her one eye glinted in the candlelight, full of sadness or some odd emotion Karp associated with the madness of women.

"Is it too late?" he asked in a cracked whisper.

"Never too late," Marlene said into his ear as she reached down into the water. "Kapitan, ze Britische convoy! Up periscope!"

"Marlene," Karp gasped, "you're going to drive me crazy. I can't take this—"

She swiveled around and wriggled and straddled Karp.

"Oh, a little bit over," she whispered. "Aahgh! That's it, oh, that's perfect. Isn't that perfect? Oh, my gosh, I'm—we're floating away."

6

A RINGING PHONE brought Butch Karp out of a love-sodden sleep, after which he hung a right and plunged back into dreamland again. It wasn't his phone anyway. He rolled over and pressed a pillow over his head, a pillow that smelled of Marlene, a cocktail of patchouli oil and sex. Karp wriggled at the returning memory. Marlene had outdone herself last night, as was her occasional and unpredictable wont, concluding with a marathon steeplechase athwart Karp's exhausted yet potent body. His crotch was still tender.

Which reminded him of another requirement of nature involving the same zone. Flinging off the quilt and sheets, he heaved out of bed. He had forgotten, however, that he was sleeping not on his own bed on the floor, but on Marlene's high four-poster, with the result that he stumbled and banged his shin painfully on the bureau close by. He cursed and looked around the sleeping platform, rubbing sleep from his eyes. Below, Marlene was visible only as a tousled mass of black hair above the back of an armchair. She was chattering to someone on a pink Princess phone. It went with her sleeping loft, which she had furnished as a little girl's bedroom in an Italian neighborhood in Queens, circa 1950. She had a white four-poster single bed with pink dust ruffles—an authentic relic of her girlhood—a white bureau, and a white vanity table, with a pink crinoline skirt and a matching bench. All bore patterns of cherubs and roses. There was also the armchair, a brocaded monstrosity that might have been French Provincial, had France been occupied in the seventeenth century by Italo-American sanitation workers.

He stood and rubbed his bumped shin against the back of his calf. Climbing down the stairs to the main floor, he padded, naked and huge, across to the tiny toilet closet.

"Yahoo!"

When Karp emerged, his girlfriend was jumping up and down on her bed, yelling and flapping her arms by intention and her breasts by default. It made a pretty sight, piquing both his curiosity and lust.

"What happened, Marlene?"

She bounded off the bed and ran over to the rail that surrounded the sleeping platform. "I was right, dammit! I knew it. That was Marino on the phone. He just heard from his lab and from the post-explosion guys at the Alcohol, Tobacco and Firearms unit. It *was* a grenade! And they had never seen that type of timer before, but it looked to them like military hardware, and—"

"Marlene, hold your horses. So it's a grenade. Big deal. I told you, they could have stolen it from a National Guard armory—"

"Yeah, they could have, if they stole it in Omsk. For your information, Mr. Smarty-pants, Terry Doyle was blown up by a disassembled Soviet RDG-5 hand grenade. The fuse fragments are derived from the standard UZRG and the charge was RPX, about one hundred grams. It all checks. Warsaw Pact, all the way."

"Oy vey," Karp said.

"No kidding. Stay there, I'm coming down. There's more." Marlene neatly vaulted over the rail into Karp's arms. She hugged him and stretched to kiss his ear.

"What else?" he asked, hugging her back.

"First say, 'Marlene smart, Butch dumb.' "

He did so, with reasonably good grace, and she continued.

"They're checking out the timer. But the big news is, when Marino got back to Rodman this morning, somebody had ransacked the room where they were keeping the evidence. Luckily, Frank had loaded the crucial stuff into a carton and taken it home. How about them apples?"

"How about them," Karp said wonderingly. "And the only people with access to Rodman at night would be—oh, shit."

"Cops," Marlene finished with grim satisfaction.

"Christ, I got to call Denton. I should have called him last night, but I was seduced from my duty . . ." He squeezed the small cantaloupe-firm buttock convenient to his right hand.

She skipped away from him and began to climb the ladder to the sleeping loft. She said over her shoulder, "Well, it's Sunday, and far too early to be thinking of business. I'm going back to bed."

Karp went over to the downstairs wall phone and dialed Denton's number. As he did, he glanced up: Marlene was in a yoga headstand at the foot of the high bed, her legs spread wide apart, her ankles rotating in small circles. Thus distracted, Karp dialed. An irate woman answered in Spanish. Dial again: a dog hospital. Karp turned his back on Marlene's gyrations and concentrated on the number.

"Karp! Where've you been? I've been trying to get you all

night." Denton sounded angry and harassed, not at all inclined to make allowances for a Sunday morning.

"I was out. What's up?"

"Our hijackers surrendered, that's what's up. At six-fifty Paris time, yesterday evening. They're coming back aboard military transport. They're scheduled into Kennedy at two-ten this afternoon."

"That's great! Where are they supposed to go then?"

"Federal custody, so I guess they'll take them down to FBI headquarters."

"Ummm. Not so good there. I can interview them at the FBI, no problem, but afterward . . . Look, Bill, we've got to end up with physical custody of those people. I'll call Bloom and get him to pull his famous strings. I want them in Riker's under our control."

"What's the matter, don't you trust the Feds?"

"Yeah, to take care of the Statue of Liberty. And speaking of trust, I think we got a little problem closer to home." Karp related to Denton what he had learned from Marlene, and got several short, sharp expletives in return.

"I find those guys, they're dead. And I'll find them if—"

"Bill. Stop. I mean, my advice is, find out what you can, but no witch hunts while this case is going on, now that we actually have a case. You don't want to drive whoever's screwing up deeper under cover before you find what the source of the pressure is. What could make cops want to screw up the prosecution of a cop killer?"

"Nothing."

"It's something, bet on it. So we've got to make sure that everything about this case is absolutely by the book—collection and custody of evidence, arrest and custody of suspects, procedure, documentation, the works. That means everything gets double-checked by you and me or people we personally trust."

"Right. You got it. Meanwhile—"

"Meanwhile, I need the flight crew and passengers taken to Centre Street. Park them in a courtroom and I'll get a gang together to do interviews. Then I'll roust a judge and get warrants for the homes and business premises of the suspects. You need to get in there fast, toss the joints, pick up any evidence relating to bomb manufacture, conspiracy, and so on. And I want all evidence in my immediate custody as soon as possible. That's critical. What else? Oh, yeah, the bomb on the plane. Where's that now?"

"The bomb? Oh, right, you don't know. It was a dud."

"A dud?"

"Yeah? Funny, right? There was nothing in that pot but air. And a brick."

Karp arrived at FBI headquarters, trailed by a small, grayish man named Murray Rothman. A court stenographer, he was well-known for his perpetual availability and his tomblike discretion. Karp was going to tackle the hijackers himself; he'd given Marlene the more onerous responsibility of rousting a couple of assistant DAs out of their Sunday torpor to interview the flight crew and passengers.

The entrance to the building was cordoned off by the familiar gray sawhorse barriers, lined with photographers and TV crews, and several television vans were parked nearby. Farther back, several hundred other people were milling noisily in the late summer sunshine. Some of these were passersby or New York gawkers, but the majority was an organized group carrying homemade signs: "Free the Freedom Fighters," "Free Croatia." They were respectably dressed middle-aged and elderly people, not the kind usually found in demonstrations in Manhattan. There was a priest with them, which was not surprising, since most New York demonstrations are so equipped. What was a bit odd was that this one was haranguing the throng.

Karp introduced himself to the uniformed lieutenant on duty. Denton's name worked its usual magic, and he and Rothman were allowed into the lobby. There he waited with cops and plainclothesmen of various organizations, all conversing cryptically or speaking strange-sounding CB talk into hand radios. Nobody spoke to Karp. He didn't have a radio.

After ten minutes they heard sirens and a convoy comprised of two NYPD blue-and-whites, a white U.S. Marshal's Service car, an unmarked car with a red flasher, and a dark van pulled up into the cleared space out front. As men piled out of the vehicles, Karp spotted Pillman getting out of the unmarked car. Several men in plainclothes, who Karp supposed were U.S. marshals, opened the sliding doors of the van. The five hijackers clambered down, first the four men and then the woman, blinking in the sunlight.

Three marshals led them to the building entrance. The cameras popped and whirred; reporters shouted questions. The crowd caught sight of them, and the contingent with signs exploded in cheers. The male hijackers lifted their handcuffed hands above their heads and waved to the crowd, smiling broadly. Karp noticed that they did not clench their fists, a gesture he had always regarded as a sort of international symbol of one's willingness to deal radically with all problems.

In the lobby Karp got his first close look at the hijackers. The men seemed in good spirits, smiling and talking loudly to one another in a Slavic-sounding language. By contrast, the woman seemed tight-lipped and worn, her blond hair unwashed and pulled tightly back, her eyes hidden behind dark glasses. As their guards took them into an elevator, Karp wondered why they were so laid back. Did they know something he didn't?

Spotting Pillman entering an elevator, he gave Rothman Pillman's office number, dashed forward, and got a shoulder in between the closing bronze doors. They stuttered back open and he stepped into the car. "Hello, Elmer," he said cheerfully. "Looks like our idea worked."

Pillman exhibited one of his large collection of scowls. "What're you doing here, Karp?"

"Fine, thanks, how're you? Well, why I'm here, Elmer, is to interview our suspects in this apparent case of first-degree murder, inform them of their constitutional rights, and take custody of them in behalf of the people."

Pillman gave a noncommittal grunt. The elevator was crowded largely with FBI personnel, and he did not want to get into a public argument he was not sure of winning. The doors opened and Karp followed Pillman down the hall to his office.

A number of agents were waiting there for instructions from their boss. Like Pillman, they were all wearing casual clothes, this being Sunday. He talked to the men briefly, after which all of them left save one, a good-looking, freckled blond with a little mustache. Pillman turned to him and gestured in Karp's direction. "Joe, this is Mr. Karp from the New York DA. He wants to interview our prisoners. Karp, Joe Stepanovic. Joe is something of an expert on Croatian affairs, aren't you, Joe?"

"Good to meet you," Karp said. "I assume you speak the language, yes? Well, if Mr. Pillman doesn't mind, we can use you as a translator. OK, here's my stenographer, let's get going."

Pillman looked askance at Rothman, who had just shuffled in to the office. "Wait a minute, Karp, I can't just let you take this whole thing over. I have to get clearance. Right now you can take yourself and your stenographer the hell out of here. I'll let you know when you can start."

"And when would that be?"

"How should I know? I told you, I have to make some calls."

"Fine. Make your calls. Mr. Rothman and I will wait right here. By the way, to save you some time, should one of your calls be to the U.S. Attorney for the Southern District, I happened to talk on the phone with Mr. Aleman this very morning just before he teed off at Easthampton with Mr. Bloom. He and Mr. Bloom agreed it was essential for me to depose the suspects at the first opportunity."

Pillman stared at him pop-eyed, his normally pasty complexion enlivened by growing blotches of scarlet on either jowl. Without a word he went into his inner office. As the minutes passed, Karp idly spun the Rolodex on the secretary's desk. Stepanovic studied the benign face of the president on the wall. Rothman sat in a chair, his stenographic machine held primly on his lap.

When Pillman emerged, he was a new man. A thin-lipped smile split his face, but stopped short of his eyes. "Well, well, Karp, looks like you get to order anything in the store. You seem to be a well-connected and popular young man. Heh-heh." He wasn't chuckling, he was just saying "heh-heh."

Karp smiled his best false smile and tried to look well-connected and popular, two qualities he knew had always eluded him. "Thanks, Elmer. Glad to get any misunderstandings cleared up. So let's get to work. I think we should start with Karavitch. Lead on."

The FBI kept a more civilized interrogation room than the ones in the Tombs or the typical precinct: a real oak table and oak chairs, no bare bulbs, and an American flag in the corner, so you could tell you weren't in communist Russia.

Rothman unlimbered his steno machine. Pillman and Karp sat at the table, and after a few minutes Stepanovic came back with Djordje Karavitch. The two men sat across from Karp and Pillman.

Karavitch looked tired. His cheeks were covered with gray stubble and his white shirt was grimy. Despite this, he carried himself well; his shoulders were squared and his eyes bright. He looked like a general—defeated perhaps, but still a general.

Karp took him in. Not nervous, even a little arrogant: a tough cookie. He began the formal ritual. He introduced himself and the others in the room. He explained Karavitch's rights under the law, including the right to remain silent and the right to have a lawyer present during questioning. He asked whether Karavitch understood, or whether he needed a translator.

At this the old man allowed himself a slight smile. "I speak English, Mr. Karp. I am a citizen of this country since 1950." This was said genially, almost patronizingly. In Karp's experience, arrested suspects who began interviews this way were hard to nail, believing some personal quality or connection rendered them above the reach of the law. They usually cracked when they found out they weren't. Of course, Karp had to admit to himself, occasionally they really were.

"Fine," he said. "Now, will you agree to waive your right to a lawyer and answer some questions at this time?"

"That would depend on the questions, would it not?" Karavitch asked. Once again a slight smile crossed his face, making the scar on his lip bounce.

"You may refuse to answer at any time, Mr. Karavitch. This is an entirely informal proceeding, although information taken down here may be used in more formal proceedings, such as arraignment or trial."

"I see," Karavitch said. "Then perhaps I can ask you a question in clarification, yes? Why is it that you are here, Mr. Karp? Have I broken the laws of New York? What is your charge? I am arrested, true? Our legal system says you must tell me the charge."

A *very* tough cookie, Karp thought. "Surely, Mr. Karavitch, you must realize that there are a large number of serious charges that could be brought against you and your associates. Kidnapping, assault with a deadly weapon, theft—"

"But none of these were committed in New York. In New York all we did was get on a plane. We did not take over the plane until many miles away."

"It doesn't matter, Mr. Karavitch. In such a case, the crime is assumed by law to have taken place at the point of origin of the journey."

Again the smile. "If this is true, then still, it is from the borough Queens that the plane takes off. LaGuardia Airport is not in New York County, true?"

Karp felt himself growing angry. He was not supposed to be fencing with this bastard, especially not on the record. Karp glanced over at Pillman, who was struggling to retain an expression of innocence that would have seemed smarmy on an altarboy. Karp considered the possibility that Karavitch had in some way been coached. But no, there hadn't been time. The suspects had been taken directly to FBI headquarters from the airport. Besides, who would have coached them? And why?

Karp rearranged his face in a flat mask, and let a full minute of silence go by, while he counted the flecks in Karavitch's irises. There was no way he was going to lose control of this interrogation. "True," he said. "Could you state your full name?"

With a series of piercingly brilliant questions, Karp got the suspect to admit his name, address, and occupation, and that he was involved politically with movements to liberate Croatia from the yoke of communism. He seemed willing to spout off about the miseries of the great Croatian people under communism until nightfall or until Rothman ran out of steno tape, but Karp cut him off.

"Right. We've established you're a great patriot, Mr. Karavitch.

Now let's talk about the bomb you placed in locker number 139 in Grand Central Station on or before Friday, September 10, of this year."

Karavitch stopped smiling. "I placed no bomb."

"One of your associates, then?"

"No bomb. No one placed any bomb. We have hurt no one, no one!"

"Well, that's interesting to hear you deny that your bomb hurt anyone, Mr. Karavitch, since I don't recall suggesting it. And you're sure that none of your associates did, either? How come? Do you watch them every minute?"

"We are an army. We are under strict discipline."

"Yes, and you're the general, right? You are responsible for what your, ah, troops do?"

"Yes."

"Thank you. I'm glad we were able to establish that. Well, Mr. Karavitch, it turns out that there *was* a bomb in locker 139, and it exploded and killed a New York City policeman. Now, as you probably know, being so familiar with our legal system, the homicide of a police officer in line of duty is murder in the first degree. You and all of your associates are subject to such a charge, the most serious charge in our legal code. Mr. Karavitch, while I do not make any promises or guarantees whatsoever, it often happens that when people assist the law, the law is more inclined to treat their case favorably. Now, would you tell me please how you obtained the explosives and the other components of the bomb you left in locker 139 on or before September 10, 1976?"

The tick of the stenographic machine went on for a few seconds. Then the room was silent, save for the creaking of chairs and the whir of the ventilation system. All eyes were on Karavitch, who remained as still as stone, his face pale and unreadable. Then he turned to Stepanovic and said something in Croatian. Karp noted that his tone when speaking that language was different from the one he used when speaking English: harder, more like the bark of command. To Karp's horror, the FBI man answered in the same language, and Karavitch began to reply.

"Stop!" Karp shouted. "Damn, Pillman! What is this? You guys are lawyers. You know the damn translator can't engage in colloquy with a suspect on the record." Pillman shrugged: "You can't get good help these days." Karp turned to Stepanovic. "What did he say? And what did you say?"

"He said that he didn't want to—" Stepanovic began mildly, but Karp cut him off. "No interpretations, Stepanovic! Give it to me verbatim."

The younger man flushed, then continued. "He said, 'I do not want to answer his questions anymore.' And I said, 'Do you want to have a lawyer present? Will you answer questions with a lawyer present?' Then he said, 'Perhaps later. Right now I am feeling faint. I am an old—' Then you cut him off."

Karp took a deep breath and continued in what he hoped was a level voice. "Thank you, Mr. Karavitch. You may go now. Please bring in Pavle Macek." Pillman nodded at Stepanovic, who stood and went to the door. Following him, Karavitch looked about as faint as the Chrysler Building.

When they had left, Karp turned to Pillman and said, "What kind of stunt was that, Elmer? No, don't tell me. But if your boy tries that again, I'm out of here, *with* the prisoners. I'll get my own goddamn translator, you understand me?"

Pillman looked away, his eyes heavy-lidded. "You could get boring, Karp, you know that?"

Karp thought of a number of replies to this, but held his tongue as Stepanovic entered the room with Macek. The hijacker seemed excited. His lanky, thin hair was plastered to his scalp, and he stank of sweat.

The questioning began as before. Macek, it turned out, was also a citizen and needed no translator. He was also a Croatian patriot. He also knew nothing about any bomb. The hijacking was a demonstration, no one had been hurt. He resented the accusation that he had had anything to do with the killing of a policeman. He wanted a lawyer.

Cindy Wilson Karavitch identified herself, hid behind her sunglasses, and asked for a lawyer. End of session.

Vlatko Raditch spoke no English, but smiled a lot. He maintained he had boarded the plane as a lark with his buddy, Milo. He thought the whole thing was a joke. Bombs? What bombs? He didn't ask for a lawyer, but it was obvious to Karp that he needed a nanny.

The last interview was with Milo Rukovina. Karp regarded him hopefully: he had the look of a weak link. During the initial questions, with Stepanovic translating, he ducked his head and removed his thick spectacles and pinched the bridge of his nose and wiped his forehead with a large, soiled handkerchief.

Karp spoke slowly and carefully, trying to control his frustration. He listened carefully to Rukovina's answers, hoping inanely that the grammar and vocabulary of Serbo-Croatian would spring miraculously into his head.

Karp read him his rights and then led him through a series of questions about the hijacking. Then he asked, almost casually,

"Mr. Rukovina, who was responsible for assembling the bomb that
you placed in locker 139 in Grand Central Station?" After this was translated, Rukovina shook his head violently from side to side, and a torrent of words poured from his mouth. "I am not, I was never responsible for the technique, for the technical details. I am the political theory, theoretician." Stepanovic translated. "I have no knowledge in this area."

Karp nodded, smiling, fixing Milo with his eyes. Then he said, very slowly, "Mr. Rukovina, who does have such knowledge?" Karp caught the "Gospodine Rukovinu—" and then Stepanovic was off with at least two dozen words, delivered rapid-fire in a low, even voice. Milo squeaked back a phrase, and then Stepanovic said something, and then Milo gasped out two words. Karp's fist crashed down on the table; Milo jumped like a rabbit.

"That's it! Mr. Rukovina, thank you. You may go now. Murray, mark the time and put away the machine. We're through. Let's have those transcribed first thing tomorrow morning, huh?"

Stepanovic left with Milo, and after packing his machine and tapes, so did Rothman. Pillman stood up, stretched, and yawned. "It's been fun, Karp. Now buzz off, I want to get home. Maybe I can still catch some of the game."

"You total shit," Karp said in an even voice. He stood up and loomed over Pillman. "I can't believe you would deliberately screw up an investigation. I can't fucking believe it. A cop got killed, and you're trying to queer the case."

"Up your ass, Karp. Don't blame me if you can't handle an interrogation."

"Pillman, in my last question there were five words besides the guy's name. Your boy comes out with the Gettysburg Address, and Milo looks like he swallowed a peach pit. The fucking translator is coaching the suspect.

"Now, I don't know what's going on, who's jerking your chain, but it's going to come out, sonny. What is it, Pillman? What's the dirty secret?"

"I don't have to take this shit from you, Karp. Get the fuck out of my office."

Karp's foot lashed out and kicked a chair across the room, a willful abuse of U.S. government property and a misdemeanor offense. Pillman did not arrest him. Then Karp careened out the door and almost collided with the returning Stepanovic in the corridor. The smaller man tried to get by, but Karp blocked his path. "Stepanovic, tell me, what does 'knees nahm' mean?"

"What?"

66

"That's what it sounded like, the last thing Rukovina said in there, his last two words."

"Oh, you mean *'ne znam.'* It means 'I don't know.' "

"Thanks, Joe. You know, I think I'm really picking up the language."

"Oh?" Stepanovic said with an uncertain smile.

"Yeah. *Ne znam*, huh? He said it, all right. But you said it, too, didn't you, Joe? Twice, in fact, during your little chat. How about that?"

Down in the lobby, Karp called Marlene's office, but got no answer. Then he dialed his own office. While he listened to the phone ring he thought about calling Bill Denton and about what he would say. The interrogation had shaken him. Karp knew more about corruption than most. He was an agent of a system that was corrupt in its every limb. But he was not himself a conspirator and was uneasy in the presence of conspiracies. He liked to be able to tell the good guys from the bad guys.

And Denton was a good guy. He had to be. But cops were being bent in this case, and Denton was brass, the highest. The possibility that Denton was not leveling with him, that his concern for bringing Terry Doyle's murderers to justice was in some way a fraud, gave Karp the screaming jitters. It meant he was absolutely alone. He decided to wait before calling Denton.

The phone in Karp's office was answered by Roland Hrcany, a fellow assistant district attorney and a friend.

"DA's office, we doze, but never close."

"Who's that? Roland?"

"Hey, yeah, Butch? What's happening, man?"

"I'm down at the FBI. I just got through interviewing the hijackers."

"Great! Did they do it?"

"Yes, hijack; no, locker bomb. Very adamant and they want to see a lawyer."

"Uh-oh."

"Yeah, right, and there's more. Listen, Roland, Marlene got you down to do the interviewing?"

"Yeah, we're having a great time. Got a case of beer and the little TV. We're watching the Yanks at KC in between; four-two, Yanks, top of the fourth."

"Who else is there?"

"Besides Marlene, that kid, Tony Harris, and Ray Guma."

"She got the *Goom* down to depose witnesses on a Sunday?"

"It was me. I said I'd fix him up with a piece of ass afterward."

"Thanks, buddy. Roland, do you think we're the only district attorney's office in the country with a full-time pimp on the staff?"

"Far from it. Most have nothing but. Hey, here's Marlene. You want to talk to her?"

"Yeah, but Roland, do me a favor. Arrange to get custody of the hijackers. I'd like them in Riker's by tonight. I want those guys buried, so nobody gets to them but us. And Roland, this case has weird shit all over it, so use cops you trust, personally. You know what I mean?"

Hrcany laughed. "Yeah. Married ones who play around. OK, will do. Here's Champ."

"Hey, cutie. How's it going?"

"Cutie, my ass. You ought to see this place, Butch. Beer on the floor, the game blasting out of the TV. Roland is showing Guma Polaroid beaver shots of women, and the great connoisseur is making his selection of the evening. For two cents I'd join the Carmelites and piss on all of you."

"If you did, could we still fuck?"

"Ah, Butch, that's the kind of sensitive remark that warms a lady's heart. I got to go. One more interview and then home and self-immolation."

"Wait, seriously—how's it going?"

"No problems. We've pretty much established that the plane was hijacked, so kidnap, umpteen counts. Assault? There was a lot of yelling and threats, but the passengers and crew were left alone physically. Except Alice Springer, one of the stews. She said this asshole Macek had his hands up her pants for half the flight."

"Did she come?"

"No, Sensitivo, she did not. She was scared shitless the whole time. Unfortunately, she seems to have accepted Karavitch as her personal savior."

"What, Stockholm syndrome?"

"Yeah, downtown Stockholm. Apparently, charismatic isn't the word. The other stew, West, agrees, except she hates the bastard's guts. By the way, what's your make? Did you see him?"

"Yeah, I did. I'm inclined to agree too. A tricky, mean, tough son of a bitch. Straight-faced denies all knowledge of the locker bomb, same with his troops. I kind of doubt we'll roll any of the others if it means putting the blocks to the old bastard. I don't think anybody wants to fuck with him, including the Federal Bureau of Investigation."

"Oh? That sounds interesting."

"Yeah, but a long story. Anything else?"

"Just one item. West also swears she spotted Macek and Mrs. Karavitch slip into the lavatory together during the flight. And she doubts they were washing their hands."

7

ON MONDAY MORNING, Butch Karp and Marlene Ciampi and several hundred other assistant district attorneys, the district attorney himself and his aides and assistants, learned judges by the dozens and clerks and secretaries in the hundreds, and brigades of police, and regiments of witnesses and victims, the bored and the anguished, squads of jurors good and true, and uncounted lawyers, young and harried or suave and grave, depending on whether they worked for the poor or the rich, and the ladies and gentlemen of the press, merciless and cynical; and, of course, a varied mob of criminals, the cause and purpose of this whole cavalcade, the petty thugs, the thieves and robbers, whether by stealth or weaponry or clever papers, the whores of both sexes, the cold killers, the hot killers, the rapists and torturers of the helpless, the justly accused, the falsely accused, together with their keepers, parole officers, social workers, enemies, friends and relations, converged, all of them, on a single seventeen-story gray stone building located at 100 Centre Street on the island of Manhattan, there to prod into sullen wakefulness that great beast, the Law.

The Law was having a bad year. Its mistress, the richest city civilization has ever known, was as broke as a piss-bum in the gutter. So among other things, the Law was starved and ill-housed and generally treated like a dirty dog. And the Law responded in kind. It sulked in its grimy kennel and refused to do its proper work, which is, after all, finding out who the bad guys are and giving them their lumps.

Instead it pretended. In that grim year, you could commit a felony in New York and have but a one-in-ten chance of being arrested, and if arrested, but a one-in-ten chance of being indicted, and if indicted, but a one-in-ten chance of actually going to prison. The people responsible for the Law refused to enforce it, instead attending only to its droppings, the criminal justice statistics.

Chief among these was the notion of clearance. Arrests were cleared by plea bargaining beyond all reason, which meant that the crooks knew you would give them almost anything to avoid going

70

to trial, because nothing loused up the system like lots of time-consuming trials. Not to mention that there was no room in the prisons, which exerted back pressure on the system, like blockage in a toilet.

Karp's boss, District Attorney Sanford Bloom, was the chief apostle of clearance, not the least of the reasons why Karp despised him. Bloom had instituted clearance quotas, which all the DA bureaus and individual assistant DAs had to meet.

Bloom's sole purpose, it seemed, besides favorable publicity and garnering useful brownie points from those in power, was to keep the system moving at all costs. Never mind that the same people were arrested again and again for similar crimes and always went free.

It had not always been this way. A few years previously, the district attorney had been the legendary Francis P. Garrahy. Garrahy had been New York DA for nearly forty years, in which time he had created one of the finest prosecutorial offices in the world, mainly because he was a great trial lawyer and hired great trial lawyers. He liked trying criminals and putting them in jail for a long time.

Karp had joined this team because it was the best. With Garrahy as coach, young lawyers were scouted, encouraged, browbeaten, pushed to the limits of their talents, and then either chucked off the team or given their shot at the major leagues: prosecuting homicides in New York County. Garrahy was tough, brutal some said, but always concerned about the men he called "his boys." Karp had loved him.

Not that the DA's office had been a paradise; it had always been a suburb of Hell. But with Garrahy in charge, there was a small chance at something like salvation, the satisfaction of a well-done job for someone who knew what a well-done job was.

And in fact, the lobby of 100 Centre Street this morning and every weekday morning, did resemble Hell enough to fool the average demon. At eight-fifty it was already crowded with people who had business in court or who worked for the court, but also with those citizens who had no place else to go.

Pushing through the mob, Karp thought, as he often did, that it was always the same crowd. Weren't there always those two obese black women with tired faces, the trio of pockmarked Puerto Rican youths, the tan dwarf with no arms, the same elderly colored gentleman with the worn gray suit and cracked wing-tips, talking reasonably to an invisible being named Clara?

And the sounds were always the same. A hundred transistors and boom boxes tuned to twenty different stations were punctu-

71

ated by shouts from the ones who yelled at their lawyers, intermixed with the continuous rumble of arguments and excuses and threats in six languages.

Add in the smell of steam heat, stale tobacco smoke, acrid coffee from the first-floor snack bar, and you could understand why the people who worked at 100 Centre Street called this area the Streets of Calcutta.

"Hey, Mr. Karp, wanna magazine?"

The man who plucked at his sleeve was slight, with thick lips in a large, pale face. His watery blue eyes were wide and intense behind round glasses patched at the hinges with cellophane tape. Neatly dressed in a blue suit and tie, he was pulling a child's red wagon loaded with old magazines.

"Yeah, sure, Warren, what you got? *Sports Illustrated?*" Karp asked amiably.

"Sure thing," said the man, reaching down for a magazine. He handed Karp a three-month-old *Sports Illustrated.* Karp gave him a couple of quarters.

"See you later, Warren," he said, moving away.

Warren smiled. "Thanks, you big asshole," he said in a loud, clear voice. "And go fuck yourself!"

Karp had a warm spot in his heart for the man everybody called Dirty Warren. Although he realized that life was no picnic for him (Warren did not have many repeat customers, and occasionally picked up lumps from those unfamiliar with the brain malfunction called Tourette's syndrome), he believed the home of the criminal justice system required the presence of someone with an uncontrollable urge to shout obscenities. And Warren was at least physically presentable, which could not be said of many of the other Calcutta regulars, the Scab Man, for example, or the Walking Booger.

Karp's office was on the fourth floor. Since he was the Deputy Director of the Criminal Courts Bureau, he rated an enclosed office with a real window. The bureau director, a Bloom crony named Melvyn Pelso, was an elegant slug, whose main functions were lunching with the great, going to meetings, and spying on Karp for Bloom. On the good side, he rarely arrived before ten and often skipped Mondays altogether, which meant that Karp could use his vastly larger office for meetings of Karp's Team.

Karp believed devoutly in rules, in Due Process, and Criminal Procedure, and the Rules of Evidence, and Probable Cause, in the Presumption of Innocence and the Punishment of the Guilty. That the management of the District Attorney's Office was truly interested in none of these things made his life more difficult, but neither depressed him nor drove him into comfortable cynicism. It just made it necessary for him to organize, unofficially, and under the table, a Team of his own.

The members of the unofficial team had gathered, as they did every Monday morning, in the bureau's outer office: a dozen young and a couple of middle-aged attorneys drinking bad coffee out of styrofoam cups and munching danishes paid for by Karp and brought in by Connie Trask, the bureau secretary.

He swung breezily in, waved, snagged a coffee and the last prune danish. "Give me five minutes," he said.

Karp went into his own office and did bureaucracy. He grabbed a thick sheaf of paper out of his brimming in-basket and threw away anything not marked "special" or "urgent." He read the survivors quickly, threw half of them away, and scribbled notes to Connie on the rest. Then he signed a group of documents having to do with promotions, requisitions of staff, expense reimbursements and supplies. They had all been initialed by his secretary, so he scrawled his signature across them. Connie never made mistakes in procedure.

Leaving his office, he dumped the finished work on Connie's desk, and went into the bureau chief's office to pursue his real job, which was making the criminal justice system produce some criminal justice, against all odds and the will of its masters.

At the long, shiny oak table the other lawyers had left a place for him. They were sitting at the table or on chairs dragged from other parts of the room. Marlene Ciampi was sitting behind Pelso's desk, swinging gently back and forth in a massive black leather judge's chair.

Karp sat and looked around the room. A few Old Guards—Ciampi, Roland Hrcany, V.T. Newbury—and the rest babies in their first or second year in the DA's office. Karp recruited the best of the annual intake into the Criminal Courts Bureau, and tried to keep them sane and productive. Even so, the turnover was ferocious.

"OK, let's get started," he said. "You first, George. What've you got?"

George Sobel stood up, opened a brown manila folder, and began talking about the robbery and stabbing of a Korean convenience store proprietor in quiet, careful sentences, like a man describing symptoms to a physician. Sobel was a good lawyer, but unprepossessing. His auburn hair was badly combed, and he was dressed in a dusty blue suit flecked with dandruff. Karp made a mental note to speak to him about his appearance.

Sobel went quickly through the details of the crime. It was not a very interesting crime, about as unusual as the arrival of the Times Square shuttle at Grand Central, and Karp wondered what the point of the case would be. In fact he was having a hard time concentrating on what Sobel was saying. He was still trying to put together the hijack case, which was becoming entirely too complex. Why was the real bomb in the locker and the fake one on the plane? Surely the other way around made more sense. Or did it?

". . . Kim was taken to Bellevue by ambulance at twelve-thirty on the morning of the fifteenth. After surgery, he gave a good description of the assailant to police—"

Hrcany, who had been leaning his chair against the wall, pushed off and brought the front legs down with a bang. A powerfully built man, he sported a fierce blond cavalry mustache and had a dark tan that he boosted with a sun lamp in his office. He looked like a refugee from Muscle Beach, slow-witted and brutal, an impression that was only half correct. "Hang on there, George, I think you lost me," he rumbled. "What does Manhattan Homicide have to do with it? I thought you said this Kim didn't die. So we're talking robbery and assault with a deadly weapon?"

"No, my Kim didn't die. My Kim is Sun Kim. The other Kim, Nam Kim, was murdered on the third of August, and Kun Park, another owner, the week after. It's a pattern. That's the point. This guy Hornreade is going around knocking off Korean convenience stores and stabbing the owners."

"How do we know this, George? And if we do, why aren't we going for homicide?"

Sobel took a deep breath. Hrcany was well known for his merciless badgering of younger attorneys. "We know, but there's no case on the murders. There was an eye on one of them: Park's wife was in the store. But the mutt was in and out in a couple of minutes. She was in the back and didn't get a real good look, and then when she saw what he did to her old man she went crazy. Ripped his belly open—same cut he used on both Kims. My Kim was lucky. Also, she doesn't speak English."

"The cops have hit the neighborhood?" Hrcany asked. "No other witnesses? Evidence? Prints? There must have been a lot of blood—"

"Yeah, we got prints on the register in the Park case, but they're crappy, same as usual. Blood on Hornreade's shoes; maybe it's Park's, maybe it's Kim's. The one who survived. That's pretty thin, but—"

"It's garbage for murder two," Hrcany said grumpily.

"That's what I thought, but the robbery assault is golden. Maybe attempted murder. We can blitz him on it."

Karp nodded. This was, of course, the reason for these meetings. The complex system that adjusted the punishment to the crime had long since eroded. To replace it, Karp and a few of his peers had erected a form of rough justice. Everybody knew who the real bad guys were. If you couldn't nail them for what they did, you nailed them when you could. Capone, after all, had died in prison on a charge of tax evasion. By carefully concentrating his resources, especially that rarest commodity, the attention of the police, and by cooking the figures when he dared, Karp could meet his clearance quotas and at the same time put a fair number of bastards behind bars for significant periods.

"Good thinking, George," he said. "Who's on defense?"

"Carcano."

"He's chicken shit. Wave the murders in his face, hint you got more than you do, and go for the max. Don't roll. Get Judge Maldonado or Kapperstein. If you can't, let me know. And let me know the hearing date, I'll goose the judge before. OK, next case. Tony?"

Tony Harris was the pick of the litter in Karp's opinion, a tall, rangy kid from St. John's with long, unruly hair. He was bright, a beaver for work, and could hit to either field. He played third base for Karp's softball team.

"This could be a Spectacular," Harris began. A chorus of groans came from the room. Spectaculars were politically sensitive but largely pointless cases that took up too much time, got plastered across the front page of the *Daily News,* and invoked the personal attention of the district attorney himself.

Harris grinned pleasantly, showing an assortment of large, crooked teeth. "The facts of the case are briefly told," he said. "On September 11, Jerold Weaver, male Caucasian, an unemployed pipe fitter from Long Island City, got his load on at the White Rose on Eighth and Forty-fifth, during which time he was heard loudly complaining about, if I may quote, 'these goddam rich nigger pimps' unquote. At around eleven that night, Weaver was seen in an altercation with a well-dressed Negro male, named Milton C. Weems, who was in the company of a female Caucasian named Molly Frumpton. Weaver was pushed violently to the pavement by Weems, after which Weems and Frumpton entered a 1976 white Cadillac convertible owned by Weems and drove off.

"Weaver then entered his '64 Dodge pickup, pursued Weems up Seventh Avenue to 56th Street. Weems stopped for a light, Weaver got out of his truck, shot Weems five times in the head with a .38 caliber revolver, got back in his car, drove off down 56th Street, ran a light, and collided with a garbage truck. The cops picked him up unconscious, with the gun on his lap." Harris then spent fifteen minutes detailing the case, its evidentiary basis, and the state of the depositions from witnesses.

Karp said, "Good presentation, Tony. Any questions, gang?"

Hrcany laughed. "I'll bite. What's the punch line, Tony? A citizen blowing away a pimp is a Spectacular? A celebration maybe, but . . ."

Harris grinned again. "Yeah, we wish. It turns out that Milton C. Weems was—you ready for this?—a deacon at Ebenezer Baptist, the owner of a sizable dry-cleaning business, and father of four. Miss Frumpton was his secretary of many years."

More groans. Karp cut in. "What do we do with it, Tony?"

Somebody cracked, "Send him to pimp recognition classes and get him another box of shells." Everybody laughed, a thin, callous laughter with no joy in it.

"Straight murder two as the top count," Harris said. "Defense is a Public D., name of Rafferty. He's talking extreme emotional as the affirmative defense, the guy was drunk and so on."

"Which is bullshit. He hated pimps so much it made him crazy? He was so drunk he didn't know what he was doing, but he followed a car, parked, aimed, and shot?"

"Don't blame me, Butch, I'm just telling it. Of course, I understand the big question is, what's the deacon doing with his lily-white secretary in Sleazeville late Saturday night?"

There was an odd tone to Harris's comment, and Karp shot back quickly, "You 'understand'? What's that supposed to mean?"

"Oh, Wharton called me to—how did he put it?—fill me in on the political ramifications. And to remind me we had nearly six hundred homicides pending trial. And that maybe Mr. Weems was not all he was cracked up to be in the morality department. He was pretty subtle, but the message was that there was no point in, quote, stimulating racial tensions unnecessarily, and that the district attorney would not lose any sleep if we accepted manslaughter one on this."

"What! What is this, fucking Alabama?" Karp said loudly to the room at large. Conrad Wharton was Bloom's administrative bureau chief and hatchet man. He was the one who kept the clearance numbers and enforced them.

"Tony," he said, controlling his anger, speaking in a tired, precise voice, "Section 125.25 of the New York State Penal Code is written in English. It's very short. Even Wharton could read it. Somebody sticks a gun in a guy's face and pulls the trigger is either intending to cause that person's death, section one, or, section two, evincing depraved indifference to human life. So let's get a

Form Two indictment upstairs, huh? And let Mr. Rafferty worry about the defense for a change instead of the district attorney."

Karp could see in the faces of the younger attorneys that he had given them something valuable, probably the only thing he could give them, since they certainly weren't going to get promoted hanging around him. He knew he could expect a nasty, exhausting phone call twenty minutes after the indictment hit Bloom's desk.

He caught Marlene's eye, as tired as his own felt. He forced a weak smile and said, "OK, Marlene, case of the week. Let's have it."

Marlene began briskly, flipping through the large index cards she used for case notes, cards covered with her small, elegant handwriting. She now wore huge, round tortoise-shell spectacles for reading, to prevent the deterioration of her good eye.

She had done a good job on the Doyle case. She called it that, rather than the terrorist case or the Croatian case or the hijack case, which was what the papers were calling it. Marlene was emphasizing that the dead cop was the fixed star around which the increasingly bizarre case revolved.

She concluded with an analysis of the gravamen of the crime: the placing of a booby-trapped bomb in a public locker constituted depraved indifference to human life under the statute, and then went on to the indictment strategy.

"We intend to indict all five participants for second-degree murder under 125.25, section two. Since Doyle was a police officer killed in L.O.D., we could go for murder one, under 125.27. That might be supported by the fact that the terrorists called the police and so might reasonably be held to suppose that the victim of the booby trap would be a police officer. On the other hand, it could be a tricky proof—it's not like a mutt gunning down a blue suit. Also, we want to sweep them all in under the felony murder clause of 125.25, which is why murder two is a better bet.

"Our position is that the crime is a direct result of a conspiracy to draw attention to a political cause by violent action. That assumes they were all in it; they all knew about the locker bomb; they're all culpable in the murder. As I said, we would also indict under section three, felony murder in connection with kidnapping, since we can construe the bombing as being in furtherance of the lesser included offense."

As she stacked her cards and resumed her seat, half a dozen people began to talk at once. Karp banged his knuckles on the table to restore order, and nodded at Roland Hrcany, who said, "It still doesn't hold up, Marlene. How do we know who planted the bomb? How do we know one of these bozos wasn't playing a solo?"

"We don't. The point of the group indictment is to keep the pressure up. They're hanging together now. They may start coming apart once it occurs to them that they're looking at going up for murder. If it was a solo, and unless they're a lot less flaky than they appear, one of them should deliver the trigger man."

"What about the affirmative defense on the felony murder?" asked Hank Schneerman, one of the junior ADAs. "They could each claim ignorance of the real bomb. They could say they thought it was going to be a phony, like the one in the plane."

"Yeah, they could. They could say the devil made them do it, too. But the job right now is to show the arraigning magistrate and the grand jury that a crime took place and that the suspects did it. And to do it in a way that will put the maximum pressure on them to improve their individual positions at their buddies' expense, which I think this strategy does."

"Butch, are we really going all the way on this one?"

All eyes turned to V.T. Newbury. He rarely spoke at these meetings, except to exercise his acerbic wit. He was a short, slightly built man with a chiseled profile and the kind of huge, luminous blue eyes that John Singleton Copley depicted in portraits of eighteenth-century gentlemen.

"What do you mean, V.T.?" Karp asked irritably. He was not getting the enthusiastic support he expected on this case.

"I mean that this is potentially an incredibly complex case. If we push for trial on this, I have the sense that you and Marlene both are going to be investing a huge proportion of your personal time in it. I'm asking whether it's worth it."

"Worth it? Shit, Newbury, they killed a cop! Worth it, my ass! What do you think these meetings are for? How come all of a sudden you're talking 'worth it'?"

"Calm down, Butch. Your virginity is safe with me. I know what we're doing here. We nail the shitheads who think they're getting away with major crimes. OK, I'm just asking if these guys are in that class. Sure, they have to be put away. But a dickhead fresh out of South Orange Law is going to go for a plea on this. The point is, do we push for the top count or not? Or is there something else going on?"

Karp was, characteristically, about to say something nasty to his best friend, who had, also characteristically, been so unwise as to stand between the wolf and its prey, when the door flung open and a rumpled, barrel-shaped man with the face of a frenzied orangutan rolled into the room. A chorus of boos and cheers burst from the assemblage. Ray Guma, the Mad Dog of Centre Street, grinned broadly and waved. "Hey, gang, stand by! I got a great case—"

"Guma, goddamn! You got a helluva nerve coming in here an hour late looking like shit," said Karp, relieved to have a less tricky outlet for his annoyance.

Guma's face fell and he looked down at his outfit. His suit was unpressed, his tie untied, his shirt unbuttoned, a day's growth of beard stood out on his swarthy face, and his curly black hair stuck out in oily disorder. "Shit? Hey, it's Monday, I had a great weekend. Give me a break." Everybody knew that after twenty minutes in the men's room he would emerge, as always, a reasonably presentable greasy Italian lawyer.

Karp looked at his watch. It was almost time to dismiss the meeting and let the ADAs go off to court. Karp was not anxious to pursue the Doyle case in greater detail, given the reception it had already received. He waved his hand, yielding the floor to Guma. "OK, Goom," he said. "Spit it out. And make it snappy."

Guma paused to tuck in a shirttail and pull up the zipper on his fly before plunging into a rapid-fire outline of his case. He spoke, as always, without notes, in a Brooklyn accent that Fordham Law had done little to improve. Guma's memory was legendary; he never forgot a face, name, or citation.

"The victim, girl named Elvira Melendez, attests her boyfriend, Alejandro Sorriendas, attempted to kill her by beating her with a kitchen chair and then throttling her with his hands. Who the hell knows how she survived, but she did, and she's in Bellevue and pissed off and willing to press. They picked up Sorriendas the day after, where he works out in Queens. Scratches all over his face, nice prints on the chair, it's a lock. So what I want to do is—"

Karp cut in, annoyed again. "Guma, what is this *bupkes*? We're trying to keep fucking cutthroats from walking here, you're selling a domestic assault?"

Guma held up his hands in protest. "Butch, for chrissakes, let me finish? This guy Sorriendas, he's a Cuban. OK, you know Pinky Billman?"

"No, is he a Cuban too? What are you talking about, Guma?"

"Pinky Billman. I know him from when he used to be a detective in Chinatown. A good guy. Now he's a sergeant in Queens narco. He says this particular mutt, Sorriendas, is tight with Sergio Ruiz. You know who *he* is, right?"

"No, I don't. Should I? Look, Goom, we got like five minutes. These guys got to make court, so—"

"Wait, wait! Sergio Ruiz. They call him 'The Serpent.' *The* bigtime Cuban heroin and cocaine importer. *Really* big time."

79

"I know him," V.T. said mildly.

"You do?" Karp exclaimed.

"Well, not personally. I get my smack from an Episcopalian bishop. But I've been working with the federal strike force on money-laundering operations connected with narcotics traffic. Ruiz's name comes up in a bunch of places. Import-export joints in Miami and Tampa, a couple of brass-plate banks in the Caymans, Bahamas, the usual. He came here about five years ago and set up an outfit called—what is it? Tel something?"

"Tel-Air Shipping, out in Queens," Guma put in.

"Yeah, right. Tel-Air. Anyway, he's big and he's smart. Nasty too, from what I hear."

"Right!" Guma agreed. "We're talking a serious scumbag. The other thing is, the Feds have clamped the lid on Tel-Air. They're building some kind of megacase, and Pinky can't get near it. So what I want to do is squeeze this Sorriendas, try to get a hook into Ruiz. I figure, go forward on the attempted murder. They'll try to cop to simple assault, but I want to wave a serious threat of trial for the attempted in their face. Whaddya say?"

Karp squirmed. He knew Guma was, quite properly, proposing the oldest trick in the prosecutor's book: squeezing a suspect for a lesser offense in hopes that he would turn his pals over for a bigger crime. But such strategies depended on a credible threat of going to trial, and the pressure on Karp to produce clearances had almost eliminated his ability to do this.

"Sorry, Goom, no can do," he said at last.

"Aww, Butch, come on!" Guma yelled, slamming his hand on the table.

"Guma, look, you can wave anything you want, go ahead. But unless your Cuban's lawyer can't read a court calendar it ain't going to get you much, because I'm not going to push Bloom for a trial slot on this one, which I would have to do because right now I'm tapped. I'm not going to let a New York County murder case, of which I got about six hundred pending, fly out the window to try a domestic in the hope that it'll help out a Queens drug bust, which according to you the Feds have got locked up. *Capisce?*"

Guma gave Karp an eloquently disgusted look and walked out, slamming the door. After a brief embarrassed silence, Karp sighed and said, "OK, that's it, gang. Time to fight crime." The attorneys rose and drifted out of the room, murmuring and upset. Karp looked at Marlene, hoping for some support, but she just shrugged and started to pack her files away in a leather attaché case. The loneliness of command, Karp thought. He touched her arm.

"Say, Marlene, you'll draw up those indictments? I want to get them to Bloom today."

"They're almost drafted. I'll have them around noon. See you later."

Karp went back to his own office and began gathering up the case folders for the day's sessions. For the next six or so hours Karp would be constantly on the move, appearing at arraignments, racing upstairs to one of the six continuous grand juries to present indictments, then picking up on preliminary hearings for any of his troops that were out sick or busy with trials. This was in addition to trying to supervise two dozen inexperienced ADAs.

He arranged the folders in ordered stacks tagged with strips of foolscap and began listing exactly where he had to be at what particular moment of the day. On several occasions he noticed that he had to be in two places at once. He made a note to talk to a couple of the court clerks and get them to adjust their calendars so he could cover everything. Karp remembered birthdays and bought a lot of good scotch at Christmas so that they would do such things when he needed them, which was almost daily.

He was just packing his files in his briefcase when his door opened and a woman entered. "You're supposed to knock, Rhoda," Karp said tiredly.

"Yeah, and you're supposed to return calls from the front office."

"Is this going to take a long time?" he asked. "I'm going to be late for court."

She looked at him aggressively, her head cocked and her dark eyes narrowed under the lavender eye-shadow. A smile close to a sneer showed on her generous mouth. Rhoda Klepp was also an ADA, but not the sort who would ever attend Karp's meetings. On arriving at the DA's office eighteen months ago, she had shrewdly observed where the power lay and had attached herself to Conrad Wharton, serving him in much the same manner as he served Bloom. As a result, she was relieved of most courtroom duties, while still continuing on the roster of the Criminal Courts Bureau, thus adding to Karp's coverage problems. It was one of the ways Wharton got back at him for failing to meet his clearance quotas.

"The boss wants to see you, Karp."

"Mr. Bloom wants to see me? That's funny, I don't have a message slip from him."

"I mean Chip." Wharton liked people to call him "Chip," but most people agreed with Ray Guma's observation that he walked like he had a corncob up his ass, and called him "Corncob."

"Oh, *Chip*. *Chip* is not my boss. See you later, Rhoda," Karp said, and, grabbing his briefcase, made to leave his office. Klepp blocked his way. This she could do well, since she was built, as they say in New York, like a brick shithouse. She had a figure of overwhelming lushness, mounting immense, perfectly conical breasts, which she enclosed in steel-girded brassieres, mighty structures that could have passed the midtown building code. As she favored frilly, semi-transparent blouses, these were literally her salient feature.

"I'd see him if I were you, Karp. He wants to talk about the Weaver thing, one. And you were supposed to get in touch with Monsignor Keene on the Brannon case last Friday. He called Bloom and he's pissed. You get the Powerhouse down on you and you're dead in this town."

Karp vaguely remembered having to call somebody from the Archdiocese of New York about a nice Catholic boy from an upstanding family who had been caught supplementing his clothing allowance with a string of B and E's on the Upper East Side. He looked down at Rhoda and for a mad instant wondered what would happen if he honked her cones, one, two. Then he turned sideways and squeezed past her overhang. "I'll make the call, Rhoda," he said. "but tell Corncob if he wants to see me, he can make an appointment. I don't work for him yet. And no deal on Weaver."

As Karp trotted down the hall to court he reflected mildly on the fact that in three short days he had managed to piss off the Federal Bureau of Investigation, his own staff, his boss, and the Catholic Church. I must be doing something right, he thought.

8

THEY ARRAIGNED THE hijackers on the murder complaint Monday afternoon. The media were out in force. The hijackers were big news and Karp wasn't the only one who bought scotch for court clerks. Also present in the hallway, watched by two bored security guards, was a cheering section of Croatian supporters. The priest with them, a strongly built man in his fifties, scowled at Karp and Marlene as they entered the courtroom, and Karp recognized him as the one who had been at the FBI building.

The gateway to the judicial system for criminal cases, arraignments have the gravity and ambiance of the turnstiles on the Seventh Avenue IRT. The accused hear why they were arrested and the magistrate sees that the complaint has been drawn up in due form and that the arrest has not been arbitrary or capricious. The magistrate usually also sets bail. Five minutes is long for an arraignment.

This one was even shorter. "Who's the pinstripe on defense?" asked Marlene, motioning to the youngish man conferring with the five prisoners at the defense table. Karp looked over and saw a pink-cheeked person in a beautifully made blue suit and a blow-dried razor cut. "Never saw him before," Karp answered, which was odd because he thought he knew every prosperous criminal lawyer in Manhattan by sight. He consulted his papers. "Name's John Evans. An oddly unethnic name for a New York criminal lawyer, and he didn't get that suit at the Legal Aid thrift shop. Could be a corporate firm's convenience guy, in which case he is out of his league. Or maybe out-of-town muscle?"

"Could be," Marlene said. "I heard Karavitch's church was taking up a collection for legal defense. Maybe they had a big contributor. I'll check it out—uh-oh, we're on."

Karp asked for half a million dollars congregate bail, on the grounds that the accused were dangerous terrorists, had killed a police officer, and had stolen an airplane, all of which might lead the court to a strong presumption that they would skip before trial. John Evans rose to object that the accused were all gainfully employed and that they had strong roots in the community. The judge was not impressed with the argument. Cop killers don't make bail in New York when the cameras are rolling. Karp got his bail and the five hijackers were bundled off back to Riker's Island.

Marlene left for an arraignment hearing on another case, and Karp ducked into his office to call Monsignor Keene. When he came on, his voice was hearty and smooth.

"Ah, yes, the Brannon boy. A terrible tragedy. I've known the family for years. A prominent family, very close to His Eminence. The father is a papal knight, and they've got any number of distinguished members of the bar. Perhaps you know Michael Bailey, the boy's uncle?"

"Yes, I believe I've heard the name." Mike Bailey owned zoning law in Manhattan and was necessarily free with political contributions.

Keene rolled on. "I've spoken to Sandy Bloom about it personally, and he assures me that we can handle the matter with no, ah, permanent damage to the reputation of the family, or stain on Billy's record."

"Yes, I bet he did, but the problem is, Monsignor, that the Brannon family also seems to have added a professional burglar to their ranks. There are seventeen counts of burglary on the indictment. Also, there's the matter of Mrs. Lepach."

"Mrs. who?"

"Mrs. Sarah Lepach. She caught little Billy on his last job and made a grab for her sable, and Billy cold-cocked her. Seventy-six years old, spent six weeks in the hospital."

"Dear God! I wasn't told. How dreadful!"

Maybe you weren't, but for damn sure Sandy Bloom knew about it, Karp thought.

"Yes. Look, Monsignor, I don't want to be a hard a—I mean, my major concern is that we don't treat this like Billy pushed a kid off a slide in the playground. Between you and me, I'm not sure that five in Attica is the right solution, but he's got to get his lumps. I tell you what. I'm willing to drop the aggravated assault and accept a lesser on the other break-ins if he pleads guilty on the Lepach burglary. He'll get six months in a youth camp upstate. And I want full restitution on all the burglaries, and the medical expenses, and I want him out of town. Military school, in Wyoming. And I want him out of trouble, forever. He gets a traffic ticket in New York, he's meat."

"I see. And his record? The publicity?"

"We can fix that if the family will guarantee the rest."

84

"I'll make sure of it. Thank you, Mr. Karp. I'm grateful to you and I'm sure the family will be too."

After he had hung up, Karp thought about equal justice under law for about three seconds, which was all he could stand. His stomach had gone queasy, which was unusual. He had a digestive system made of Teflon over lab grade ceramic. He'd grabbed a potato knish and a Pepsi off a cancer wagon at lunchtime, and this was clanking around in his vitals like a brick in ammonia. Maybe he was getting old. He was struggling to remember the five basic food groups essential to good nutrition when Connie Trask buzzed him.

"It's upstairs. Are you in?"

Karp said that he was. You can only avoid your boss so long. After that he might begin to suspect you don't like him.

After the obligatory wait to establish relative status, Bloom came on the line. He got right to the point.

"Chip's been having difficulty reaching you."

"We're both busy men. What can I do for you?"

"A couple of things. First of all, your numbers look like shit. Mel Pelso says you're not following policy on assigning trial slots."

"I'll try to do better. It would help if old Mel would venture into a courtroom occasionally and clear some more cases. With some coaching I'm sure we could teach Mel how to accept a plea to a lesser."

Bloom chose to ignore the remark. "Now, this Weaver thing—"

"Is murder two. The facts don't allow anything else, and I intend to try, absent a guilty plea to the top count."

"I don't think that's wise."

"You don't? Then overrule me. You're the DA. It's your signature on the indictment." Of course, Karp knew that the DA would not take the heat for a direct and publicly verifiable overrule. He wanted Karp to take the heat.

"Well, think about it," Bloom said lamely. "And speaking of indictments, they just brought this hijack thing up. What do you think you're doing here, indicting *all* of them on second-degree murder? It's absurd! The damn case is complicated enough without trying to prove five people, two of whom speak no English, all had guilty knowledge about a booby-trapped bomb. I suppose you want to go to trial on this one too?"

"Yes. It's a good case."

"Is it? Well, you'll get to explain your legal reasoning tonight on television."

"Oh?"

"Yes, Carl Weber called for an interview. The taping is sched-

uled for seven-thirty in my office. They want it for the eleven
o'clock local news."

"You'll be there too?"

"No, I have a prior engagement. You'll be on your own."

"Uh-huh. Umm . . . ?"

"Yes?"

"You going to sign those indictments?"

"Oh, yes, I'll sign them, all right, and I—" Bloom was about to
say something else, and thought better of it. Instead he snapped,
"I have another call," and clicked off the line, leaving Karp to
consider why, for the first time in living memory, Sanford Bloom
had turned down the chance to be on television. He went to the
door and stuck his head out.

"Connie, where's Marlene?"

"In Part Twenty, I think." Connie kept all the bureau ADAs'
schedules neatly under her short Afro. "No, wait. Tony's got that
today. She's out of the office, at a funeral. You want me to find
out whose?"

"No, don't bother. I'll catch her later." Karp knew whose funeral.

The funeral was in Queens. Where else? Half of Queens is
covered by cemeteries. The weather was appropriately funereal:
gray, cold, and windy. Marlene had never been to an inspector's
funeral before and was impressed. There were hundreds of uniformed cops with black-taped badges, the pipe band of the Emer-
ald Society playing dirges, plus representatives from other police
forces. The New York Police Department buries its dead well.

Terry Doyle's entire chain of command was there, except for
Jack Doheny, who was still in the hospital. She spotted Bill Denton and Pete Hanlon in a group of senior officers, all in full
uniform, and made her way over to them. She greeted Hanlon and
introduced herself to Bill Denton. Hanlon looked drawn and nervous. They talked briefly about the funeral and how the widow was
taking it. After a while the other officers drifted away, leaving her
with Hanlon and Denton.

"How's the case going?" Denton asked.

"OK, on the surface. We got the indictments in today."

"What do you mean, 'on the surface'?"

"I mean, we know one of the five we got pulled the trigger on
Terry, but we don't know which one, and how many of the others
knew about it. That could be a problem. And Butch thinks the FBI
is trying to queer the case."

"Any idea why?"

"None. But it's worrying. There's also the issue of where they got the explosives and the trigger. Which reminds me: Inspector Hanlon, I need names of people with expertise in this kind of explosive device."

Hanlon frowned. "I'll have my office draw you up a list."

"How about off the top of your head? Who's the best? You must know. And given the circumstances, I'd prefer it to be somebody unconnected with the federal government." Marlene flashed her most winning and innocent smile. It was a stroke of luck getting Hanlon here alone with his boss. It would make it hard for him to dissemble, if that was on his mind.

Hanlon cleared his throat heavily and looked down at the ground. When he lifted his face again she saw the tension in it. His voice was strained. "Sam Rackwood is about the best there is in this country, but he's with the Feds, ATF."

"Who's the best in the world, Pete?" Denton asked in a flat, quiet voice.

"Um, I don't know . . . maybe Taylor? G.F.S. Taylor, if he's still alive. He lives in England—London somewhere. I heard him speak once at a course in Glencoe. My girl has his address at the office." Hanlon's face looked pinched and raw, and not just from the cold wind off the bay. "I'm not sure you can get to him, though," he mumbled distractedly. "Taylor's supposed to be an odd bird."

Marlene wrote the name down on a pad she took from her bag. She smiled brightly. "That's OK," she said, "I'm an odd bird, too."

"Butch, you're still here! I was going to leave you a note." The head sticking through the opening in Karp's office doorway was large, square, and covered with orange fuzz, like industrial carpeting. The door opened wider and a big, cylindrical body pushed through. Fred Slocum dressed cheap and ugly. This evening his ensemble comprised pinkish-tan double-knit slacks and a baggy polyester sports coat in charcoal, red, blue, and orange nubbles, worn over a pale green shirt showing a clean crescent of T-shirt at the open neck.

Karp looked up from his work and rubbed his face. It had the rubbery feel you get after a Novocain session. His stomach was still sour and producing acrid gases that stung his throat. "Yeah, I'm still here. I got to go upstairs and get taped for TV at seven-thirty, so I figured I might as well stay here and get rid of some paper." He glanced at his watch. "Shit. It's quarter to seven."

"You going on TV? What, this hijack thing?"

"Yeah, Carl Weber's doing the interview."

"That asshole," Slocum sneered. "He'll pull out a little piece of paper in the middle of it and say, 'Mr. Karp, our investigation shows that in 1948 you took a copy of *Dick and Jane Visit Grandma* out of the New York Public Library. That book has never been returned. Do you deny it?' "

Slocum did an accurate imitation of Weber's portentous drone, and Karp grinned. "Yeah, right, I better watch my ass. So what was the note going to be about?"

"Oh, yeah. Max Dorcas. Old guy, runs a little hole-in-the-wall joint in Grand Central, luggage sales and repairs. It's right across from the locker where they left the bomb. He made the little guy, what's his name . . .?"

"Rukovina?"

"Right. He's sure he saw him and another guy put a big pot in the locker last Thursday. He remembers it because he wondered why anybody would put a pot in a locker—a package, a bag maybe, but a pot?"

"What about the other guy?"

"Zilch. High collar, low hat. He thinks he had a mustache. But he's sure on Rukovina."

"Great, Fred, that's enough. That's the first piece of evidence tying any of the gang to the real bomb. Great work!"

Slocum shrugged. "You want me to set the lineup?"

"Yeah, let's do it first thing tomorrow. And, Fred, I'd appreciate it if you went out to Riker's and brought them in yourself."

Slocum frowned slightly and shrugged again. "Sure, whatever." He turned to go. "By the way, you ought to get some air. You look crummy."

Karp wrinkled his nose. "I feel crummy. I had a shitty lunch, or something. Take care, Freddy."

"Yeah, you too. Tell Weber to fuck himself."

After the detective had gone, Karp bent to work again, but surrendered to his feelings of unease after a few minutes and threw his pencil down. He did need some air. He also needed to talk to Marlene. But her office was dark when he went by, so he trotted down the four flights of stairs and through the lobby into the darkening street.

Karp stood on the steps of the courthouse in his shirt-sleeves and filled his lungs with cool evening air. It helped, a little. Traffic had thinned out and the air was purifying itself, aided by a stiff breeze from the river, six blocks away. The sky was still slate blue over the west side of Foley Square, and the street lamps were coming on. Under one of them a dark young man in a red warm-up jacket leaned against a white van and combed his long, straight hair. He regarded Karp neutrally in the manner of New Yorkers. Karp looked away and watched Dirty Warren pulling his red wagon down Centre Street.

Two TV station vans were parked illegally in front of the courthouse, and Karp assumed they were connected with the taping. When a church clock called seven-fifteen from Little Italy, Karp went back into the building for his date with the millions. As he did so he wondered once again why Bloom was declining the same date, and even more, why the major late evening television news show had assigned its chief investigative reporter to do the interview. Did they know something he didn't? Join the crowd, he thought.

In her apartment, Marlene examined herself in her long mirror. She had put on a full black wool skirt, a rose silk blouse, and her grandmother's jet beads. She also wore knee-length black boots, her black eye-patch on her bad eye, and her black kid gloves on her bad hand. She wanted to look slightly military, conservative, no-nonsense, just right for a date with a seventy-two-year-old retired Brit soldier.

It had turned out that the famous G.F.S. Taylor did not live in London at all, but in New York (naughty Inspector Hanlon!). Not only that, he was at home when Marlene called and told him breathlessly why she simply *had* to see him (she always found it helpful to take ten years off her age and thirty points off her IQ when asking men for interviews over the phone). And not only was he home, but yes, he was free for the evening and would not at all mind if Miss Ciampi dropped by.

The Northumbria was an imposing apartment house on West 77th Street, just off Central Park West, with a liveried doorman and a slow, paneled elevator, the kind of place occupied by widows of wealthy garment magnates. It smelled of furniture polish, steam heat, and old paint.

She rang the bell of Taylor's apartment and waited. A minute passed. She was about to ring again when the door was flung open, revealing a tall, spare figure in a gray cardigan and baggy tweed trousers. The man had a great beaked nose capped with bushy eyebrows above and a ragged, thick mustache below. His right cheek was a mass of twisted flesh, like the tallow at the bottom of a guttered candle, and he wore a patch on his right eye. After a moment of stunned silence, G.F.S. Taylor laughed, a set of barks like small-arms fire, and said in a loud voice, "You must be Miss Ciampi. I see, ha-ha! I see we can shop for spectacles together. Do come in."

Marlene followed Taylor through a narrow hallway lit by dim wall sconces into a large, high-ceilinged living room. There was an odd smell to the place, strong tobacco, mostly, but with a medicinal overtone like a doctor's office. She wondered if the old man were sick.

The room had a well-kept but impersonal feel to it, like the lobby of a good hotel in a provincial capital. A heavy mahogany sideboard, two Duncan Phyfe couches, and a chinoiserie end table set on a worn oriental rug. Art-deco lamps threw fuzzy circles of light against the ceiling.

Taylor bade her sit on the silk couch and offered her sherry. He poured from a crystal decanter and sat down on the couch opposite. "So how did it happen?"

"What, this?" she asked, touching her face.

"Yes."

"That's interesting. I thought the English were supposed to be deathly afraid of asking personal questions."

He smiled broadly, a wolfish but not unpleasant smile. He had very large yellow teeth. "Well, I'm hardly English anymore, am I? I've been here since '48 more or less. And besides that, my mother was a Serb, and Serbs love asking personal questions. And besides that, you've come here to pump me for some information, which on the phone you were not at all anxious to specify. And so one likes to know with whom one is dealing. Don't you agree?"

Marlene shrugged. "All right. A bomb went off. A letter bomb."

His one eye, shining in its nest of dark wrinkles, widened with interest. "Really? Spring or pull cord?"

"Pull cord, C-4 with a chemical primer. I was being a jerk; I had diagrams of the damn things in my desk."

"Yes. Still, that kind is hard to spot. And hindsight is not something readily available in the bomb disposal business. But then you're not in that business, are you? You said on the phone something about the district attorney? You have some identification, of course. I'm sorry, but . . ."

Marlene dug through her bag, found her wallet, and displayed her photo ID, which he studied briefly and returned. "You'd be surprised," he said apologetically, "how many people nowadays want to cadge free advice about blowing things up. One has to be careful."

"Speaking of which," said Marlene, "how did you . . . ?"

He laughed, bark-bark-bark. "Yes, it's not exactly a good advert for the firm. It was during the war, quite near the end, actually. I was training a group of partisans in bomb disposal techniques, defusing devices the Jerries and their friends left behind. We were billeted in a little mountain village near Jajce. That's in Yugoslavia, you know. I was sleeping on the floor near the stove. It was bitter and the stove was roaring. Some big Montenegrins from one of Brkovic's units stumbled in during the night. They were clumsy with cold and they crowded around the stove. Of course, it went right over and landed on a haversack of incendiary bombs. I woke up with my head on fire."

"My God! What did you do?"

"Went right through the window and landed in a snowbank. Saved my life, with the results you observe. Remarkable, really. I spend two years taking apart bombs with the Royal Engineers in UXB work during the Blitz, then over to Jugland with McLean, ten months of antidemolition, defusing mines in the cold and dark, with an electric torch in my teeth and my fingers numb. Not a bloody scratch. Then I go off like a torch in the safety of my bed. Hilarious, when you think about it, but it does rather put one off—how shall I say—making firm plans."

"I guess I know what you mean. Since I got blown up, life seems, I don't know, unattached. You lose the smooth progress everybody else seems to expect. You're sort of ready for whatever happens, but you can't really take it seriously.

"I mean, I'd like to get my face fixed. Not the eye, the face. Just, ah, not to be gorgeous or anything, but just move back to neutral. I don't like seeing what I see in people's faces when they look at me. Sometimes, anyway. When I'm feeling bitchy, I use it, rub it in their faces. Afterward, I feel worse. Also, there's the principle of it. If I was a cop injured in L.O.D. there'd be no question—full reconstruction, full medical. But DAs, forget it. Also, the letter I opened, it wasn't for me. The state says they're not responsible. I could sue, get a contingency lawyer, but I don't just want an out-of-court, I want my—my *rights!*"

She stopped, startled by the flood of what she had said. He was observing her calmly, smoking some strong foreign cigarette. She felt her face flush with embarrassment.

"Whoosh! God, I didn't mean to get into all that."

"No, no. It's quite all right, really. Sometimes one must . . . discuss. It even helps if the other person is an utter stranger. Or old. The old hear lots of secrets, you know, presumably because the silence of the tomb is relatively close . . ."

Now Taylor seemed embarrassed. He busied himself refilling their glasses and lit a cigarette for her. "So, Miss Ciampi," he said brightly, "what is your puzzle?"

"Marlene, please."

"Marlene, then. And I'm Goddy."

"Short for Godfrey?"

"No, not at all. The G stands for Gilbert. It's the initials, G.F.S. They called me Godforsaken at school, clever but long-winded, and you can't go about calling someone 'God,' especially not me. So Goddy it was, and has been."

Taylor barked and produced a toothy, ingenuous smile, and Marlene laughed. You could imagine him dressed in an Edwardian sailor suit at six. Then he leaned back and waited for the unfolding of the tale.

Marlene delivered it with her usual terse precision. Taylor sat placidly, hearing her out, occasionally massaging his face with a long, bony hand. His fingers were stained yellow from the powerful cigarettes.

"A solenoid, did you say?"

"Yes, to trigger the grenade cap. I thought it was peculiar at the time. I mean, why not just detonate electrically? It doesn't make sense."

"Not our kind of sense, no. But suppose someone fancied the idea of producing a little delay between the sound of the solenoid firing the cap and the explosion. Anyone close enough to hear it couldn't possibly get away. Someone trying to defuse a bomb, for example, who, of course, would know exactly what that sound meant. Someone might get an odd kind of pleasure out of imagining what went on in the minds of his victims during those five seconds."

Taylor's voice had slowed as he said this, as though he were dwelling in some precinct of old memory.

"Goddy," Marlene said carefully, "you sound like you were talking about someone you know."

He snapped to. "Was I? Well, one met all kinds in the war. There were a few who might have fit. I daresay they're all dead now, of something slow and ghastly, one hopes. Now as to this mysterious timer—"

"I have it with me."

"Do you? Splendid! Let's have a look."

She took the zip-lock plastic bag with the timer scraps out of her portfolio and handed it across the table. He held it up carefully and shook it. Then he reached into his shirt pocket and pulled out a monocle, which he screwed into his good eye. "I hate this thing. It makes me look like a stage colonel."

"Pip-pip, and all that."

"Quite. Let's see what we have here. This was what triggered the solenoid, eh?" Taylor manipulated the debris carefully through the plastic. He seemed fascinated by the little bits of metal. Finally he stopped and said peevishly, "Dammit, there's no bloody light in this mausoleum." He sprang to his feet. "Come with me. I'll show you where I really live. But no smoking."

She followed him down the hallway and through a side door into another room. The light was so much stronger here it made her blink. The peculiar odor was stronger as well, and Marlene realized with a shock that it was the heavy, headachey scent of nitroglycerin. The room was lit by a huge overhead industrial fluorescent fixture. Taylor had converted the apartment's master bedroom into a study-cum-workshop. One wall was lined with bookshelves, another with steel shelving containing cartons and odd bits of equipment. One wall was taken up by a long, black-topped laboratory table that held a large illuminated magnifier, a binocular microscope, and various power tools: grinders, drills, a miniature lathe. There was a comfortable armchair and a neatly made-up cot in one corner of the room. Taylor actually did live here.

Marlene wandered around the room as he sat down on a stool by the lab table and began to remove the parts from the bag with a tweezers and place them delicately on an enamel tray. As he did so, she examined a framed coat of arms on the wall. There was a crown at the top, then a pick and shovel device, then the outline of a coffin with the top slanted to show it was empty. Underneath that was a scroll with a motto in Latin: *Sepulchra multa non corpes habemus*. A label said, "64th Bomb Disposal Detachment—Royal Engineers."

"What's this mean, Goddy?"

"What? Oh, that. Poor Latin, I'm afraid. It means 'We have many graves, but no bodies.' The brass didn't like it, so it never became official. It was supposed to be bad for morale. What tripe! Probably had the highest morale of any bunch in the war. I mean, risking your life without having to kill anyone—who could ask for more? A marvelous bunch of men, that was, the poor bastards. All right, what have we here?"

He was peering through his magnifier, holding each piece of debris up and rotating it. He said, "Ah, Marlene, would you be so good as to reach me down that little bottle with the blue label? Yes, that's the ticket, thank you."

Taylor placed a few drops of clear liquid on the broken shaft of metal. "This should bring up the serial numbers," he explained.

"What do you think it is?" she asked.

"I'm afraid I know what it is. I just want to make certain."

He brushed the dissolved charring from the pieces with a little swab. They gleamed dully in the strong light, like gunmetal. "Here, come have a look." He backed away from the magnifier and let

Marlene look through it. The pieces were lined up on the enamel tray just as they had been in Marino's lab, but the markings were much clearer: kmf = DO 1.44 Ze er 15 M.

"What's it mean? Is it Russian?"

"Hardly. It's a Dozy, as we used to call them."

"You've seen one before?"

"Bloody right, I have. The Jerries started using them on aerial mines in late 1940. Then after the Blitz was finished, they issued them to engineer units all over the Eastern Front and the Balkans. Clever shits, weren't they? Look, there's no bomb so dangerous as one that everybody thinks has been made harmless, right? So they build a time-delay fuse with its own power supply, which doesn't start until the power leads to the main detonator have been cut. The UXB man pulls the fuse, clips it, gives the all clear, and the navvies start moving in with their tackle. Then, boom! Good for morale, eh?"

"Goddy, hold on a second. You're telling me this is a Nazi timer?"

"Well, I don't know about Nazi, but it's a German Dozy timer, all right. Look at the markings. The 'kmf–DO' is missing the R in front. It stands for Reichskriegsmaterialfabrik Dortmund. The '1' is for the Mark I model, the '44' is the year of manufacture. The rest should say, 'Zeitzünder,' time-delay fuse. The '15' is the time in minutes it takes to go off once triggered.

"It's a marvelously simple and sturdy device. I understand the East German army still uses a variation. You see, if you even remotely suspect there's one involved, you daren't cut any wires at all. It's even dicey removing anything metallic from the body of the bomb, because you never know where the cutoff trigger might be. That means—"

"Wait, Goddy. You said the East Germans were using it. That could mean it came with the Russian grenade. Maybe the same supplier."

Taylor chuckled. "No, dear girl. Whatever the East Germans use or don't use, this particular little bugger was made in Dortmund in 1944. It's straight from the Wehrmacht to you, with love. Someone's had it in their toy chest for nearly thirty years."

9

ALL THINGS CONSIDERED, the taping had gone rather well, Karp thought as he walked downtown the following morning. Being interviewed for television was a lot less of a strain when you kept in mind that TV—and all journalism for that matter—was a division of show business. At close range, Weber had struck Karp as a prematurely aging man of no particular intellect or distinction, what they called an empty suit around the courthouse. It was difficult to speak intelligently to someone who was not in the least interested in what you were saying, but merely in his own appearance of interest and perspicacity. Besides, he had a thin scum of pink pancake makeup on the collar of his shirt. You couldn't take a guy wearing pancake makeup seriously.

Weber's questions had probed at the gory details of the bombing and whether police incompetence had contributed. Karp declined to elaborate on the first and asserted strongly that there was no evidence for the second. He recalled thinking at the time that somebody was making a point of inserting this accusation into people's minds; it must be common gossip if Weber had picked it up.

The reporter had also asked about the character of the defendants, about whether they were not, as they claimed, struggling against communist oppression, albeit with deplorable methods and unfortunate results. The implication was that with all the horrible crimes in the city, the DA's office had better things to do than harass a bunch of freedom fighters whose only real crime was that some clumsy cop blew himself up taking a bomb out of a locker. Weber felt it necessary to mention several times that no one on the plane had been injured. Karp had, with difficulty, remained calm under this barrage, answering in as dull and legalistic a manner as he could generate, that a crime had been committed and that it was his duty to prosecute it on behalf of the people out there in television land.

But toward the end of the ten-minute session Weber had suddenly asked the jurisdiction question: "Mr. Karp, it seems to me that there are other district attorneys involved in this case. The killing took place in the Bronx, did it not? And the airport is in Queens. Yet you seem to be in sole charge. Has some kind of deal been made with the other DAs?" Karp was surprised by this, as being out of character with the rest of the interview. Why should a television audience, why should Weber, give a hoot about jurisdictional issues? Warily Karp had answered, "I don't know about 'deal.' When more than one DA's office is involved, one of them usually takes the lead, to coordinate evidence and so on. There's only one set of cops, so . . . it just makes for a better case."

Weber pressed on. "And in this case it's you, correct? You have full responsibility?"

"Right. It's my case."

"And you intend to put these people in prison, despite the complexities and conflicts we've mentioned?"

"Yes," Karp had said bluntly, and the camera had hung on his face for what seemed like an unusually long time as Weber summarized the interview in a few brief sentences and signed off.

This morning, as he entered 100 Centre Street, Karp found he was famous for Andy Warhol's fifteen minutes. A couple of people he knew waved to him in the Streets of Calcutta. Roland Hrcany shouted across the hall and mimed the rolling of a camera and the crouch of the news photographer. Apparently, Dirty Warren had seen him too.

"Hey, Mr. Karp, I saw you with that Carl Weber. You looked real good," he said with a boyish smile.

"Thanks, Warren."

"Hey, you gonna be on TV again? There was all these camera guys here before. With lights and things. Shitfaced motherfucker! I'll kill ya, you bastard!"

"No kidding? No, not right away, Warren, it was probably for something else, some big shot."

"Hey, you're a big shot, Mr. Karp. They should put you on TV more." Karp now noticed a TV cameraman with a portapack camera shuffling rapidly toward the elevators. Instantly Warren snapped into a brilliantly accurate imitation—facial expression, carriage, movement—of the cameraman for about three seconds. Then he returned to his ordinary bland expression. The mimicry, like the obscenities, was entirely unconscious.

"Magazine, you scumbag shitface?" he inquired politely.

Karp laughed and picked an old *Cosmopolitan* off Warren's wagon, leaving a dollar on the pile. More newspeople were crowding the bank of elevators, struggling to enter the cars. Connie

Trask, looking worried, pacing and biting her lip, brightened when she spotted him.

"Butch! God, am I glad I caught you! They're going crazy up there."

"Sounds like business as usual. What's going on?"

"No, really! We got a riot in the office. I wanted to catch you before you landed in it, and I—"

"Wait a second, Connie, calm down. A riot?"

"It's the Croatians, from Brooklyn. There's God, I don't know, two hundred of them up in our office, yelling and screaming and tearing things up. They're yelling for you, too. That's why I thought I better come down."

"Yeah, thanks, Connie. How about building security, you call them?"

"Yeah, first thing. They sent two guys, a big help."

"OK, I'll take care of it. Go to the snack bar and get yourself some coffee or something. OK?"

"All right. Great way to start the day, huh. Hey, I saw you last night on the news. You looked good."

As Karp dashed into a nearby office and picked up a phone, he began to realize why he and not Bloom had been cast as the featured player in this case on TV. Cursing himself for his own stupidity, he dialed Bill Denton's number.

It took two hours for the tactical cops to drag the Croatians out of the Criminal Courts Bureau offices and down to the waiting paddy wagons. Used to dealing with radical kids or unruly members of minorities, the cops were disconcerted by having to manhandle respectable middle-aged people led by a priest.

Karp stood in the fourth floor hallway, guarded by an immense black TPF sergeant, and watched the last of them being muscled out. A fiftyish woman with a neat blond perm and a sky-blue pants suit squirmed in the grip of two six-footers. She caught sight of Karp as she was dragged by and let out a stream of spittle-laden vituperation in two languages.

The TPF sergeant said, "Karp, you better watch yourself, these nice folks don't like y'all one bit."

"Free the Five! Free the Five! Long live free Croatia!" the woman shouted as the stairway door closed. The stairwell was echoing and booming with similar shouts. The sergeant snorted.

"That's it. You'll be OK, now. The chief's got building security beefed up for the next week at least."

"Thanks, Sarge. Any bloodshed?"

"Naw. These folks're all talk. And we got orders to be real

gentle. This demonstration'd been a bunch a brothers, there'd a been hair on the walls. Croatians, my ass!"

Karp thanked the sergeant again and went into the office. A dozen or so attorneys and clerical workers stumbled around in the wreckage, setting up desks that had been overturned and clearing up drifts of scattered paper. He acknowledged their greetings and a scattering of compliments about how well he had looked on television. Hrcany came up to him and handed him a large hand-lettered picket sign. "Here," he said, "you might want it as a souvenir." The sign said:

KOMMIE-LOVER KARP
FREE THE FIVE! !

"The price of fame," Karp said ruefully. "Roland, if I ever go on television again, would you be a friend and kick me in the ass?" He gestured broadly to the wrecked office. "Christ, look at all this crap."

Roland started to leave and then snapped his fingers. "Shit, I almost forgot. I found you another witness. Guy name of Emil Koltan. He's a waiter down at the Buda Restaurant."

"Oh yeah? What's his story?"

"The story is, I'm having dinner with my dad last night at the Buda, which is the place to go for serious pirogi and paprikash, and we get to talking to Emil. Him and my dad go way back, before '56 even. So they're bullshitting about money, how hard it is nowadays, et cetera, and Emil's talking about how he takes these odd waiting jobs, like banquets, weddings, and so on. I'm not really listening until I realize his tone has changed, to like confidential. He's asking my dad for advice, and he's talking about a private dinner he did for a Croat fraternal organization."

"When was this? The dinner."

"Just last week, the ninth. It seems these four guys at Emil's table were a little high and talking freely because they figured nobody could understand them, which was a good bet because they were speaking Serbo-Croat. Little did they know that our boy Emil, though a Hungarian, understands Serbo-Croatian. He was raised in one of the border areas that kept switching around during the last century or so. Anyway, he got the gist of the conversation, which was that they were giving one of them the needle about screwing up something important. Emil says 'the little one, with thick glasses' was the goat. Turns out, it was putting a bomb in a locker in Grand Central."

"Holy shit, Roland!"

"Yeah, wait, there's more. They're also talking about stealing a plane. One of them, Emil says, 'the big one, old, but like a bull,' is like running a quiz show, snapping out questions about what everybody is supposed to do, making sure they know their parts—"

"Karavitch."

"Sounds like it."

"Unbelievable! But Roland, why didn't this waiter tell anybody about this?"

"Come on, Butch, what's to tell? They were laughing and joking—it could have been a play, or a practical joke."

"About bombs and boosting airliners?"

"Butch, they're Croats. Emil's a Hungarian. How does he know what a bunch of Croats would find funny? But when he saw them on TV after the hijack and recognized them—"

"He can ID them?"

"Sure. Except for the chick. She wasn't at the dinner. So he gets concerned and decides to talk to my dad next time he's in the Buda. My dad is sort of a pillar-of-the-community type, big lawyer, owns property, so a lot of the old country people like to grab him and spill their guts in Hungarian, maybe cop some free legal advice. Anyway, he did, and there I was, and the rest is history. Here's his name and address." Hrcany handed Karp a piece of paper. Karp took it, kissed it loudly, and flung his arm over Hrcany's shoulders in an athletic hug.

"Roland, I'm peeing in my pants. Between Emil and Max Dorcas, Rukovina is going to crack like an egg, that little scumbag. That's it, that's the case in—ah, shit!"

Karp grimaced and slammed his right fist violently into the palm of his left hand. "What's wrong, Butch?" Hrcany asked.

"Dorcas, dammit! There was supposed to be a lineup for him here this morning. Look, Roland, thanks a million for this. I got to call Spicer now to get the lineup going and I'll tell him to send a man for Emil too. See you later."

Karp got Fred Spicer on the second ring. "Fred? Karp. Look, things are rolling. I want to do that Max Dorcas lineup right away, and I got another witness in the same case that I'd like you to send somebody for, also right away. OK, here's his name—"

"Hold on there, Butch, just a second. The Dorcas lineup? Christ, I canceled that, must of been a little past nine."

"You canceled it? Without asking me? Why in hell'd you do that?"

"There was a riot going on, Butch, hey?"

"What the fuck does that have to do with it, Fred? We weren't

99

going to do the lineup in the goddamn Criminal Courts Bureau office. Shit!"

"Well, I just thought it was wiser not to, that's all," said Spicer, beginning to huff. He was a reasonably good administrative cop, if inclined to be lazy.

Karp gritted his teeth and sat on his rising temper. Spicer could screw up his life more than just about any member of the police department, and Karp could not afford any more problems at present. "OK, OK, Fred. Sorry I snapped. Schedule the Dorcas lineup for tomorrow first thing. I'd like Slocum to bring them in from Riker's himself."

"Yeah, he said you wanted him to. Hell, Butch, I got better things for my guys to do than haul scumbags from the jail and back. I'm short as hell now, as it is, and—"

"Fred, bear with me. Believe me, it's important. But more important right now is picking up this witness. Name's Emil Koltan. Here's the address." Karp read off an address in the 80's off East End Avenue. Spicer said he would get right on it, which Karp doubted but couldn't do much about.

After hanging up, Karp went into his office, undamaged except that somebody had scrawled "FREE THE FIVE" across his frosted glass door in pink lipstick. He calmed himself by sheer force of will, put in a couple of hours of paperwork and made a dozen or so phone calls, including one to Denton about the waiter Hrcany had found. Around eleven Marlene Ciampi walked in, as usual without knocking.

"Where have you been this fine morning?" Karp asked sourly. As always, his first sight of Marlene in the morning made his heart bump with love, but today he resented it. Roland's news had elated him and the conversation with Spicer had cast him down again. Those events, coming on top of the TV appearance and its sequel, made him feel jerked around, a feeling he particularly hated.

"I didn't know you were a Cosmo girl," said Marlene, pointing to his desk. "This gives us something else in common." Karp realized he had been carrying the magazine he had bought from Dirty Warren around with him all morning. He cursed and threw it in the trashbasket.

"Silly you," said Marlene, perching her bottom on the edge of his desk and shaking out a Marlboro. "Now you'll never know the seven ways to tell if your boss is romantically interested. Hey, I saw you on TV last night."

"Yeah, right. How was I, great?"

"I thought you were the sexiest thing since Marshal Dillon. I was wet to the knees."

"I was set up. Fucking Bloom wants a patsy to hang if this case goes sour, and right now it looks like a good bet. I can't believe the shit that has gone wrong." He briefly filled her in on what Hrcany had told him and about what had gone down with Spicer. She puffed smoke and listened, then said, "Take it easy, Butch. It's a complex case. It's going to take us awhile to settle down all the aspects. Now, you might be interested in another little wiggle I happened to turn up—"

"It's not *that* complex, Marlene, for crying out loud! You wrote the goddamn indictments. That's what we should be concentrating on. The gang left a bomb. The bomb killed a cop. We got to convince twelve people it went down that way and that's all she wrote. Period."

"If they let you."

"If who lets me? What's that supposed to mean?"

"Butch, while you are pursuing the great simplicities, somebody is trying to screw up the case. You have to believe that, and you know as well as I do that there are about a thousand ways to taint a case like this. A couple have already been tried."

"So? We stopped them."

"So far. But they only have to score once, and they'll keep trying. Which is why we have to find out who they are. And soon."

Karp leaned back in his chair and massaged his scalp. He felt exhausted and irritated. "They! Who's 'they,' Marlene, tell me that! What are we going to do, go off on some paranoid wild goose chase after some fucking conspiracy we don't even know exists? We got six hundred homicides . . . ."

"I know how many homicides we have, Butch," said Marlene quietly. "And there's no need to start shouting at me."

"Ah, Christ, I'm sorry, Marlene, but what do you expect me to do? I'm hanging on by my fingernails here. I just have to play it straight defense, that's all. And hope we can catch all the shit. OK, I'm calmed down. Now, what was the little wiggle?"

Marlene had decided on the spot not to tell him about what she had learned from Taylor, at least not yet. Or about what she planned to do with the old soldier. "The wiggle? Oh, nothing much. I found out where John Evans is from, is all."

"Evans? Oh, the fancy suit at the arraignment."

"Yeah. He works out of Washington, D.C. For Arthur Bingham Roberts."

"Oh, that's just great. Marlene, where the hell do these

101

schmendriks get the bread to hire the most expensive criminal lawyer in the United States?"

"Oh, I wondered about that, too. So I went down to the Fifth Precinct, where they booked those yo-yos who were here this morning. And I got sort of cozy with Father Peter Blic."

"Who?"

"Father Blic is the priest at St. Gregory's in Greenpoint, where the Croat cheering section comes from. Our suspects are his parishioners."

"And the parish raised the money?"

"Oh, sure, they had a bake sale and bingo and put together enough to hire Arthur Bingham Roberts for about twelve minutes. No, this weekend somebody delivered a check to Father Blic, with a note that said that Mr. Roberts had been contacted and was interested in the case. The check was for twenty K."

"I can see his interest. Are you going to tell me who the check was from?"

"Well, you know, I asked Father Blic that very question, because, as I told the dear man, I was so impressed by the Christian generosity shown by the benefactors of those brave freedom fighters, that I had resolved to make a special novena for them. So he said that while he didn't know the actual donor, the check was drawn on the account of a law firm called McNamara, Shannon, Shannon and Devlin, and maybe that would help."

"Hmm, sounds like a bunch of Croatians, all right. What's their story?"

"I don't know yet. That's for this afternoon. What do you think?"

"Not much. They're no criminal firm, though. Is that it?"

Marlene got off the desk and went to the door. "On the Doyle front it is. Oh, by the way, I sent my injury appeal up through channels. It's probably sitting in Corncob's in-basket. Any little thing you can do—"

"Sure, babe, I'll try, but you know how it is."

"Alas, I do. See you." She gave him a lopsided grin and slipped out.

Shortly thereafter, Marlene locked herself in a booth in the ladies' room and began weeping silently. Mouth wide open, tears gushing, she hugged herself and rocked back and forth, howling softly, her mind blank. After about ten minutes she mopped her face and blew her nose with toilet paper. These sessions had been occurring with increasing frequency during the past year. The overwhelming feelings would unpredictably burst like a summer squall, and then she would excuse herself from whatever she was doing and dash for the bathroom. Spiritual diarrhea, she called it privately, and told herself that it was a cheap substitute for therapy.

But in her heart of hearts she knew better. Something was wrong inside. Things had to change. She thought about what Karp had said about defense. Or *dee*-fense, as he pronounced it in the jock manner. Defense was not enough, it was not enough to be tough. She wanted to be rescued. She wanted love, a family. She was thirty-one. She wanted Karp to rescue her. If only he could see beyond his arrogant mission to save the world. Oh, Butchie, she thought, I know you so well and you don't know me at all. I'm going to have to rescue you first.

Marlene left the booth and went to the sinks and mirrors to repair what was left of her face. While she was brushing her hair, Rhoda Klepp came out of one of the booths and occupied the next sink. Since there were ten sinks, this was an invitation. Marlene did not particularly like Rhoda Klepp, but neither did she join in the vituperation heaped on her by the other ADAs. The DA's office was hiring more women these days than it had when Marlene had started out, but it was still largely a men's club, and Marlene felt a guilty impulse toward sisterly solidarity.

"How's it going, Rhoda?" she said heartily.

"Oh, so-so," replied Rhoda, not taking her eyes off herself in the mirror. "I'm doing the briefing for the monthly targets meeting this afternoon. Chip is such a perfectionist, you wouldn't believe it. And Sandy too. Never a false move. I think he's running for president. He always keeps an extra suit in the office in a cleaner bag—God forbid he should get a wrinkle or spill something. Also, he's got ties. A riot! He tapes phone calls, you know that?"

"Uh-uh. What do the numbers look like this month?"

"Not that great. I don't think Sandy is going to be very pleased with them."

"Oh?"

"Yeah, people are going to get creamed. Your, ah, whatchama-callit . . ."

"Karp."

"Especially. I can't believe how he goes out of his way to piss people off. Not just Chip, everybody. The cops too."

"Which cops are those?"

"Oh, you know, stuff you hear. I really shouldn't be talking about this." She finished her makeup and backed away from the mirror. She turned this way and that, tucking and pulling at her blouse and adjusting the underlying cables and supports. Marlene stared at this performance, and Rhoda caught her looking. "Make you jealous?" she asked.

"You certainly have a nice figure, Rhoda," Marlene said evenly.

"Yeah. I used to hate it. But now I love when men stare at my body. You can see them trying to look away, but their eyes always drift back, like little machines, the assholes."

"Uh-huh."

Rhoda seemed to take in Marlene for the first time. "It's power. I guess it's probably hard for someone like you to understand that. I mean . . ."

"Right. Look, Rhoda, I sent an administrative appeal up to, um, Chip's office. Do you know if it got there?"

"Oh, yeah, I think I saw that lying around. What about it?"

"Is he going to sign it?"

"Well, that would depend, I guess. I mean we've got to worry about the precedent. We need to check with the general counsel and the insurance people. And so on."

Marlene was struggling to control her rage, afraid that in another moment she would lose it all and commit a class-A felony. She cleared her throat and said softly, "I hardly think that precedent is a concern. How many ADAs do they suppose are going to be bombed in a year?"

"Well, it's the principle, then. Ramifications. Whatever," said Rhoda blithely. As she picked up her handbag and prepared to leave, she favored Marlene with a look of amused contempt. "Get smart, honey," she said. "You're a bright girl. Why should Chip hassle himself to do you a favor? You hang around with Karp, some of the smell rubs off, you understand? And now you're farting around with this stupid skyjack case, which every time he hears about it the DA wants to vomit. You understand what I'm saying? You could really have a future around here if you changed your attitude, hung around with the right people, worked on the right cases, steered them the right way."

"Will it give me big tits too?" Marlene asked spontaneously, half to herself.

"What?"

"Nothing, Rhoda," she said. "Have a nice day."

After Rhoda left, Marlene kicked the wastebasket as hard as she could, twice, making a satisfyingly aggressive clamor. On checking her datebook, she found she was scheduled to interview a woman named Doreen Moore who was accused of stuffing her four-year-old daughter in an oven and roasting her alive.

Rhoda Klepp meanwhile went to the monthly targets meeting, a vastly more comfortable duty. Karp went too, although it was by no means comfortable for him. The monthly targets meeting was where Wharton got to torture Karp, and he had to sit there and take it. The idea was that each bureau would commit to clearance targets and then be held accountable for them each month. As it turned out, however, Karp's boss, Melvyn Pelso, made the commitments, which he did without consulting Karp or anyone else who knew what was going on in the courtrooms. Pelso got the credit for heroic commitments, and Karp got the blame for failing to meet them. Theoretically, he could have met them, provided none of his attorneys was ever sick or ever took a day off, and provided virtually every defendant pleaded guilty to the top count of the indictment, and especially provided that he practically never went to trial.

Since none of these provisions were met, he always flunked. Today was worse than usual. Because of the events of that morning, Karp had not had a chance to review the cases he had proposed for trial and which he had to defend to Wharton. To his dismay, he found included among them the case of Alejandro Sorriendas.

Karp found Guma in his office, feet up on the desk, smoking a White Owl and reading the *National Enquirer*. "Don't strain your mind with that stuff, Guma," he said. "You might have to use it someday."

Guma smiled around his cigar. "Hey man, I'm a trial lawyer. I got to keep up with the masses, get a feel for what people will swallow. How about this? 'Mom Cuts Off Arm to Feed Starving Kids. Dad Watches.' "

"Speaking of trials, you rat, I just got my ass reamed because you stuck that piece-of-shit Sorriendas attempted homicide on the trial roster, so Wharton could give me his little smile and say, 'Gosh, Butch, things must really be slack in Criminal Courts if we're going to trial on a domestic assault, hah, hah.' How the fuck do you expect me to stand up for the real cases when you pull crap like that?"

"Butch, calm down."

"Why? I thought we had an agreement, and I get up there and get shafted."

"Calm down, Butch. It's OK. I just needed something to flash at Sorriendas and his lawyer. I figured you'd catch it and dump it and no harm done."

"Bullshit, Guma. That list went into typing last night, without Sorriendas. You had your girl type your version, and then you slipped it into the box upstairs so it would be Xeroxed for the briefing book."

Guma took his cigar out of his mouth and put his feet down on the floor, his face an artful amalgam of hurt innocence and belligerence. "OK, guilty! Guilty, your honor! Big fucking deal. Butch, listen to me, baby. Do I ever steer you wrong? This thing goes down the way I think, you're gonna be golden."

"No way, Guma. And just don't pull shit like this, man . . ."

Guma held up his hands and smiled disarmingly. "Butch, Butch, what're we fighting here? We're the good guys, remember? The white hats. Come on, look, I got a half hour. I'll buy you a coffee, some danish, we'll talk."

It was hard to argue with Guma, Karp had found from long experience, since he had no use for either logic or consistency, and had the endurance of a sumo wrestler. Karp allowed himself to be ushered down to the snack bar on the first floor. When they were settled in the smoky fug with their bad coffee, Guma said, "Look, Butch, these are serious bad guys. Just give me a little juice to squeeze Sorriendas with, and I know we can crack something. Not just the dope, homicides too."

"Oh, yeah? Which one?"

"Come on, how do you think Ruiz got to be a smack czar in five years? Giving out Green Stamps?"

"No trials, Goom."

"OK, OK, no trial. But let me squeeze Sorriendas anyway. Get some cops to follow him around, roust him, like that. Whaddya say?"

"I say, if you can get one of the guys to do it, and it doesn't screw up any of our other investigations, and it's cool with Spicer, I could care less."

"Jesus, Butch, thanks a lot. What a prince! Hey, but put a good word in, huh?"

"Sure, talk's cheap," said Karp, standing up. "It's been real, Goom. See you round."

For the remainder of the court day Karp ran around through the dirty hallways, doing the People's business. Once he caught sight of Marlene leaving a courtroom with a crowd of people. He waved at her, but she didn't respond. She looked depressed and drawn. He made a mental note to call her later that evening to find out if she had learned anything about the Croatians' unknown benefactor.

By six the building had cleared out, except for the cleaning people clattering the waste baskets and maniacs like Karp, who were just beginning the most productive part of their working day. For an hour or so he plowed through the day's intake of case files, assigning them to the various attorneys under his command and making brief notes on strategy for the ADAs, who would see them for the first time the following morning. Then he reviewed the stack of cases that he would handle personally, and made notes about the police officers and witnesses who would have to be scheduled for the rest of the week. Around eight, feeling peckish, he went out through the echoing hallways and into Foley Square.

He walked up Baxter Street to a hole-in-the-wall Chinese take-out joint, where he ordered a quart of chicken chow mein and a large Coke to go. Waiting for his order in the steamy, brightly lit place, he mulled over the Doyle case. Whenever he thought about a case, he thought visually, as if he were figuring out a basketball play, with bodies moving rapidly in space, rearranging themselves constantly in relation to each other and to the three constants—the ball, the basket, and the rules of the game. He often diagrammed cases in the same way.

He slid a take-out menu sheet from the stack on the counter and turned it over to its blank side. Using a pencil stub he drew in the center a circle marked "BOMB-HOMICIDE" and from that a line connecting it to another circle marked "CROATS" with the names of the hijackers in smaller circles within it. The names "Karavitch," "Macek," and "Wilson" were connected in a triangle, with a question mark in it. A line from "Rukovina" led to the "BOMB-HOMICIDE" circle. Rising up from this line were two balloons. In one of them was the name "Dorcas" and in the other the name "Koltan." Another line led from the "CROAT" circle to one marked "A.B. Roberts." This line had a question mark and a dollar sign on it.

He drew another line from the "BOMB-HOMICIDE" circle, at the end of which he drew a little square labeled "Device." He put a question mark over it. Then a line from that box to a circle marked "COPS," with another question mark. Inside the "COPS" circle he wrote the names "Denton," "Hanlon," and "Spicer." He put a question mark over the last two. Then he paused and chewed the pencil, and finally put another over "DENTON." Then he crossed it out. Then he drew it in again, but faintly.

Finally he drew a large circle around the whole diagram. On its periphery he drew circles marked "FBI" and "BLOOM," with large question marks over both of them. Under "BLOOM" he wrote "knew K. name—Denton/ screwup/ TV?" Under "FBI" he wrote "translator/screwup/coaching/how?/why?" That's the case in a nut-shell, folks, he thought. He counted up the question marks. Too

107

damn many. The real question was, which ones were important and which represented the usual crap that accumulated in the wake of a murder investigation cruising through a sea of corruption?

Somebody was trying to get his attention. "Oh-dah ready," said the man behind the counter. Karp took the heavy brown bag with the bill stapled to the top of it, and then folded the diagram and put it in his pocket. As he left he noticed a dark young man looking into the restaurant window. He seemed to be staring right at Karp. Then he took a comb out of his jacket pocket and, using the window as a mirror, began combing his long black hair. As he did, he cocked his lean jaw with a peculiar little bounce at each stroke of the comb and narrowed his eyes, as if seeking an image of perfection.

Karp went back to his office, squirted packages of hot mustard and soy sauce over the chow mein, and gobbled it down. As he was chewing up the last of the ice in his Coke, the phone rang.

"Karp. We doze, but never close."

"Hah, hah. Karp? Fred Slocum. I've been trying your apartment."

"Silly you. What's happening, Fred?"

"All kinds of shit. You hear the news about Max Dorcas?"

"No, what?"

"About half an hour ago somebody tossed a fire bomb into his store."

"Ah, shit! Is he hurt?"

"No, he closed up at six-thirty. But the place is totaled."

"Anybody make the guy who did it?"

"Sonny's checking. Newsstand guy says it looked like a Puerto Rican, dark guy, medium build. Didn't get a good look at the face, needless to say."

"You talk to Dorcas yet?"

"Yeah. He's pretty busted up over it. And I didn't have to tell him what happened. Somebody called him at home and told him to develop a lapse of memory. They said the next fire he'd be in the middle of it, tied to his wife."

"Godammit! What does he say?"

"Well, he's not too enthusiastic about being a good citizen anymore. I'll work on him, but . . ."

"Yeah, I know. Freddy, who knew about Dorcas? I mean, being a witness and spotting Rukovina."

"In details? Me, Sonny, you, Spicer, probably the C. of D. Anybody you told. In general, that he was a witness in the case? Who knows? The lineup wasn't no big secret. I mean, this isn't the Manhattan Project."

"Not yet, Freddy, but who knows? Did you get to Koltan?"

108

"Who?"

"Emil Koltan. He's another witness. Christ! You mean Spicer didn't tell you to bring him in?"

"Not me, Butch. Never heard of him. Maybe he told Sonny or one of the other guys."

"Right, but somehow I doubt it. Look, Freddy, he's really key. Could you go and pick him up right now?" With mounting anxiety, Karp read the name and address off to Slocum. The only people who knew about Koltan, besides the Hrcanys, were Karp and Spicer. And Denton.

After urging speed and security on Slocum, Karp hung up and tried to make sense of these new developments. He unfolded the Chinese menu diagram and spread it out on his desk. It didn't tell him anything more than it had at the take-out. He remembered what Doug Brenner had said at the clam bar on City Island—if something's moving funny, there's got to be a mover. Denton? It seemed incredible, but he had to consider it. Maybe that story about Kenny Moran and Terry Doyle was bullshit. He could check it out. But why would he put Karp in charge if it was a tank job? Bloom? Always a possibility. Did Bloom have something on Denton? But what about the FBI?

He picked up a pencil and drew a wavery light line connecting the circles marked "Bloom" and "Denton." Then he smiled and drew near the center a stick figure with a frowning face and marked it "Karp." He drew a heavy jagged line coming down from "Bloom" and striking the stick figure.

A shadow played across the glass on his door. Karp's stomach churned and he stood up, sweeping the diagram into his desk drawer.

"Knock, knock, anybody home?"

Karp was surprised at how much adrenaline had just pumped into his system and slightly ashamed. He sagged back into his chair, feeling faintly queasy, and called out, "Yeah, come in."

V.T. Newbury opened the door and entered. He was dressed in a dirty Burberry trenchcoat, a faded blue sweatsuit, and sneakers, and carried a briefcase. He sniffed the air and said, "I've been running and you've been gorging on Chinese. Oriental decadence." He sat down on Karp's wooden side chair. "What's wrong? You look sick, man."

Karp grinned weakly. "It must be the MSG. What are you doing here so late? What is it, eight already?"

"More like eight-thirty. I came to pick up some printouts for the strike force."

"You getting anywhere with that shit?"

"Yeah, but it's slow. Of course, we're just errand boys for the Feds, nor do they trust us that much to begin with. We're not untouchable, you know."

"You'd think after Watergate, and Hoover, they'd have developed a sense of shame."

"Minor lapses, my boy. Oh, speaking of which, I ran into your old buddy Pillman the other day."

"How was he?"

"In rare form. I made so bold as to ask him about the Tel-Air operation. You remember, from Monday?"

"Yeah. Guma's pride and joy. What'd he say?"

"Tel-Air? What's Tel-Air? Playing it very close indeed. It piqued my curiosity, though. So I thought I would use some of my own connections in the financial community to noodle around, trace some transactions and so on."

"The cousins."

"You got it, boss. Oh, yeah, cousins. You'll be interested to know I got through to Andrew at the State Department. One of his school buddies is in intelligence liaison and Andrew tried to quiz him about all those mixed signals during the hijack negotiations. Much clearing of throat and sideways looks, but it turned out that Langley was showing inordinate interest in the affair from minute one, as soon as we knew the identity of the gang."

"That's the CIA?"

"Yep. Also, this Simon Dettrick I told you about, the spook in Paris? No longer there. Leland called me. Apparently Dettrick flew home on the military jet that carried the hijackers back to New York. Also aboard was Jim Toomey, the guy from the New York FBI office."

"Oh-ho! You think these guys maybe discussed the situation with our friends? Maybe gave them a little free legal advice, the scumbags?"

"It's a possibility. Well, I'll leave you to your musings. See you in court."

V.T. rose to go. As he went out the door, something popped into Karp's mind. "V.T., wait a minute. Cousins made me think of your father. He knows the New York corporate law scene pretty well, doesn't he?"

"You could say that. Why?"

"Could you ask him about a firm called McNamara, Shannon, Shannon and Devlin?"

"What about them?"

"Just what their business is, who they represent. Marlene told me they just issued a big check for the legal defense of the Croats.

It looks like they're hiring Arthur Bingham Roberts. I'd like to know who's that interested in these assholes walking away from this."

V.T. whistled softly through his teeth. "Offhand, I'd say it was a gift from God."

"What do you mean."

"Well, I needn't trouble Father on this one. The fact of the matter is that McNamara, et al. get about ninety-five percent of their business from the Archdiocese of New York. I'd bet that the check was Powerhouse money. What's wrong? You look like you just ate a rat."

"Oh, nothing. Some things are starting to come clear. Thanks, V.T., see you later."

After Newbury had left, Karp took out his diagram. He crossed out the question marks over "Spicer," "Denton," and "Hanlon," replacing them with heavy check marks, and drew a heavy circle around all the policemen. A thick jagged line came down from this circle to strike the stick figure. Poor "Karp"! Then he made a heavy line from the police to "FBI" and to "BLOOM."

Then he made another circle floating in the upper right of the page and labeled it "CIA," and connected it with a thin line to "CROATS." Question mark on that; involvement, but who knew what it was? Almost done. In the upper left he drew a heavy-sided box. An arrow came down from it and touched the dollar sign near "A.B. Roberts." Another arrow flew over to the "COPS" circle. He pressed hard on this arrow, thickening it and doodling little circles and arabesques around it. Then he doodled a steeple on the heavy-sided box, and on top of it, a cross. He studied the diagram for a long minute, then folded it up carefully and placed it in his trouser pocket. "Holy shit," he said out loud. "Holy shit."

10

KARP WALKED HOME through the deserted streets of down-town, the fateful diagram folded into a small square and stuffed in his wallet. The night was cold and damp, and he was wearing only a thin raincoat over his rumpled suit. The chill he felt in his vitals did not, however, have an entirely meteorological origin. He felt utterly alone, abandoned, a lost child on unforgiving streets. This feeling had quite overcome his natural skepticism about conspiracy. His thoughts raced in idiotic confusion, looking for some strong refuge, something undeniably real. The law? Obviously, a sham. Justice? A silly joke. Love? Give me a break! Religion? Vain mumblings of tribes.

From forgotten depths, bred in a hundred schoolyard brawls, his paranoia of Catholics blossomed like a noxious weed. He had been raised in one of the borderland areas that dot the five boroughs, this one deep in Brooklyn, where Kings Highway and Flatbush Avenue join. Go northwest from this junction and you are in Midwood, among the Jewish middle class. Karp had lived on this side of the border, but barely. Go south and you are in Flatlands—solid Irish and Italian. East is East Flatbush, now heavily black, but when Karp was growing up a mixed province of white ethnics: Italians, Poles, Germans, Hungarians.

Although native New Yorkers know that New York is not the melting pot of legend, tolerance generally prevails among the adults populating these zones. But the male youth of an age to wander the streets and play in the concrete schoolyards were subject to outbursts of tribal barbarism that would not have been misplaced in Beirut. Karp had been a husky, strong kid and had two big brothers, but he spent a lot of time in the streets and he took his lumps. He learned early that you get your lumps largely from persons who do not share your eth. In Karp's case, in the Brooklyn of the late forties, these were almost always flat-faced, snub-nosed, pale, light-haired, blue-eyed kids: Irish, Poles, Catholics.

Of course, this had been a long time ago. Karp's family had become more prosperous and moved out of the city to a homogeneous suburb just before he had gone west to college. Religion and ancestry were not big issues at Berkeley in the mid sixties. Karp's Jewish consciousness and the associated paranoia approached absolute zero. Back in New York, working for the DA's office, he was vaguely conscious of something called the Archdiocese of New York as a force to be reckoned with, like the police and the mayor's office, and the Chase Manhattan Bank, but he had never given it any particular thought. In fact, until he had caught that case on the boy burglar—Brannigan? Brannon?—he had never been asked to deal directly with the Church. Uh-oh. Why not? Because he was Jewish? Because he didn't know the secret signs? Then why now? Why did they insist he deal with it now? Part of the plot? Was there a connection between the Croats and Brannon? Ridiculous. But just as ridiculous was the confirmed fact that the NYPD was conspiring to prevent him from prosecuting a case against five people who had killed a cop. And that the Church was footing the bill for the killers.

Before he dived into a troubled sleep that night, a vivid image from childhood burst into his mind. He was walking home along a Brooklyn commercial street holding his grandmother's hand. He did not particularly like his grandmother; in fact, she terrified him. She was a broad, powerful woman from the backwoods of Galicia, a creature out of the sixteenth century, subject to fits of rage and unpredictable violence.

On this occasion she had been angry about something, and Karp was being pulled quickly down an unfamiliar street. At a corner was a larger, dark brick building with turrets and an iron-bound oak door. A church or a parochial school. In a tiny iron-railed enclosure before the building stood a life-size white statue of a gently smiling woman with her hands outstretched, palms upward. Karp remembered pulling toward the statue to get a better look, but his grandmother had hauled him roughly away and mumbled some dreadful curse in a mixture of Yiddish and Polish. Then she spat on the ground.

Karp dragged himself out of bed the next morning, feeling headachey and bilious. He threw himself on his rowing machine and exercised violently for half an hour, until his muscles screamed and his vision was red with pain. Then he took a hot shower. Physical pain was the best medicine he had found for the mental agonies of the night.

This time it didn't quite work. The headache was gone and his belly was ready for another influx of dreck, but the queasiness remained in his spirit. Something was cooking, that was for sure, and in some way he was in the pot. On the other hand, he thought, how could you go to a friend and tell him that the Catholic Church, the NYPD, the FBI, and the district attorney were conspiring against you? What could he say? What about the KGB, Butch? They miss the boat? No, his friends would be very kind, and after a while, so would the doctors at the sanitarium. No, for a while at least, he would have to play it uncomfortably solo.

And since at work Karp was normally sociable and frank to a fault, the new Karp attracted attention. He began to lock his desk. He started using public telephones for certain outgoing calls. He stopped talking about the Doyle case. He began to insert long pauses and hard stares before his responses in conversations, as if mentally reviewing the dossier of the person speaking. "Want to go for coffee, Butch?" Pause, beat, beat beat. "Yeah, OK."

Two days after this new Karp had emerged, Ray Guma buttonholed V.T. Newbury outside a fourteenth-floor courtroom. "Hey, wait up a minute, I got to talk to you. Look, V.T., you notice anything strange about Butch recently, last couple days?"

"Umm, well, a little diffident, perhaps. Secretive?"

"Secretive? He's acting like he's in a Gestapo movie, for crying out loud. Listen to what happened today. I got this case, a homicide, a domestic, a grounder, but it's got a little twist to it. Lady in the Village turns up dead, Bleecker Street. So, needless to say, the cops look for the old man. He ain't at work, skipped the last two days. The cops hit the streets, ask around. This is Comer and Defalco from Manhattan South, by the way. So what happens? A priest from St. Joseph's shows up at the precinct with a story. It turns out the victim, Mrs. Bendiccio, has been playing around. She goes to the priest to spill her guts—not confession, just unburdening, she's not sure she wants to dump the boyfriend, maybe she wants to know how much time she's got to do in the barbecue in the next life, whatever.

"Anyway, she tells the priest the boyfriend's got a hot temper, she's scared that if she dumps him and goes back to Augie, he'll go batshit. When the priest hears she's been whacked, naturally he comes in and lays the story on Defalco and Comer. Even got a name for the boyfriend, Ted Mores."

V.T. glanced at the hall clock. "Goom, what does this have to do with Butch?"

"Wait, I'm getting to it. OK, it's no trick finding either man. Hubby stumbles home, surprised as hell to find somebody choked his old lady while he was off on a binge. Ted goes, 'What girlfriend?' clams up, wants a lawyer. An insurance guy, married, lives in Peter Cooper.

"Naturally, I want to tell Karp about this, get his sense of how to play the case. OK, I go to his office. I knock. He *unlocks the door*. He's locking himself in the office now, in case you don't know. I go in, he rushes back to the desk and clears some papers off, in a hurry, like he doesn't want me to see them. So I tell him the facts of the case. When I get to the part about the main informant being a priest, kaboom! He goes pale, jumps up, starts pacing back and forth. He starts asking all these crazy questions. Is Ted Catholic? Is Comer the cop Catholic? I ask him why he wants to know, he clams up. 'Oh, just curious, you know.' In a pig's eye I know. And there's other stuff . . .''

Guma's voice faded. He scowled and chewed on his lower lip.

"Sounds grim," V.T. agreed. "What do you think? You think he's flipping out from the strain?"

"Flipping out? You mean going crazy? Like he wasn't crazy already? I'd have to think about that. Guy who lives in an apartment with no furniture, works eighteen hours a day, seven days a week, at a job where his boss is looking to put the blocks to him any way he can, which also pays him around three tenths of what he's worth—I don't know what word you might use to describe such a person, but 'crazy' might not be entirely out of line."

"Not 'dedicated'? 'Devoted to justice in all its multifarious forms,' perhaps?"

Guma smiled. "Same thing in this shithole. But really, you know and I know that Karp is the best trial lawyer we still got around here, and he's been carrying the joint on major crimes since Garrahy kicked off. In the office the guy is ice. You've heard him on cross-exam. Other DAs, they can't resist the little dig at a hostile witness. Pisses off the judge, confuses the jury. And Butch? He treats these bastards like gold, gets the story, in, out, bingo. The jury thinks he's God, *they* wouldn't treat this obvious asshole that good. And so on.

"Now this. And it's connected to this goddamn hijack case, I know it is. But what I can't figure is, how come Karp is suddenly so interested in religious persuasion when as far as I know—and I've known the guy seven, eight years—he never made a peep about it before. The reason I ask is that if Karp is all of a sudden going to turn into a pain in the ass—and he is the only boss around here that isn't—then maybe I got to seek some serious career counseling. I'm too old to put up with assholes."

"I see your point. Have you talked with any of the others? Roland? Or Marlene?"

"Roland? Who knows what Roland is thinking? Guy's a fucking animal. Roland thinks Karp's losing it, who knows what he'll do? You heard the expression, 'If you have a Hungarian for a friend, you don't need any enemies'? That's Roland. They made it about him."

"And Marlene?"

"Ciampi? She's not exactly your connoisseur of sanity at the present time. You know she heads for the can on a daily basis for a good honk? Or so my informants inform me."

"Well, she's had her troubles."

"So what? I got my troubles too. Am I carrying forty cases? Fuck, yeah. Is my ex taking me to court for the orthodontist bills for two kids: four, five big ones? Fuck, yeah. I'd a known that, I would've kicked their teeth out before the divorce. You see anything wrong with my teeth, V.T.? They work. They eat food. Women and children don't run screaming when they see me on the street. Well, theirs are just like mine, couple of gaps is all. Five grand, which I haven't got, she's taking me to court. So you see me sitting in the crapper bawling? No fucking way."

"And the bottom line of this is . . . ?"

"Talk to him, V.T. He respects you. Talk to Marlene. Find out what's going on. He's got a hard-on for the pope? Fine, we'll fix it, anything. Butch goes off the rails, man, we might as well turn this place over to the mutts."

Bill Denton finally caught up with Karp late in the week, after four rounds of telephone tag, which Karp had engineered by calling back when he was sure Denton would be away from his desk. A standard bureaucratic trick, but not foolproof if the person you are trying to avoid has your private number and doesn't mind using it.

"Karp, where've you been? I been trying to get you for days."

"Oh, busy. You know."

"That's the problem, I don't know. What's happening on Doyle?"

"We've started with the grand jury, just a couple of witnesses. I'm expecting to finish up the presentation tomorrow. There shouldn't be a problem getting an indictment, and we can arraign on the indictments early next week. One lawyer is representing the bunch of them, so there's only one set of motions to take up time. Assuming everything goes as expected."

"Any reason it shouldn't?"

"Not aside from the stuff you know about already. The FBI acting up. People intimidating witnesses. Riots. Cops trying to mess with the evidence. Nothing we can't handle. Expect the unexpected, as you always say."

"Yeah. I've been looking into that. I've got to admit, it could be you were right. Something funny is going on, and it's connected to this case."

"Oh? Any hot leads?"

"Some stuff," Denton said vaguely, "it hasn't jelled yet. By the way, you're still holding the physical evidence, aren't you?"

"Some of it. We have the stuff from the homicide scene. Your guys are still holding whatever they pulled out of the defendants' apartments and business premises. Which I'd like to see, by the way. I've asked Spicer about it, more than once."

Denton grunted indifferently. "You think it's safe? Where you've got it, I mean?"

"Yeah, it's safe, Bill. And where it is, that's where it's going to stay. And since we're talking about the evidence in the case, maybe you could lean on old Fred to come across with what he's got. It might be helpful to know what the evidence is before the trial."

"You got it, Butch," Denton said. He paused. Then he said, "Is there something wrong, Butch? You sound funny all of a sudden."

"No, nothing. Just working hard."

"Oh. Well, take it easy, then. We wouldn't want anything to happen to you."

"No, we wouldn't, would we, you fucking hypocrite dirt bag!" Karp said to the dead phone after Denton had broken the connection. This is great, he thought, talking to myself. Me and Dirty Warren. I wonder how much he clears from the magazines? Maybe it's not too late to think about a second career.

He dialed Marlene's office number. He let it ring ten times and then put it down. He looked at his watch: six-ten. He had a date with Marlene that evening, during which, he had just about decided, he was going to tell her the whole tangled story and show her his diagram. If she bought it, he would at least have an ally and be done with dissembling to the woman he loved, and if she didn't, she could take him over to Bellevue and have him committed. Or laugh. Maybe a good yuck would blow the paranoia away. But it couldn't come from inside him. He was void of yucks.

His phone rang, and when he picked it up it was Marlene. "Hi, I'm home. What a day! I'm totally finished." Her voice sounded thin and distant, like a tape played on a cheap Walkman rip-off.

"You OK?"

"Not really. This Moore thing is getting me down."

"Did you happen to look into the source of that defense check in Karavitch? At those lawyers, Shannon Shannon and so on?"

"Oh, Christ, I knew I forgot something. Damn. Look, I'll get on it tomorrow."

"No, that's OK, I'll get one of the cops on it. It's their job."

117

"OK, great, thanks. I'm sorry, but this case is just draining the crap out of me. For some reason I can't cope with it."

"What's the problem? I thought it was open and shut. Depraved indifference homicide, Form Two. They claim somebody else sneaked in late at night, put the kid in the oven?"

"It's not a technical problem, Butch. It's not a legal problem, putting asses in jail. It's an emotional problem. It's *my* problem; I can't get it out of my head. The scene. The corpus of the crime, as we say. She's trying to get mellow with Cecil in the bedroom, but little Taneel is crying. Four, the kid is. She won't stop. She whips the kid with a belt. Still no good: damn kid won't stop. She can't stand the noise. She drags the kid to the kitchen and puts the girl in the oven, and she wedges the door closed with a chair. She turns on the flame. How come? How come she turned on the flame? I asked her that, 'Doreen, how come?' Shrug. Dunno. Story of her life. Goes back to the bedroom, suck on some 20-20, do a little skag, Cecil puts it to her, she so fine. All the time the little girl is shrieking, roasting alive. She can't hear the screams too well, but the stench—"

"Marlene, stop. It's a case. Do your job. Put 'em away and move on."

"Right. Stay cool. I'm getting this advice from Mr. Uninvolved here. One of the great obsessives of the Western world. Sorry, no can do. This one has got to me. Put 'em away? Sure. Doreen Moore is eighteen. That means she had the kid when she was fourteen. Fifteen in the slammer will do her a lot of good, learn her not to burn up her babies. Case closed. Oh, yeah, you want to hear the cherry on top? Doreen is preggers again. I love it. Dickens was right, you know. You spend every day swimming in shit, the smell rubs off. Not in those words, of course."

"You can't do this to yourself, babe. The Doreens aren't your problem."

"No, you're right. They're not. It wasn't my baby either. I don't have any babies."

"Marlene, I'm coming over. We'll go out, get some dinner, we'll talk—"

"Butch, no. I'm wiped. You don't need me this way. Look, call me this weekend, we'll get together. But not tonight."

Karp stared at the dead phone for a while, then dialed her number again. He hung up before it had a chance to ring. Then he packed his briefcase, grabbed his coat, locked his desk and his office door, and went out.

Karp walked the two miles from Centre Street to his building on Eighth Street almost every evening when the weather permitted.

His route home took him up Broadway through SoHo. One of Karp's secrets was that he occasionally hung a right on Grand, walked up Crosby, past Marlene's loft, and stood in the deep doorway of the building across the street, watching her lit windows. Once or twice in the summer he had seen her sitting on her fire escape. He had hidden, feeling like a fool, unable to help himself.

He did this again that evening, leaning back in the shadows, watching, thinking about whether it was remotely possible that— no, not Marlene, it was too enormous to contemplate. He must be losing it, even to form such a thought.

Just as he was about to push off, he saw a blue Ford pull up outside her doorway. A stocky middle-aged man with a gray crew cut got out and rang her bell. A minute later, Marlene came out, got into the front seat with the man, and was driven away. For some reason he was not particularly surprised. Automatically he wrote the license plate number down in his pocket diary and slowly walked home. Once there, he took off his shoes and his tie and ate three aspirin. Then he lay down on his bed and looked at the ceiling. This is it, he thought. Rock bottom.

The next day, a Friday, Karp took *People* v. *Karavitch et al.* to the grand jury. Taking a case before the grand jury was not a difficult task. Quite the contrary. Prosecutors like grand juries, and grand juries return the favor. The ADA presents his evidence that a crime has been committed within the jurisdiction and that a certain person has committed it. The grand jurors, twenty-three sober citizens, almost always nod gravely and bring in the indictment. The certain person alleged to have committed the crime is neither present nor represented.

The actual proceedings were about as exciting as applying for a driver's license. The grand jury met not in a regular courtroom, but in a dim chamber with a curious resemblance to a law school lecture hall. The jurors yawned and shuffled in a row of seats facing a raised platform for the DA, the stenographer, and any witnesses that might be called.

The room was void of judge, defense lawyer, spectators, or press: a prosecutor's paradise. *Karavitch et al.* was but one of ten-odd indictments Karp had to deliver that morning. When the jurors were ready, Karp called his witnesses: Detective John Hammer, a bomb squad member who had been at Grand Central on the day Terry Doyle removed the pot from the locker; Captain Arthur Gunn, the pilot of the plane; and Sandra Mollo, a passenger, the woman Karavitch had slugged. After they had finished

119

their various tales, Karp asked if any of the jurors had any questions. They did not.

Thanking them for their attention, Karp left the grand jury room and waited in the antechamber, a room with the ambiance of a bus station, filled with witnesses, ADAs, and cops. The grand jury took about as long to consider the indictment as the Supreme Soviet takes to consider a proposal by the Politburo. In a few minutes a loud buzzer sounded once in the antechamber: the jurors had indicted. Two buzzes meant rejection, three that they wanted to see the ADA again.

The five hijackers were thus duly accused of "the crime of murder, committed as follows: that the defendants in the County of New York, on or about September 10, 1976, under circumstances evincing a depraved indifference to human life, recklessly caused the bomb blast death of the deceased, Terrence James Doyle, who at the time was performing his lawful duties as a police officer, by leaving an explosive device, to wit: a bomb, inside locker number 139 in Grand Central Station." Next case.

Which was, by coincidence, that of Billy Brannon, boy burglar, a coincidence that unfroze Karp's brain and started him thinking aggressively again, his natural mode, with the result that at the end of the morning's work he emerged from the grand jury room a new man.

The new man went back to his office and rummaged in a side drawer littered with the pink telephone-message slips pertaining to every call he had returned over the past year. A primitive system, but it worked. He found the one he wanted and made an appointment for the following morning with Monsignor Francis Keene.

Marlene came into his office around five, sat down on his side chair, and lit a Marlboro.

"So what's up, babe? Feeling better? You sounded real bad last night." Karp said this to his blotter as he shuffled papers.

"Oh, I guess. How about yourself?"

"Doing good. Can't complain." Shuffle, shuffle.

"Uh-huh. Not according to V.T. He says you're freaking out. He says Guma says so, too."

Karp looked up and stared at her. Her eye was cool, with that drift of pain beneath that always broke his heart. "That's a lot of crap, Marlene, and you know it," he said angrily.

"Do I? I think you're acting peculiar, too. Secretive. Not that you shouldn't have secrets, but this . . . whatever, is screwing up the gang. You're—I don't know—snapping at people, giving funny looks."

"Look who's talking. Freaking out? Secretive? Check yourself out, kid. You want to know the truth? I'm fine. I'm eating, I'm playing a little ball. I'm doing my job—"

"Butch—"

"—which right now is nailing the guys who put Terry Doyle away, which I intend to do, despite—"

"Butch, wait a—"

"—despite the goddamn DA and the FBI and Hanlon and Denton and the police department and the fucking Powerhouse—"

Marlene got to her feet and stuck her face in his. "Butch, stop! What are you talking about? Denton? The *Powerhouse*? What?"

"What am I talking about? It's a secret. How do you like that?"

"Butch, this is Marlene. We're on the same side. We spill our guts—"

"OK, let's spill our guts. You start. Tell me about NGH 615."

"What?"

"The tag on the blue Ford last night. The old dude with the crew cut?"

"I don't believe this. You're having me *watched*?"

"No, I'm not 'having you watched.' I was worried about you, sentimental asshole that I am. I went by your place to see if I could cheer you up, you're too beat to go out, right? Hey, I don't control your life, but when I go by, and I see you sneaking out with—"

"Sneaking? Sneaking! I was on the fucking job, you jerk! Renko Span is an *informant*, for chrissakes. When I said I was whipped and I couldn't see you, I meant I didn't have the energy for a goddamn crazy insensitive conversation like the one we're having right now."

"What kind of informant?" he demanded suspiciously.

"I met with this bomb expert, G.F.S. Taylor, about the device itself, the trigger. OK, we talked, we got friendly. Karp, he's seventy, for God's sake, and he let on as how one, he fought in Yugoslavia during the war, and two, he's still palsy with a couple of Yugoslav emigrés in the city who might have known something about Karavitch back in Croatia. Renko Span is one of them."

"And what does this have to do with the case?"

"With the case? Not much, maybe. It might tell us a lot about who's so interested in making sure that there isn't a case, and why."

"Save yourself some trouble. I already found that out," he said glumly. "The 'who' anyway. Here, you might as well have a look at this. Since we're spilling our guts."

Karp dug out his wallet and removed the diagram, wrinkled and softened like an old map. He spread it out on the desk, and Marlene stood behind him, resting her hand lightly on his shoulder, under the circumstances a gesture of the deepest intimacy. Karp tried not to think about that or about how Marlene's wiry body radiated heat like a coke oven.

"What is it? You reorganizing the office?"

"No, it's a picture of who's screwing who and who's trying to bag this case. I still can't believe it, but I can't draw any other conclusions from the evidence. What I don't understand is why." Karp quickly described what he had learned about the source of the legal defense funds and what he thought this implied.

Marlene whistled softly over her lower lip. "Oh, ho. That's interesting. I always wondered what they did with the collection cash. Very interesting. Where does the FBI come in?"

"I'm not entirely sure. It may sound strange to say it like this, but maybe Bloom saw this as an opportunity to put it to me. He set me up to run the case, he's got me established as the push behind trying these people. Maybe somebody in the Feds owes him a favor. The case gets screwed up, dismissed, and Karp carries the can. Bloom can even say, 'I told you so.' "

"Could be, could be," she said. She lit another cigarette and started pacing the small room, her head down in thought, her hands on her hips. "It seems a little tortuous, even for Sandy Bloom. Maybe not for Wharton, though. And the cops . . .?"

"A natural. That's why they call it the Powerhouse. The connection between the Archdiocese of New York and the police department is well-known. Couple of words in somebody's ear, the message gets around. Besides,—"

"Besides what?" Marlene had stopped pacing and was looking at him sharply.

"Well, you know: cops, Irish, Church. There's a connection." He shrugged.

"Oh, yeah. Father Feeney gets all the micks together and says, 'Me bhoys, the Holy Faather needs this case put in the tank, so as ye've a hope o' heaven go out an' corrupt th' evidence—"

"Come on, Marlene—"

"No, you come on. I can't believe this. It's—it's like those posters those nuthouse fundamentalists put up—the pope is taking over the world. Beware, America!"

"Marlene, it's not like that . . ."

"No? What's it like? Frank Marino's a Catholic. You think he's bent? Jack Doheny? Luke D'Amato? For that matter, the kid herself. I'm a mackerel snapper, too, Butch. You want to see the ruler marks on my hand from the nuns?"

"That's not the same and you know it!" Karp shouted. "Now cool down. I just meant that since the year one the NYPD has been run by the Irish establishment, and the Church in New York is run by the same guys, the same families in a lot of cases. I got the Arch paying for a bunch of cop killers, I got cops bent all over the place, I got witnesses being intimidated or disappearing when only the cops know who they are. You can see the train of thought, can't you?"

"I can, and it sucks. Karp, that's like saying if the check for Roberts came from Hadassah you'd suspect all the Jewish cops and judges and ADAs, including present company."

"Maybe I would," Karp said, a little lamely. A lot of the starch was going out of his beautiful, scary pattern.

"Horseshit, darling, absolute horse doody! Now look. There *is* a conspiracy. But we have absolutely no evidence that everybody that's interested in queering this case is working in the same conspiracy. And so we have to be guided by one of my favorite prosecutorial aphorisms: let the case grow out of the evidence; never squeeze the evidence to fit your idea of the case. You know who taught me that?"

"No, who?"

"Butch Karp, back in the days when his brain was still working. Baby, listen to me. First of all, pull the team together again. It's too much for one person, even you. Let's work the angles independently. Sure there's a church angle. Go ahead and see where it leads. I'll follow up on the bomb and the Yugoslavs. Let Guma and the cops work the street, the neighborhood where these guys hung out and made their scene. V.T.'ll handle the Feds."

"What about Hadassah?"

She laughed. "Let Roland do that. And the cops—which reminds me, have you told Denton about this?"

"Are you kidding? He's got to be in on this. Come on, Marlene, an Irishman gets to be a superchief, he's not plugged in at the Arch?"

"God, Butch, sometimes you amaze me. I realize all these Christian denominations might be a little confusing to a nice Jewish boy from Brooklyn, but still . . ."

"Marlene, what are you talking about?"

"Bill Denton. Irish, sure. But he's C. of D. because he's probably one of the ten smartest cops they ever had on the job and because after Knapp, when they were looking for brass that wasn't tarnished, somebody recalled that Bill Denton had never accepted

as much as a cup of coffee, so he got the post. I mean, he still has
to be somewhat discreet: he wears a green tie on St. Patrick's day
and all, but Bill's people're from Belfast. He's a black Protestant.
Come on, Butch, don't punch the goddamn wall, you'll hurt your
hand."

11

"How do you feel now?" Marlene asked tenderly. It was nearly midnight. Karp's head was nestled in the crook of her shoulder, and they were both lying against the warm, damp sides of Keystone Plate-E-Z while perfumed water lapped at their skin. "Uh-hum," said Karp, master of words. He was busy making little waves by moving his chin. Each time the trough of the wave passed Marlene's breast, the nipple would glint in the reddish glow. Karp found this unutterably amusing. Marlene had arranged the glow by flinging an article of underwear over one of her photographer's lamps during the evening's steamy prelims.

"No, really. How's your hand?"

Karp raised his huge mitt above the glittering surface of the water. "Looks OK. A little swelled up maybe."

"You nut. It really drives you crazy when you're not perfect, doesn't it?"

"I guess. That business about Denton really got to me. I mean, all my instincts told me he was straight, and then I get involved, possessed, by this conspiracy theory, and I start accusing him of throwing the game. In my mind only, thank God. I'd have to leave town if I had told anybody about this. Meanwhile, I got to call him first thing tomorrow, and tell him about the check from the Archdiocese. Maybe it'll help him get a lead on who's running the game for the cops. Better late than never. Shit, the whole thing makes me nauseous." He shook himself in irritation.

Marlene hugged him and kissed him lightly on the head. "Let it go, Butchie. Nobody likes to think they're a little bit of a bigot, especially not us educated liberal types. It wouldn't have mattered if you hadn't gotten scared by this case and played it so close. Jesus! Goom would have blown that crap to smithereens in a New York minute. That's why you have compadres, right? Keep your sweet ass straight, right? But it got you in a weak spot. A little Jewish paranoia. God knows, you've got every right to be paranoid. They *are* out to get you." She twirled his wet hair in her

125

fingers and sighed. "Everybody has a weak spot. You have to compensate . . ."

"Yeah? What's yours, Marlene?"

"Mine? Why, it's you, of course," she replied without an instant's thought.

"It was Pretty Boy Floyd," said Denton, his voice over the phone tight with anger.

"The outlaw, Oklahoma knew him well," Karp said.

"What?"

"Nothing. A song. What do you mean, Bill? Who's Pretty Boy Floyd?"

"Bob Floyd, our Deputy Police Commissioner for Public Affairs."

"Oh, him." Karp knew him by reputation and from countless TV interviews, a beautifully dressed man with almost movie-star looks and a deep, resonant voice that could express nonsense believably. "The PR guy. An empty suit, I thought."

"Yeah, but ambitious as the devil and a pillar of the Church. I knew it was him the minute you told me about the check this morning."

"How come you're so sure? Did you brace him on it?"

"No point. He'd deny it, and I haven't got the clout or the solid evidence to roll a D.P.C. No, I talked to your friend Fred Spicer. It seems Pretty Boy called Fred in for a little chat right after the hijackers got booked. Suggested that the powers that be would not mind one bit if these guys got dismissed. Suggested that an up-and-coming lieutenant might find the path to captain smoothed out when the time came.

"This is subtle, you understand—it happens all the time, and Floyd is the guy from whence it comes, especially when the source of the pull is our friends in the Powerhouse. In a situation like when Vice hits one of those faggot bars in Soho or under the West Side Drive and they find out the guy in the pink dress is none other than Father Flanagan, Floyd says a few words in the precinct captain's ear and the papers get lost. Or maybe the captain calls Floyd, tells him he already lost the papers, picks up a few brownie points."

"So Spicer thought it was business as usual? But, shit, Bill, this is murder, and a cop . . ."

"I said he was subtle. The hint was also put in that it was a fuck-up at Rodman Neck. Doheny was drunk, Doyle and the boys were playing grab-ass with a live charge. Bingo."

"He believed that?"

"Why not? People tend to believe what's convenient, especially if they hear it from authority. He's helping the Church, his job, and his career. As far as he knows, there's no crime, or not much of one. It's not like he's walking some child rape monster. You think he's going to ask questions? Spicer?"

"Yeah. A certain tendency toward the lazy. So how did you play it when you got the story?"

"Very soft. He assumed I was in on it, and I didn't bother to correct him. I suggested that you were in on it, too."

"You did? Why the hell . . . oh, yeah, right."

"Right. I figure Spicer and whoever he's got working with him are concentrating on screwing up the evidence you've got. Scaring off witnesses. Trying to grab the evidence at the range. They try anything else, it might be a good idea if they didn't bother much about whether you knew about it or not."

"Good thought. Um, it just occurred to me. Has Floyd got anyone else working for him? Besides Spicer."

"That I don't know, but it's a good bet. Spicer assured me that neither he nor any of his gang were involved in torching that store in Grand Central. I believe him; it's not his kind of thing. The Feds, now—"

"Yeah. The problem is, it's going to be hard filtering the evidence. Some cop walks in here with a manuscript called 'How I Wasted Terry Doyle' in Karavitch's handwriting, I'm going to break out in a cold sweat."

Denton laughed sourly. "Yeah. Just remember, everybody, every detective on this case, runs through the New York DA squad. Anybody comes to you from left field, you can figure him for a setup. Uh-oh, I got a call waiting. By the way, how do you figure the Church angle?"

"I don't. I got an appointment with somebody at the Arch who owes me a favor, maybe I can squeeze him a little. I'll keep in touch."

When Karp put down the receiver, his private button lit up at once. He had a call, too. It was Guma.

"Butch, dammit, you hear what happened?"

"They found Hoffa?"

"Yeah, right. Sandro Sorriendas turned up dead. In his place up in Washington Heights, a knife job."

"Who? Oh, yeah, your Cuban dope kingpin. The cops like anybody for it?"

"They do. Are you ready for this? The girlfriend, Ellie Melendez. What bullshit!"

"Why don't you like her, Goom? He busted her up pretty bad.

Maybe she figured to get her licks in before he got around to it again and finished the job."

"Butch, I know this lady. She's a bird. Scared of her shadow. Could she start for the Jets? No. Could she tackle a tough mutt like Sorriendas with a knife? Same answer."

"Why do the cops like her?"

"You know cops. What they like is a simple clear on a homicide, and the simplest is a domestic. He got whacked in the middle of the night, she was there, so they got their opportunity and motive. No forced entry. Case closed. On the other hand, he put up a helluva fight—defensive wounds, the place is wrecked. No way Melendez is going to chase him around the room with a combat knife."

"What's her story? I gather that if she didn't do it, at least she saw the whole thing."

"She hasn't said word one since they booked her. Shakes, yes. Crying, yes. But no statement. Or so they say. I haven't laid the famous Guma charm on her yet, which I intend to do this afternoon."

"Good luck. By the way, who *do* you like for it?"

"Ruiz, who else? Who has apparently dropped out of sight, according to Pinky Billman."

"Guma, you got Ruiz on the brain. Think about how many other kinds of people could have killed an uptown Latino dope handler. Maybe he was parking his pork someplace he shouldn't have. Maybe somebody is trying to give Ruiz a message, knocking off one of his boys. You don't know . . ."

"I know, Butch, believe me. It's on the street. Sandro and Ruiz had words in public last Thursday. I think it was about Melendez, as a matter of fact, but I'm not sure. Also Pinky gets a call from one of his snitches, guy named Arpado, day before yesterday. Says Sandro is pissed off, maybe he'd like to put it to Ruiz, but he's scared shitless. He also wants to know if Pinky is straight arrow, because everybody knows that Ruiz has protection. So the story is on the street. If somebody sold the same story to Ruiz, which is a reasonable bet, the Serpent's going to go for the knife, guaranteed."

"Who's protecting Ruiz that everybody knows?"

"Aha! I figured that would get your attention. This we don't know exactly. Like I told you the other week, the Feds got that Tel-Air place in Queens staked out. They're making movies, they're tapping phones. Nobody else gets a taste, though, and nobody's supposed to make waves, might fuck up the big federal case. Meanwhile, the way I hear it, Ruiz is running all the dope in the world."

"Let him, I could give a shit. But if he killed somebody in New

York County, his ass is mine. Keep in touch on this, Goom, I'm starting to like it."

"I knew you would. By the way, welcome back to Planet Earth, jewboy."

The Streets of Calcutta were more jammed than usual when Karp went down to get some coffee. The temperature had dropped fifteen degrees the previous night, and an icy rain outside showed no sign of diminishing. This stimulated in New York's legions of street people an intense desire to exercise their right as citizens and see justice done in open court. As a result, the place stank like a wet dog.

It was unusually noisy too. Spats and shoving episodes exploded like ladyfingers and echoed off the high ceilings. Karp's attention was drawn to a particularly loud argument. Munching a doughnut, he wandered over and shouldered through the knot of people surrounding the protagonists. A security guard had a half-nelson on a dark, wiry young man with a huge black mustache, who was struggling and yelling in some guttural language. Two other security guards were attempting to reason with an enormous and oddly costumed being, whom Karp recognized as the Walking Booger.

The Booger was to filth what Fred Astaire was to ballroom dancing. Even squeaky clean he would have been no treat. He had a harelip and a cleft palate, a huge nose reddened and eroded by some disease, and tiny, red-rimmed eyes. His cratered face was fringed by rank, coarse hair and a beard that for many years had relieved its owner of the necessity of ever wiping his nose. He was making violent gestures and adding incomprehensible roars—"Ahnk orhn Ink, 'm!"—to the general din.

Karp now observed that the center of the controversy was Dirty Warren, who was lying among a scattering of magazines at the feet of the dark mustache, who was trying to kick him. Warren was dabbing at his mouth with a blood-stained handkerchief and staring around him with a bewildered expression. Karp leaned over and helped him to his feet.

"What's going on, Darryl?" Karp asked one of the guards.

The guard, a husky black man with a shaved head, looped his finger a couple of times close to his forehead. "Aw, the same old shit. Dirty Warren called this gentleman here a bad name, and this gentleman popped him one." He turned to the gentleman in question and roared, "Goddamn it, shut up, you!" The stream of foreign invective from the dark mustache subsided to a low rumble. "So the Booger sees this," Darryl continued, "and goes for this guy. Ripped the front right off his jacket. He's some kind of

Turk or Pakistan, some damn thing. Thinks his momma insulted, old Warren call him a motherfucker. I try to explain, Warren calls everybody motherfucker. He don't care, he want to beat Warren's ass. Shit, I never saw the old Booger get mad before."

"Me neither," Karp said. "A good thing, too."

"Yeah, he's a solid citizen, the Booger. You know, some of these bondsmen send him on errands. He carries checks around sometimes, big cash too. Honest as the day is long."

"He ever get mugged?" Karp asked, fascinated.

Darryl raised his eyebrows. "You think some skel gonna hit *him* for cash? Get his butt kicked *and* stink for a week." He turned and addressed the crowd, "OK, folks, the party's over. Let's break it up." The crowd started to drift away. Then he said, "Frank, take our friend here to the security room, let him cool out. Booger, you gonna be good now? You gonna buy this man a new jacket, right?"

"Ank ark 'n gnphnk."

"Good boy. Warren, you try and watch your mouth sometimes. Go sell some magazines."

"OK, Darryl, thank you," said Dirty Warren meekly.

As Karp walked toward the elevators, he reflected that a man with a high school education had just disposed of an assault and battery and property damage case with perfect justice in three minutes for a public cost of about twenty-eight cents. Not for the first time he questioned the social utility of his profession. The elevator came. Just before the doors closed, Karp caught a glimpse of Dirty Warren on his knees, gathering up his tattered stock. The little man's face went blank as he drifted into one of his strange fits of being possessed by another personality. His eyes became lidded, his head cocked to the side, and his hand moved up to caress his hair, in a detailed parody of male narcissism. Karp felt a shock of recognition. He had seen that exact gesture before. But where?

At one that afternoon, Karp was sitting next to Marlene Ciampi in the jury box in a fourteenth-floor courtroom. The only other occupant of the box was a tall, thin man half hidden behind *The New York Times*. There was no jury because this was merely the arraignment on the grand jury indictment in *Karavitch et al.*

The case was called. "Where the hell are they?" Karp asked under his breath.

"I'll go see," Marlene answered and slid quickly out of the box and down the courtroom aisle. Karp felt a tremor of uneasiness: the possibility that "something" might happen to the hijackers was never far from his mind. He looked out at the spectator seats in the courtroom. A scattering of print journalists and dozing streetniks, but most of the seats were occupied by Croatian supporters, including that indefatigable cheerleader, Father Blic.

"Are the People ready in *Karavitch et al.*?" asked the judge. Benjamin Devine was a spare, elderly man who ran a no-nonsense calendar court.

Karp rose. "Your Honor, the defendants are not present at this time. It's possible they were delayed in traffic. May we have a second call on this case?" The judge grunted his assent and the clerk called the next case on the calendar. Karp sat down. The Croats murmured to one another and stayed put.

"Excuse me, please, but do you think there will be much delay?" Karp twisted around to face the man behind the *Times*. A foreigner, was Karp's first thought. The man wore his graying brown hair swept straight back, longer at the top and shorter at the sides than was fashionable in New York. Also, he spoke with the faint roll of an accent, one that Karp had heard before. "You see, I have an appointment in two hours some distance from here, and if there is to be a long delay, I must call—"

"No, I doubt if it'll be that long. They probably got tied up en route." Karp paused, then gestured to the Croatian spectators. "Ah, are you with them? The, ah, Croats."

The man started and then smiled broadly, showing uneven brown teeth. "Me? No, no, not at all. Oh, allow me . . . Terzich." He stood slightly and thrust his hand forward. Karp shook it awkwardly over his shoulder and introduced himself as well. "I have been retained by the court for translation. And you, of course, are the famous prosecutor of this case. I have seen you on television."

"Uh-huh. That's interesting. A translator, huh? Is there much call for Croatian translators in New York, Mr., ah, Terzich?"

The man smiled again, shyly. "Well, not very much. I am called from time to time. I am a professor of Slavic languages at Columbia. Associate professor."

"And originally you're from . . .?"

"Yugoslavia. Like them." He gestured at the cheering section.

"But you said you weren't a Croat."

"I am not. I am a Serb. From the Vojvodina."

"But you can translate their language?"

Terzich chuckled. "It is the same language, Mr. Karp. We are the same people, divided by a common language, as I believe Mr. George Bernard Shaw said about the Americans and the British. This is why it is called Serbo-Croatian."

"Huh!" Karp said. "Then what's Yugoslavian?"

The associate professor chuckled again. "Well, this is difficult to explain in one breath. There is a joke in Yugoslavia that we have two alphabets, three religions, four languages, five nationalities, and six republics. But Serbo-Croatian is one of the languages and two of the alphabets. You see, we southern Slavs became literate rather late in history. The Church gave us our writing, and those who were converted by Catholic missionaries took up the Latin script, and those who were converted by Orthodox missionaries took up the Cyrillic script."

"Like Russian?"

"Very like Russian. The Catholic south Slavs became Croats; their Orthodox cousins, you might say, became Serbs. Since then, of course, the history of the two peoples has been very different. Which causes many problems. And one of them has come to rest on your doorstep, I think."

"The case, you mean?"

"Yes. You could say that this case began in 1389. That was when the Turks crushed the Serbian empire at the Battle of Kossovo. Thus began five hundred years of appalling slavery for the Serbs, and centuries of nearly unending combat for the Croats, who found themselves on the front line of European resistance to the Turks. As a result of this . . ." Terzich stopped abruptly and smiled a sheepish smile. "Forgive me, Mr. Karp, I am carried away by my subject. The occupational disease of all professors is to lecture at the slightest provocation."

"No, that's OK," Karp said. "It's just hard to believe you would think that the motives for a crime could be traced back to things that happened so long ago."

"Yes, this is what Americans believe generally. You have abolished history, have you not? Your Henry Ford says, 'History is bunk,' and you nod, yes, the past is dead, only the future is real, and we can change this as we like. Perhaps this is true for you, though I doubt it. But in Yugoslavia we breathe history like the air. We cannot escape it, even when it carries, you might say, traces of poison.

"And so must you, because, believe me, there is no way to keep this history bottled up inside Yugoslavia. You are surprised it escapes and kills one policeman? Sixty years ago, it started a war that killed ten million people and changed the world. Perhaps even your life was changed by this little event, Mr. Karp. The First World War? Perhaps someone got shot instead of married. Perhaps someone decided that Europe was no longer healthy and made the voyage to America. So it is possible that you owe your existence to something that began inside my country."

132

Terzich paused and nodded his head in the direction of the Croatians. "These people are living out a kind of historical dream. The defendants you are prosecuting they consider heroes. They were all raised on tales of dashing Croat warriors in red cloaks, killing Turks, killing Austrians, killing Serbs, all for the freedom of Croatia and the glory of its holy church."

Karp shook his head. "But it wasn't any blow for freedom. They failed. It was a screwup from the start. They killed an innocent man for nothing."

"An innocent man. In a five-hundred-year war, Mr. Karp, believe me, the notion of innocence does not survive. In Yugoslavia we have a monument *honoring* the man who started the First World War, the greatest slaughter of innocents that history records. And failure does not matter, either. The Serbs failed for nearly five hundred years and won in the end. At what cost you can have no idea. You have an expression in this country for someone who habitually uses foul language: 'He curses like a priest's son?' That cannot be right—"

"Curses like a preacher's kid," Karp volunteered.

"Just so! Very colorful and very American. He curses like a preacher's kid. In Yugoslavia we say instead: 'He curses like a Serb on a stake.' This is from the Turkish practice of impaling rebels on stakes. The sharpened pole is inserted between the victim's legs, up through the body cavity, and out just under the shoulder, the skilled impaler being careful not to hit any organs or blood vessels that would cause a quick death. Then the butt of the stake is stuck in the ground, and the condemned man is left to die in sight of all his friends and relatives, who, of course, are prohibited from helping him, on pain of suffering the same fate. Such a death can last for days. The expression I referred to tells enough about how our heroes of that time responded: they did not pray, or beg for mercy.

"But still, failure upon failure, the revolts did not stop. At Nis, south of Belgrade, the Turks built a tower ten meters high out of the heads of Serbian rebels. How many heads is that, I wonder? It would be an interesting calculation. And why did they rebel? So that they could have a flag and a king of their own? Not at all. Mr. Karp, do you know what a janissary is?"

"Some kind of soldiers, weren't they?"

"Not exactly. Imagine this, Mr. Karp. Imagine that you have a son, a beautiful, strong son. You nurture him, you teach him all you know, you love him more than your own life. At the age of nine he is the strongest and bravest and most intelligent boy in the village, the natural leader.

"Then, one day, the thing happens that you always knew would happen but are powerless to prevent. A squadron of Osmanli cavalry rides into the village. The spahis dismount and race through the houses, driving all before them with their whips. Holding back the villagers, they line up the boys of nine and ten. Their *beg* walks down the line, inspecting them like cattle. Of course, he picks your son, puts a collar around his neck, and drags him off to become a janissary, to be circumcised and converted to Islam, to fight for the sultan, to rule over provinces. A brilliant idea, actually. To strip the conquered people of their best stock and use these men as soldiers to keep the subjects pacified. Perhaps you will see your son again, as a proud man in a green turban, ordering your friends and relatives to be impaled. Can you imagine it? And this went on for five centuries.

"So when the Serbs finally got their own nation, they fought for it like demons. Serbia lost a higher proportion of its sons in the First World War than any other nation. In that war and in the two Balkan wars before it a third of the population perished."

"And what about the Croats?" Karp asked.

"Ah, the Croats, our cousins. They were heroes, too, but of a different kind. They became cannon fodder for the Austrian Empire in its great struggle against the Ottomans. Perhaps we would be wearing turbans and speaking Turkish right now, Mr. Karp, had it not been for the brave Croats. The Germans kept them on a tight leash nevertheless. There is a monument in Zagreb that commemorates the execution, in 1573, of the Croat peasant rebel Matija Gubec. The Germans seated him on a red-hot throne and crowned him with a red-hot crown. A typically witty German response to the Croat desire for independence.

"And after the danger from the Turks was past, they remained useful to the Germans. Croat troops crushed the revolution of 1848 in Vienna. As a reward, the Germans gave their country to Hungary. Another witty comment. The Croats fought the Hungarians, though, and later they fought the Serbs for the Austrian empire during the First World War. Why not? Fighting was all they knew.

"And when at last, after so many centuries, the Slavs in the Balkans had a nation they could call their own, the Croats kept fighting against Yugoslavia. They did not want to share a nation with ignorant Serbians and dirty Bosnians. Perhaps they had learned too much about a certain kind of pride from living so long on the German leash. And perhaps they learned too much treachery from their German masters. So that they welcomed these masters when they returned in 1940 and crushed Yugoslavia. And then they had their precious Croatia, a fascist puppet state that the Nazis set up for them. And all the good Croat nationalists put on black uniforms and became *ustashi*, little Slav brothers of the S.S., and went out to massacre the Serbs, Jews, Moslems, and anyone else who polluted the precious soil of Croatia.

"The *ustashi*. I do not think we have time for me to tell you about these people and what they did in those years. Perhaps, if you have the opportunity, you can ask Djordje Karavitch."

"Karavitch?"

"Yes. In 1940 he was one of the first to sign up. A great Croat leader in those days, believe me. Ah, Mr. Karp, I think someone is trying to attract your attention."

Terzich pointed to the rear of the courtroom, where Marlene was making come-hither gestures. Karp got up and walked over to her. "What's happening?" he asked.

"It's OK. They're in the pens. A water main broke on Houston Street and the van from Riker's had to make a big detour. Look, I can't stay for this, I'm due to present to the grand jury in ten minutes. I'd like to talk to my witnesses before I go in."

"No problem. Hey, let's do something tonight, dinner in the Village, movies?"

"Like real people? Oh, be still my heart! OK, meet you after work."

Karp watched the big courtroom doors close behind her and then strode down the aisle to the prosecutor's table. In a few minutes the door connecting the courtroom to the holding cells opened, and the guards brought in the five hijackers. They marched over and sat down at the defendants' table, where they were joined by Terzich. The Croatian audience burst into cheers and clapping, which Judge Devine suppressed with vigorous poundings of his gavel. The clerk called the case.

"Are all parties ready?" Devine asked. Both Karp and Evans murmured that they were. "Will counsel waive formal reading of the charges?"

Evans stood up. "We will, Your Honor, and at this time we would like to interpose a plea of not guilty and make an argument for bail."

"Go ahead."

Evans cleared his throat. "Your Honor, I must confess that I fail to see the presumption under which these defendants were denied bail. Surely there is no question of these particular defendants appearing for trial. I would point out to you that they have no criminal records, that they all are employed, and that they have solid roots in their community. They enjoy the support of their community, the depth of which you can gauge yourself right here in your own courtroom. Fifty people at least have left their jobs and homes to come down here today. It strikes me as gross injustice to have people of this caliber languishing in jail for an incident that can be clearly traced to the incompetence of a group of police officers. Your Honor, we believe that setting these people at liberty on fifty thousand dollars' bail for each defendant is more than justified by the present circumstances."

Evans sat down to murmurs and scattered applause. Devine banged his gavel angrily. "Another disturbance and I will order this courtroom cleared. Mr. Karp, do the People wish to be heard?"

"Yes, Your Honor," said Karp, getting to his feet. "Counsel has asked for bail on the basis that the defendants have roots in the community. Certainly that is one premise for bail. But there is another condition: that is the nature and character of the crime itself, which counsel has seen fit to slough over. Let me address that omission. These well-rooted people hijacked an airliner and subjected over fifty innocent people to terror and torment. They planted a bomb that was specifically designed to explode in the face of anyone who tried to disarm it, a bomb that killed a young police officer who was attempting to do his sworn duty of protecting the people of this city. These crimes exhibit a callous disregard for human life and safety. That they were committed by well-established, educated people does not detract one whit from their heinousness. Indeed, it exacerbates it; it shows them to be not common criminals impulsively striking out for revenge or material gain, but malicious, merciless, and deadly conspirators.

"Moreover, I would call the court's attention to one salient fact: the last time the defendants had their freedom, they chose to hijack an airliner on a one-way journey to a country of refuge. Counsel may be prepared to bet that they will not do so again if freed, but the People are not. The defendants should be remanded with no bail, and we are prepared to try this case forthwith."

Evans came out of his chair like a shot. "I expected this contentious bombast from someone with your reputation, Karp," he said loudly. "This kind of cheap dramatics can only aggravate tensions in the community and lead to further violence."

Karp looked at Evans as if seeing him for the first time. "I'm sorry, are you talking to me?" he asked mildly, and was rewarded by the deep flush that rose up the defense lawyer's pink cheeks.

The courtroom was filled with rumblings and shouts of anger. Devine flailed away with the gavel, and when he could make himself heard again, he said sternly, "Mr. Evans, Mr. Karp, you can exercise your wit on each other on your own time. I don't like private duels in my courtroom. Is that understood? Good. Bail is denied. Defendants are remanded until trial. Trial date is set six weeks from today."

* * *

In the van going back to Riker's Island after the hearing, Karavitch observed the effect the judge's refusal of bail had produced in his colleagues. Macek stared at his handcuffs, as if willing them to disappear. He had not looked Karavitch in the eye since they left Paris. Rukovina was trying to explain to Raditch, without notable success, what had just happened in court. Milo, at least, was positively enjoying captivity. Being in jail convinced him that he was one with the Croat martyrs of old. They were a bunch of clowns, Karavitch thought. Except for him. And the woman, of course. Nobody could call her a clown.

Although they were in jail, Karavitch and his friends were far from forgotten. A torrent of mail had begun from the moment of their arrival, mail that included cakes, soups, locks of hair, plum brandy (confiscated) and enough religious material to outfit a seminary. The redoubtable Father Blic was a daily visitor. The man was in terror lest the federal government enter the case and start dredging up material from the war years. Only that week an elderly Lithuanian had lost a deportation appeal. He had been accused of working the night shift at Majdenek. Blic did not know the details of Karavitch's war record, but he could guess.

Karavitch would listen gravely to these appeals and counsel caution and patience. The last thing he wanted Blic to do was to stop the federal government from taking charge.

Today, however, on his return he had received a phone call from one much higher in the ranks of the church than Father Blic.

"It's me."

"Yes, I recognize your voice," Karavitch replied. "I observe that your influence does not extend to judges."

"That was unavoidable. You didn't expect to be let off with a warning, did you? Are you comfortable? Do you need anything?"

"Comfortable? I have been in worse places. It is like living in a barn, with animals."

"It won't be for too much longer. Things are working."

"Oh? What things?"

"Well, obviously, it's not something I care to discuss on the phone. In fact, it's best that you have no direct knowledge."

"But, in general . . ."

"In general, there are certain flaws in the case against you. If we push at the right vulnerable points, it will collapse."

"Yes? And this prosecutor, Karp, he will allow this to happen?"

"What he wants is irrelevant. We are working many levels above Karp. He is no longer a factor in the case."

12

THEY LEFT THE movie theater around eleven. The sky was pouring black ice onto the city. The film, a heartwarming French romance, had warmed their hearts as advertised, but their flesh was freezing. Neither Karp nor Marlene had an umbrella.

"We better stay at my place," Karp said.

"I hate staying at your place. It's like sleeping in the morgue. I get up in the morning, I feel like I'm at my own wake."

"Thanks a lot, Marlene. And after I went out and got you a TV—"

"Yeah, that TV. A fourteen-inch black-and-white from Sri Lanka, and you've been bringing it up for two years. Let me ask you, have you maybe purchased a table to put the TV on, or do I still have to balance it on my ankles lying in bed? And how about the fridge? This seems like a good night to suck on some instant iced tea. Really cozy. Besides, I've got to get to work tomorrow, which means I've got to go back to my place, wash, feed the cats, change clothes, and fight traffic both ways. Which is going to be a Chinese whorehouse tomorrow with this weather. No thanks." She rooted around in her oversize bag and extracted a crumpled package of Marlboros.

"Marlene, why are you being like this?"

"Like what, Butch? It's a pain in the ass, that's all." She looked up from under the shelter of the marquee. "Looks like it might be letting up. Let's walk over to Sixth. We can start walking downtown. Maybe we can pick up a gypsy cab." She strode off, puffing blobs of white smoke like a switch engine. He sighed and followed her, moving carefully over the rain-slick paving.

At the corner of Waverly and Sixth Avenue, she produced a piercing whistle between two fingers, then a stream of violent curses when the yellow taxi failed to stop. He touched her arm and said, "Marlene, it's one-way north here. These guys are all going back to the barns."

"Shit! OK, let's walk over to Seventh."

"Dammit, Marlene! I don't feel like walking!" This statement was so uncharacteristic and said with such vehemence that it brought her up short. She looked into his face. Even by streetlamp light she could see that his face had a gray, unhealthy look. There were tiny, glittering beads of sweat on his upper lip. "God, Butch, you're sick," she exclaimed. "What is it?"

"Nothing. I'm not sick."

"Yes, you are. You look like you're in pain."

In fact, Karp was in agony. The first shot of wintry weather always caught him unawares; during the intervening year he made himself forget what cold and damp did to his injured knee. He was walking on what felt like a mass of hot razor blades.

"Come on, let's get out of the rain," said Marlene, pulling him under a shop awning. As he followed, she saw he was limping. "It's your knee, isn't it?"

"No. It's OK," said Karp automatically, grimacing in pain.

"Bullshit, Butch. If you're hurting, we'll go back to your place. Why didn't you just say so?"

"No, it's OK, I can walk."

"I can't believe this! Now, look, I'm in charge. We will go to your place. On the way we will stop off and get some tea, some honey, a lemon, and a flat pint of Christian Brothers. I will put you in bed, tuck you in, and feed you hot tea and brandy."

"And? And?" said Karp, rolling his eyes and pretending to pant like a Newfoundland dog.

She giggled. "We'll see. If you're good."

They walked slowly up Sixth to Eighth Street, sticking close to the buildings to avoid the freezing rain. After stopping at a liquor store and a mini-mart, they entered the recessed doorway of Karp's apartment house; a large man emerged from the shadows and blocked their way. Marlene gasped and stumbled back against Karp, who felt the jolt of adrenaline, the fight or flight syndrome that is as characteristic of a stroll through Manhattan as dog shit. The man stepped into range of the streetlight's glow and Karp immediately relaxed. He was no mugger but a middle-aged, well-dressed white man. He was also soaked and thoroughly distraught.

"Excuse me, please, but could you help me?" he asked, smiling. He was stocky and had a face like hundreds of others in the garment district or diamond district. Karp had a couple of uncles with the same look. The slight accent clinched it. "I am sorry to bother you, but I have locked myself out of my car." He smiled in embarrassment. "It's a rental. I was driving out to the airport. I have a seven o'clock flight tomorrow morning, so I make a plan to turn the car in, stay at the Sheraton, get a good night's sleep—"

"Where's the car?" Marlene said.

"Please, all I want, you should be so kind, just call for me Avis, they'll send a man."

"Nah, that'll take hours. Is that it?" Marlene pointed to a beige Galaxy parked in the no-parking zone in front of the building. Its parking lights glowed yellow in the rain. "OK, here's what we'll do. Butch, let me have the keys. You guys watch the car so somebody doesn't boost it. I'll be right back."

"Marlene, what . . . ?" Karp began, but she just smiled, unlocked the lobby door, and vanished.

"What is she doing, the young lady?" the man asked.

"Don't ask me, mister. I'm usually the last to know. You from out of town?"

"Me? No, from New York, West End Avenue. Oh, excuse me—Abe Leventhal." He stuck out his hand and Karp shook it. "How come you ask? Oh, the rental. Listen, I bought a Chrysler, new last year. So I'm a schmuck, I believe you should buy American. Five times it's in the shop, if you can believe it. The brakes go down to the floor. I'm driving along, the door comes open by itself. No wonder they're going broke. My brother-in-law tells me, 'Buy a Mercedes, buy a BMW, they never break down.' Listen, if they last forever I wouldn't touch them, from those *momsers*. God forbid I should buy a German car! So I'm renting two days a Ford. It didn't break down yet, I figure I'm lucky. Ah, what is this?"

Marlene had emerged from the lobby holding a wire coat hanger. "Right, let's get this gentleman into his car," she said briskly, and went past them into the street. Bending the hanger double, she pushed it down between the window gasket and the glass. It took her about ninety seconds to spring the locking mechanism and open the door.

"This is marvelous!" exclaimed Leventhal, beaming. "You saved my life. Who would believe in New York strangers would help you out like this? I wouldn't believe if my own family would go out of their way like this. Listen, I got to do something nice for you. You got a stereo?"

"He doesn't," Marlene said.

"Okey-dokey, I tell you what. Here's my card." He reached into his back pocket, yanked out a wallet the size of a softball, and handed Marlene a card. It bore a crowned loudspeaker and the legend, "ABE LEVENTHAL, THE STEREO KING."

"Come by the store anytime, pick out anything you want: loudspeakers, tuner, turntable, whatever. You can have it at cost." He shook hands with both of them, repeating his thanks, got in the Galaxy, and drove off.

"What do you think of that!" Marlene said with wonder. "We

140

did a favor for somebody and we didn't get shot or otherwise abused. Call the networks. And you're going to get a stereo practically for free. New York must be changing."

"Yeah, could be. And maybe Edmund Gwenn will be Santa in Macy's this year. Marlene, where did you learn to jimmy a car like that?"

"Wouldn't you like to know. God, I'm freezing. Let's go in and make some hot drinks. Oh, no! You don't have any pots."

"I have a pot. It was in the stove when I moved in."

"Terrific! We'll chase out the spiders and make some toddies and think about our new stereo. Gosh, Butch, this could be the beginning of a whole new era. Next year, a table!"

The following morning, Connie Trask observed the big smile on Butch Karp's face and flashed one in return. "My, my, don't you look happy. Your horse come in?"

"Oh, much more spiritual than that, Connie. What's on for this morning?"

She frowned. "Well, I hate to do this to a happy man, but you're loaded." She consulted her desk calendar. "There's a Paul Flanagan, a detective sergeant, waiting to see you right now. He wouldn't say about what. Then at ten-thirty you got to be uptown to see Father Keene. I got Brenner to pick you up at ten. Then one o'clock, you got the monthly report with Wharton. Tony Harris is working on the report, he says he'll have it by noon. Two o'clock is the Weaver arraignment, you said you wanted to be there when Harris does it. Then V.T. wants to see you. I put him in for three-thirty, and Ray Guma at four. Is that OK?"

"Yeah, I guess. Can't Pelso go to the meeting with Wharton?"

"He could if he wasn't in Bermuda. Some big-time international ee-vent. When you going to get some of those free travel goodies, Butch?"

"Soon. I'm scheduled for a trip to North Dakota when Hell freezes over."

Karp strode toward his office, his good mood diminished but not entirely gone. Marlene was incomparable when she made her mind up to delight, as she had last night with her erotic nurse routine . . . Of course, she could just as easily transmute into an abusive monster, for causes that were beyond his competence to divine. He had decided long since that his only choice was to hang in there and take it, and hope that Marlene would work things out herself.

"You're Sergeant Paul Flanagan? Roger Karp."

The man waiting for Karp in his office was wearing a natty tweed sports jacket, charcoal slacks, and faintly tinted aviator-style glasses. The two men shook hands and Karp waved Flanagan into his wooden visitor's chair.

"So what can I do for you?"

Flanagan reached into his breast pocket and extracted two sheets of paper. He handed one to Karp and said, "You know what this is."

Karp glanced at it. "Yeah, it's a copy of the note found in the locker with the bomb that killed Doyle. What about it?"

Flanagan smiled and handed Karp the other sheet. It was the same message, but it was not a copy. Karp felt a tremor of apprehension. "Where did you get this, Flanagan?" he snapped.

The smile grew wider. "I typed it myself. On Milo Rukovina's typewriter. And I checked it out with the lab. It's the same type-writer that typed the note in the locker."

Karp leaned forward in his chair and stared at the other man with such intensity that the detective's smile faded and he asked nervously, "Is something wrong? I thought it was pretty good evidence."

"It is. It's very good evidence. It links Rukovina and the other conspirators to the actual placing of the bomb. Tell me, how did you happen to come across this piece of very good evidence?"

"Oh, just luck," Flanagan said modestly. "It turned up as part of a routine investigation. Of the bombers and their associates. I figured I'd see if the type on this typewriter we found matched up with the manifesto they got the papers to print." He gestured to the two sheets on Karp's desk. "And there it is."

"Right, there it is. Good work, Sergeant. By the way, are you new on Fred's squad? I don't think I've seen you around before."

"Oh, I'm not with the DA squad. I'm BSSI."

Karp raised his eyebrows. "Oh? That's interesting. Why would the Bureau of Strategic Surveillance and Intelligence want to run its own investigation on this case?"

Flanagan shrugged. "It's routine, like I said. A political bombing—"

"Yeah. These guys are a little to the right of the people the Red Squad usually gets involved with, no?"

Flanagan shrugged again and smiled. "Hey, I just follow orders, man."

Karp tapped a pencil on his desk and looked again at the two sheets. He sighed wearily, his good mood entirely evaporated now. When he looked up at Flanagan and spoke, his voice was calm and careful.

"Sergeant, I'm going to assume that you're just what you appear to be, a cop following orders, and that you're not involved in any conscious effort to obstruct justice. And I'll continue to assume that, as long as I believe you're answering the questions I'm about to ask you as honestly as you can, with no more of this happy horseshit about routine investigations."

A flush broke across Flanagan's cheekbones, and his jaw tightened. "What the hell are you talking about, Karp?"

"There isn't any investigation of the Doyle bombing besides the one that I'm running out of this office. If you're not working for Fred Spicer, and indirectly for me, you're not working on this case."

"That's bullshit."

"No, it's not. And if you like, I'll get on the horn to the C. of D. and you can hear it directly from his own ruby lips. But you probably don't want me to do that, because Chief Denton doesn't like cops who try to screw up investigations."

Flanagan's face faded several shades toward white, and he chewed his lip nervously. "OK, wait. What's going on here?"

"I don't know, Sergeant, but I need to find out. Why don't you tell me how you came across this stuff?"

Flanagan pursed his mouth and thought for a few seconds, assembling his story. Then he said, "You're right, there's no investigation. Couple of days ago, Wednesday, a guy calls me, says he's got evidence on the Doyle case, on this guy Rukovina. I tell him, go see Spicer, he's got the action on that case. But he says no, he wants to go to BSSI, nobody else."

"Did he say why?"

"Yeah, I asked him that. He said he didn't trust you—I mean those guys." Flanagan paused, but when Karp remained silent, he went on. "Anyway, I set up a meet, and he takes me to this apartment house in Yorkville where Rukovina lived. We go down to the storeroom in the basement, where they keep bikes and stuff. And there's the typewriter. It's got Rukovina's prints all over it. Oh, yeah, I forgot, I got lab reports on that too. That's it."

"And . . . ?"

"And nothing. That's it. I went to the lab, got a rush on the prints and the type comparisons. Then I came down here."

Karp looked the other man full in the face. "Sergeant, don't act dumb. Who was the guy, what was his name, where did he come from, why is he ratting on our friend Rukovina? Give!"

Flanagan looked away. "Oh. This I don't know."

"Fuck, you don't. Was he a regular snitch?"

"No way. Look, I swear I never saw the guy, before or since."

"Yeah, maybe, but you know who he is. And I need to know."

"I'm telling you, goddamn it! He was just a guy . . ."

Karp reached for the phone. "I told you I'm not fucking around,

Flanagan. In about five minutes I will have Denton on this line, and you will be ordered to report to his office forthwith, and you will spill your guts. After which, if I'm any judge, you will spend the rest of your career working in a blue bag out of some precinct in the South Bronx." Karp started to dial. Flanagan cleared his throat heavily. Karp stopped dialing and glanced up.

"OK, OK. I wasn't supposed to tell you anything. Shit, man, I don't know what the fuck is going on. They told me this was coming down from the DPC level."

"Floyd, right?"

"Yeah, how did—"

"Never mind. Who was the guy?"

"Yeah, I can see how I'm getting hung out to dry here. Well, fuck them." Flanagan smiled ruefully. "The guy didn't give his name, as a matter of fact. But I figure, I'm not going to go to no DA with no fucking homicide evidence without knowing who the guy is who's giving it to me. So I set up my partner to tail him. After we break up in Yorkville, he takes a cab and Jimmy follows him to Columbia. It turns out the guy is some kind of professor. Name of Terzich. Stefan Terzich."

"Ah, shit!" Karp yelled, flinging his pencil against the wall.

"No, honest, that was his name," Flanagan said hastily. He wiped his forehead with the heel of his hand.

"Yeah, right, I believe you. It figures." Karp found himself staring at the twitch in Flanagan's lower lip. "So tell me," he said after an uncomfortable pause, "what does Professor Terzich do, when he's not professing?"

"What d'you mean? Like private life?"

"No, public. I'll give you a hint. It has something to do with translation."

"I don't know what you're talking about."

"Flanagan, you're playing games again. If you were suspicious enough to check out your informant as far as you did, you must have also learned that he's the court-appointed translator in the Karavitch case. Two of the defendants, Raditch and your boy Rukovina, don't speak English. That means when they appear in court, they have to have a translator. More important, the translator has to be present when their lawyer confers with them. You understand this, Flanagan? The translator is privy to the protected relationship between client and lawyer guaranteed by the Sixth Amendment. He can't go and rat out his whatever, his translatee, to the cops or the prosecution."

"Yeah, but why is that any skin off your ass?" asked Flanagan. "You didn't get him to do it."

"That's not the point. I'm responsible for the legality of the evidence I present. If I showed up in court with that tainted typewriter and presented it as honestly come by in the course of an investigation, not only would the case be garbage, but the State would have good cause to boot me out of there on my ass, not to mention disbarment proceedings, if they believed that I had guilty knowledge of the taint and presented it anyway. Which I'm willing to bet they had somebody in the wings prepared to swear to. Probably Terzich, those sons of bitches!"

"Who you talking about, Karp? You saying you were set up? This whole thing is a setup to get you?" The cop was frankly incredulous.

Karp shot him a sour look. "Did somebody set this up? Does Howdy Doody have a wooden dick? Come on, Flanagan. This thing was scripted, choreographed, and directed from minute one. Not specifically to get me, no. Springing Karavitch and company is the main thing. But I think I was the cherry on top. That made it extra sweet. And I'll be honest with you—I would've rolled too, if I didn't know that there was an absolute lock on this investigation by the C. of D. himself. No fucking way you could've told me something new that I hadn't got from him or one of my guys first."

"So who was it?" Flanagan asked.

Karp didn't answer. He leaned back in his chair and stared at the ceiling for a minute. Then he said, "All right, Sergeant, here's what we're going to do. I will get a stenographer in here and I will ask you some questions. Then we will get this Q and A typed up and you will sign it. Then you will go back to fighting the red menace and forget all about this case, unless and until somebody tries something like this again, at which time you will come see me immediately. Understood?"

Flanagan understood. Two hours later, Karp was alone in his office, looking at the neatly typed Q and A transcript and the lab reports about the typewriter and the fingerprints. He stuffed these papers in a large manila envelope, sealed it, signed his name across the flap, and stuck cellophane tape over the signature. He addressed the front of it to himself.

Brenner was waiting for him on the White Street side.

"We're going to 52nd and Madison, no?" Brenner asked as Karp slid into the front seat.

"Yeah, let's go," Karp grunted.

"Oh, you're in a good mood today. Is there any truth to the rumor that you're planning to convert, providing the pope drops all this crap about Jesus?"

The laugh bubbled up inside Karp and burst out, filling the car.

Once started, he found it hard to stop. Brenner glanced at him sideways, a doubtful smile on his rough face. "Hey, it wasn't that funny. You OK, Butch?"

Karp wiped his streaming eyes. "Yeah, it's OK. You had to be there. Look, swing left here and hit the post office. I got to mail a registered letter."

Monsignor Francis Keene's office in the archepiscopal chancery was small but cozy, and had a nice view of Madison Avenue. One wall was all books; another was bare, except for a crucifix. The narrow wall behind the substantial mahogany desk was covered with framed photographs, some of Keene with groups of priests and others showing Keene in a football uniform.

Keene himself looked like a chunk of native basalt, a former lineman who had fought fat to a standstill in his middle years. His gray hair was closely cropped around his squarish skull, and his face was organized around a large crumpled nose and dark, bushy eyebrows.

A jock, was Karp's first thought on entering the office. He tried to imagine him wearing one of those funny hats priests wore in the movies. It was difficult. So was imagining him at prayer.

Keene had a big hand and a hard grip. He ushered Karp into a brown leather chair and sat down himself behind the desk. Karp glanced at the photographs. Keene caught his eye and smiled. Karp said, "I see you used to play some ball."

"Yes, starting defensive tackle, three years. A small Catholic school in the Midwest."

"Yeah, Notre Dame. I think I've heard of it. You look like you could still go in for the sack."

"On a good day, Mr. Karp," Keene chuckled. "But thanks anyway. I believe you played some ball yourself."

Karp felt an uncomfortable reprise of his recent paranoia. Somebody had taken the trouble to investigate his background and convey it to Keene. "Yeah, but not a contact sport."

"Like the law, in that respect, no?" Keene smiled and leaned back in his chair. "Well, Mr. Karp, I have to tell you that Billy's family was very pleased with the disposition of his case. We all owe you a debt of gratitude. If there's anything I can do—"

"Actually, Monsignor, there is something. I'm given to believe that you're sort of a troubleshooter for the, ah, the—"

"The Church, Mr. Karp? Yes, I imagine you could call me that. The Archdiocese does what it can to avoid unnecessary embarrassment, and I try to help where I can. Although I do have other duties."

"Yeah, right. So I thought you might know something about a murder case I'm working on right now."

"A murder case? Involving clergy?"

"No, it's this Karavitch case. The gang that hijacked the plane to Paris. They also left a bomb that exploded and killed a cop. Terry Doyle, his name was."

Keene's eyebrows came together in a frown. "I'm not sure I see the involvement of the Archdiocese in this affair."

"Let me help you out. These defendants were barely out of their handcuffs when somebody sent a check for twenty K to one of the most expensive criminal lawyers in the country for their defense. The source of that check was the Archdiocese."

"I see. And . . . ?"

"And I'd like to know why."

Keene looked out at Madison Avenue for a moment, his brows still wrinkled. Then he turned back to Karp. "Supposing it were true—I'm not sure I have to give the prosecution that sort of information."

"Of course you don't. You could kick me out of here this minute. But I suspect that the main point of the aid, and the reason for the discreet way it was handed out, is to keep the lid on some connection these guys have with the Church. A lid that I will do my personal best to pry off if I don't get the answers I want."

"I wouldn't advise doing that, Mr. Karp," said Keene, his voice rumbling.

"Why? Because it might harm my career? If you know enough about me to know I used to shoot hoops, you also know it would be real hard to screw up my career any more than it is already. Now we can fence around some more and trade threats, or you can tell me what I want to know and I'll be out of here. And like you said, you owe me one." He tried a frank and boyish smile. "What do you say?"

Keene shrugged and smiled back. "You want to know why the Church is helping to pay for the defense in this case? It's no big mystery, Mr. Karp. You appear to have, if I may say so, a certain tendency toward morbid suspicion. I imagine it must be a natural occupational hazard of your profession. Not the law; I mean the business of catching criminals. I've noted it often in my many friends on the police force. I find it interesting because it is the diametric opposite of a hazard in my own profession, which is credulity, the tendency to look for the good in people.

"There's a passage in Sartre I've always liked. He describes how once during the Resistance he was trapped in a cellar with an old priest. They were both hiding from a Gestapo search. Sartre asked the priest whether there was any wisdom he had distilled about the human condition as a result of hearing thousands of confessions. The priest replied, 'Most men are better than they believe they are.' I would suggest as a corollary: 'Most men are better than other men believe they are.'

"We should keep that in mind when we talk about Djordje Karavitch. The story is rather complex, as you might imagine, since it took place in the Balkans in the midst of war. Do you know anything about Yugoslavia, Mr. Karp?"

"Croats and Serbs, you mean?"

"Exactly! Croats and Serbs. The Croats are, of course, Catholics. The Serbs are not. It may be hard to imagine in these ecumenical and irreligious times what it once meant for a nation to be so constructed. Yes, there is Ireland, but what goes on in Belfast is the palest shadow of what has happened within our own time in Croatia. But how they believe! It is a sad statement on our world that the faith needs oppression for its fullest flowering. The Irish. The Poles. The Croats."

"You mean under the Turks?"

"Oh, no, I mean the Serbs. When Yugoslavia was formed in 1919, it meant surrendering the Croatian people and their religion to the domination of an alien faith. Like Ireland under the Protestant Ascendancy. The Serbs were on the winning side in the First World War, you see, so they picked up the marbles—the courts, government jobs, army, police.

"The Church helped where it could. It supported youth groups, unions, political organizations, anything to keep alive the spirit of a Catholic Croatia. I should add, to a greater extent than would be the case today. In politics, at any rate."

"What does this have to do with Karavitch?" Karp asked irritably.

"I was just coming to that. From his earliest youth, Karavitch had been active in Catholic and nationalist organizations. He was a devoted follower of the great Croatian leader, Stefan Raditch. When Raditch was murdered in 1928, Karavitch was plunged into despair. In the end, his faith sustained him, as I trust it still does. He became an editor of a Catholic newspaper in Zagreb and a prominent youth leader. Of course, he was constantly harassed by agents of the central government.

"During the war he fought hard against the communists, and afterward—"

"Wait a minute. You mean World War II? The communists in Yugoslavia were on our side, weren't they?"

Keene paused and answered with more than a hint of annoyance, "Things were very complex in those years, as I've said. In any case, after the war it was, of course, impossible for Karavitch to stay in Yugoslavia, and so it was arranged for him to come over here."

"Arranged? By whom?"

"Friends, I suppose. I don't see that it bears much on the present situation. Pavle Macek came over at that time as well."

"And that's the story?"

"Yes. You sound surprised, Mr. Karp. Mr. Karavitch was for many years a fighter in the cause of Catholic freedoms. You are yourself Jewish, I understand. Perhaps you are a member of a Jewish organization. If that organization wished to aid in the defense of someone who had fought against anti-Semitism and had been arrested for some outrage against, let us say, an Arab embassy, I daresay you might approve of that organization coming to his aid. It's the same here. The Church has an obligation to see that he has a decent defense, however misguided his recent actions. Surely you would not dispute his right to defend himself, or our right to aid him?"

"No, not at all. I don't even object to being fed this line of malarkey I've been getting from you. What I do object to strenuously is cops messing up my case against these rats because you, or somebody in your line of work, leaned on a deputy commissioner with political ambitions."

Keene rose slightly out of his chair, like a tackle coming off the scrimmage line. His face flushed and his neck seemed to swell around his stiff white collar. "What the devil are you talking about?"

Karp stood up. "If you don't know, I strongly suggest you find out, Monsignor. Now, you know very well that a case against whoever slipped the word to Pretty Boy Floyd for obstruction of justice would probably not get very far. But I will file such a case if—"

Keene was on his feet now. "Are you threatening me?"

"Threaten you? How can I threaten you? You're the Powerhouse. Look, Monsignor, the war stuff I could care less about. Karavitch carried water for the Germans? So what? It was a long time ago, and there's plenty of VWs in New York. But your boy killed a cop, also a good Catholic, by the way, and so I'm going to put him away for it if I can.

"That's why you got to call off the fellas, Monsignor. I mean it. Like I said, I can't threaten you, but I guarantee you, the cops put this one in the tank, you'll never make cardinal. Talk about embarrassment, for the Church and all, if this ever got out. Which it will. Hentoff would eat it up with sour cream. And besides, Monsignor, it's not nice. You hired yourself a good lawyer. Now play fair." Karp gestured at the photographs as he strolled toward the door. "For the Gipper, huh?"

In the car, Brenner asked, "I see you're smiling. How did it go?"

Karp leaned back in his seat and stretched, then rolled the window down to dispel the effects of Brenner's White Owl. "It went OK. We had a frank exchange of views about morality."

"Oh, yeah? Who won?"

"Me, so far, I think. But on points."

Just past one, Karp found Tony Harris waiting for him outside the DA's conference room on the eighth floor of 100 Centre Street. He was carrying a fat sheaf of wide green-and-white-striped computer printout, the kind computer jocks call elephant toilet paper. His tie was pulled down and his long wispy hair was disheveled.

"Thank God. I thought I was going to have to go in there alone," he said with relief, handing the sheaf to Karp.

Karp glanced at the summary tables on the front page. "You should, as part of your education. It's the world's greatest display of lawyers who have never been near a courtroom. They should be stuffed and sent to a museum. How do we look?"

"About the usual. Clearance rate's up a point, five down off our quota. It looked worse this morning. They fucked up the programming. We had *negative* rates for a couple of crime categories. I got them to do a rush for us, since it was their goof, and—"

"Hold on, Tony. You know about this computer shit?"

"Yeah," Harris replied sheepishly. "I was a business admin major before I switched to pre-law. I did some COBOL programming at Syracuse."

"No kidding?"

"It's no big deal. The jerks picked up a canned program from LEAA and loaded it without testing. It was in a different version of COBOL and the address parameters were slightly different, so the counts were off. What I did was—"

"Stop, you're talking Chinese. Listen, Tony, can you get into the computer and, like, mess around with it?"

"Theoretically, sure. If I had the passwords and access to a terminal. Why?"

"Nothing," said Karp. "Just a thought. Look, I got to go for my whipping. See you later."

Conrad Wharton prided himself on starting meetings on time. He was talking to the assembled group of bureau directors and assistants, each with a stack of printouts on the table, when Karp walked in, five minutes late. He immediately stopped talking, and Karp took his seat in silence. He always performed this embarrassment ritual. Karp had continued to come late.

Wharton resumed his commentary, which he delivered in a rapid-fire nasal monotone, confident and empty. At calculated moments he would purse his cupid-bow mouth and stare at one or another of the men to see how his wisdom was being received. His mouth was a curious shade of bright pink, like the candy-lipsticks favored by small girls. His hair was white-blond, short, and thin and his face was round, bland, and nearly beardless. He looked like a sweet doll until you looked into his eyes, which were blue and calculating.

He finished his speech, some administrative business about new forms and an admonition to purchase no new furniture during the upcoming fiscal year without a written justification attached to the standard requisition. Most people took notes, for Wharton liked people to write while he was talking. Karp diagrammed basketball plays.

Wharton flipped through his printout and said, "This month makes the sixth straight month the Criminal Courts Bureau has failed to meet its clearance quotas. I think that's a record." He let out a dry, humorless chuckle: "Hegg, hegg, hegg." Most of the people around the table laughed politely. Karp looked up from his paper and regarded Wharton blankly. "Oh? Gosh, Conrad, I thought we were doing real good. You sure Data Processing got those numbers right?"

Wharton frowned. "What do you mean?"

Karp picked up his printout and let it flop down on the table. "This was run off a program written in the wrong version of COBOL. The address parameters are screwed up. I caught a bunch of mistakes myself, and as you know, Conrad, I'm not any computer expert. Hegg, hegg, hegg. How do we know any of this is worth discussing?"

A flush dawned over Wharton's peach fuzz. "That was a minor problem and we fixed it."

"Maybe," Karp said. "But we ought to make sure. Did any of you guys notice any errors this month?"

This was, of course, an invitation to mutiny. Even professional ass-kissers will turn on their tormentor given a reasonably safe opportunity. For months Wharton had been heckling them about their "stats" and telling them "figures don't lie." Now it seemed they did lie, and the chance to pin their bureaus' shortfalls on the system was irresistible. The meeting was soon out of control.

151

Wharton bluffed for a while, but then had to call in Rich Wool, a skinny, long-necked character who ran the information system. He, in turn, had to call in a squad of data weenies, pale, slug-like creatures who blinked in the unaccustomed glare of the above-ground and talked incomprehensible jargon at one another. After fifteen minutes Wharton dismissed the meeting as hopeless and retired to his private office in a huff, trailed by Wool and his weenies flapping unfolded reams of printouts.

Karp was about to descend the stairs when he remembered his promise to Marlene about her compensation claim. He went into the Admin suite and tried to find out from various clerks and special assistants what had become of the claim jacket. It was on Mr. Wharton's desk awaiting signature. Karp sighed and headed for Wharton's private office. He walked up to the secretary, a good-looking brunette, and said, "I got to see him. Two minutes."

"He's in a meeting."

Karp brushed by her. "Two minutes," he said. "He'll see me. I'm one of his favorite people."

Wharton had a big window office and new blond oak furniture. He had an American flag, a state flag, and a little platform for his big oak desk, so he could look down on visitors. The only visitor at that moment was Rich Wool, who by the look of him had just gotten a monumental reaming.

Wharton looked up, scowling. "Yes? I'm in the middle of something."

"This'll only take a minute. It's urgent," replied Karp blandly, not moving and obviously not intending to move. Wharton glared and then gestured for Wool to leave, flicking his hand as if brushing off an insect. Wool scuttled out the door.

"All right, what is it?"

"Marlene Ciampi, one of my people, has a request for workplace-injury compensation in your office. I'd like to know what its status is."

"Oh, yeah," said Wharton, his mouth pursing toward a smile, "that thing. Well, its status is, we're considering it."

"And when will you stop considering it?"

"Oh, that depends on a number of factors. We could expedite it quite a bit if we could make a few, ah, adjustments."

"What are you talking about, Conrad?"

Wharton leaned back in his huge judge's chair and put his feet on the desk and his hands behind his head. He had tiny feet encased in soft tasseled loafers. He smiled. "Butch, my boy. You know how things are done around here. You give a little, you get a little. You cooperate with me, I cooperate with you."

"Like how?"

"Like changes in attitude. Like being a team player. Like not being such a hard-ass on this Weaver case. Like relaxing a bit on Karavitch."

"Let me understand this, Wharton. You're suggesting that I throw two murder cases and in return you'll do your job and sign off on a legitimate compensation claim? Is that the deal?"

"Throw cases? Nobody's talking about throwing cases, Butch. Just a matter of easing up, a change in emphasis. And from what I hear, the Karavitch case almost kicks itself out of court. The evidence seems shaky in a lot of ways, don't you agree?"

"I can't believe I'm hearing this, even from you, Wharton. God damn, you're a pimp!"

Wharton's feet came off his desk with a bang. He stood up, his fists clenched and his jaw working. "Don't you speak to me that way in my own office! Who the hell do you think you are? You ape! Do you have any idea what it takes to run a prosecutor's office in a city this size? Let me tell you something: your precious Francis P. Garrahy sure as hell didn't. Have you got any idea what shape record-keeping was in when we got here? You know what we found? Big bottles of black ink and boxes of steel pens, and goddamn ledgers. We've been trying for two years to move this office into the twentieth century and we've done pretty well, despite everything you and your asshole friends have done to mess things up.

"I've tried to help you, God knows, and I've gotten nothing in return but contempt and juvenile misbehavior. Fine! You'll hang yourself sooner or later. But then you have the unmitigated gall to come in here, with your goddamn attitude and ask me for a favor for your little piece of ass—"

Karp lurched forward, put his massive hands on Wharton's desk, and brought his face to within inches of Wharton's own. Wharton drew back instinctively and fell into his chair.

"Wharton," said Karp slowly, straining to keep his voice calm. "I'm sorry I called you a pimp. I don't know what you are, but you sure as hell don't have the balls to be a pimp. I'm trying to be nice now. I'm trying not to kill you, because if I did, I would probably walk on a temporary insanity plea, which is against my principles. So let me ask you once again, when are you going to stop sitting on this goddamn claim?"

Wharton sat up, his face blazing and dappled with nervous sweat. "When? I'll tell you when. I'm going to stick that claim in her retirement file. She'll get it when she's eligible for Social Security. Now get the fuck out of my office before I call a guard!"

13

"How DID IT go?" Tony Harris asked him. It was three-fifteen, and they were sitting side by side in the empty jury box of a courtroom on the twelfth floor, waiting for the arraignment of Jerold Weaver, the man who had gunned down the dry-cleaning magnate under the impression that he was ridding the city of a pimp. Karp was there to observe and advise, and also to dissipate the rage built up during his interview with Conrad Wharton. He could still feel it pounding in the pulse at his temples and churning his stomach.

"Don't ask," he replied. He massaged his belly and wondered whether he was going to have to start gulping antacids like the old farts who worked in the courthouse. He realized it had been a grave error to allow his temper to flare out of control in front of Wharton. He had always understood at some level that Wharton—and Bloom himself, come to that—had allowed him to survive this long because they wanted his complicity in what they were doing. They admired and despised him at the same time. They wanted him as their tool, as a cog in the mechanical justice system they had constructed. Amazingly, with all their power, they sought his approval.

For this reason they let him get away with stuff. Especially Wharton, who patronized him at every opportunity, and treated him like a political imbecile, a naughty boy who would come to his senses, given enough patience and plenty of firm but fair punishment.

Karp could play that game, too, and had, scaling his resistance and contempt just a hair short of the level that would force them to admit that he would never come across. He knew he had exceeded it this afternoon, and he knew why. Bloom and Wharton had to be involved in Flanagan's evidence. It was too lawyerly a plot. The poisoned bait was too custom-designed to appeal to a prosecutor's appetite for it to have come from any other quarter. "*Why* is the question," he said out loud.

"What?"

"Oh, nothing, Tony, just mumbling to myself." He brought

himself to focus on the case at hand. "I see we have Sleepy Sam
Lepell on the bench. His Honor is not exactly an ornament of the
profession, but he's not a bad guy, if you don't confuse him with
the law. He's about a year from retirement, but his brain retired
about ten years ago. On the other hand, he is not going to pressure
you to accept a cockamamie man one on this. Rafferty's slick.
He'll try to focus attention on the defendant's emotional state at
the time of the shooting, and he'll offer years in the can, zero to
twelve, fifteen, the limit—"

"Because of the max-out rule," Harris said.

"Right, because of max-out, he only has to serve two-thirds the
max time. It's the zero that counts. He could be walking in eighteen months, the little shithead. But the judge gets credit for the
stiff fifteen of the max. Crazy, but that's show biz. Which is why
you hold out for the top count, murder two."

The clerk called the Weaver case, and Harris got to his feet and
collected his case files. "Go get 'em, baby," Karp said. Harris gave
him a stiff smile. He was nervous, not because he was unprepared,
but because of the nasty politics surrounding the case.

Rafferty, a thin, dark-haired man in a shiny gray suit, had
moved into the well of the court. The guards brought in Jerold
Weaver and escorted him to the defense table. Weaver had a
jug-eared monkey face and a wide drinker's nose set in the middle
of it. He looked used up and confused.

The judge asked for the plea. Rafferty said, "Not guilty, Your
Honor. And may counsel approach the bench?" Sleepy Sam beck-
oned with a plump white finger, and the two attorneys advanced to
the oak presidium. Karp couldn't hear what the three men were
saying, but he could easily guess, having done the same thing
countless times himself. Rafferty would be making his offer to
change his client's plea to guilty in return for a reduction in the
severity of the charge, which was particularly important here,
because murder was the one exception to the max-out rule. If
Weaver went up for murder two, he would spend a long, long time
in a very unpleasant place.

What Rafferty had to give, therefore, was his guilty plea; what
he wanted was an essentially meaningless sentence. What Harris
had to give was his consent to the reduction in charge; what he
stood to gain was another precious clearance. If the bargain went
through, moreover, the judge would avoid the annoyance of a trial
and get credit for a stiff twelve- or fifteen-year sentence.

Things were not, however, going smoothly in the shadow of
Judge Lepell's bench. A shadow of annoyance flickered across his
normally unfurrowed brow. Karp grinned. Harris was making waves.

155

Rafferty would up the ante year by year to the maximum the law authorized for first-degree manslaughter, while at the same time suggesting elements in the case that would make for a difficult conviction at trial. Harris would hang tough. He had an unambiguous murder with no procedural impediments in sight and a reliable eyewitness who had observed the killing across the width of a car seat. It was a training-wheels case for a prosecutor.

The conference ended with Sleepy Sam clearing his throat and remanding the case for trial. Defense and prosecution left the bench and walked back through the well of the court. Karp could see that Tony was disturbed; his lips were tight and there was a band of red across his high cheekbones. Rafferty said a few words to his client. Then he motioned to Harris, who walked over to him. The defense lawyer guided the younger man to the side aisle of the courtroom and there engaged him in a brief conversation. Rafferty was smiling; Harris nodded a couple of times, then left, and walked over to the jury box.

"What was that all about?" Karp asked, frowning.

"Oh, nothing much. It got a little hot up there and Rafferty was saying no hard feelings. The usual bullshit. And he wanted the remand date moved up a couple of days. He had a conflict and I told him no problem." Harris noted Karp's expression and asked, "Is there a problem? I thought we did OK."

"Yeah, right. Then you go and let a lawyer take you aside in front of the whole courtroom and the goddamn defendant and have a little private conversation. What do you think Rafferty is going to report to Weaver about what you discussed?"

Harris flushed. "How do I know?" he asked defensively. "And why should I care?"

"You care because everything that goes on in a courtroom bears on the case. OK, maybe it's not important in this one, but you get a rep as somebody who likes to go aside for little chats with the defense and someday, in a real close one, some shyster is going to say to the judge, 'Why, Your Honor, I was led to believe just now by Mr. Harris,' et cetera, et cetera. Or some client is going to complain that he saw Harris and his lawyer talking and his lawyer told him that Harris said the fix is in. And so on.

"You understand? It's a cloud on the case; maybe a little cloud, but little clouds get together and make thunder. You're in open court, you conduct your business in the open, on the record, where possible."

Harris said, "OK, sorry," and turned away to shove papers into his briefcase. Karp felt a pang of remorse. He said, "Hey, Tony, it's OK, you did good. I didn't mean to lecture you, I just got a hair up my ass today."

Harris smiled his crooked smile. "Nah, it's good training. See you." He took his bulging briefcase and walked off up the center aisle to his next case. He had to swerve to the side to avoid the small figure of Rhoda Klepp, who was homing in on Karp like a reentry vehicle on the first day of World War III.

"There you are," she said without preamble. "You're never in your office and nobody ever knows what you're doing. I've been looking all over the building for you." She walked into the jury box and cocked a plump hip on the railing.

Karp stood up and stretched. "This is a courtroom, Rhoda. I spend a lot of time in courtrooms because I am a lawyer. Law-yer. See the guy up there in the black robe? He is a judge. Juh-udge."

"Cut the bullshit, Karp."

"You better watch it, Rhoda. You start hanging around in courtrooms, you might meet a criminal, maybe catch a disease of some kind."

Klepp rolled her eyes and curled her upper lip, an expression she used when she heard something she thought was stupid. Among the bureaucratic levels she frequented, this was an effective signal, since it meant she was liable to carry poisoned tales about the wit of her interlocutor to her masters, Wharton and Bloom. Karp ignored it. In fact, Karp avoided looking at Klepp entirely, since he did not want his gaze to wander anywhere near those mighty cones. As he examined the ceiling moldings, Klepp tightened her jaw and went on. "The boss wanted to find out what's happening with Weaver. It's today, isn't it?"

"Was. He's remanded for trial. The clerk can give you the exact date."

"Trial, my ass. I'll get it back on the calendar for another hearing. The boss wants us to accept a plea on this one."

"Oh?"

"Yeah. I wish you could take a hint sometimes, Karp. It'd make life easier for everybody. You heard about the dope they found in this asshole's car?"

"Whose car, Weaver's?"

"No, Karp, Weems's. A gram of toot in the glove compartment. It looks like Mr. Weems wasn't quite the pillar of the community the press has him cracked up to be. Liked the high life. So did his secretary, it turns out. I hear she—"

"What is this, Klepp? We're investigating the *victim*? The guy was shot dead in the street, for chrissakes! We got the killer. Who cares about the victim's bad habits?"

Klepp favored him with a small, superior smile. He was looking at her now. "Karp, don't be a schmuck. There's a political aura about this case that you don't seem to understand. The black community is not going to stand up for this guy—he's an embarrassment now. It's a good case for building points with the rednecks. We let him cop to man one, put him away in Attica for a couple. With any luck some dude'll knife him and—"

"Rhoda, shut the fuck up!" he said with such vehemence that she actually did. He bent over and put his face close enough to hers that he could see the little lumps of mascara on her eyelashes. She leaned away from him, but she couldn't move far because of the rail of the well. He lifted his enormous hand in front of her face and counted on his fingers. "One. Focus on this, Rhoda. I don't care about politics. It's just boring assholes playing stupid games. Two. It doesn't matter if anybody will stand up for the victim. That's what we get paid for. It doesn't matter what the victim did or was. He's the fucking victim! Am I making contact? We care about what the defendant did. Three. Over my dead body will you cop a plea on Weaver." Karp backed away and strode out of the well. Rhoda came after him. "You maniac! You're dead already," she shouted.

Sleepy Sam woke up and tapped his gavel. "Miss, please! This is a courtroom."

Back in his office, Karp found out what she meant. There was a sealed envelope in his in-basket, marked "CONFIDENTIAL" and "URGENT." In it was a letter from Bloom, thanking him for his work as Assistant Bureau Chief of the Criminal Courts Bureau and informing him that his services in that capacity would no longer be required, effective close of business the following day.

Ray Guma squashed his cigar into the tin ashtray and looked in silence at the small woman seated across the dirty, Formica-topped table. They were alone in an interrogation room on the fourth floor of 100 Centre Street. Elvira Melendez's gray prison uniform hung slack on a body that, except for high, pointed breasts, was like a twelve-year-old's. She had beautiful, black, heavily lashed eyes. Those eyes were filled with terror.

Guma was trying to be gentle with her, which was difficult, because gentleness was not his strong suit. For forty-five minutes he had been trying to get her to come across with some information about the Sorriendas murder, with no result except shrugs, monosyllables, and frightened glances from those huge eyes whenever he mentioned Ruiz.

From a pack Guma had brought, she was slowly smoking Kents,

one after the other, blowing the smoke in strong twin plumes from her nostrils, tapping the ashes into the tin ashtray. Suddenly Guma sprang from his chair. "This is bullshit," he said. "I feel like the Gestapo. You're scared shitless, and I'm trying to help you, and it's not working. Look, I got an idea. I'm starving, you're probably hungry, eating baloney sandwiches in the jail, right? Let's get out of here, grab a bite to eat, maybe have some laughs. What d'ya say?"

She looked at him blankly. He put on his suit jacket and came around to her side of the table. He took her hand. "Come on," he said, pulling her to her feet. "Hey, we'll get some Cuban food. *Arroz con pollo.* Biftek with lime and a big pile of those weird French fries. Flan. You like flan? Shit, honey, I haven't had any flan in years. There's a great place in the Village, on Eleventh Street—Yglesias or Ysidro, begins with a Y, anyway."

She was still staring at him. She fingered the label of her prison dress. "But how . . ."

"Oh, I got an old raincoat in my office you can wear. Don't worry, I'll bring you back, you won't get in trouble with the jail. Hey, I'm an officer of the court, right?"

"You can do this?"

Guma beamed. "Is Fidel a commie?"

They ate, or rather, Guma ate. She picked at her rice and beans and drank three cups of *café con leche.* And smoked. Guma raved about the food, cracked jokes in bad Spanish with the waiter, and watched her. Once she almost smiled.

When the plates were taken away and the place was nearly empty, she said, "I'm not what you think I am."

"What do you think that is?"

"A slut. Someone who lives with gangsters. You're treating me like a person, even though I know you're just trying to get me to talk about what happened to Alejandro. Even the pretense that you care about me means something. For a long time no one has even pretended."

"What are you, then?"

"At one time I was a schoolteacher. Now I am a slave," she said, "to him. *El Serpiente.*"

"I thought you were Sorriendas's girlfriend."

She snorted. "Him! Ruiz gave me to him as a present. Perhaps he was drunk, or he bet me in a card game and lost. It wouldn't be the first time, you know. Not nearly. Alejandro was not the worst of them, either."

"He busted you up pretty bad."

159

"Yes, he did. Ruiz came one night with Hermo, one of his men, to have a party. Ruiz made me do things with him, with Hermo, in front of Alejandro, you understand? He couldn't do nothing, anything. He just drank. Then, when they went away, that's when he beat me up. I could understand that. But Ruiz is beyond understanding. You know about machismo. Domination of women, yes, but honor and courtesy are also there. Ruiz and women, it's not machismo, nothing to do with honor or courtesy.

"In the old days, in Santiago de Cuba, he was with the Batista police. There were stories. Girls from the barrios would disappear, then later they would find the bodies on the dump. We were neighbors, you know, in Santiago. I would see him on the street, and he was always polite, like an ordinary man. My family was in politics, so we were protected. After the revolution, in Miami, he began to come around. We were no longer protected, and he was no longer polite. When my father died, three years ago last May, all this began."

"Didn't you ever try to get away? Or go to somebody for help?"

She lit another cigarette and pumped smoke for a silent minute. Guma could hear the rattle of dishes in the kitchen and the murmur of Spanish voices. She said, "I have a family. They live in Hialeah. My mother and my baby sister. She is eleven. Ruiz has told me in great detail what will happen to them if I don't do what he wants. So there is no escape for me. But as long as I am with him, I think he will stay away from them, I think.

"But maybe not. Now that I'm in jail . . . who knows? That's why they call him what they do. Who can understand a snake? So you see why I can't help you. But thank you anyway for all of this."

"What if I could arrange protection for you and your family?"

She smiled sadly. "What, the police? You think the cops in Hialeah are going to guard an old woman and a kid forever, every place they go, to school, to the store, all night?"

Guma looked her in the eyes and put his hand on top of hers.

"Not the cops," he said. "And believe me, it won't be forever."

Karp stayed in his office the rest of the afternoon. He read the letter from Bloom a couple of times, but the message didn't change. The phone didn't ring once. Word gets around. At three-thirty V.T. Newbury walked in, holding a fat accordion file and looking cheerful. He sat down and said, "Roger, my boy, I'm going to make your day."

"If it's not the Nobel Prize, forget it," Karp replied glumly. He passed Bloom's letter across the desk.

V.T. read it and raised his elegant eyebrows. "Hmm, this could be serious. We'll have to do something about it."

"Like what? I only wish I had decked that little motherfucker."

"There, there, it's not worth getting excited about. We'll think of something. Meanwhile, there's this." V.T. pulled a sheaf of papers out of his file.

"What is it?" Karp asked without enthusiasm.

"The synopsis of my brilliant exploration into the origin and ownership of Tel-Air Shipping, Incorporated. We owe a debt of thanks to my brother-in-law Derry, who has long been a name to conjure with in offshore funds. Also, that kid, Harris, is some kind of computer ace—very helpful. So here's the story: Tel-Air began in 1973 as a Cayman Islands corporation . . . what's wrong, Butch?"

"V.T., you're not computing. I just got *fired*. The candy store is closed. You understand what that means? It means politics as usual in the Criminal Courts Bureau. No more team. No more Tel-Air. We got a dead dealer. We got a greaser chick who looks good for it. Case closed, one more clearance. She's got a history of getting beat up by the victim—JoJo the Dog Boy could walk in off the street and cop her to man one. She didn't actually do it? There's a killer loose on the streets? Who gives a shit? We're all Wharton's robots now, cranking out pleas. Not me, baby. I am *gone* from here."

"Butch, snap out of it. Of course you got fired. I'm just surprised it didn't come down sooner. Christ on a crutch. You've been on borrowed time since Garrahy died."

"So?"

"So they've shot off their nukes. What else can they do? They think they've won, which is the best time for a counterattack."

Karp shook his head, which was starting to ache. "Bullshit, 'counterattack.' With what, paper clips? No, that's it, V.T. I gave it my best shot and I crapped out. I should've played along more, schmoozed up to Wharton and all of them on the eighth floor. I didn't, I blew my cool, I lost. And fuck it all."

"What about Doyle, you going to blow that off too?"

"Shit, no! Doyle's different. I'm at least holding some cards on that one, as long as Bill Denton doesn't get hit by a truck. But that's it, ace. No Tel-Airs. I'm going home."

"Suppose they're connected?" V.T. said in a neutral voice.

Karp, who was shrugging on his suit coat and walking toward the door, whipped around with his arms still half in the sleeves. He looked like a falcon with its wings folded, swooping out of the sky.

He stared at his friend. "What's connected, V.T.?"

"Gotcha!" said V.T., breaking into a broad grin. "It's tenuous but interesting. You have to have a devious mind—"

161

"V.T., don't screw around with me now."

"Fine, I'll just skim the high points."

"Yeah, leave out the parts about which relatives gave you what stuff."

V.T. sniffed. "To me, those *are* the high points. However. To resume, Tel-Air is a privately held Caymans corporation, which means it's just a brass plate on a lawyer's office down there in the sun. I won't go into how I got hold of this information, but Ruiz owns forty-nine percent of the company. The directors are all stooges of his, except one, who represents the majority shareholder, someone named George Paine. He's not important; in fact, he may not even exist. But the shareholding firm is very important.

"Now here's where it gets tricky. Control of Tel-Air is lodged with another offshore called Delmaris Investments. Ruiz is on the board of that one, together with two other men, Luis Cabrone and Bernardo Gelles. OK, think back a couple of years—Watergate, Vietnam protest, Daniel Ellsberg's shrink, the Carl Hoffman break-in. Got it?"

Karp scrunched up his brows, then shrugged. "Sorry, V.T., I'm drawing a blank."

"Ah, the tragedy of Alzheimer's and so young! Carl Hoffman? Worked for the Pentagon, realized that senior people in Vietnam and Washington were covering up the real numbers of Viet Cong and N.V.A. troops, inventing body counts. Spilled his guts to the *Washington Post*? Later somebody broke into his apartment, looking for incriminating stuff."

"Oh, yeah, now it comes back. They found out the guys who did it were on the FBI payroll as 'informants.' A big scandal."

"Right, a big scandal. And the names of the guys they nailed for the break-in? The envelope, please: Luis Cabrone and Bernardo Gelles. You like it? Wait, there's more. OK, we got black-bag guys on the FBI payroll connected to Tel-Air and Ruiz. Let's go back to the companies. Delmaris Investments has only two investments. One is Tel-Air. The other is—are you ready for this? Southeastern Air Ferry Service, Limited."

"Who?"

"Butch, children in rompers know that Southeastern is a CIA front. They ran the whole Guatemalan operation through it. So Ruiz is linked to CIA too. And not only that. It looks like Ruiz and his merry band were used as police and counterinsurgency trainers, plus some other fairly nasty odd jobs, when the CIA helped to whack out the Arbenz regime in Guatemala.

"So that's the corporate connection. Look at Tel-Air more closely and what do we find? Nothing much. The firm has almost no assets. They rent a warehouse out in Jamaica, Queens, and a couple of vans. For a shipping company they do remarkably little shipping. They don't have any bank loans, they're not in commercial paper either. But do they have a cash flow! For the last six months it's averaged around two hundred K monthly. They maintain a small wash account in Mercer Trust, dozens of small deposits, all cash, very cagey.

"Every month or so Ruiz cleans it out, and he or one of his men gets on the direct Swissair flight from Kennedy to Geneva. They're not pricing cuckoo clocks. Every dime goes into a numbered account at the Credit Vosges.

"Only two commodities can generate that kind of loot with no visible honest economic activity. One is dope, which we know he's into from Guma. The other is arms. That would explain one peculiarity: we can't find any supplier for his operation. Plus if he's using Tel-Air to launder his cash, and if almost all his capital goes into the bank, and if all the cash from the bank goes to Switzerland, what does he use for dope buys? He's not growing poppies in Queens, and DEA is positive he's not buying overseas. His volume would make waves for sure and attract the attention of the wise guys in Marseilles and Palermo. That's a tightly held franchise.

"Another fact: in March 1976, during a period when our government was trying to put the screws on El Salvador by cutting down on military aid, a 'private' group based in Salvador purchased five hundred and thirty thousand dollars' worth of weapons from a French consortium. The same month, Ruiz's account at Credit Vosges showed withdrawals of approximately five hundred and fifty thousand dollars in Swiss francs. Don't ask. DEA corrupted a Swiss bank clerk. Conclusion: Ruiz is getting dope, both heroin and coke, from somebody, for free, selling it here in bulk, and using at least part of the proceeds to buy guns. Any ideas about who could be the middleman?"

"CIA?"

"Two points. But to be fair, I doubt that it's official CIA, not like it was in the Sixties, fucking out of control. There must be dozens of former or even current CIA guys now who are running, or could run, entirely renegade operations funded by self-generated sources. Ruiz's operation looks like one of those."

Karp tapped his fingers on his desk. The headache was building into a rare skull-buster. He massaged his face and neck and wondered idly where Marlene was right now. He'd have to call her before he left.

"So? What do you think?" V.T. asked. "Pretty neat, huh? It sure as hell gives you something to work Elmer Pillman over with."

"True. But a connection? Bunch of Croats, bunch of Cubans, neither likes the reds very much, maybe both have a CIA handle, but . . . or am I missing something?"

"Just one detail. The agent who was the chief executive officer of Southeastern, who is reportedly close to Ruiz, just happened to be on the plane with the Croats on the way back from Paris and has gone into deep bye-byes since. Our mysterious friend Dettrick. Coincidence? Maybe, but there's also those swarthy guys dashing around and burning down luggage stores in Grand Central Station and otherwise threatening witnesses in the Doyle case. They're sure as hell not middle-aged Croatian refugees. Maybe they're Ruiz's people doing a favor for Daddy."

Karp thought about this for a while. "OK, there's a connect, but only through Dettrick. Let's say Dettrick's behind the game to spring Karavitch et al. or working for somebody who is. What we don't have is the why."

The door opened and Guma walked in, looking rumpled and tired. When he saw V.T. sitting in the only visitor's chair, he went out and dragged in a wheeled secretary's chair and sat down. Karp said, "Goom, what we want to know is why."

"Why is a crooked letter, as Mama used to say. Why what?"

"Did V.T. fill you in on a possible link between Ruiz and the Doyle thing?"

"Yeah, a little. The CIA connection, right? Sounds like a fucking movie. What about it?"

"We were wondering why a collection of dope- and gun-running renegade Cubans with CIA connections would suddenly take an interest in Croatian national independence."

Guma shrugged. "Search me, Jack. Why don't we pick up Señor Ruiz and ask him?"

"Good idea. But why should he tell us anything?"

Guma swiveled around on his chair, wearing a triumphant and not entirely pleasant smile. "Because I have his tiny *culliones* right in my hand. Elvira Melendez will testify that she saw Sorriendas get slashed to pieces by Ruiz and a pal of his, Esteban Otero, a guy they call Hermo. We just finished the Q and A."

"Brilliant, Guma!" V.T. said. "How did you swing it? I thought she wouldn't talk at all."

"Besides my charm, which is the stuff of legends, I arranged for some protection for her and for her family down in Miami."

"Protection?" Karp said. "I thought the People were protecting her in the Women's House of D. And who did you get in Miami, the cops?"

Guma shifted uncomfortably and worked his mobile face as he

164

searched for a plausible lie. Finding none suitable at hand, he decided to come clean. "Well, actually, she's not in jail. I got the bail reduced and sprung her. She should be on a plane for Miami in about twenty minutes. Also, I dropped the charges on her. She's a material witness now in a case against Ruiz and Hermo Otero. I already filed the complaint."

Karp whistled softly. "My, you've been a busy boy. So the Melendez family is to be reunited in beautiful Miami. Uh-huh. And who did you say you had watching them in the world capital of Latino crime? The South Miami police force?"

"Actually, it's Hialeah. But, uh, I didn't actually involve the local cops."

"Guma, not the Feds."

"Shit, no. What kind of jerk do you think I am?"

"Who, then? A private security firm? With what for money?"

Guma threw up his hands. "All right, already! It's under control. I made a couple of calls to some people I know and it's all arranged, no money involved."

"These people have names, Goom?"

Guma squirmed. "Yeah, just some people I know in North Miami Beach, from the old neighborhood, you know? Jimmy Guardino, and, ah, Tony Buonafacci. They're actually gonna stay in Tony's place."

V.T. was having a hard time stifling a case of the giggles. Karp felt it welling up in him too, but he struggled to keep his expression neutrally stern. "Ah, Guma, let me get this straight. You parked our material witness and her family with Tony Bones?"

"Yeah. Come on, guys, it's OK. Look, Tony doesn't like Cuban dope dealers, right? For business reasons. And on the personal angle, he's a family man. He don't go for the shit Ruiz was pulling, with the girl and all. Also I figure anybody who could go one-on-one with Joey Gallo and walk away has got to have the edge on a bunch of Cubans. Hey, what's so funny?"

After Karp and V.T. had finished laughing, Karp wiped his streaming eyes and said, "Mad Dog, I love it! You made my week. And you know why I love it? Because I'm not responsible anymore. No more loneliness of command. I can appreciate your work for the artistry it is. It'll be one of the comforts of my declining years."

Guma said, "V.T., what's he talking about, 'not responsible'?"

"Karp got the sack today. He's no longer our glorious assistant leader."

"What? How the hell did that go down?"

In a flat, tired voice, Karp recounted what had happened in Wharton's office. As he did, he found to his surprise that he could not summon the feelings of rage he had felt at the time. He was not calm, exactly. It was as if something was missing in him that had been there before—a certain feeling of invulnerability. With a start he recognized it as something he had experienced before, when his knee had been smashed and he had lost the dream of physical perfection. He wondered what it was he had lost in Wharton's office.

When he had finished, Guma got to his feet and started pacing the little room. "Goddamn it. We can't accept this. No way."

"Guma, it's OK," Karp said tiredly.

"It's fucking not OK," cried Guma. "It took me years to break you in. How am I gonna get away with stuff if I got some new asshole breathing down my neck? And it will be an asshole, you can bet on it."

"Got any suggestions? Anybody?" V.T. asked.

"Short of sucking Wharton's weenie in Macy's window, I can't think of anything I could do that would get them to change their minds. I'm not sure I even want them to, if you really want to know."

"Oh, Butch, for chrissakes, cut out that crap," Guma said, his voice rising. "You're not quitting on us now. What we gotta do is get rid of them."

"Guma, be real . . ."

"No, we can do it. Wharton first. Without Wharton, Bloom is like a prick without balls."

"A happy conceit," V.T. said. "Guma, do you think that this is the moment we've been waiting for? I wonder . . ."

"The moment? What do you mean, V.T.?"

"I mean for the creation of a situation so cosmically, so transcendently embarrassing that the victim would be rendered incapable of participating in public life for years, and which would be so constructed as to hold the perpetrators entirely harmless from retribution. I mean—"

Guma's face lit with comprehension. "Shit, yes! This is it! This is finally it! It's time for the Big Prank."

"What are you guys talking about?" Karp asked.

So they told him.

14

K ARP WALKED HOME up Broadway that evening around half past five. The sky still held some steely light in the west, and traffic still roared in the streets. Usually when Karp went home, the streets of these commercial districts were deserted. No more late nights, he thought: from now on I'm a five o'clock shadow. He had even left his briefcase at the office.

Karp also continued to ponder *Karavitch et al.* and was troubled. He thought he had a reasonably accurate picture of the sequence of events that had led to the death of Terry Doyle, and of course he knew who had done it. What he still lacked was an understanding of motivation. And motivation was the key to this case. "The question is why?" Karp said aloud, banging his fist into his hand as he walked along, just another New Yorker talking to himself on the streets of the world's largest open-air aftercare clinic. He stared in embarrassment and glanced furtively around. A man leaning against a wall with a flat pint of Orange Rock looked at him without interest. At least he wasn't hearing voices. Yet. Suddenly he wanted more than anything to talk to Marlene. He cut right on Grand Street and walked over to her loft. Her window was dark and her two cats, Prudence and the immense and ragged Juris, were sitting on her front step, which meant she was out. Karp considered sitting down and waiting with the cats. Instead he kicked the wall hard enough to hurt his toe and frighten the cats away. Then he went to a lunch counter, where he purchased two leaden potato knishes and a can of Pepsi, and walked home.

At his door, Karp realized immediately that someone had entered while he was gone. The deadbolt was open and he could smell cigarette smoke. He felt a jolt of fear. Someone had tried once to murder him in this apartment, and that incident returned to his mind in all its hideous detail. Perhaps Flanagan had told someone about what he had told Karp, and about the Q and A. And someone had sent a hitman? Who left the place stinking of smoke? Who didn't know enough to relock the door? No, it had to be some asshole snooper, one who didn't expect him home until much later.

167

In a rage Karp ran through to the bedroom and kicked the door open. He burst into the room, with his fist cocked back next to his ear. From the bed, where she was lying, reading a Barbara Cartland, Marlene Ciampi said, "Put down that knish, big boy, I'm harmless."

She giggled. So did Karp when he realized he was holding the uneaten pastry in his assault hand.

He let out a long breath and threw himself down full-length beside her. "My God, Marlene, I thought you were a prowler."

"Yeah, you forgot you gave me a key."

"True. I give out so many." He examined the knish. "Hell, I could have hurt you. This thing must weigh thirty pounds."

"Yes, and it has sharp edges too. Suppose you put it away and tell me how surprised and thrilled you are to see me, and then I might let you chew on my face for a minute."

When they came up for air, she asked, "Well, aren't you going to thank me?"

"Uh, that was the most marvelous kiss I ever had in my whole life."

"Not that, you goon. Oh, shit, you didn't even notice. Wait, put your hands on your eyes. Don't peek!"

He did as she asked and felt her leave the bed. In a moment there was a click and Mick Jagger burst into the room, singing about Jumping Jack Flash. "Ta-daaah!" she cried. "Surprise! Isn't it great?" She danced a few sexy steps, and Karp noticed that her legs were bare under her swirling full skirt. "I got it today. KLH speakers, Kenwood amp and tuner, sixty watts per channel. Dual Pioneer cassette deck. Leventhal even delivered. You won't believe how much."

"How much?" Karp asked, noticing the glowing stereo for the first time.

"A hundred-twenty even. The markup must be amazing. Anyway, what do you think?"

"Um, it's great, Marlene. Thanks, I'll give you a check."

"Oh, screw the check. I wanted to do something nice for you. A little civilized pleasure in your bleak life." She sat next to him on the bed again. "Come on, give a little! Doesn't it make your day?"

"Yeah," he said in a dull voice. "Really." He got off the bed and took off his tie and jacket. "I'm sorry, baby. I'm a little depressed. Bloom canned me today."

"Canned you? What do you mean, from the DA? He can do that?"

"No, not yet. Just from the deputy slot. I'm not your boss anymore. Just a plain ADA. But I think I need to start looking for a new job."

"But why? What the hell happened?"

Karp shrugged. "Some bullshit thing. I got into a fight with Wharton. We had words. It was about you, as a matter of fact."

"Oh?"

"Yeah, I asked him about your appeal and he said he was going to hold it up if I didn't—what was the phrase?—something about changing my emphasis, easing up. I guess I lost it. Called him a pimp."

Karp went over to his closet and changed into jeans and a gray sweatshirt. He sat down next to Marlene on the bed. She was sitting in its center, legs crossed, hunched over, her hair falling across her bad side like the wing of a shot crow. She was smoking hard. Karp took her hand and kissed it.

"So. What do you think of that? Want to turn on some hot music on my new stereo, maybe lose ourselves in fleshly delights?"

She said nothing. Her hand was like a fresh-killed chicken in his. He touched her shoulder and asked, "Marlene . . . what is it? What did I do?"

She drew a deep breath and swallowed hard. "Oh, nothing," she said at last. "It's just, I wish you would think for once. I keep hoping you'll think about something else besides your fucking cases."

"What are you talking about?"

"Me. I'm talking about me. My claim. Have you got any idea how fucked up I am financially? Or my family?" She looked up at him and with a brusque gesture swept her hair away from her scars and the black patch over the empty eye. "Do you know what this cost?"

"You had insurance . . ." Karp began lamely.

"Bullshit, insurance. You think the kind a coverage I had takes care of *this?* I had the fucking minimum. Why not? I'm young, healthy, I'm going to live forever, why spend the extra thirty-six forty a week, right? I had to go to my parents, Butch. My parents. They blew their savings. They took out a second mortgage, twelve per cent. My mother told me; my father, he'd kill her if he knew she did. He's sixty-four. He's a plumber. It's funny, I never told you that, and we've been going together two, three years.

"Butch, his back's fucked up. The plumber's disease, right? He was supposed to take it easy. Couple of years ago my brothers chipped in to send them down to Florida, Fort Lauderdale, after Christmas. Maybe start thinking about selling the house in Queens, get a condo or something. That's shot to hell now, isn't it?

"Last Tuesday my mom calls me up. She was crying on the phone. He's going out on jobs. He's lying on his back on wet

169

concrete, goosing pipes. He comes home white from the pain, can't even watch the news on TV. She's crying, but she doesn't say it, you know? When are they going to give with the money, Marlene? This isn't right."

"Marlene, I'm sorry, I really am. I didn't realize. But . . ."

"But what, Butch?"

"But what did you expect me to? What could I do?"

She swung her feet down off the bed on the side opposite him and started to feel around for her shoes. "I don't expect anything, Butch. They're not your parents, it's not your face."

"Come on, Marlene. Don't."

She stood up and turned around to face him. "Don't what? Don't be angry? I am angry. Goddamn angry!" She started to storm around the bedroom, tossing various possessions into her large leather shoulder bag.

Karp felt an unfamiliar kind of anger rising in him as well, anger compounded of self-contempt and guilt. "Where are you going?" he snapped.

She stood at the foot of the bed, hands on hips, chin thrust out, her face dark and furious. "Out. Home. I don't know. Away!"

"Fuck that! You're going to stay and work this out. I want to know first of all what you expected me to do. Say, 'Yes, Chip, anytime you want a killer sprung, hey, be glad to oblige. You got a little political problem, want to shit-can a good case? Give ol' Karp a call.' What did you want me do, Marlene? Lean over and yank his crank?"

"Yes! Yes, I did!" she cried out. "I expected you to lean a little, compromise, stroke the bastard, for chrissakes. There are a million ways you could wriggle out of any deal you made. What the fuck does it mean? Here's a flash, baby—you're not going to save the world in this job. You're not Gary Cooper, high noon has come and gone, and I'm sick of it. This crap about 'a man's got t' do whut a man's got t' do'—it's exhausting. It's murdering me—"

"How about you, huh?" Karp shouted. "Tell me you want to throw Karavitch. You want to ride out tomorrow and tell Bobbi Doyle that we're going to let the guys who blew her old man's head off walk away because it's inconvenient for some politicians if we bring them to trial, and besides, Marlene needs a new face!"

"Oh, fuck you, you bastard! You bastard! You don't care about Bobbi Doyle or my face or my family or me. You just care about you, you and your fucking pride. A fucking Jewish prince is all you are. Well, you can yank your own crank from now on, you bastard, because I am taking my little guinea ass out of here. Enjoy the music!"

With that, she grabbed her trenchcoat off the closet doorknob and made for the door. Karp reached for her arm, but she eluded him and went across the living room, her steps striking gunshots on the naked wood. He ran after her and threw his body in front of the outside door. Letting out a string of shrill curses, she tried to shove around him, but he grappled her, pulled her to his body, swaddled her struggling arms. Holding her close like that, he felt an unexpected and unwanted jolt of sexual energy. Embarrassed, he held her away from him at arm's length, holding her upper arms tightly. She promptly kicked him in the shin, hard.

He gasped, but did not let go. She kicked him again. Between gritted teeth he said, "Kick all you want, kid, but let me tell you something. Look at me, Marlene! They won, if we're doing this to each other. This is what they want. They don't want us to care about each other or love each other. I don't just mean you and me. I mean the whole team. They want us to hate and fuck each other over. That's what gives them their power. And that's all they're interested in.

"And about what you said. Yeah, I didn't think about you, and I should have. Big-time lawyer, I should know how to cut a deal, even with a scumbag like Wharton. But I didn't and I fucked myself and I fucked you too, and I'm sorry as hell about it. Now, let me make you a promise. I will get you the money. I don't know how yet, but I will get it. Not just because I love you and you're you, but because it's right.

"As for Wharton, it's open war now. He's going to play hard-ball, I can play hardball too. We got a thing going I think will settle his hash for good."

"What thing?" Marlene asked suspiciously.

"I'll tell you later, providing we're still compadres." Karp released her shoulders and stood away from the door. "If you still want to go, you can," he said, his gut twisted in a knot.

She didn't go. Instead she leaned against the door post and began to cry, silently as she had done so often in the ladies' room. Her tears smeared her eye makeup around her good eye so that it looked like she wore two patches. After a while she stopped, exhausted. Karp scooped her up in his arms and brought her to the bed. She curled up on her side. In a small voice she said, "I'm sorry. I'm crazy." Karp was silent. He unfolded a blanket from the foot of the bed and threw it over her. In a few minutes she was asleep. Karp turned down the volume on the stereo and lay down beside her without undressing, but it took a long, long time before he too blacked out.

When Karp awakened he was alone. It was early morning. His

shirt was unbuttoned and his jeans were lying crumpled at the foot of the bed. Sometime during the night he had come out of sleep to feel Marlene's mouth on his face and neck, then her hands running over his body, caressing him and pulling off his clothes, and then her mouth again, tongue and teeth, moving slowly down the length of his body. He had lain there utterly passive, the way he knew she wanted him to be just then, and watched by the dim light of the stereo dial the ever fascinating sight of her dark head over his groin, moving slowly up and down, up and down.

Or perhaps it had been a dream. He checked himself out in the bathroom mirror, saw the marks all over him, and smiled. There was a note stuck in the ceramic toothbrush holder. "Sorry about all that last nite," it said in Marlene's neat script, "I believe you. Gone to see Taylor's Yugos re: Karavitch—in around noon. Crazy bout you (so to speak) M."

The note brought the events of the previous day slamming back into his mind. His smile faded. He sat down on the bed, picked up the phone, and dialed Denton's office. He identified himself as Roger Karp from the DA's. His office informed him that the chief was on his way to work and forwarded the call to his car phone.

"What's up?"

"All kinds of shit," answered Karp, "but I'm not sure I want to talk about it over a car phone."

"It's that bad, huh? OK, tell you what—I'll swing by your place in ten minutes. We can talk there."

When Denton arrived, Karp had showered, shaved, and dressed for work. The detective looked around the living room with a bleak eye and said, "Karp, I can't stand this. I'm going to drag you down to Goodwill and get you some furniture."

"I got a stereo."

"Great, I'll squat on the record player. Very relaxing. OK, what've you got?"

Briefly, Karp went over the events of the previous day. When he had finished, Denton pursed his lips, puffed his cheeks, and blew out a stream of air. He looked down at the immaculate tips of his brown Italian shoes. "Well, well," he said. "A fancy piece of work. You really think the Church, the CIA, and the FBI are conspiring to queer our little case?"

Karp shrugged. "Yeah, a hair too paranoid, isn't it? I forgot to tell you, I'm also picking up broadcasts from Venus through my fillings." Denton hesitated a bit before acknowledging the remark with a thin smile and a short laugh. He should have been here last week, Karp thought as he continued: "But basically, I don't think it's a real conspiracy. It's more like these Croatians were connected across a number of different scams, buried stuff, some of it pretty deep in the past. Nobody expected this hijack, nobody expected a cop would be killed. But it goes down, and a bunch of people are running around in a panic, doing dumb things, but independently. And I don't think institutions are involved as much as individuals or groups of individuals acting for themselves."

Denton raised his eyebrows. "That's interesting. Why do you say that?"

"Um, just a feeling right now. Look, if the Church or the FBI, as institutions, had a serious beef with us on this, if it was something attached to the case that was, ah, innocently embarrassing, let's say, there's a zillion ways we could accommodate them. Christ, we're not morons, we do it every day. They'd come in for meetings, we'd discuss it, horse trade a little, and come to some agreement. But the various parties in this mess don't want to come out in the open with their problems. They prefer to work in secret and do crimes to prevent these guys from coming to trial—suppression of evidence, arson, kidnapping . . . by the way, is there anything on our Hungarian waiter witness yet?"

"Koltan? No, we're still looking. You think these Cubans snatched him?"

"It's a possibility. There could be a murder, another murder, connected with it too."

"What, the boyfriend?"

"Yeah, Sorriendas. I read the Q and A that Guma got off Melendez last night. I'll send you a copy. According to her, Sorriendas was real nervous the last few days before he got it, drinking heavily, raving. From what she gathered, Ruiz was setting up to whack somebody out and the boyfriend didn't want any part of it."

"Did he say who?"

"No, just that it was somebody *muy importante* and that it would bring a lot of heat down. Sorriendas figured, and he was probably right, that he was set to take the fall if it did. She thinks, and I think, that he was ready to spill his guts and Ruiz aced him to prevent it."

"Who do you like for the target?"

"Karavitch and company, who else? It's sure as hell a good way to stop them from coming to trial, and I have an idea that whatever it is that lots of people don't want to come out is sitting inside the heads of our defendants." Karp paused for a moment. "Bill, I don't like them in Riker's."

"Yeah, me neither. OK, this is today's agenda. First thing, we hit Ruiz and round up him and his merry band. Then, in case we haven't got them all, or in case one of the other players gets the same idea, I'm going to move the bunch of them. You remember the place in The Bronx where we stashed Frank Siggi and his wife last year?"

"The place on Mt. Vernon Avenue? Yeah. I like it. But what if I need access to them?"

"What's your mother's maiden name?"

"Gimmel. Why?"

"I'm going to tell my guys to release the prisoners only to you or Brenner personally. If you have to call, identify yourself as 'Roger Gimmel Karp.' "

"Roger Gimmel Karp, a name to conjure with," Karp said. "I can't believe we're doing this, Bill. It's a movie! I'm expecting to hear the director yell, 'Cut!' "

Denton shook his head. "It's a pisser, all right. But I can piss, too. I know a guy in FBI headquarters, works for the Assistant Director, Investigations. We'll see if we can put Elmer Pillman through some hoops. As for the DA, that's touchy. I'd give a lot to know what Bloom's end of this looks like."

"Probably not much. Terry Doyle is just a number or part of a political chip he's playing. Bloom's most likely doing a favor for somebody he thinks might help him out someday, or some guy he owes a favor to." Karp imitated Bloom's fruity voice: "Sure, Jim, no problem, we'll take care of it. Regards to the family."

Denton chuckled at this and Karp went on. "The critical question is the motivation of the other players. The cops? Simple, cops follow orders, and not only orders. They follow hints, raised eyebrows, grunts, especially if they want to make captain at forty. The CIA? Who knows, except what I said before. It's probably personal and not institutional. I'd really like to have half an hour in a small room with this guy Dettrick."

"What about the Arch?" asked Denton. There was concern in his voice. Superchiefs are politicians, and in New York politicians do not lightly take on the archbishop or his works.

"Same thing, a private scam that went slightly off. Maybe our boy Karavitch did something naughty in 1943 and they knew about it and vouched for him anyway. If they can fix it for twenty K and a little discreet pressure, fine."

Denton snorted and glanced at his watch. "Anything else, Butch? I haven't stood up this long without a drink in my hand since I walked a beat in the old two-seven."

"Bill, I love it when you pretend to be a crusty old harness bull at heart. Yeah, there is one thing that bugs the hell out of me. Here's Karavitch, old guy, sitting pretty in the U.S., a citizen, got a hot young wife, a reasonable income. Why in the world does someone like that decide to pull a crazy stunt like he did, steal a plane, leave bombs around? I can't figure it. And if I can't figure it, the defense will set it up so that the jury can't figure it, either. And you know juries. If they don't buy the story, as a story, who knows what they'll do?"

Denton considered this for a moment and answered, "I take your point. I don't know what was going on in Karavitch's mind, but I've known a lot of murderers. Besides the crimes of passion and the real loonies, every mother's son of them killed for one or more of the classic big three."

"Love, money, or revenge."

"You got it, son. My next paycheck says our boy was on one of those. I'd check his finances. And I'd check his hot young wife."

"Yeah, you're probably right. You know with all the political bullshit around this case, the basics tend to get lost—motive, means, opportunity, and all that. Shit! I just remembered something. Listen, Bill, can you drop me at Centre Street? If they haven't bricked up my office yet, I think I got an angle."

Riding downtown in a cab, with her underwear stuffed in her bag and still squishy from the night's exertions, Marlene felt like the Whore of Babylon. The driver, a dark, skinny youngster, kept eyeing her in the rearview. She pulled back her hair and said, "I have one eye, see?" He cleared his throat and pretended not to hear her, but he also stopped looking.

Half an hour later, bathed and dressed in a nubbly dark gray silk suit and a frilly blouse, she felt slightly better, and when Peter Gregorievitch pulled up in his blue Ford, she was able to muster a bright smile. The old man was the only person in Marlene's experience who habitually left the driver's side of the car to open and close the door for his passenger, like a chauffeur in a movie. But you could see by his eyes and the way he carried his thin body that he was no servant.

They drove through the early morning traffic in silence. Peter Gregorievitch was not a talker. This was her third such trip with him without a word spoken. At the meetings to which he had delivered her, Taylor and Renko Span did the talking.

He drove her to a tan five-story house on Tenth near St. Mark's Place. As he drove off to look for a parking space, she entered the building, pushed a button, and was buzzed through the street door. This building, unlike most of the others on the block, lacked the stigmata of vandalism. The mailboxes were intact and shining. The hallways were odorless except for the must of old paint and steam heat. Peter Gregorievitch was the superintendent of this building.

The man who opened the door of 326 looked like a taller Nikita Khrushchev with more warts. "Ah, Marlene," he cried, flinging his arms wide in a dramatic gesture of welcome. "So good of you to come again." He ushered her into the apartment with a bow. "Our friend Goddy is here, as you see. And Peter is . . . ?"

"Parking the car. Hello, Goddy." G.F.S. Taylor was sitting at a round table covered by a pale, striped cloth decorated with peasant embroidery. When he saw Marlene, he rose and took her extended hand. "Delighted, as always."

They all sat down. Span poured strong, thick coffee and served a sticky, baklava-like pastry. Marlene ate three pieces as pleasantries were exchanged. Peter Gregorievitch soon knocked and joined them at the table. After a while the coffee cups and dishes were cleared away.

Taylor had told her beforehand, "It may take some time for these men to trust you. They are not trusting sorts." The first interview had been stiffly formal. Marlene had talked about her family and her work; Span and Taylor had exchanged anecdotes about Yugoslavians and Englishmen. The second meeting had been easier; they had brought out the slivovitz and had become mildly drunk. The conversation had turned darker: Taylor and Span had talked about the war and Marlene had repeated for the benefit of the two Yugoslavs the story of her maiming.

Now Renko smiled at her during one of the lapses in the small talk. His small, dark eyes had a look of intelligent appraisal that belied his manner as genial host. "Marlene, how nice it is for old men like us to have the company of a delightful young woman. This does not happen often, so we ask ourselves, Peter and I, why is it we have the pleasure of your company? You come with our old comrade Goddy, so we know that you do not mean us any harm, not that there is much you could do to us. Of course, there are those who would like to harm us if they could."

"You mean the communists?" she asked.

"Pah! We are communists, Peter and I. In Yugoslavia there are left only social fascists, and those jailed or dead. My dear girl, those who are driven in limousines and have hunting lodges and palaces are not communists.

"However, you must understand that there are groups over here who do not wish for the survival of Yugoslavia, communist or capitalist. Peter and I are Yugoslavs first, you understand? People know us, here and in Europe and in our homeland. You should know that there are people who would like to make anticommunism an ally in their fight against Yugoslavia. The existence of people such as Peter and I, who love Yugoslavia and oppose the regime is—how should I say it?—inconvenient. So, my dear lady, you will forgive us if we are suspicious. Of course, this may be but the imaginings of old men who still believe they are important enough to harm."

He hunched his shoulders and shifted his eyes, hamming a man on the run, and then laughed. Marlene and Taylor joined him, and then Marlene said, "Renko, look, what do I know about all this political stuff? I'm a kid from Queens, you know? Vote straight Democratic, always have. But Goddy said you might be able to help me out. Why kid around—you got to know why I'm here. I got a dead cop, killed with a Russian weapon hooked to a booby trap Goddy says came from World War Two. It's not your usual man bops old lady with closest available object. I'm lost here. Any way you can steer me on Karavitch or his gang, where they got the stuff, their motivation, anything, I'd be grateful. If not, hey, it's not a total loss. I learned how to drink slivovitz."

Renko Span cocked an eyebrow and shot a meaningful look across the table at Taylor. To Marlene he said, "Ah, Marya, you are so frank, you put us old conspirators to shame. Okey-doke. I speak to you straight out. You must hear a story—no, two stories. The first story, it happens in 1944 in the winter. The Nazis and their allies are retreating from Yugoslavia. The Soviets are threatening to cut off their retreat, and so they are moving north and west as fast as they can run. They know they are whipped, but like dogs they seek to destroy what they cannot hold. We partisans, of course, are harassing them always, and from time to time fighting pitched battles, which we now have the strength to do. I am captain of a unit operating in the Vojvodina.

"One day we are moving along a road through a forest. Suddenly we hear voices, a baby crying. People come out of the forest. They are Serbs, and also some Jews, from a village nearby, very ragged and hungry. Peter, tell me, what was the name of that village?"

"Vrcevo," said Gregorievitch around his pipe.

"Vrcevo. Yes, of course. Well, the people told us that the day before this they had heard that Germans were approaching. How many Germans? we ask. Thousands, we hear.

"This is always the answer—'thousands.' So I send some of my boys into the village to scout. Soon they return—it is deserted, unharmed. This is strange, but we don't complain so much because we have been fighting hard, we have wounded, and it will be good to sleep in a house for a change. Or even a barn. So we go with the villagers down to their village.

"We settle in. The villagers go about their tasks. All is quiet for five, ten minutes. Then boom, boom—explosions from the houses, fires, screams. I think, mortar barrage, but there are no shells screaming through the air. Then I think, booby traps.

"So it was. The Germans had placed booby-trapped explosives through the whole village. We found out later that it was a unit of the Thirteenth SS Division. At the time we wondered why they had expended so much effort on one small village, and later we learned that the Germans were conducting a training exercise, showing troops from different parts of their army skills that would be useful for slowing down the Russians during the retreat into Hungary. Of course, they used a real village. Two of our men and seven villagers were killed and many wounded.

"I sent a messenger to battalion headquarters for engineers. The weather was turning bad, and these people had no shelter and no way to prepare the little food they had saved. We had to clear the traps from the village. So that afternoon, comes three men. They go through every house, the church, barns, every place. They find, oh, perhaps twenty, thirty bombs, mostly antitank mines and artillery shells. These were hooked to detonators that they connected to different things people would use—a stove door, a cupboard, even stairs. Very clever this all was.

"But we think by evening we have outsmarted them. Our men began to unhook the trip wires and remove the detonators. We start to move the explosives to a shed, because we wish to use them. Then, boom, boom, boom! The bombs we thought were safe explode."

"Dozies, right?" asked Marlene, excited. "The Germans had the booby traps rigged with the same kind of time-delay fuse that killed Terry Doyle."

Taylor grinned. "They had indeed."

"And you were one of the three engineers, right? Which is why I'm here. OK, the Germans used Dozies in Yugoslavia. What's the connection with our guys? Or is there . . . ?"

"There is another story, which is not mine to tell." Renko Span nodded at Peter Gregorievitch.

The others waited while Gregorievitch fiddled with his pipe and made rumbling sounds in his chest, as if all his words were buried there under a cover of ancient debris. When he began, he spoke slowly and distinctly, pausing from time to time to run his hand over the gray bristles of his head. "This was in Krushak, which is on the road to Senta, in the north. It was eight days after Vrcevo.

"We were camped. A boy comes to us, nine or ten. He says, 'Come, please, everyone is dead in my village.' So we go down. It is true. They have killed the whole village. We can tell it is *ustashi* who have done it, because of the women." Here he paused, rubbing his head, seemingly stunned by the grisly memory.

"What does he mean *ustashi,* and what about the women?" Marlene asked Taylor in a low voice.

"The *ustashi* were irregular troops of the Croatian fascist regime," Taylor answered.

Gregorievitch resumed. "The women were all piled in a heap in the Orthodox church, naked. They had all been murdered, some in a horrible way. Impaled, but not as a man is impaled. Also, we found the pregnant ones, those that showed, they slit their bellies open. Always this was done, I cannot understand why—to kill a woman and an innocent baby before it is even born. We found the men, mostly old men and children, in a shallow trench nearby. They had all been shot. I have seen many bad things in the wartime, but this was the most bad thing, in Krushak.

"The boy with us had escaped by hiding under a chicken coop. But he saw it all. These were *ustashi,* he said, but there were also German soldiers. From his description of their uniforms and insignia we knew they were Prinz Eugen."

"That's the Thirteenth SS Division again," Taylor said. "These were two companies en route to link up with the main body of the division at Senta, and creating havoc as they went."

"So," Gregorievitch went on, "we went back to our commander and told him what had happened, and he decided our battalion should set an ambush for these Nazis and their friends. We marched like madmen through rough country to get in front of where we knew they had to pass, in a place where the road twists around three hills. We killed many of the SS, but some escaped. They were well armed and fought like wolves. We killed all the *ustashi* except for three. Two escaped with the SS. We saw them drive away in a half-track, too fast for us to follow. The third we captured. I will not say what we did to him, but I think in the end he told us the truth. He said that the leader of the *ustashi,* one of the two who escaped, was Djordje Karavitch."

"My God!" Marlene said in a breathless voice. "That's how he picked up the Dozy. Damn it, Renko, this guy's a war criminal—why wasn't he turned in?"

Renko smiled wanly. "He was many times. But always nothing was done. Who knows why? Perhaps he has friends who protect him. Perhaps the government here thinks he is a great anticommunist patriot persecuted by the regime in Yugoslavia. Emigré politics are complicated, my dear."

"How did he get out of Yugoslavia anyway?"

179

"Oh, that is easy. There was such confusion at the end of the war. We made a search for him, you can be sure, because of Krushak. Peter, would you get the poster?"

Gregorievitch rose stiffly from the table and left the room, returning in a few moments with a large, soiled brown envelope. From it he took a yellowing sheet of paper protected by tape and clear plastic food wrap. He laid it on the table. Marlene saw a poorly printed photograph of a young man in a black uniform, with light hair and light eyes, a strong nose, and an air of serious purpose. Seated at a desk, he had a pen in his left hand as if he were about to sign a document. Behind him in the photograph was a large poster marked with the backward-seeming letters of the Cyrillic alphabet, showing a handsome soldier in a Nazi uniform bayoneting a monstrous soldier marked with a hammer and sickle. There was Cyrillic and Latin text above and below the photograph, and Marlene could pick up the name "Karavic" in the latter.

"Wanted dead or alive, huh? Look, Renko, this is terrific. I'd consider it a great favor if you'd let me borrow this for a day to make copies."

Renko smiled. "Of course you may. Obviously, the case you have is interesting to us. We would like to see this man brought to justice even after so many years."

After that, despite the early hour he brought out a tray with a dusty bottle and four small crystal glasses. They all tossed molten plum brandy back in their throats and said, *"U nasdravi j'e!"*

As Marlene and Taylor were leaving, Span clutched her sleeve and spoke so that only she could hear. "Marlene, this man, he will be in prison a long time?"

"Karavitch? Yeah, if we nail him on the murder charge."

"If? There is some doubt that he did this?"

"Not in my mind, but you can never tell what will happen in the mind of a jury. And there can't be, as we say, a shadow of a doubt, or the guy walks."

Renko clutched harder, and Marlene, looking at him in surprise, saw that his normally genial face was contorted with sorrow and worry. "This must not happen!" he said in a hoarse whisper.

"Sure, Renko, but, hey, what's wrong?"

"If this man is walking the streets now, Peter will find him and kill him. Do you understand? Since the plane and the pictures in the newspapers and the TV, he has thought of nothing else. So . . ."

Marlene disentangled herself and patted his arm. "Renko, we'll do our best" was all she could say. He nodded. Then he asked,

"How could I lose Peter Gregorievitch after all these years? Who else would I talk to?"

In the street outside, she turned to Taylor and said, "I'm glad you took me there. Those are great old guys. Oh, sorry—I didn't mean—oh, hell."

Taylor laughed. "Yes, age is an insult in the U.S., isn't it? What a peculiar people you are! Sometimes I forget and think I'm at home, and then all of a sudden it's like bloody Timbuktu. Yes, they're very decent old chaps. They don't talk to everyone, you know. You have a way of bowling people over, I think. Quite charming in its way."

"Thank you for that too," said Marlene, smiling. "Oh, yeah, I almost forgot. A couple of other things. One, the Soviet grenade—where did they get it? Two, about Karavitch coming out of the woodwork after all these years. You would think that with his background, he'd want to keep the lowest possible profile. Any ideas?"

"Only vague ones. There's someone who might be able to help you more, and I think I can get you in to see him, if you're game. Name's Dushan."

"Another Yugoslav?"

"Yes, but one of a rather different cut."

"How so?" asked Marlene.

Taylor looked around and inhaled the peppery fumes of St. Mark's Place sharply through his mustache. "Well, to begin with, he's a spy."

15

KARP LOOKED OUT the car window at the gusts of sleet and the frozen working classes while Denton did business on his phone. An unseasonable blizzard had dumped almost two feet of snow on New England, and Fun City was bracing for an imminent transformation into a hellish, snarled winter wonderland. Karp was not looking forward to facing his former staff; worse would be the various degradation rituals that Wharton had no doubt cooked up.

On entering his office, he found two symbols of his demotion already waiting in his box. One was a thick stack of case files. He was no longer excused from feeding the insatiable maw of the Criminal Courts Bureau and would have to prosecute these this morning with about two hours of preparation. The other was a brief note from a man named Harvey T. Arnoldson announcing that he was the new Deputy Bureau Chief. Could Karp arrange to visit him at his convenience?

Karp decided to get it over with. It was an uncomfortable meeting on both sides. Arnoldson was about fifty, with long graying hair and the kind of sideburns that had gone out of fashion in 1970 for everyone but truckers. He had been doing solid but undistinguished work in the Frauds Bureau since he had passed the bar exams and had been as surprised as anyone when the promotion was dumped in his lap. He was careful and slow and followed orders, which was why he had gotten it.

They exchanged pleasantries and agreed that it was an uncomfortable situation. Arnoldson said Karp did not have to hurry about moving his office. Karp thanked him. Arnoldson said he expected a weekly report from all of his attorneys and expected them to make their numbers. Karp said he would so report and would try his best on the numbers. More pleasantries. Good-bye.

Karp was not particularly concerned any longer about being fired or about having to report to Bloom's babysitter. Either everything would be changed within weeks, or he would be on the street. Meanwhile, he had to blaze through the morning's cases and then follow up on his angle.

He had remembered something Marlene had said about Mrs. Karavitch and one of the others. He thumbed through the Q and A transcripts and found the right section: the flight attendant, Daphne West, had observed Cindy Karavitch going into the can with Pavle Macek, presumably for some in-flight service, while her hubby was schmoozing in first class. Had Karavitch known? Was the hijack connected in some way to the ancient comedy of an old man betrayed by a young wife? Not enough information yet, he thought, but the existence of a love triangle was a crack in the solidarity of the group into which he could insert the thin edge of a wrecking bar.

If the district attorney's ministers had thought that they could wear Karp down by piling on cases, they had misjudged their man. Br'er Rabbit was back in the briar patch. Court work was a tonic after the wrangling tedium of bureaucracy, and by three o'clock, when his last appearance concluded, he was juiced up and happier than he had been in months.

When he got back to his office, the first thing he saw was a big sheet of computer paper pinned to the wall above his desk. On it someone had drawn a cartoon of an unnaturally tall Karp playing basketball with a squat figure who could be identified as Conrad Wharton by the large corncob emerging from his rear. The iconography was simple: Wharton was tripping him under the basket, but he was still making the shot. It had been signed by virtually every member of the Criminal Courts staff, and most had written messages of support and encouragement.

Karp stared at it for a long while, chuckling and grinning like a maniac. Then he noticed a manila envelope taped to the wall, so it would not be lost among the drift of paper on his desk. It was from Marlene. In telegraphic phrases she summarized what she had learned that morning and said she would try to nab him that afternoon. She closed with a lewd suggestion that warmed him from his heart on down. Included in the envelope was a copy of the wanted poster from Renko Span.

He studied the face on the poster. It was remarkable even through the heavy grain of the photograph: the long, predatory nose, the wide mouth with its corners slightly raised to indulge the photographer, the broad, intelligent forehead with the light hair slicked straight back. The pale eyes looked straight into the camera and conveyed intensity of feeling and a certain grim seriousness. A righteous reformer, Karp thought, not a machine guy. This guy wouldn't make deals.

Something didn't jibe. There had been a cynical, mocking cleverness about the man he had questioned that did not fit with the face before him. This guy in the photo looked tough, but he believed in something. Karp had considerable experience in sizing up bad guys, and he had figured the man in the FBI interrogation room for a serious criminal, the kind that believes in nothing but himself and his ability to outsmart the world. Of course, he thought, people change in thirty years. And the face was a good match—the nose and eyes were unmistakable. This was Djordje Karavitch in his salad days. Karp realized with a bit of a shock that the picture had been taken when Karavitch was about thirty-three, about the same age as Karp himself. He shuddered. He did not want to think about the future just now. He pinned the poster above his desk.

An hour later, as he was plowing through the preparation of the next day's cases—calling witnesses, arranging for police officers to appear, scratching notes on yellow paper—Connie Trask buzzed him to say that Fred Slocum needed to talk to him right away.

"Butch?" said the detective, speaking loud to make his voice heard above the buzz of noise in his office. "We went into Tel-Air about an hour ago."

"Yeah? How'd it go? You get Ruiz?"

"We got zilch. Denton laid on a big operation, stealers from half the precincts in Queens, tacticals, machine guns, mortars, tanks. But the place was cleaned out. Nobody there but an old watchman, he hasn't seen anybody since Wednesday. Ruiz has a big place in Forest Hills and we hit that too. Also zilch. He's running."

"Crap! The bastards were tipped."

"Probably," Slocum agreed. "I tell you, though, we stirred up a hornet's nest out there. There was a bunch of *federales* on stakeout in a couple of vans around Tel-Air and they went crazy. Queens detectives wasn't thrilled, either, but Denton was running the show so they had to smile and eat it. Lots of dire threats, though, from the Feds."

"I'm trembling."

Slocum laughed. "I'm sure. We'll find them, though. Denton's got an army working the case. The guys thought it was a little weird, the C. of D. putting the max on for a shitty case like this—a skel gets knifed, who gives a rat's ass?"

"It's more complicated than that, Fred."

"I figured. When you get around to it, the foot soldiers would appreciate you sharing the details."

Karp ignored this last remark. He had just thought of something. "Fred," he said, "what's the situation with the physical evidence in Karavitch? From his place. What've you got and where is it?"

184

"Uh, there ain't much, maybe half a carton of stuff. We got some papers from Karavitch's place, a calendar marked with the dinner they all had before they took off, a receipt for the plane tickets—like that. It's stuff that ties them to Croat political bullshit and the flight, but shit, we know they're crackpots and we know they were on the flight. On the bomb, we're thin. We went over Macek's repair shop and the super's shops in all the buildings that Karavitch managed, figuring maybe they built the bomb in one of those places. Forensic found some wire and some insulation in Macek's shop that matched up with the bomb fragments, but what the hell, one piece of wire looks like another piece of wire. They found some brick dust too, in the same place."

"Brick dust, huh? Does it match?"

" 'Not inconsistent with the samples found at the crime scene and in the body of the deceased.' You know how Forensic is. But same difference—brick dust ain't fingerprints."

"Fingerprints ain't fingerprints, if it comes to that. But what do you think? Macek built the thing in his repair shop, right?"

"Sounds like it to me, but try to prove it."

"I'm not sure I'll have to. You didn't find any explosives, huh?"

"Not a trace."

"That figures. Where's the stuff now?"

"I threw it all in an old carton I picked up in Macek's shop. I got it here."

"Great, Fred—look, do me a favor. Could you drag that carton down here? I want to take a look at it."

After Slocum had dropped the carton off, Karp examined each of the plastic envelopes. As Slocum had said, it was not much, some small tools, assorted debris, and a stack of papers, all in a small, open corrugated carton that still had bits of Styrofoam excelsior from the original packing. But he hadn't planned to learn much by inspecting himself. Picking up the phone, he called Marino at Rodman Neck and then Doug Brenner for a ride.

Jamaica Bay looked like the North Sea by the time they got to the police range at Rodman Neck. The sun was obscured by clouds the color of dirty sidewalks, and the wind off the bay shot through Karp's raincoat, pierced his body, and flew out the other side. His knee ached and he almost limped as he climbed the stairs into Marino's building.

The bomb squad captain was waiting for him with another man, whom he introduced as Sergeant Dalker, the officer in charge of the bomb-sniffing dog unit, also housed at Rodman. Dalker, a thin man with a fox-like face, was holding a German shepherd on a short leash. The dog's name was Rosie. As he spoke briefly about the capabilities of such animals, Karp noticed that he had the odd habit of asking the dog for concurrence whenever he made a statement about her.

Karp explained what he wanted and they set up the plastic bags, opened, in a row on the floor. Dalker led Rosie along the row. When she got to the seventh bag, she made a whimpering noise deep in her throat.

"Is that something?" Karp asked.

"Could be," said Dalker, squatting down next to the dog's head. "What is it, Rosie? You smell something?" In the bag was a hacksaw. Dalker looked over his shoulder at the other two men. "It's possible that the saw was used on or near some explosives, maybe to saw through a dynamite stick, or more likely, somebody with explosives on his hands used the tool. But the trace is faint and Rosie's not sure, are you, Rosie?"

The dog drew a blank on the other bags. In vain they went through the routine two more times with the bags in different order. Karp looked at Dalker, who shrugged and waggled his hand from side to side. Karp sighed and said, "OK, guys, thanks, it was worth a shot." He put the carton down on the floor, and he and Brenner started sealing the bags and tossing them in.

Then Rosie barked and lunged forward and started to claw at the sides of the carton. Karp stumbled backward out of her way, startled. "What's that all about?" he asked. "Rosie changed her mind?"

"No," Dalker said, "it's the damn carton." Unloading it swiftly, they placed it in the center of the floor. The dog stuck her nose in it, shook it with her teeth, whined, wagged her tail, and did all the other things that explosive-sniffing dogs do when they find explosives. "There was high explosive packed in that carton for quite a while," Dalker said. "Right, Rosie? Wasn't there?"

As Dalker talked sweetly to his dog, Marino said, "Butch, most explosives will volatilize over time. If they're packed in something absorbent like cardboard or this styro, the packing absorbs some of the vapors, and naturally that's what the dog smells."

But Karp was hardly listening. He was staring at the top flaps of the carton. They had been hanging down on the outside, probably since Slocum had picked it up casually in Macek's repair room, so that nobody had noticed the top of the carton when it was closed. Rosie's prodding nose had lifted it and exposed the outside of the flap.

On it was a glossy, neatly typed label addressed to P. Macek at his shop. Though it was much covered by dust and grease, Karp had no trouble reading the fat red letters of the Tel-Air logo printed across the top.

"Doug, this evidence we got here, I want you to bury it," Karp said an hour later as the two of them sat in the car outside the dark mass of the Criminal Courts Building. "Take it someplace and hide it. And I don't want anybody but you, me, and the Chief of D. knowing where it is."

"Yeah, I'll hide it in my kid's closet. You want me to drop you home or you going in?"

"No, you go home," Karp said, sliding out of the car, "I got some calls to make and I'm supposed to meet up with Marlene later."

In his office, Karp found that the person he most wanted to call also wanted to call him, and pretty badly, it appeared. His secretary was gone for the day, but while he had been out she had plastered the back of his chair with taped-on pink phone message slips marked "URGENT," all from Elmer Pillman of the FBI.

They made him wait a full three minutes on hold, with no Muzak, just to put him in his place. When Pillman got on, he came right to the point. "You asshole! Do you realize what you've done? Do you realize how much work you just blew to hell today?"

"Why, Elmer, what are you talking about?" Karp asked mildly.

"Don't play dumb with me, you shithead!" Pillman roared. Karp could feel the scowl through the phone lines and moved the receiver a few inches away from his ear. Pillman sounded like a tiny man shouting into a bucket: "The fuck-up you pulled out at Tel-Air. Six months of work. The DEA, the ATF, the Bureau, even your own goddamn Queens narco! And you trash the whole thing because you think, you *think*, there's a connection with some goddamn spic knifing."

"Tel-Air? Elmer, what makes you think I had anything to do with going into Tel-Air?"

Silence. Then a bellow of rage. "What? I'll tell you what, asshole! I just talked to your boss, the DA. *He* fingered you. How do you like that, jerk-off?"

"Gosh, if he said that, then Mr. Bloom is sadly misinformed. I'm just an ordinary New York County ADA, Elmer. I don't command squadrons of men in Queens County like you do. As I understand it, that operation was set up by Chief Denton personally. Maybe you should talk to him, since you're so upset. Wait a second, I'll get you his number."

"I've got his goddamn number!"

187

"Oh, yeah, how silly of me. You're the liaison between the Feds and the NYPD. My, my, I bet your colleagues are pissed at you, Elmer. I bet they're blaming you for the mixup."

"Karp, you motherfucker, I swear to God I'll get you. You'll wish you never were born before I'm through with you. If you think you can fuck with the Bureau and get away with it, you—"

"But I'm not fucking with the Bureau, am I, Elmer," Karp broke in, his voice grown hard. "The Bureau has nothing to do with it. This is your show. It's a solo all the way. So I'm only fucking with you. You see, Elmer, I know about you and Ruiz, and I know why you've been trying to queer my case against Karavitch and his little gang. It took me awhile, but I finally found out. Good-bye, Elmer."

Karp hung up and looked at the sweep hand on his watch. In less than fifteen seconds the phone rang. Karp picked it up and said gently, "Yes, Elmer? More talkies?"

"I didn't like what you just implied," Pillman said lamely.

"You didn't? What a sensitive nature. I wouldn't have thought it, considering how you're always screaming at people and calling them bad names."

"Cut the bullshit, Karp. We need to talk and not over the phone. How soon can you get up here?"

"Never is how soon, Elmer. I'll be in my office for another hour. If you'd care to stop by, I'll see if I can squeeze you in." Karp hung up and quickly dialed a Massachusetts number. A pleasant female voice answered, and Karp asked to speak to V.T. Newbury.

"Well, well, how fortunate," said V.T. when he got on the line. "I'd been meaning to get in touch with you all day. What happened? Is the despicable Ruiz in custody?"

"Afraid not. I think somebody tipped him, and he's on the run. But that's sort of what I needed to talk to you about. We found out that the Ruiz operation supplied the grenade that blew up Doyle."

"Ah-ha! The missing link. How did you find that out?"

"Tell you later. Right now I probably got Pillman coming over here in ten minutes. I just told him I know all about him and Ruiz and why he's trying to bag Karavitch et al., and he's going to pump me to find out if I'm bluffing."

"And are you?"

"For shit's sake, V.T., of course I am. All I know for sure is the grenade connection; beyond that it's Blank City. That's why I'm calling you. You're into all this conspiracy jazz. I need some ideas, and fast."

"I'm flattered. OK, let me think." For what seemed like an

endless interval, Karp sat with the earpiece growing sweaty around his ear and listened to V.T.'s breathing and the tuneless whistle he always made between his teeth when he was deep in thought. Finally he came back to earth. "Right. Let's start with the two facts we know for sure: one, Pillman is trying to queer the case, and two, Ruiz supplied the bomb. Now, the strange thing about these two facts is that they don't fit together."

"What do you mean?"

"Because there is no way that Pillman would have authorized, or allowed, or paid for, Ruiz giving explosives to Karavitch's group. It's off the charts."

"Why?"

"Because whatever else he is, Pillman has been an FBI agent for over twenty years. He may be corrupt, but I can't conceive of any FBI agent abetting domestic violence for any reason."

"What if somebody is blackmailing him? Ruiz, maybe."

"Still no go. And for another reason. As they used to ask us in law school, who benefits? Why should Ruiz want to give grenades to the Croats or help them out with a little thuggery? For Pillman? No way, because why would Pillman want to help the Croats? It doesn't make sense—it's circular. The Cubans must have been mobilized by somebody else. From Ruiz's point of view, slipping a grenade or two to somebody or breaking a few heads is merely a sideline, something he'd do practically as a favor for whoever is making his operation possible. But it's not Pillman. You don't know the guy the way I do, Butch. This is a bureaucrat, not an entrepreneur. The only critical question is why Pillman is shielding Ruiz.

"Now let's add another fact. Before he came to New York as deputy, Pillman was stationed in Miami, where he helped to break up a group called SOBA. This was a bunch of militant right-wing Cubans who were planting bombs on people they didn't think were sufficiently anti-Castro. A very classy piece of work, by the way, and Pillman got a lot of credit for it. This was in, like, '68 or '70. I'm pretty sure Ruiz was there around then too, and he was tight with a lot of former Batistianos. Pillman could have used him as an informant maybe a provocateur, maybe skirting the edges of legality."

"V.T., damn it, why didn't you tell me this stuff before?"

"Because I was thinking CIA, not FBI. They're in two separate, noncommunicating compartments of my brain, as they are in real life. You remember, we were going to use the possible CIA link with Ruiz to beat up on Pillman. But what if there's a much closer link? What if somebody's beating him up from the other side?"

"How do you mean?"

"Say it's like this. A connection is created between Karavitch and the Cubans. Pillman doesn't know about it. He's just going about his business fighting evildoers. The Karavitch case lands in his lap. But as soon as he starts working on it, he gets a call, say—and this had to be almost as soon as the names of the skyjackers were made public—he gets a call telling him that Ruiz is involved. Immediately he knows that the Croats can't come to trial, because if they do, they might rat on Ruiz and his operation, and then Ruiz or one of his people might rat on Pillman. Alternately, somebody who knows about Ruiz and Pillman is pressuring Pillman to lay off the Croats. There's your blackmail. Either way, it's in Pillman's interest, if he can do it without being too obvious about it, to prevent the Croats from coming to trial. Q.E.D."

"That's very fancy, V.T., very fancy indeed. For some strange reason I like it."

"Why, thank you, Butch. I hope it works. Oh, one other thing. I know it's late notice, but why don't you come up and stay with us this weekend? We have plenty of room and since you're not a big shot anymore, you can take a weekend off now and then. I invited Guma too."

"Oh, yeah?"

"Yup. The Big Prank rolls next week. We have to do some last-minute strategizing, at which you are perfectly welcome should you care to risk one-to-five in Elmira. Also, I'd like you to meet Annabelle. And bring La Siciliana. You both could use a break."

"What about the snow? There's supposed to be a blizzard up there."

"Not to worry. The plows are out and I got through OK this afternoon. Besides, it's tapering off."

Once broached, the idea of spending a weekend with Marlene in the country was overwhelmingly attractive. He could not remember offhand the last time he had so indulged himself, probably years. He agreed to come that evening if Marlene was willing, and V.T. dictated what seemed like an impossibly complex set of road directions.

A few minutes after he had finished with V.T., Karp heard the outer door open and then footsteps crossing the deserted outer office. A shape loomed up against the frosted glass and then Pillman entered.

He was pale, his eyebrows hairy knots, and his wide frog's mouth was compressed into a razor line. Karp motioned to the chair and Pillman dropped his blocky body into it like a sandbag. He eyed Karp sourly for a moment and then rumbled, "So? I'm here. What have you got?"

"Well, Elmer—"

"Goddammit, Karp, don't call me 'Elmer.' Pillman, everybody calls me Pillman."

"OK, Pillman, what've I got? I've got you trying to queer my case on *Karavitch et al.* I've got you protecting a major narcotics trafficker and gunrunner. How's that for openers?"

"It's garbage. You're blowing smoke."

"How about Miami? How about what you and Ruiz pulled on the SOBA people? I've got that too. Still garbage?"

Pillman licked his lips. He was even paler now. "How the fuck . . . ? You've got Ruiz, haven't you, or Hermo . . . Ah, Christ, what a mess. Look, Karp, you got to understand, these people are informants. They're flaky, but they're valuable assets, you understand? OK, Ruiz runs dope and guns, but if not him, a million other guys. Meanwhile I keep a line on some really dangerous people, the kind who blow up airplanes and assassinate politicians."

"What about assassinating New York police officers? Is that in the class of excusable crimes?"

Pillman snorted and twisted his mouth into a parody of a patronizing smile. "Karp, that was an accident. I mean real assassinations—the Kennedys, King—"

"Pillman, stop it. Let's understand each other. You were naughty in Miami: illegal wiretaps, bag jobs, and worse: one of Ruiz's boys turned out somebody's lights just to build up machismo with the SOBAs." Karp was spitballing, but he could see from the shocked expression on Pillman's face that it was an accurate guess. It's always murder, the unexplainable infraction, he thought, as he plowed on: "OK, that means you and this mutt are married. But I could care less, Pillman, believe me, about what went down then. It's none of my business. Are we in Miami? It's snowing up to your ass out there.

"But, Pillman, when your little shithead supplies the bomb that goes into a device that was designed, no accident, designed to kill the man defusing it, and did in fact kill said man, a New York City police officer performing his lawful duty, then I do care."

Pillman's jaw had dropped and a look of unfeigned shock and incredulity had captured his face. "Wha-what?" he sputtered. "What was that about the bomb?"

"Ruiz supplied the Soviet grenade the Croats used to make their bomb. Come on, Pillman, don't tell me you didn't know that."

"I didn't. I didn't, I swear to God! Oh, Christ, this is it, it's all over."

Pillman was so genuinely distraught that Karp was taken aback.

But he pressed on: leaning toward Pillman, he locked the other man's gaze to his and said, "You didn't, huh? OK, say I believe you on that—how did you know there was any connection between Ruiz and the Croats? Why are you screwing up the case?"

"I got a call. Right after we got the word on the hijack. The caller told me that two of the hijackers, Rukovina and Raditch, had been involved in that assassination of the Yugoslav consul-general in Marseilles. They'd arranged for and delivered Soviet weapons for the hit to a group of Croats in France. Ruiz had supplied the weapons."

"Why Soviet weapons?"

"Why do you think? It makes Belgrade think the Sovs are supporting separatist movements in Yugoslavia—so it works against the possibility of reconciliation between Yugoslavia and the Kremlin. It also stirs up the Croats and other separatist factions in Yugoslavia."

"Who would want that?"

"Us for starters. Yugoslavia is a pain in the ass. They're a big hole in the south flank of NATO. They're neutral commies, but if they ever hooked up with the Warsaw Pact, which they could do tomorrow, it'd be a disaster. It'd be much better to have a set of reliable anticommunist states in that strip. Or so the thinking goes."

"Whose thinking, Pillman? Who called you?"

Pillman squirmed and held out his hands in a supplicating gesture. "Come on, Karp. I can't tell you that. We're talking national security here. This is big time."

"OK," Karp said flatly.

"OK? What does that mean?"

"It means OK. What do I care what kind of games you're in as long as you're not playing on my court? The only reason I give a damn about this spy bullshit is so I can find out who's queering my case and make them stop. They want to start wars? Fuck 'em, I'm 4-F."

"But what are you going to do? I mean about Ruiz?"

"Ruiz killed a guy named Sorriendas and he did it in the County of New York, so if we can catch his ass I will put him up for murder two. If he wants to cut a deal by ratting on you, or whoever he's involved with in dope or guns, I will tell him to get fucked. People don't kill people in New York County on my watch and then walk, I don't care what kind of spying they did for somebody. If the narcos want to lay extra charges on him, or the Feds, fine, that's their business. Everybody will get their shot.

"On the Karavitch thing, it's even simpler. If everybody would just get out of my way, it's a lock. They go to trial and let a jury decide. That's how I work. They pay me to put asses in jail, not run exposés. And you will stay out of my way from now on, Pillman, won't you?"

He smiled nastily and Pillman slowly nodded his head.

"So I think Elmer is cooled out, too," Karp said to Marlene as she snuggled in his lap. It was an hour after Pillman had slunk out and Karp was feeling pretty good. He had proudly narrated the afternoon's events, only moderately distracted by the pressure of her small, hard breast jammed against him or the warm nuzzling on his neck.

"That's my man," she breathed, "I'm sitting in his lap squirming like a snake, and he's recounting macho triumphs." She ground her bottom into his lap. "Uh-oh, I can feel it—it's grown another two inches. Jesus, Butch, another day like today you'll have to tape it to your knee."

"Marlene, why do you like to make fun of me? I already said I was sorry. And I thought you cared about this case."

She drew back, looked at him seriously for a moment, and then kissed him on the cheek. "I do care, baby. And it's great about the evidence and Pillman and all the rest. Really. But my caring machine is wearing out, you know? I'm not like you, not straight and determined. There's something missing, you understand? In my life. And I'm being consumed by this damn claim—"

"I said I'd—"

"Yeah, yeah, you did, and I believe you, but still—shit, I need a smoke." She got up off his lap and began casting through her bag for her Marlboros. When she had lit up and the little office was blue with smoke, she added, "What I need is a break."

He stood up. "And a break is what you're going to get. We're going up to V.T.'s this weekend, lie around, play in the snow . . ."

"Oh, Butch, really? Hot damn!" She ran to him and gave him a bear hug that flexed his ribs. "When do we leave? Oh, boy, this is just what we need, a little nestling under quilts in a four-poster, far from the madding crowd and the fucking city."

He grinned and said, "We could leave right away. All we have to do is pack. I'll run up to midtown and rent a car."

"Oh, don't do that, I got a car we could use. Let's go now! I'll pick you up outside your place in what? Forty-five minutes?"

"Marlene, you can't drive. You only have one eye."

"The hell I can't. Half the people driving in New York are totally blind. Besides, it's only a couple of blocks. You can drive

193

us up to the country." Before he could object, she had blown him a kiss and run out.

An hour later Karp was dubiously eyeing the vehicle Marlene had driven up to the curb. It was a 1957 Chevrolet Bel-Air, pink on the bottom and white on top. The rear end was considerably higher than the front, and it had wide-track Eagles on the rear wheels and speed-shop stickers all over the rear quarter windows.

"This is the car? Where did you get it?"

"It's Larry's, from Larry and Stu in the loft downstairs. They're in Bermuda for three weeks. Larry found it in Biloxi when he was down visiting his mom and fell in love with it. Isn't it great? Hey, let's get in, I'm freezing my genuggies off here."

In fact, the temperature now hovered in the low teens and the air was filled with swirls of gritty snow. They loaded the suitcases into the car and got in. Karp sat behind the wheel, a custom job made of welded chain that was about half the size of an ordinary wheel. It had a large green plastic knob attached to it at the two o'clock position. Marlene slid in next to him. "Look, Butch, a make-out knob. That's so you can steer with one hand with your arm around your best girl."

"Marlene, this is a stick shift," he said, examining the huge chrome shaft sticking out of the floorboards. It had a white plastic skull on its end with red jeweled eyes.

"Yeah, right, a Hurst shifter. We got 446 cubes under the hood, too. Let's roll, big boy!" She looked at him oddly. "Karp, don't say you can't use a stick shift. That's like saying you can't get it up."

"Oh, no, sure I can. It's just, I don't drive much." The truth was that Karp had not driven a car more than half a dozen times since law school, where he had owned a sedate secondhand Plymouth with automatic. He had perhaps three hours' total experience with a stick shift, logged at age seventeen on his brother's VW.

The important thing, he recalled, was not to stall. He pressed the accelerator gingerly. The engine rumbled. Muffling had obviously been of secondary interest to whatever redneck maniac had built this car. He recalled vaguely that something called a tachometer had something to do with shifting. There was a large black gauge bolted to the top of the dash that jerked every time he goosed the gas. That must be it. He cautiously depressed the clutch and slid the skull in the direction first gear was in the 1951 VW.

"Hey, let's go," she said, "time's a-wastin'."

The tach went from one to seven. He decided four was a safe bet. He pointed the wheel away from the curb and tromped on the gas until the needle hit four. The air was filled with an ear-rattling roar that sounded like a dive bomber taking off from a carrier. Karp smiled bravely at his best girl and popped the clutch.

Twenty minutes later, they were barreling north on the Saw Mill River Parkway through a mild blizzard. The snow was bone dry, forming dancing pinpoints of brilliance in the headlights.

"Good thing there's no traffic," Marlene said. She was curled up in the suicide seat, her high boots tucked up under her black wool skirt, trying to light a cigarette with shaking hands. "You're, ah, quite a driver there, Butch."

"Thanks," he said hoarsely around a tongue as dry as flannel.

"But, um, maybe you should shift out of second. You'll get better mileage. Third's probably up and to the right. If you want."

"Yeah, oh sure, I was just warming her up," he said, reaching over to do it. But as he looked down, he had occasion to notice for the first time something odd. "Say, Marlene? This car has no ignition key."

"Yeah, well, actually, it doesn't really need one."

"Oh? Why not?"

"Well, I sort of forgot to get the keys from Larry, so I sort of jumped the ignition."

"You boosted this car? That I'm driving?"

"Don't be mad, Butch. It's cool, honestly."

"Oh, shit, Marlene! What if we get stopped? That's it, curtains. No job, no future. You lunatic, don't you realize that assistant district attorneys are not supposed to do crimes? Christ, Marlene, ½ sometimes I don't know . . . Oh, God, is there registration in the car? At least if we have the goddamn registration . . ."

Karp began to look for it, behind the front visor first, and then stretched across to pop open the glove compartment and fumble inside it. The car veered back and forth across the road, as he yanked out a handful of assorted material.

"Butch, take it easy, it's all right!" she cried as they hit the shoulder.

"It's not all right. Turn on the dome light. OK, what's this: map, map, tire bill—oh, shit." He held up a plastic baggie. In the yellow light she saw that the bag contained a miniature wooden pipe, a packet of Zig-Zag cigarette papers, and a half ounce of brownish vegetable substance that Karp doubted very much was Bugle cigarette tobacco. He let it drop to the seat.

"I can't believe this. This is not happening," he said in a faint voice.

"We could throw it out the window," she suggested brightly.

195

"Good idea, Ciampi. I'm sure the car isn't dirty down to the floorboards. The trunk is probably full of toot, for chrissakes."

They drove in strained silence for a minute or two. Then he gradually became aware that odd splatting sounds were issuing from between her clenched lips.

"What's so funny, Marlene?"

She exploded into hysteria, thick, choking, exhausting laughter. "Karp," she gasped at last between guffaws, "we'll cop a plea . . . we're first offenders . . . they'll give us—they'll give us six months suspended . . ." and she started laughing uncontrollably again. And it was, after all, pretty funny, and so he started to laugh, too, harder and harder. He had to wipe the tears away so he could see the snowy road.

When they had finally quieted down, she snuggled up to him and he put his arm around her and used the make-out knob to steer. She said, "I love this. I want to drive through this blizzard with you forever and never stop."

"Sounds good. We'd have to stop to get food. And pee," he said, always the sensible one.

"No. We'd keep driving. We'd never eat and we'd pee in the backseat." She turned on the radio. It was tuned to a rock station and the Birds playing "Eight Miles High."

"We'd have to stop to . . . you know, do the dirty," he said, acutely aware of her pointed tongue scrounging around his right ear.

"No, we wouldn't," she whispered.

Then she pulled away from him and he was aware of her bouncing on the seat. In a flash she had reached up and hung a pair of rose silk bikini underpants on the rearview mirror. "I've wanted to do this all my life," she said, "and the moment has come."

"Marlene, what are you doing? Stop that! Ahhgh, there's the turnoff!"

The Chevy shot across three lanes onto the Taconic Parkway as she unzipped his fly and began to fumble within. "Mar . . . stop it, we'll get killed!" he yelled.

"Who cares? It'll be a once in a lifetime experience. Ah, there he is. Yumm."

"Wait, I'll pull over," he gasped as her head descended.

" 'on't 'ou 'are!" she said, her mouth full and moving like the pistons in the straining 446, just as hot but much slower. With a final noisy lick she raised her head, flicked off the dome light, and heaved her naked thigh across his lap. "Marlene, this isn't wise," he wheezed.

"Yeah, it's real foolish. But I'm dying for you. It's going to fry like a sausage. OK, let me just . . ."

She reached under her full skirt and clutched the blazing item shooting up from his groin like a Hurst four-speed stick, pointed it into the right place, and sank down with an audible slurp and a grunt of pleasure. "Don't slow down, don't, don't slow down," she hissed around the teeth she had sunk into the curve of his neck. In a minute the first wave of climax rolled through her, and she yelled over the scream of the engine and the tires, over the pounding of the music.

Karp's life was passing across his eyes as he wove S-shapes on the snow of the Taconic State Parkway and jammed his hips up to met Marlene's frantic bouncing. The tiny part of him still capable of thought was trying to figure out how he could have predicted that a stable and idealistic young lawyer would spend the last few seconds of his life fucking a crazy woman while going sixty-five miles an hour through a blizzard in a stolen car loaded with dope. But after a short while that part of him was completely extinguished, and he surrendered to the oblivion of pleasure.

16

THEY DIDN'T DIE. To Karp's immense surprise, not only did they survive, but they were able to navigate the worsening blizzard and arrive at their destination at eight o'clock. They were just in time for dinner.

Their hostess, Annabelle Partland, owned an isolated farmhouse in the hill country outside Great Barrington, Massachusetts, and as they pulled the Chevy into the snowbound farmyard, all they could see of her was a person wearing an immense orange parka, the kind used in Antarctic expeditions, and a fur-lined hood pulled tight around a face. When the car engine was finally turned off, Karp found his ears ringing in the unaccustomed silence. As he stepped out into the freezing wind he could actually hear the snowflakes striking the windshield.

Marlene threw her red parka up over her shoulders and dashed for the house, with Karp and Annabelle behind her, lugging bags. The door lintel was so low that he had to duck to enter. As he did, he noticed a carved wooden sign over it, which said:

I haven't got any.
And I don't want any.

In the mud room inside the door, Annabelle shucked off her great garment and hung it on one of a row of wooden pegs. When her hood came off she released a mane of pale coppery hair vibrating with static, and a round, wide-mouthed, pleasant freckled face. She was wearing a gray Ragg sweater, a set of Oshkosh overalls much stained with clay, and high woolen leg warmers patterned with Icelandic designs. She smiled at Karp and said, "My, you certainly don't look prepared for this blizzard." He took off his Yankee baseball jacket and stamped the snow off his high-top sneakers. "Yeah, right," he admitted. "I don't get out of town much."

"Well, you're *really* out of town now," she said and led him down a narrow passageway to a small dining room, where a table

198

was set for six and where Marlene was already pouring herself a glass of red wine. V.T. came out of the kitchen, wiping his hands on a dish towel.

"Hi, Butch, Marlene. What's happening," he said cheerfully.

"Grand theft auto," Karp answered.

"Pardon?"

"Ask her," he said. "For the record, I'm an unwitting accessory."

"Karp, you rat! V.T., this man is going to turn my ass in to the law because I . . . oh, never mind, it's entirely too tedious to go into right now." She stuck her tongue out at Karp, then looked around the beamed, candlelit dining room. "Gosh, this is a great place, Annabelle. When did you get it?"

"In 1793," she said. "Let's eat."

An hour later, Karp was sitting with Marlene on a couch in the low-ceilinged living room. They were stuffed with white bean soup and sausage washed down with quantities of thick French wine. Marlene, mellow and slightly drunk, was smoking. Karp was staring at the fire and playing with a smooth rock he had picked up off the walnut coffee table. A stereo was playing a McGarrigle Sisters record.

Cold sober and just starting to relax from the drive, he looked around the room, fascinated. It was filled with remarkable objects. On the walls, besides dozens of paintings and drawings, some richly framed, others stuck up with pins, there were elaborate tufted quilts that looked like the vestments of extraterrestrial priests. The rugs on the polished wide-planked floor were irregular in shape and had the energy of bright animals. Pots and ceramic sculptures in fantastic variety sat on shelves, on tables, or were scattered in rows on the floor, some like stones from a riverbed, some like relics of ancient civilizations, some like silver and neon explosions. The furniture was a mix of heirloom antique and extravagant crafts. The couch on which they sat was a Duncan Phyfe upholstered in blue silk, on which a variety of embroidery work had been flung, together with a collection of odd pillows that were themselves soft sculptures. The chairs placed at either end of the coffee table were artful constructions of smooth tree-limbs laced together with rawhide, hemp cable, and soft, quilted leather.

"This is some place," he said, breaking the silence.

"Yeah," Marlene answered, "not your usual motel modern. What do you think of old Annabelle?"

Karp shrugged. "She seems pretty nice. V.T. is obviously her total slave. He wants to marry her."

"Yeah? Will they?"

"It's in doubt. V.T. wants to stay in the city and Annabelle refuses to leave here."

"I don't blame her. In fact, I sympathize entirely. She's in her own place, and she's her own boss. I really like her, which is strange, because when I walked in here, for about two seconds I was blinded with envy. But she's, I don't know, so completely herself. Like the Wife of Bath. 'I am my own woman, well at ease.' "

"Like the sign on the door—'I don't have any . . .' "

"Right. Every woman's secret wish—to be ten forever, with all your toys arranged just so and infinite playtime and no nasty boys to break in and mess things up."

Karp looked at her as she stared into the fire. The good side of her face, fine-boned and noble, caught the glow of the flames and seemed to shine with its own light, like a cameo carved from a red gem. He fought down the intense desire that gripped him. He said coolly, "Boys, huh?"

"Yeah, or men. Oh, naturally one wants a man on tap, should one wish to fuck one's brains out on the odd evening. Oh, shit, Butch, your expression. You take everything so personal."

"I thought sex was personal."

"Yeah, sure, but I was talking generally. Never mind, it's just girl stuff. God, I needed this break." She gestured broadly to the room. "Look at this. This is a beautiful place. Remember beauty, Butchie? Funny, in school I hung around with a gang of artists, sculptors. musicians, whatever. After a while, I started to think they weren't, I don't know, serious? Solid?

"I would talk to them, and they would just smile or joke. It finally struck me that they had nothing to say, or what I mean is, if they had something to say, they would draw it, or sing it. I couldn't understand it then. It pissed me off, all the shit going down in the world, and they're farting around with paint.

"So I switched to pre-law and started hanging around with political types. Engaged, but bor-ing."

"Smash the state?"

"No, never those guys. Male chauvinists, every damn one of them. Serve the people and squash your old lady, it never fails. No, more like Free the Tanktown Seven. A bleeding heart."

"I'm surprised you didn't go into public D."

"Yeah, only I figured the wretched of the earth get more lumps from the skels than they do from the cops. Besides, there's the power—"

"Ah, power, my favorite subject," V.T. said as he entered the room, holding a bottle in one hand and four stemmed glasses in the other. "Annabelle decided to break out one of these in your honor. A '70 Margaux, the beverage of the ruling classes. Her father sends her a case for her birthday every year, in the hopes that the wine will befuddle her into marrying a bond salesman and moving to Darien."

As he poured the wine, Annabelle entered, checked the fire, and flung a couple of chunks of applewood onto it. Sitting in a leather chair, she pulled an embroidery hoop out of a canvas bag and began to stitch, in between sips of wine.

"Hey, V.T.," Karp said, "you sure Guma said he was going to come tonight?"

"He said, but you never know with Raymond. We'll have to make do without him for the nonce. Meanwhile, you can tell me all about Ruiz the Serpent and his Soviet grenade."

Karp recounted the events at the bomb range and the carton that linked Tel-Air and the Croat bombers, and then related his conversation with Pillman. "So you guessed right, V.T.," he concluded. "Ruiz must have whacked somebody in Miami, and Pillman went along for the ride. You should have seen Pillman's face when I slipped that in."

V.T. said, "Uh-hmm," and stared into the fire.

"V.T., you're thinking something."

"Yes, I am. This is really puzzling, isn't it?"

"You noticed. Well, spit it out."

"That call that Pillman got right after the hijacking, saying he should lay off Karavitch because Ruiz supplied the Croats in Marseilles with Warsaw Pact weapons, and two of the Croats on the hijack were involved in it—that's puzzling."

"Why? It was bullshit anyway. Whoever called must have figured the Grand Central bomb came from that same load, but why tell Pillman that? Better let him think he's covering up for something besides a New York cop killing."

Marlene said, "That can't be right, Butch. According to Pillman, he got that call before Terry was killed."

"Oh, right. Yeah, so either Pillman's lying or—"

V.T. cut in, "Or the phone call was the truth. The caller was really concerned about the Marseilles connection. Rukovina and Raditch were really involved. Somebody was using them as mules to carry munitions to Croat terrorists. Which means the Grand Central bomb wasn't part of any conspiracy outside our little band in New York."

"Right," Karp said. "Now I'm with you. I've been thinking that's the key to understanding this case. The political, the institutional stuff, it's just smoke. Really, it's all private: secrets, ripoffs, ambitions, egos."

"Why is that different from the way it always is?" asked Annabelle calmly. She got three blank looks from the others. "I mean," she continued, "that sounds to me like the ordinary life of institutions—just what you said—secrets, ripoffs, ambitions, and egos. The odd thing is why you're surprised."

There was a brief, embarrassed silence into which V.T. said, "Umm, the point is, dear, it's not supposed to be that way, which is why it's interesting. Watergate was an aberration, after all."

"Was it?" Annabelle said, more sharply. "How come you're so sure?"

"Because they screwed up, Annabelle," Marlene said. "Just like our guys screwed up. That's the problem with conspiracies. Christ, it's hard enough to get anything done in real life out in the open, with the full force of the law, and public opinion working for you. It's almost impossible to do anything that's both illegal and secret, if it requires a lot of organization and lots of people working together. Almost all criminal action is massively simple and stupid."

Annabelle shrugged and picked up her embroidery hoop again. "You may be right. What do I know? It just seems to me that things could hardly be as dreadful as V.T. says without some form of connivance between the bad guys and the supposed good guys."

"Oh, connivance!" exclaimed V.T., laughing. "That's a different story. Do we have connivance, Butch?"

"Lots of connivance, V.T. Yeah, you see, Annabelle, we all work for a guy, connivance is like his middle name. Not the same as conspiracy, though. More opportunistic."

"That's the point," put in Marlene. "Nobody plans that things should be screwed up. It's just the sum of everybody working a private angle in the public business. And Bloom has a real big angle."

"Yeah, but be fair, Marlene," Karp said. "Bloom is a master at covering his tracks and letting somebody else catch the shit. For example, I'd give a lot to know who called him after the hijack. You remember I told you Denton told me that he knew Karavitch's name before the cops or the TV had it. Even more, I'd like to confirm my hunch that somehow old Sanford was involved in getting that cop to plant the phony evidence on me. That would be a crusher—disbar city. But there's no chance in hell of us ever finding out."

"Yeah, unless you could get hold of his tapes," replied Marlene.

"Tapes? What tapes are those?" he asked.

But he did not get an answer just then, because at that moment all the lights in the house went off and the stereo stopped playing. Marlene gave a little shriek of alarm.

"Oh shit, it's a CIA hit team," V.T. said. "They tracked us here and now they're going to silence us because we know too much."

"I thought you said there wasn't any conspiracy, V.T.," said Annabelle.

"That was just a story to ease your mind, dear. I just want you to know that I'll defend you to the death or until it becomes personally inconvenient, whichever is first."

"That's my man," said Annabelle, standing up. The fireplace lit her with the eerie glow familiar from countless horror movies. With the music silenced, they were aware of the sound of the wind humming through the trees outside. "I don't want . . . to die," Marlene said in a quavery voice.

They all laughed and then V.T. stood up too. "You're too tough to kill, Ciampi. Actually, it's probably ice on the lines. It'll be morning before we have power. We'll get some lights."

So they spent the rest of the evening in companionable semi-darkness, lit by kerosene lamps turned low. Karp and Marlene snuggled under a pile of afghans on the couch. Their hostess and host did the same on the hearth rug.

The darkness brought on an intimacy among these four private people of a kind that occurs with children at a pajama party or soldiers on the night watch. They told spy jokes and cop jokes to suit the theme of the evening. V.T. got his guitar out and they sang sentimental songs. They popped popcorn over the fire and toasted marshmallows and finished off another bottle of Margaux.

Marlene said dreamily, "This is just like Girl Scout camp. I'm going to wake up in a bunk with initials carved in the wall, and discover that my entire adult life has been just an unusually long and violent nightmare." OK by me, she said to herself.

Karp thought, this is real life: friends, good food, fun, furniture. Why have I given this up? He could sense Marlene's happiness. Relaxed vibrations issued from her like waves of heat from the fireplace. And she was singing; she hadn't really sung since the bombing, and she was singing the saddest songs she knew, which meant she was really calm and happy. She sang "Dutchman" and "Wagoner's Lad," and a song in French that V.T. knew how to play, full of misery. Then she sang something Karp had never heard her sing before, about a maiden who gave herself for love to an enchanted knight, and rescued him from the Queen of the Fairies. She sang full-bore, high and wild, with V.T. beating out a strong rhythm on the flat of his guitar. Karp did the same with a pen on an empty bottle, a skill he had picked up in kindergarten and not much improved since.

Around midnight Guma blew in, looking like the abominable snowman, in the company of a blond who was so obviously what she was that she might have been wearing a T-shirt with "BIMBO" written across it. Guma's car had conked out at the bottom of the hill and they had trudged three-quarters of a mile through deep snow in street clothes and shoes. He was drunk, inevitably, since he considered driving so boring that he always got tanked to the nozzle before any long drive.

The woman, whose name was Sunni Dale, was about to succumb to hypothermia, having climbed the hill in the open-toed heels she wore in her nightclub act. Guma, it seemed, had invited her out for a drink with some friends, without bothering to tell her that the venue was a mountainside a hundred and twenty miles off. Guma flopped on the couch and was snoring in about four seconds. Annabelle took charge of the woman and hustled her off to a steaming tub. Karp and Marlene lit their way to bed by candlelight.

Their bedroom was tiny and cold. They shivered and giggled as they pulled off their clothes and scrambled naked under the thick pile of quilts on the antique spindle four-poster. Down in the trough provided by the ancient mattress, they intertwined every available limb in an effort to keep their body heat from draining into the icy, crisp sheets.

"This is crazy," Karp said, "there's no heat in this house. They'll find us frozen and blue in the morning, like in Jack London."

"Be quiet," she answered. "This is the second most romantic single moment of my entire existence."

"What was the first?"

"Sweeping into the Copa on prom night on the arm of Rocco Tedeschi. I wore a powder blue strapless. Everybody died."

"You went out with a guy named Rocco?"

"Yeah, so what? Butch, I'm Italian. Anyway, he was gorgeous and bad and my folks hated him. It was perfecto. He was the one who taught me how to drive, and also how to drive cars that belonged to other people. What a night! Later I let him go almost all the way. Just the tip in. He popped in about three seconds, making me a true woman while allowing me to save my technical virginity for my Comp Lit professor two years later."

"That's pretty romantic. Speaking of which, what was that song, about the knight and the fairy queen?"

"Tam Lin? It's a good one. What about it?"

"I don't know, I liked it. The part where the fairies turn him into different animals and she keeps holding on to him."

She kissed his ear. "Is that what you want? To be rescued from the Queen of the Fairies?"

He laughed. "The Queen of the Fairies is named Marvin Belkin and he hangs out on Christopher Street. He's never shown any special interest in me, but . . ."

"God! Will you look at that!" Marlene exclaimed.

The candle, which they had placed on the windowsill, had gone out, a victim of one of the bedroom's vagrant drafts, and in the instant of its extinction, as the reflection of its flame died in the window, the moon burst from a nest of shining, ragged clouds and flooded the room with cold silver.

"Yeah, it's pretty," he said after a moment.

"Pretty? It's ravishing! Moonlight on the newfallen snow, snuggling under perfumed quilts in an eighteenth-century farmhouse—I could stay here forever!"

"Tell me about the tapes."

"Tapes? Oh, fuck a duck, Karp, you really know how to enhance a mood. You're as good as drugs."

"Sorry. But really—"

"But really, I don't know shit. Iron Tits once vouchsafed to me in the girls' crapper that Bloom had some sort of Nixon arrangement for taping conversations, but . . . shit! What's that noise?"

The house had begun to vibrate with a strange thumping, like the sound that might be made by a spastic dragging a dead calf over a barrel. There was a thump at the door. "Sunni, goddammit, where are ya? I can't see shit."

Marlene giggled. "Mr. Guma, Esquire, retires for the evening." The steps receded down the hallway. Then they heard a door opening and a muffled conversation that resembled the audio portion of a Punch and Judy show. Then silence.

"Anyway," she resumed, "that's all I know about the tapes, but I would guess they're kept pretty tight."

"Uh-huh, I guess."

"Mmm, I can see the wheels turning. But how could we get our hands on them? We don't even know where they're stashed."

"I don't know. I'll think of something."

"Yeah, I bet. Christ! What's *that* noise?"

"Umm. Sounds like somebody getting nooky on a creaky old bed, not unlike the one we currently occupy. I would guess Guma from the force of the thumps." They listened breathlessly for a few minutes. "Ha, a screamer. I figured her for a moaner, like you," he observed, stroking her back and kneading her small buttocks, hard as handballs.

"Jesus, it sounds like Moloch fucking a piece of bombazine, in

Henry Miller's immortal phrase. By the way, I'm not a moaner,"
she said, throwing a leg over his hip and pulling him even closer.
"I'm a gasper. Oh, my, you're getting my attention now. Let's see
what's going on down here." She pulled away and he felt fingers
flickering over his belly.

"Uh-oh, it's disappeared."

"It's the cold."

"Yeah. Maybe I should blow on it."

"No, Marlene, I think you mean 'suck,'" he said. "'Blow' is
just a figure of speech."

The roar of a snowplow awakened him, and the first thing Karp
saw was the rear of his beloved, who was standing by the window,
looking out, dressed in a heavy white sweater and nothing else.
Her delicious round bottom and the enticing space between her
slim thighs were at his eye level. He stared for several pleasurable
minutes until she caught his eye in the window's reflection and
turned around.

"What are you looking at?"

"The greatest ass in North America."

"Fah, it's way too fat."

"Bullshit," he replied, lifting the covers, "come on back to bed,
and let me use it."

"Yuk! You're turning into an animal. You're as bad as Guma.
No, I'm getting dressed. I want to get out in this glorious day."

"Don't play in the snow," he said grumpily, pulling the quilts
over his head.

But after a while he got dressed, pulled on some old galoshes he
found in the mud room, and went outside. It did not seem possible
that a sun so bright could yield so little heat. The air was as clear
and hard as lead crystal, and cut his nostrils. He crunched through
the drifts, following Marlene's deep footprints across the farmyard.
As he neared the huge barn, Marlene caught him behind the ear
with a snowball. He scooped up a handful of snow. "OK, Ciampi,"
he snarled, "you're dead meat." He heaved, she ducked, giggled,
and ran into the barn. He picked up some more snow and set off in
pursuit.

After the brilliance of the snowy morning the barn was like a
coal mine. He stumbled over lumber and bounced off posts while
his eyes adjusted. He heard a sound and saw Marlene moving
toward the foot of a ladder leading to the barn's loft. He fired and
had the satisfaction of seeing a white burst of snow against the
back of her red parka. She laughed and ran up the ladder, and he
followed her.

"Look, isn't this great, Butch? We could have a dance," she said, twirling in the center of the barn's great loft. The loft did have something of the disco about it. Although it was gloomy under the eaves, the wall was pierced by chinks and knotholes, which lit the floor and the far walls like random spotlights. At the far end was a perfect square of absolute blueness where the loft door opened to the sky.

Marlene began to hum "The Blue Danube." She put her arms around Karp and led him into a clumsy, shuffling waltz. She upped the tempo little by little until they were whirling breathlessly across the dusty floor. They stopped. Karp kissed her hard. Her hair smelled of wood smoke. She pulled away and looked at him, her expression odd and unreadable. She stared at the blue square for a moment, then turned back to him, and said, "It looks like a swimming pool from the high board. It's a swimming pool for birds."

He yawned and started toward the ladder. "Yeah. Hey, let's go back to the house and see what's for breakfast."

Marlene didn't answer. Karp heard her footsteps against the boards. He spun around and saw her running full tilt toward the open door. He realized with mounting horror that she was not going to stop. With a cackling yell she launched herself into naked space, and a last image of her against the blue heavens was burnt into his mind's eye: her thin, jean-clad legs spinning like egg beaters, her red parka flapping, her arms wide, her black hair a crazy halo around her head.

For a moment he was paralyzed, frozen between the impulse to run toward the door where she had vanished and the more sensible idea of going down to ground level. In the absolute silence he could hear the blood pound in his ears. Then he broke loose and hurled himself down the ladder and out to the front of the barn.

The square door was a black eye patch against the silvery wood, thirty feet up. Beneath it was a huge pile of snow pushed up by the plow. Karp ran to it and clambered up its side. At the top there was a Marlene-shaped hole, chillingly gravelike, and at its bottom was Marlene, looking like a frozen princess.

She appeared to be unconscious. His heart in his throat, he leaped into the hole, knelt down, and touched her face. "Marlene!" he wailed.

Her eye opened and her tongue stuck out at him. "That was great," she said. "I want to go again."

"You crazy idiot!" Karp yelled. "You could have killed yourself. There could have been a piece of goddamn farm equipment under the snow." He climbed up out of the hole and looked around. "Hey, you jerk! Will you look at this?"

Marlene stood up. Karp was pointing wordlessly at a large lump in the snow pile, from which emerged the corner of a rusted metal frame and several long curved steel teeth. "You missed that by about two feet."

Marlene giggled. "Yeah, it would have been a harrowing experience."

"Stop it!" Karp bellowed, grabbing her shoulders. "It drives me crazy when you pull stuff like that." He shook her and the words gushed out of him without thought. "You can't do this to me, Marlene. You're not some wacky kid. I love you! I can't stand this stuff, and your on-and-off shit. This isn't real life. I want to be with you. I want to get married."

Marlene looked up at him with a broad grin. "Well, well," she said. "Well, well, well, well, well."

"Well, well, what?"

"Well, this sort of bowls a girl over, Butch. My heart's all a-flutter. But, ah, there's a couple of things . . ."

"Like?"

"Like, if we're going to get—how can I put it?—engaged, you are going to have to meet my family."

"I'm not marrying your family."

"I beg to differ, but in any case I do not intend to sit through another Sunday dinner making polite conversation with nice un-married Italian certified public accountants, who have been getting older and more desperate-looking in recent months."

"OK, right, meet the family, you got it. You'll want a ring too, I guess."

"You guess right, buster, and I want it flagrant. I want my mom happy, and my cousins squirming in envy. And I want to get married in white in St. Anthony's on 97th Street in the County of Queens."

"Come on, Marlene—"

"No, you come on. You ask me to marry you, you unleash long-buried lower-middle-class instincts. Well, what about it, is it a deal?"

"It's a deal. But you got to promise to stop trying to kill yourself and pulling weird shit."

"Fine, no problem," she said. Then she wrapped her arms around him and pulled his mouth down onto hers.

"There is one little detail, though," she whispered into his ear.

"What's that, babe?"

"You're already married, remember?"

"Oh, yeah, that."

"That. And while Vatican Deuce has made the Church more liberal, I kind of think they draw the line there, you know?"

"All right, all right, I'll take care of it," he said grumpily, his romantic mood vanishing. The last he had heard of his first wife was that she had repaired to a lesbian commune somewhere in northern California. It was going to be a pain in the ass to track her down.

"And I'll wait for you forever, my prince, but meanwhile, my feet are freezing," she said. "Cheer up, big boy, I appreciate the thought anyway. Hey, I'll race you to the house."

"Guma," Karp said, "how would you like to torpedo the district attorney?" The power had come back on and the two men were sitting in the kitchen of the farmhouse, watching snowy figures play football on a small black-and-white TV. Unshaven and hung over, Guma was eating potato chips and drinking Carling and occasionally banging the side of the TV when its image displeased him. The three women and V.T. had gone to town for supplies in Annabelle's pickup truck. Guma scratched himself and thought about Karp's question. "Yeah, sure I'd like to. Who wouldn't? What'd you have in mind?"

Karp told him about Bloom's tapes and about what might reasonably be supposed to be on them. Guma listened attentively, then said, "Sounds great. You thinking about pulling a burglary?"

"Shit, no! That would be wrong. Besides, we might get caught. No, it occurred to me that Iron Tits is the key to this little problem."

Guma snorted. "Yeah, Rhoda Klepp—Wharton in drag. What about her, the bitch?"

"Well, where could he keep the tapes? There must be a shitload of them. OK, you know the DA's outer office? There's a row of file cabinets along the wall to the right. One of 'em's got a big security bar and a humongous lock on it. I figure the tapes are there."

"Yeah? So what? How're you gonna bust in there?"

"Klepp. She's got a key. I saw her open it once. You know that big ring of keys she jangles around with? It's on there."

"You gonna ask her to lend you her key?"

"Goom, be real. No, I figure, ah, if somebody got close to her, got her relaxed, sort of, it might be possible to borrow them for a while. I'd sure like to listen to those tapes."

"Well, shit, Butch, ask her out. Take her to Radio City and buy her an ice cream soda. She'll come across, no problem."

"Hey, Goom, come on, this is out of my league. I freely admit it. I'm not man enough to take on Rhoda Klepp. In fact, there's only one man I know of who could really pull it off."

Guma looked at Karp for ten seconds, waiting to hear the name. Then the light dawned and he grinned. "Oh no, you sneaky guy. Uh-uh, include me out. No fuckin' way. Hey, look at this asshole, he's gonna try a fourth-down pass."

"Why not, Guma? I thought you were always up for a new challenge."

"Hey, Karp, give me a break. I got a nice thing going with what's her name there, Sunni. I want to work on it, let it blossom, you know? I don't need any challenges right now, OK?"

"Guma, you just met the woman last night."

"Hey, what can I say? It was magic."

"Guma, you're missing one of the great experiences. Imagine those incredible mazumas unleashed. They'd stalk you across the room like a beast of prey. Also, I hear she's into every depravity."

"Depravity, hey? Talk to a German shepherd, then. Talk to a fuckin' pony. Not me."

"You're chicken."

"I stopped listening, Karp. I'd like to help out, but let me put it to you this way: I wouldn't fuck her with *your* dick."

"Guma won't do it," Karp said to Marlene later that evening. "Any ideas? I guess I could try."

"Yeah, but you wouldn't get far without genitalia, and I'll cut off your first move in that direction. No, I'll work something out. I'll catch her in the little girl's room one time and lay a trip on her. I owe her one anyway."

Shortly after lunch on Sunday the blessed isolation Karp and Marlene were enjoying was cut short by a telephone call from Bill Denton.

"I'm going to ruin your weekend," he said.

"You already did. What's up?"

"They found the waiter, Koltan. In a dumpster in Canarsie."

"Ah, shit. The poor bastard. How'd he get it?"

"They tied his hands behind him with wire and cut his throat. Butch, these guys are going crazy. Their scam is coming unglued and I think they figure they got nothing to lose. I got extra guys with the hijackers and all the people I can steal looking for the Cubans, but who knows? Lot of places to hide in the city, and they could have left already. By the way, did you get that stack of shots I sent over?"

"Yeah, Ruiz and company, real beauties."

"You recall seeing any of them yourself? I mean recently."

"No, not that I recall. It'd be hard to miss Ruiz, the little fucker really looks like some kind of reptile. Why do you ask?"

"Well, there's one figure in this case who's wandering around with nobody watching him, and I'm getting a little concerned."

"What figure is that, Bill?"

"You."

Karp laughed. "Come on, Bill. Mutts don't waste ADAs."

"Yeah, but these aren't your usual mutts. And as I recall, somebody tried real hard to punch your ticket a couple of years back. With that letter bomb."

"Yeah, there's that. Well, what do you suggest?"

"Get back to the city as soon as you can and stay put. I'll get Brenner to babysit you for a couple days, until we nail these assholes. Oh, yeah, speaking of assholes, your friend Flanagan has turned up missing too."

"Flanagan? Oh, crap!"

"What is it?"

"Nothing. I just thought of something I had to do." It had occurred to him that the Q and A he had taken off Flanagan was sitting in its sealed envelope on the floor of his bedroom. If anything happened to the detective, he would have no proof of a conspiracy to introduce tainted evidence into *Karavitch* et al.

"OK, Bill," he said, "we're leaving in a little while. I'll talk to you Monday."

It took them nearly an hour to dig the car out, and they left about four. The roads were icy and Karp sweated bullets on the mountain turns. It was nearly six when they hit the clear pavement of the Taconic, a black canal between the mounds of snow pushed up on its shoulders by the plows. The sky had gone dark purple when he decided he needed some coffee and pulled into one of the Taconic's rustic rest stops.

He was waiting at the take-out counter for his order, thinking about nothing in particular, when he happened to look out the window. At that moment, with an intensity that prickled his scalp, he was overcome by a feeling of déjà vu. A good-looking, swarthy man was using his reflection in the restaurant window to comb his long black hair. As he finished, he cocked his head at an angle and tossed it back so that a lock of hair fell just so over one eye.

Karp felt the ice form in his belly. He had seen that man before, doing just that in the window of a Chinese restaurant. He had seen that gesture reproduced in the crazy mimicry of Dirty Warren, which meant that this guy had been hanging around Centre Street for weeks. Now that he had seen Denton's pictures, he realized that he was looking at Esteban Otero, the man who had helped to kill Alejandro Sorriendas. Hermo.

He picked up the paper bag with his order in it, paid, and walked out, trying not to shake, trying to think, trying not to look at the man four feet away. He walked toward where he had parked the Chevy, but a large green station wagon was parked in his slot.

His stomach dropped and he tasted acid on his tongue. He turned slowly in a circle, searching for the pink car. A string of curses directed at Marlene appeared on the screen of his mind. Where the hell was she? He looked back toward the restaurant. Hermo was gone. He started back to the restaurant. There was a phone there, maybe he could call Denton—

An enormous blast erupted behind him. He stumbled and almost dropped the bag of coffee as he spun around.

Marlene was sitting in the Chevy's driver's seat, grinning. He walked to the driver's side and she rolled down the window. "Hell of a horn," she said. "It's a diesel air jobbie."

"Marlene, what the fuck are you doing?" he choked out between clenched teeth.

Her grin faded. "I was just getting some gas. I didn't want to bring the car back empty. Butch, what's the matter?"

"I just spotted one of Ruiz's men. He's been following me. We got to get out of here. Move over."

"Get in!" She leaned over and jerked the passenger door open.

"Marlene, move over! Stop playing around!" he shouted.

"Butch, listen. You want to get away from these guys? Get in. You can't drive worth a shit. Hey, is that them?"

In her rearview mirror she had spotted a white Econoline van pulling out of a slot. There were two men in the front seat.

Karp looked. "Yeah, that's them." He felt drained. "OK, you drive." He got in and Marlene stomped on the gas. The big engine screamed. She slammed into gear, popped the clutch, and the big Eagles on the rear wheels squealed, spinning wildly and sending up clouds of stinking rubber smoke. Then the treads caught and the car took off, hitting sixty by the time it reached the end of the exit ramp.

"So far, so good," she said after a few minutes. "Are they following us?"

He peered through the rear window. "I can't see them. But it's getting dark. That was quite a takeoff, Marlene."

"It was *comme il faut* at the Tastee-Freeze on Linden Boulevard. Some things you never forget. It's a good thing we got this car. I can blow the doors off anything but a Ferrari. Assuming it holds together. Oh, crap, look at this!"

They had crested a hill and before them stretched the taillights of a monumental traffic jam. She hit the brakes, skidded sideways, corrected, and slowed to a crawl behind a Volvo with a loaded ski rack.

"Shit, if there wasn't this goddamn snow I could cut across the median or go down the shoulder. Can you see them yet?"

"I don't know. Yeah, I think that's them. About four cars back."

"OK, let me try something."

They inched along in the center lane for about five minutes.

"Um, Marlene, what's the plan? You going to try to get us to a phone?"

"Yeah, after we lose these guys. Pretty soon now. We should be real close to the Tuckahoe Road exit." When the exit sign appeared, she hit the brakes and the car rolled to a stop. In seconds, horns were blaring behind them and drivers were rolling down their windows and poking their heads out. "Marlene, what's going on?" he said anxiously.

"Wait a minute. I'm getting some maneuvering room." The left and right lanes continued to move forward, and then they too were blocked by cars far back in the center lane attempting to get past the obstacle. A clear space of about five car lengths opened up. Marlene gave it the gas and the car screamed forward. Then she leaned on the horn.

It had a spectacular effect. Half a dozen cars in the right lane leaped into the snowy shoulders of the road as their drivers instinctively wrenched their wheels away from the terrifying sound. Marlene barreled past them and tore up the exit lane at fifty. There was a scream of brakes and a metallic crash behind them.

"What happened?" she shouted.

"Our guys tried to pull right out and cut off somebody. Shit, they're still coming."

She drove east on Tuckahoe Road. In the rearview she could see the headlights of the van glaring against the snow as it left the exit ramp in pursuit. A quarter mile later, she whipped the Chevy into a high-speed turn down a suburban lane.

"What are you doing now?" he asked. The van had also made the turn, and the headlights behind them were getting closer. There wasn't another car in sight.

"My Aunt Agnes lives here," she replied. Karp stared at her. Her lips were tight and she held the wheel in a white-knuckled, stiff-armed grip, hands in the ten of four position.

"Your Aunt Agnes? What are you talking about?" he shouted.

"Don't yell at me, goddammit. I have to concentrate. OK, here comes the hill. Hang on to something."

The street was a one-laner that wound through a neighborhood of large houses set back from the road. Suddenly she accelerated and spun the car across the road in a skidding left. When the car had straightened out on the new road, Karp looked ahead and gasped. The headlights shone out on nothing. Then the front of the car dipped and he was looking down a long, straight, steep hill coated with glistening black ice.

The rear wheels gently shifted to the left, farther and farther, until they were descending the hill sideways, gathering speed. Karp felt a scream well up in his throat. Marlene was shouting something, but everything was moving too fast for him to concentrate on what she was saying. The lights of houses and shadows of trees tore by in a monochromatic blur like an old movie in a broken projector.

Then it struck him that she was in control. By delicate twitches of the wheel and dabs at the gas she played the car as it continued its slow spin around the compass, at last reaching the right way around, pointing down.

The hill bottomed out and began a more gradual upgrade again. Marlene headed its nose into a snowdrift and set the brake. "Watch," she said, turning and facing the rear window.

The white van came flying around the curve and started down the hill. It hit the ice and began to skid. Karp and Marlene saw its brake lights glow red on the snow as the driver jammed on the pedal. The van spun like a top, caromed off a pile of snow, smacked a buried car, toppled over onto the driver's side, and skidded down the hill like a runaway carnival ride. Leaving the roadway entirely, it ripped through a high privet hedge and ended up smoking in the middle of a broad, snowy lawn.

Marlene backed out of the drift and drove slowly away. She was shaking with released tension. Karp felt a heavy pressure in his chest; it went away when he started breathing again. "That was incredible! How the hell did you learn how to do that?"

"Aunt Agnes's hill? We used to do it every winter when we were teenagers. It was a trip. The one who spun the car the most times won."

"Yeah, but what if the guy in the van knew how to take ice?"

"Well, I thought about that, and then I figured, Cubans? From Miami? On black ice? I figured it was worth a shot."

"I guess. I'm glad I went to the bathroom before, though. OK, where to?"

"Well, why don't we drop in on Aunt Agnes? I'm starving and she's always good for a feed. And we can call Denton from there. Besides, you said you wanted to meet my family."

17

"THEY'RE TEARING UP the street again," Fred Brenner said disgustedly. "I'll drop you at the corner here." Karp shrugged and opened the door. The clanging explosions of air drills rattled down Centre Street from its junction with Canal and reverberated between the Courthouse and the Federal Building across Foley Square. "You sure you can make it by yourself?" the big detective asked solicitously. Karp shot him a sour grin. At Denton's insistence, Brenner had been continuously with Karp since he and Marlene had returned to the city the previous night. He'd even set up a folding cot in Karp's pristine living room.

"I think so," Karp said. "By the way, I go to the can around two-thirty, and I like soft paper. Be there." Brenner laughed and pulled away in a screeching U-turn down Canal.

Karp walked past the Courthouse to Pearl and stopped in at Sam's. The little luncheonette was thick with the smell of bitter coffee, toast, and grease, the air almost like a food itself. He unbuttoned his coat and ordered a coffee with two bagels to go from Gus, the current Sam, a squat person with a striking resemblance to Yassir Arafat. Karp was about to leave with his order when V.T. and Guma came in, with a smiling Dirty Warren in tow. V.T. and Warren were their usual impeccable selves; Guma, unshaven and uncombed, looked like a man just arisen from bed.

Gus scowled when he spotted Warren and began to shake his head. "Hey, uh-uh—"

"It's cool, Gus," Guma said. "He'll be good."

"No shoutin'."

"Right. Just a little quiet breakfast. We'll sit back by the john. Hi, Butch, come on back. We're just putting the finishing touches on you know what."

"Sure. Hey, V.T., sorry we had to run. We had a great time."

"Glad to hear it. You have any problems getting home?"

"You could say that," Karp replied. When they were seated, he related the story of the encounter with the white van. "So you're a hunted man," said V.T. when he had finished. "That's pretty exciting. Can I have your Yankee jacket if they get you?"

"You ought to get out of town, Butch. Until they catch those assholes," Guma said.

"Yeah, but I can't right now. The trial's in a few weeks, and I got to watch the store or Bloom will let them cop to mopery. Of course, if I had something solid on Bloom, that'd be a different story. Like those tapes—"

"Oh, no, we went through that already."

"Guma, I'm risking my life here, and you won't risk . . . I don't know what."

"My balls? No thanks."

"What are you guys talking about?" V.T. asked. Karp told him. "Goom, I can't believe my ears. Passing up the match of the century? Klepp and Guma, my God! Alert the networks!"

"Fuck you and the horse you rode in on, Newbury," said Guma, starting in on his prune danish and black coffee. The others were silent, except for Dirty Warren's random muttering of curses under his breath. Finally Guma slammed his cup down in the saucer. "OK, goddammit! I'm not promising anything, but I will try. One try, that's all. If I draw a blank, or I get any shit from that bitch, that's all she wrote. You understand?"

"Perfectly," Karp said. "Nobody could ask for more. Right, Warren?"

"Right, Mr. Karp. You jerk-off motherfucking dickhead."

Outside the luncheonette, Karp paused to fix his collar and button his coat. The wind blowing up Pearl Street was making the crowd hunch over and the perpetual steam plumes from the manholes jitter in wispy rags. He spotted the big guy almost at once. He didn't seem to be taking any trouble about hiding himself. He climbed down from a large van that was parked across the street, a blue Dodge this time, parked tight so that Karp couldn't read the plates.

Another swarthy guy. He leaned against the front of his van, his dark eyes studying Karp calmly. He was about six-two and broad across the chest and shoulders, a weightlifter type, and wore a navy blue track suit with running shoes and a tan down vest.

Ruiz's second string looked a lot more impressive than the first, Karp thought. Or maybe this was the first team. As he began to walk down Pearl toward Centre, the weightlifter followed. He was not interested in losing the big man. On the contrary, what he wanted was a conversation with this dude in the company of the Chief of Detectives.

Arriving at his office, Karp threw himself into his chair, still with his coat on, and called Denton. "They got another boy on me."

"You said you were coming over here this morning."

"I got work to do, Bill. I'll be over afterward, maybe five-thirty. I'll bring that Flanagan stuff over, too."

"I'm worried about you, not the evidence. Why don't I send Fred?"

"For what? To sit in my office and read comics? Chief, nobody is going to pop me in the goddamn courthouse. No, I'll tell you what you *can* do. Let's follow this guy and see who he works for. Maybe he'll lead us to Ruiz."

"I was going to suggest that, too. What's he look like?"

As it turned out, the plainclothes detectives dispatched by Denton could find no trace of the weightlifter in the blue track suit. All they could do was to circulate his description to security and put out a bulletin for the guy.

Karp thus went through his hectic day with the back of his neck tickling. He found himself studying the faces in the crowded courtrooms, seeking the guilty look, the quick turning away of somebody who had been watching him. Of course, he found nothing—or rather, he found too much. Looking for suspicious people in the New York criminal courts was like looking for communists in the Supreme Soviet.

By three, he was irritable and nervous and wishing he drank liquor. Marlene had gone off somewhere; "out of the building" was all she'd told the secretary. Karp arranged and filed the ragged cardboard portfolio of case papers he had dragged around with him all day, the high point of which was the presentation of a homicide case to the grand jury. It was a simple case. A woman had left her abusive husband, and he had found her and shot her five times. Karp had no trouble getting an indictment. As far as he knew, the CIA was not interested in the affair, nor were the Vatican, the FBI, the KGB, or the Elders of Zion. It was his kind of case.

Marlene had to visit the fourteenth-floor ladies room three times before she found Rhoda Klepp. She sidled up next to Rhoda's sink and began to comb her perfectly combed hair. For this occasion she was wearing the most debauched costume she felt she could get away with in the office, a size-three lavender sweater dress that buttoned down the front, with the top six and the bottom four unbuttoned. You could count her rib bones.

She sighed loudly. "God, I'm beat," she exclaimed. "What a weekend."

Rhoda glanced over and did a double take. It wasn't that Marlene looked slutty, it was just that she had shaved the line between low-class lawyer and high-class whore to near transparency. "Oh? Where did you go?" she asked casually.

"Up to V.T. Newbury's place. What a scene! That woman he hangs out with is too much. You've heard of Annabelle Partland? I wouldn't call her a porn queen exactly, more of a classy erotica sort of thing, but she's into some incredibly kinky scenes. I mean internationally—the Velvet Underground, the Hellfire Club and all that West End stuff in London, and of course that thing that was in all the papers, with those Greek millionaires in Juan Les Pins? You remember, with the corrupt little girls?"

"You're putting me on, right?"

"No, really," Marlene laughed, "I mean, my dear, I'm no blushing virgin, but this was a bit much for even me. She showed us a film some guy had made, starring her and a couple of dudes, one of whom is now a big TV star, but I'm not supposed to say who. We were positively writhing by the time it was finished. After that it was every girl for herself and no holes barred."

Marlene hesitated before using this last line: its grotesque vulgarity might spill the beans. But no, she observed, Rhoda was now looking at her without her usual supercilious air, and her vixen face exhibited instead that mixed expression of disgust and fascination of a rubbernecker at a fatal automobile crash.

"Hey, swinging," Rhoda observed, too flatly. Her brain was reeling. It was simply not possible that Marlene Ciampi, whom she had patronized as being hopelessly naive, could have attained this level of sophistication. Not to mention that Marlene was apparently a delicious source of gossip and scandal of which Rhoda had been completely unaware. It could not be tolerated.

"Um, who was there?"

"Just me and V.T. and Annabelle. And Butch, of course. Naturally, it didn't get really weird until Guma showed up. Now, there's a hunk!"

"Guma? You think Guma is a—a hunk?" Rhoda asked incredulously, wrinkling her nose.

"Yeah, well, I guess you got to get to, ah, know him, if you get what I mean."

"You're joking."

Marlene fixed her with a level stare and did her best Joan Crawford. "Darling, you have absolutely no idea. You know, Rhoda, as you get older and more experienced, you'll find you have certain needs, needs that can't be satisfied by some pretty boy. The man is a master. What an imagination! Not to mention the equipment!"

"The e-e-quipment?" Rhoda stammered.

"Giganteroso. And indefatigable."

"Umm, you mean you and, ah, Guma—"

"Did I ever! Oh, he spent most of the evening in a threesome with this pro he brought and Annabelle, but I got my licks in. So to speak." Marlene started to titter involuntarily and managed to turn it into a dirty laugh. It sounded utterly phony to her own ears, but Rhoda didn't seem to notice. In fact, as Marlene had correctly judged, Rhoda was hooked. Although she was a habitual petty liar herself, and shrewd enough in detecting the little inconsistencies and fibs of office life, a piece of malarkey as enormous as what Marlene was handing out was quite outside her experience.

"Hmm, but Marlene," said Rhoda, her mouth dry, "I thought you and Karp were an item."

"Oh, we are, we are, but what has that got to do with it? Oh, you mean fidelity. Going steady? Like in junior high? Seriously, I mean, it *is* 1976. We *are* capable of some sophistication. He has his—how can I put it—his interests, and I have mine." Marlene finished her face and picked up her bag to go. "By the way, you might consider giving that a fling yourself. Of course, he's picky. God knows, with his reputation in certain circles he could have any woman in town."

"Who, Karp?"

Marlene laughed hysterically. "Karp? How silly! No, Guma! On the other hand, he might be a little too piquant for somebody your age. I don't know. I mean, he had this bag of implements he brought back from Thailand. Annabelle volunteered, of course. I thought the poor woman was going to have a seizure—" She glanced at her watch. "My God, I'm due in Part Thirty-three two minutes ago. See you."

Marlene ran down the hall and into the stairwell. There she commenced to laugh so hard that she had difficulty negotiating the stairs. Her nose ran, her eyes teared; she gasped and wheezed. Later, going about her grim business in court, an image kept jumping into her mind bringing to her face a loony grin unsuitable to the venue: Rhoda Klepp, naked and wet, flopping around on a sandy beach like a landed salmon—in her mouth, firmly hooked, a cylindrical pale lure carved into the shape of an equally nude Guma, cigar and all.

Guma stood in the men's washroom, his hair oil, comb, cologne, and deodorant arranged on the edge of the basin while he ran an electric razor over his blue jowls. As he did so, he was smoking the first El Producto cigar of the day, a habit he had pursued since the age of sixteen. It slowed down the shave, especially around the mouth, but he didn't mind. He did his best thinking at such moments, and at this particular moment he was thinking about Rhoda Klepp and about his approach. He reviewed his standard repertoire: Little Boy, Tough Guy With Heart of Gold, Noble But Injured and in Search of the Right Woman. He doubted any of these would work. Although the personality of the woman was hardly ever a factor in his romantic life, in the case of Rhoda Klepp he had to make an exception. His heart was not in the chase, and where the heart would not go, it was unlikely that the more operational units of anatomy would follow.

He now began to consider how he could weasel out of his deal with Karp. Suddenly he smiled. After all, he had promised only to try. He put down his razor and patted cologne liberally on his face and neck. An elderly court clerk came in to the men's room and stepped up to a urinal. Glancing at Guma, he said, "Hey, Ray, who's the lucky girl?"

"Rhoda Klepp," Guma said. The clerk laughed so hard he had to stop peeing.

An hour later, Rhoda Klepp was talking to her secretary in Wharton's outer office. When she was done, she turned to go back to her own office. That's when she saw Guma leaning casually against a wall near a potted palm. He was chewing gum. She gave him what she thought was a cool and sophisticated look. At the same time she was unpleasantly conscious of the flush that was running up her cheeks. He strolled over to her. In a neutral voice he said, "Hey, Rhoda. Wanna fuck?"

"Sure," she said, surprising the hell out of both of them.

By five, the only item left in Karp's portfolio was the sealed envelope with the Q and A from Flanagan. He told Connie he was walking over to Police Plaza to deliver something to Chief Denton and that if Marlene called, he would meet her in her office around six. He left the building by the Baxter Street exit. They were still tearing up the pavement, and the sounds of the drills echoed like gunfire through the narrow, walled-in streets. He examined the road and the sidewalk carefully. No blue van, and in any case, with traffic clogged as it was, it would be impossible for a vehicle to follow him on foot. No weightlifter either. Of course, there could be others on his tail. A short, wiry man wearing a brown parka crossed the street toward him. The man scowled and muttered something in an unfamiliar language, then moved on. A threat, or a guy who just remembered he had to pick up the dry cleaning?

Karp fought down his paranoia. Taking a deep breath, he started walking toward police headquarters three blocks away, his hand on the envelope deep in his coat pocket.

The old police headquarters, on Centre, was a baroque domed pile easily confused with a church. It had obviously been designed, at least in part, to overawe the proletariat with the greatness of the law, or failing that, to hold off an attack in force. The new building was a triangular modern structure that looked like the world headquarters of an insurance company. It was on a street that had been renamed Avenue of the Finest. Hype is cheap.

Karp wasn't carrying any bombs or weapons, so they let him in and he took the elevator up to the fourteenth floor, where the superchiefs have their offices. He introduced himself to Denton's secretary and said he'd like to see the chief for a minute. Her eyes widened in surprise. "You're Roger Karp? But you're supposed to be in Bellevue."

"What are you talking about?"

"The chief just rushed out of here about ten minutes ago. Somebody called from Bellevue Emergency and said they had a Roger Karp who'd just been shot on the street and was asking for Chief Denton."

Karp's belly knotted. "OK, there's some kind of scam going on," he said carefully, trying to control his breathing. "When the chief calls back, tell him I was here and that I'll call him later this evening, OK?"

She looked concerned. "Mr. Karp, is there some kind of trouble? Maybe you should stay here. I could call his driver and get the message to him right now."

Karp merely shook his head. He was holding an envelope containing evidence that somebody high up in the NYPD had tried to destroy a case against a cop killer. Given the phony call from Bellevue, the last thing he wanted was his whereabouts broadcast over police radio.

He left the building and began trotting back to the courthouse. He was not at all surprised when, out of the corner of his eye, he saw the weightlifter step out of a doorway and follow him at the same slow trot, like two joggers on the path around the reservoir in Central Park.

The courthouse was closing down when he arrived. The weightlifter did not follow him, but continued trotting past the entrance as if on a more important errand. Karp walked up the fire stairs to the second floor, to one of the vast depositories of court records that occupied almost all of the courthouse's first three floors. The room was dim and empty. He went to a file cabinet, pulled open a drawer, and yanked out a file at random. *People* v. *Dodd*, 1947, a routine burglary. He stuck the envelope in the file and returned it to its place. He knew where it was, but for anyone else it was now as lost as it would have been at the bottom of the Mindanao Trench.

In the main lobby, by the guard's desk and its metal-detecting frames, Karp made some small talk with the guards, then made a show of checking his wristwatch. "Hey, it's five-forty," he said. "Got to run. Good night."

I've established the time of death, he thought, make it a little easier for whoever picks up the case. Walking out onto the wide sidewalk facing Collect Pond Park, he heard a shout and spun around. The weightlifter was running toward him, his mouth open. As Karp started back for the entrance, he heard the pneumatic drills clanging up the street, and a part of his mind wondered why they had started again. Something popped like a firecracker next to him, and he felt a hard jolt in his upper arm.

Then, without quite understanding how, he was lying with his cheek on the cold pavement. His ears were filled with the sound of the drills. His shoulder and side hurt, his nose stung and dripped. Some huge weight was resting on his back. He tried to push off against it, but the pain grew unbearably when he did so.

He opened his eyes and saw gray concrete through a blur of tears. Something hot hit the back of his neck, skittered across his face, and bounced, tinkling, onto the sidewalk. He blinked the tears away. There was a squat brass cylinder lying a few inches from his eye. Dozens more littered the pavement, and as he watched, others fell from above. The deafening racket continued, and he could smell a sharp firecracker stench.

He at last made the connection: somebody was firing an automatic weapon about four inches from his left ear. He heaved upward and tried to roll. He might as well have been under an Oldsmobile. He heard the roar of a large engine and the squeal of tires, and saw the bottom half of a white van tear off down the street. The side was open and a man was lying in the doorway, his arm hanging down, the hand smacking against the roadway. The hand was bright red.

Then someone lifted him off the ground. He was being carried over someone's shoulder. He saw the pavement swiftly moving beneath. His arm flopped down and he was engulfed in agony. A wave of nausea rose from his gut, and he lost his struggle to remain conscious.

He awoke lying on his back in a dark, shaking, rumbling space. The pain was gone. Instead he felt a comfortable warmth and his face seemed covered with soft flannel. He had spent enough time in orthopedic hospitals to know the feeling. Somebody had given him a shot of morphine. People were moving around him in the darkness. They were talking softly in a foreign language, a guttural, rolling language that was oddly familiar. His mouth was bone dry and when he finally forced a few words out, he croaked.

"What's going on? What's—what—"

"Relax, you're all right now," said a woman's voice in accented English.

He tried to sit up, but there was something across his chest holding him down. "What the hell is going on? Who are you?"

Suddenly there was light. Karp blinked and saw that he was in a van, tied to a stretcher. Somebody had just turned on the dome light. Kneeling over him, looking concerned, was a familiar face.

"Leventhal?" he asked in amazement. "The Stereo King?"

"Yes, Mr. Karp, it's me."

"But what the hell . . . what are you, working for the Cubans?"

Leventhal shook his head, then said something in the foreign language. Karp tried to gather his thoughts, but the dope was making his mind slow. The language, what was it? He couldn't control his mouth. It felt two feet wide. "Crosse? Kwats? Yugo-Yugoslob? Woo?"

The Stereo King reached up and flicked off the dome light. Karp closed his eyes and drifted in and out of drugged sleep for a while. The voices murmured around him. What was that language? It wasn't Serbo-Croat. He remembered the interviews with the hijackers in the FBI office. It wasn't German either. Karp's grandparents had spoken both German and Yiddish. Recalling his grandparents was what did it. Grandparents. Funerals. Shul. The voices in the darkness were speaking Hebrew.

"Goddy?" Marlene Ciampi said, "we got problems and I need your help." She was amazed at how calm she was. She was also amazed that when Bill Denton had called and told her that Karp had been snatched in front of the courthouse in a hail of lead, she had not told him about her Yugoslavian connection. Which was why she was on the phone with G.F.S. Taylor.

"Why, my dear, whatever is the matter?" he asked.

"Somebody just tried to machine gun Butch Karp in front of the courthouse."

"Good God! New York gets more Balkan every day. Renko and Peter will feel quite at home soon. You said 'tried,' so I presume he's not dead."

"No, I don't think so. But . . . there was blood on the sidewalk where he was lying."

"And where were the police?"

"Well, the detective who witnessed the thing was waiting for Karp at the wrong entrance. By the time he heard the shots and ran around the building, the whole thing was over. It couldn't have lasted more than a minute."

"I see. And how can I help?"

"Well, there were two groups, see. One tried to whack him out and the other saved him but kidnapped him. It'd be good to know which is which. But I'd lay odds that one of them is Ruiz's Cubans and the other is—"

"Beg pardon. Ruiz?"

"Oh crap, I'm sorry, Goddy, just some other thugs in this case, a bunch of guys who used to work for the CIA and are doing free-lance evil."

"Um-hmmm. The CIA, you say. How interesting."

"Why?"

"Oh, nothing, nothing. Just thought of something. Now, who did you say the other gang was?"

"That I don't know. I'd sort of like your opinion on whether they could be Yugos. Maybe Croats."

There was a long pause on the line. "We'd better talk, and not by phone. Why don't you come to my place? Half an hour."

And he hung up before she could say anything more.

In fact, they did not talk much in any case. When Marlene arrived at Taylor's apartment and they were seated in the stuffy parlor, the old man simply gave her a slip of paper with an address written on it.

"Marlene, do you recall the last time we saw Renko, you asked me whether I had any idea of why Karavitch would become active after all these years, and I said I would try to set up a meeting with a man named Dushan, who might know more about it?"

"Yeah, I do." She held up the paper. "This is him?"

"Right. I think it's time for you to see him. And, Marlene, these are very serious, very dangerous people you are going to meet. Not like Renko. But I think that if Croatians are involved in this shooting match today, Dushan will know. More important, he might tell you, provided he thinks he can get something from you in return." As he said this, his expression was so grave that Marlene had to grin. "Wow, real spies," she exclaimed, "this is a first for me. Do I have to eat the paper?"

He returned the smile, but faintly. "I'm serious, my dear. If you get into trouble, I'm not sure I have the resources to extricate you. And I'm not sure you have anything to bargain with."

"Oh, I think I do. I've got Karavitch and his friends for starters, which I bet was the reason this guy agreed to meet me in the first place."

Taylor looked uneasy. "Well, yes, of course. But still, do be careful."

"Sure, Goddy, I know. Hey, Ms. Caution, that's me. Don't worry so much, you're starting to look like my mother." Marlene stood up and hoisted her shoulder bag. "OK, I'm going now—"

"Marlene, perhaps we should call in the police—"

"Shit, Goddy! That's the last thing we need. All we're after is a little information. Denton's got enough to do. Besides, if I sit still, I'll go crazy. No, now I'm really going, and Goddy . . . ?"

"Yes?"

"Whatever they do to me, I'll never betray you—"

"Get out of here, you lunatic!" Taylor cried, grinning now.

"Except hairy spiders. If they bring out the hairy spiders, you're finished, sorry."

The address was an old, anonymous ten-story building in the far east Thirties. The door to suite 503 was marked "KOR IMPORTS" in dull gold letters. Inside, Marlene found a tiny reception area containing a tan vinyl couch, a coffee table spread with copies of *People* magazine and a two-day-old *Post*. There was a tourist poster on the wall: blue sea, rocky shore, JUGOSLAVIE in white letters. Marlene went up to the little sliding window, behind which sat a hard-faced blond woman reading a magazine. "I'm Marlene Ciampi," she said. "I'm here to see Mr. Dushan."

The woman looked at Marlene unsmilingly, put down her magazine, and punched a button on her intercom. She said a few words in a Slavic tongue, waited a second, and hung up. She indicated a door at the far end of the reception area with a twist of her head, and returned to her magazine.

The inner office was lit only by a small gooseneck lamp on the desk in the center of the room, the bulb of which was pushed down to within a few inches of the desktop. There was a man seated behind the desk. Marlene could see that he was large, but nothing beyond that; his head was a dark lump.

"Mr. Dushan?" she asked, more loudly than she had intended.

"Yes. Please have a seat." The voice was deep, his English only slightly accented. "Forgive the illumination. I think it would be convenient if you did not see my face at present."

Marlene arranged herself on a straight chair before the desk. "Oh? Would I know you? Are you famous?"

Dushan ignored this and said, "How can we help you, Miss Ciampi?"

Marlene took a deep breath and said, "A friend of mine, an assistant district attorney of New York County, was kidnapped this afternoon. Somebody tried to shoot him, and another group of people picked him up and drove off with him. Someone suggested that you had knowledge of . . . certain groups that might be involved. So . . ."

She trailed off. Talking to a stranger in the dark like this in circumlocutions was more disconcerting than she would have believed possible. It was like going to confession. She began to feel irrationally guilty and let out a nervous giggle.

"Something is amusing?"

"No, I was thinking of confession. Telling things to someone you don't really know in the dark. Waiting to get bawled out."

A low chuckle. "Yes, and then forgiven. You are a Catholic, then?"

"Terminally lapsed, I'm afraid. But, uh, about Karp—"

"Yes, Mr. Karp. As to that, perhaps I can help you, and perhaps not. Perhaps we can help each other."

"Like how?"

"Something will emerge. As in the confessional. So. Let us begin by exchanging what we know of this situation. Mr. Karp is engaged in prosecuting a Croatian terrorist cell for the murder of a policeman. Someone tries to shoot him, and someone else rescues him from this shooting and spirits him away. It is not unreasonable to suppose that Croatian terrorists are involved. Which is, of course, why Colonel Taylor sent you to me. Tell me, how much do you know about Djordje Karavitch?"

"What's to know? He helped kill a friend of mine. And I heard what he did in the war from . . . some friends. He's a dirtball. Why do you ask?"

"A dirtball? What an interesting expression! No, Karavitch is a fascinating man. I say this although I am his enemy. A brilliant scholar, a brave fighter, a great patriot, a leader of men. But another of the millions driven insane by the events of this hideous century. It is true that many of the *ustashi* were gutter people— dirtballs, as you say—but Karavitch somehow stood above them even though he drenched himself in blood."

"You mean in that village? Krushak?"

"Ah, so you know about Krushak?" There was surprise in the man's voice. "Very good. But there were many such places, very many. In one little town, for example, in the wine region, a group of *ustashi* slashed the throats of the entire population over a wine vat. Over four hundred men, women, and children. They wished to see how much Serbian blood the vat would hold."

"And Karavitch was there?"

"Who knows? He might have been, certainly. Karavitch worked directly for Andrija Artukovic, the Croatian Minister of Police, who was responsible for organizing the murder of four hundred thousand Serbs and Jews. So, then, here is a man hunted throughout Europe, a fascist murderer; we are searching for him, the Soviets, the Allies—I ask you, how could such a man escape?"

"I don't know. Somebody must have helped him."

"Yes, somebody did. At the end of the war the Catholic Church established an organization called Intermarium, the purpose of which was to help Catholic activists escape from Soviet-occupied territory. They did not, of course, ask any questions about what these good Catholics were doing during the war, whether they were murdering Serbs or Jews, for example. One of their agents, a priest named Dragonovic, specialized in helping Croatian fascists, including the *ustashi*, helping them escape. A ratline, as they call it. We know that Dragonovic and Intermarium provided fake transit papers to a man calling himself Karavitch for a journey from Hungary to Trieste in early 1946.

"Now, you understand that in Yugoslavia in 1946 we had more important things to do than to hunt down every fascist trying to leave the country. The nation was a ruin. We had lost ten per cent of our population. But Karavitch we wanted. So we sent people to Trieste, where we knew he was staying. And he was gone. Not just gone from Trieste, gone from the Intermarium ratline. He vanished."

"Where did he go? Do you know?"

A long pause. Marlene was dying for a cigarette, but was afraid to make a light. The pleasant voice continued. "We think he was hired by your army's counterintelligence corps to run a network of agents in the Balkans. In 1948 the network closed down and Karavitch entered the United States, where he has been living peacefully ever after. It is a not uncommon story."

"So why tell it? What does this have to do with Karp?"

"I tell it to impress upon you the importance we attach to Djordje Karavitch, and to convince you that it is in the interests of justice that he be returned to Yugoslavia to face his punishment. As for your Mr. Karp, we have reason to believe that he is being held by elements of a Croat terrorist organization. This organization will attempt to negotiate an exchange—Karp for Karavitch and his group. We would like to be present when this exchange takes place."

"Uh-huh. And how are you going to arrange that?"

"That is where you come in, Miss Ciampi. You see, the police have hidden Karavitch, as I'm sure you're aware. I'm also sure that you know where they are hiding him. It would not be difficult, I think, for you to alert us when and where the exchange is to be made."

"Wait a minute there," she said sharply. "You're talking about a hostage situation. There'll be police brass in charge, and SWAT teams and, Christ, you'll never get within a mile of the place."

A chuckle rose from the gloom. "No, no, it will not be that way at all. It will be very simple, which is why they have taken Mr. Karp. Surely you can see this. It is, after all, Karp who has responsibility for the prisoners. He can order them moved anywhere he chooses, just by making a phone call."

"Karp wouldn't do that."

"Oh, I think eventually he will. If I were you, I would pray that he does not make any trouble for them. These are extremely unpleasant people, Miss Ciampi."

She chewed her lip and tried to order her thoughts. She fought the feeling that all this foreign-intrigue crap was over her head. It was a deal, just a deal with a bunch of scumbags. And she knew how to deal.

"Yeah, right. But tell me, I'm a little slow here. What's your end?"

"Pardon?"

"Your end. What do you bring to the deal? I mean, you tipped me off, thanks a lot, but why don't I go to the cops right now? Why do I stooge for you so you can grab Karavitch?"

Another of those low chuckles. "Ah, yes, I was getting to that. Of course, we have a man with these people."

"A man . . . ?"

"Don't you think that we have infiltrated all these traitorous little groups? This is Balkan politics, Miss Ciampi. We have been happily betraying each other for six hundred years. Yes, one of our people is with Karp at this very moment. My end, as you put it, is to make sure that when Karp has done what they want him to do, he does not get a bullet in the head. Now, do we have a deal?"

She was about to say, "How do I know I can trust you?" like they do in the movies on such occasions, but decided the question was not worth asking, since she knew the obligatory answer. She felt stiff and tired. "I'll await your call, Miss Ciampi," said the voice. Marlene stood up and stretched. "You forgot to say, 'Do not talk to the police," she said, but even as she said it, she sensed that the man had slipped away in the darkness.

*   *   *

"Most of it is tommyrot, of course," said G.F.S. Taylor, putting down his second beer of the evening.

"Like what?" she asked.

"Well, to start, that business about wanting Karavitch for war crimes."

"Don't they?"

"Marlene, the Yugoslavs want to forget the war. There was a bloodbath of sorts in Croatia right afterward, and then they sensibly decided not to pursue the issue. Their goal was to knit the various minorities together again. Dragging the odd Croat against the wall, fascist or no, would not have helped that end. Look, Karavitch was a small fish compared to Artukovic, and he got away. Hell, even Pavelic, the bastard who ran Croatia for the Nazis, got away. The Yugoslavs didn't send special teams after them. No, it won't wash, dear."

"But Peter Gregorievitch hasn't forgotten."

"Peter is a maniac. A lovely man, but an absolute nutter, at least on this issue. A bit of old Balkan there, you might say, blood for blood, forever. If Yugoslavia is going to survive they'll have to put that sort of thing behind them." His one eye stared into space for a while and he sipped at his beer.

At length Marlene said, "So you think that business about what's-his-face, the Catholic underground, was bullshit too?"

"God, no. Monsignor Krunoslav Dragonovic ran an escape service for hundreds of Croats after the war, on Church money, and CIA money too. There was a warm, chummy relationship back then between the Agency and anybody with a claim to an anticommunist past. Christ, they hired half the SS! By the way, do you know where Dragonovic is now? In Zagreb, enjoying a comfortable retirement. Has been since '67. I see you're surprised, but I always rather suspected the old crock was playing both ends against the middle. Get the bad Croats out, but slip a few good Red Croats in amongst them, as a little favor to KOS."

He noticed her frown. "KOS. Yugoslav military counterintelligence. I rather think you just met their New York chief."

"Dushan, huh? That's not his real name, of course."

"Needless to say. Rather fanciful nom de guerre for a good communist, incidentally. It's the surname of the last tsar of the Serbian Empire. Very strange people these."

"Yeah, you could say that. So what's his angle? Why does he want Karavitch? More important, can he do what he says? Does he have a guy with Karp now?"

Taylor waited a long time before answering, examining the dregs in his glass and pulling on the yellow ends of his mustache.

"His angle. I have no way of knowing for certain, mind you, but it must have something to do with Karavitch's current activities. It's quite possible that Karavitch never entirely severed his connections with U.S. intelligence. As for whether he can help Karp . . . well, let me say that any Croat organization potent enough to pull off a kidnapping in broad daylight under fire is likely to have been infiltrated by Dushan's people. I notice you didn't think to ask him why, if he really had someone on the inside, his man didn't ring him up the minute Karp had arranged for the switch."

"Yeah, shit, that was dumb. So why does he need me?"

"Why, indeed? But the real question is whether any Croats have him, and there I would say that I rather doubt it. Most of the Croat nationalist organizations in New York are talking shops. I don't know of one offhand that could pull it off. I'm guessing, mind you, but I think Dushan's bluffing."

"But, Goddy, what should I do? I need a plan."

"Perhaps it's early for a plan. I'd say play along for the time being. Keep in contact. Wait. I'm sure you realize that among the people who would not like to see Karavitch go to prison in America, Mr. Dushan ranks fairly high. If you pretend to play his game, perhaps he will not think to try another, one you know nothing about. But the only real player for the immediate moment is your Mr. Karp. Nothing can happen until he arranges for the switch. Another beer?"

They drank for a while in silence while the Soho bar filled up with local people. Marlene scanned the faces. One of them could be Dushan and she'd never know it. The thought gave her the willies.

"Goddy," she said, "why didn't Dushan want me to see his face?"

Taylor shrugged. "Probably thinks the less people who know him in his unofficial capacity the better. A cautious man, and every right to be."

"But what's his official capacity? Is he really in the import-export business?"

"No, he uses that office as a convenience."

"So what does he do?"

Taylor told her.

She grinned wolfishly. "Got the plan," she said.

17

KARP WOKE UP with his arm in a cast, a throbbing pain in his head, and a dry taste like old pennies in his mouth. He was lying on a comfortable bed in what seemed like an ordinary bedroom. It was morning and pale, wintery light poured through sliding glass doors. Besides the bed, there was a bureau, a low table, and an armchair. In the armchair sat a slight, dark-haired young woman, dressed in jeans, a yellow turtleneck, and hiking boots. She was knitting a small white woolen garment.

She looked up and when her dark eyes met Karp's, she smiled. "Good, you are awake. How do you feel?"

"Like hell. What time is it, where am I, and what happened to me? And who are you?"

She laughed, a pleasant girlish noise. Her English was slightly accented. Karp realized he'd heard it before, in the van, last night. "So many questions," she exclaimed as she got up and approached the bed.

"How about some answers?" he snarled. "Hey, what's that?"

"A thermometer. I must take your temperature."

"You some kind of nurse?" he mumbled around the glass rod stuck in his mouth.

"Yes, sometimes, and you are my prize patient. Let us see . . . good, you have no fever. Now I think I will bring the chief in. For your questions—"

"Who's the chief?"

"Wait," she said and dashed out of the room.

Like I could go anywhere, he thought sourly. He sat up stiffly and managed to prop a pillow behind his back with his good hand. In that position, by craning his neck, he could just see out through the glass doors. Bushes and barren trees, a patch of gray sky. When he looked back, Ben Leventhal was standing in the room, with the young woman hovering deferentially in the background. He was wearing a blue ski sweater and corduroy trousers, and had hiking boots on his feet too. He no longer looked like any of Karp's uncles.

Leventhal smiled. "So, you are back among the living. How are you feeling?"

"Not bad, considering. Somebody shot me, right?"

"We extracted you from an assassination attempt, I'm happy to say."

"And who might 'we' be?"

"Ah, excuse me. This is Devra Blok, who has nursed you back to health, and I am . . . but we have already met. You remember the night your charming young lady helped me with my car. Ben Leventhal."

"Yeah, the Stereo King. This part of your one-year guarantee, Leventhal? Parts and labor and if somebody tries to shoot you, the firm brings in a bunch of commandos? It sure as hell beats the shit out of Korvette's."

Leventhal laughed. "I'm glad to see you're in good humor, Mr. Karp. I trust you're comfortable and if there's anything you need—"

"How about a phone?"

The man frowned with his eyes, but kept a broad smile on his mouth. "I'm afraid that won't be possible just yet. Perhaps later."

As he turned to leave, Karp said, "She said you would answer questions."

"So I will. But you are recovering from a serious injury. I don't wish you to strain yourself."

"You know a guy about six-two, two-forty, curly dark hair, looks like a weightlifter? Drives a blue van."

Leventhal seemed surprised at the question. "Yes, that would be Yaacov. He works for me. Why?"

"Tell him thanks."

"I will. You're very observant, Mr. Karp."

"I try to be. Where am I? Upstate? Connecticut?"

"Upstate."

"Could you be a little less vague?"

"Not for now."

"Do you know who tried to kill me?"

"Yes. A man named Sergio Ruiz and some of his friends."

"Any idea why?"

"I think you should rest now, Mr. Karp."

"Come on, Leventhal, it'll ease my mind."

"Please—"

"OK, OK. How about telling me why the Israeli army is interested in saving my skin."

"Israeli army?" Leventhal's face was a picture of surprise. He turned to the woman. "Devra, the man is hallucinating."

"Or marines, or commandos, or whatever you are, because for

damn sure you're not a bunch of audio salesmen. And you're not Croats, because I heard you speaking Hebrew back there in the van before I passed out. What are you, yeshiva *bochers* from Williamsburg? Who else talks Hebrew? OK, the only people I know who might have an interest in wasting me are Ruiz and his guys, who you say you defended me from, and some of Karavitch's friends, of which he apparently has an unlimited supply.

"But why Israelis? Why have Israelis rescued me and why are they kidnapping me? You needed a *minyan*? You're pissed off because I'm dating a *shiksa*? No, it's got to be Karavitch."

Leventhal performed an eloquent gesture of wonderment, holding his palms up and looking from side to side as if summoning support from an invisible crowd. "Mr. Karp, I have absolutely no idea what you are talking about."

Karp fell back on the pillows, exhausted. He had less strength than he had thought. "OK," he said weakly. "Fine. You're not interested in Karavitch. Nobody's interested in Karavitch."

Leventhal's face became grave. In a quiet voice he said, "Ah, I think you have got it right, Mr. Karp. In fact, nobody is interested in Karavitch. Djordje Karavitch has been dead for thirty years. He died in Trieste in 1946, murdered by the man you are prosecuting under his name." With that, Leventhal stalked out of the room. Devra Blok resumed her seat and took up her knitting again.

At her vanity mirror, wrapped in a silk kimono, Rhoda Klepp was considering how she was going to control the situation she had created for herself with that uncharacteristic burst of impetuosity. Sex was, she well knew, merely a question of control, once you cut through all the bullshit: a question of who screwed whom and who got screwed. Usually it was a pretty straight deal—you gave, you got, and Rhoda usually arranged it so that she got a little more than she gave, which was how she had reached her present status. In her world, sex was a tool, useful, if mildly distasteful, like giving dinner parties for a lot of boring, powerful people.

But Marlene had confused her with her tale of a different world, where people conducted themselves with abandon. Abandon! That was the problem. Rhoda still hadn't figured out how you could get the benefits of abandon (in terms of having something to boast and condescend about) and still maintain total control.

A difficult problem, but not, she thought, beyond her powers. The trick would be to destroy his confidence. Booze and a show of boredom usually worked for her. After that, when he had been reduced to the pliable schmuckhood that she knew occupied the center of all male-kind, she would let him do his stuff. It would be something to talk about, at least, like drinking warm mescal from a bottle with a dead worm in it: the act disgusting, the retelling—the chance to be the center of attention—delicious.

She finished her face, stood up, and let the kimono slip down, examining her naked body like a carpenter testing the edge of a chisel. Let him drool over that, she thought. Afterward, she would bring out the costumes. And the equipment.

Guma sat on the white Haitian cotton couch in the large living room of her Murray Hill apartment and finished his third scotch. He'd been there only twenty minutes. A Burt Bacharach record was playing on the stereo. There had been some desultory conversation about what to "do" on their "date," but both of them knew why he was here. He looked around the room. Where would she keep those keys? Lots of white, three large abstract paintings, chrome, glass, with bright plastic accents: science-fiction modern. All it needed was a robed and hypercephalic envoy from the Council of Scientists.

Rhoda was clinking things at the bar. Then she came toward him holding two drinks. She was wearing a kind of black pajama outfit, silky with little shiny threads woven into it, the sort of thing the Viet Cong would wear if they shopped at Bloomies. The top was half unbuttoned, and as she bent over to set the drinks down, Guma could see an entire large, white breast even without craning his neck. She seemed to take a long time arranging the drinks, ashtray, nut bowl, and chip-and-dip tray on the low glass coffee table. Guma casually reached out and slid his hand under the breast, hefting it slightly.

"Pound and a half," he said. "My old man ran a meat market. I used to work there Saturdays." He withdrew the hand, wondering why he felt so absolutely non-horny. Maybe it was the range of expressions that flickered across her face: outrage, horror, contempt, and simulated arousal.

"How interesting," she said. She arranged herself at the opposite end of the couch and drank from her vodka gibson. "I'd rather hear about Thailand. Marlene Ciampi's been telling me all about your exotic tastes."

"She has, huh? What would she know about my exotic tastes?"

"A lot, according to her. She described your performance last weekend in great detail."

This is definitely not going to happen, Guma thought, and what the fuck is she talking about? He took a deep swallow of his drink, and observed her watching him closely. She's feeding me scotch like they were going to bring back Prohibition tomorrow. She's trying to get me drunk? Me? He smiled inwardly and an idea began to take shape.

"Yeah, that. Well, I was a little off that night." He drained his glass. "Hey, how about another drink? No, don't bother, I'll get one for both of us."

Rhoda considered herself an experienced drinker. She knew how much she could take and never took any more. On the other hand, she couldn't very well expect this jerk to drink alone. She decided that matching him one for two would be safe.

How serious a miscalculation this was she did not realize until around midnight. By then everything was moving in slow motion, and she felt like her skin was covered in masking tape. There was loud music playing on the radio. Guma kept moving in and out of her field of vision. He didn't seem to be weaving much for a man who had drunk twice as much as she had, but then, how could she tell?

"Time to get th' show onna road!" she said out loud. "Hey, Guma, y'creep. Time f' some o' that kinky stuff. I got it all, all the stuff. Hey, where are ya?"

She stumbled into the small kitchen. Guma was peering into a cabinet. "Hey, hey whatcha doin'?" she asked.

Guma looked up from his work. Rhoda was swaying like seaweed in the tide. Her black jacket was hanging entirely open and her pointed breasts rocked rhythmically from side to side. The motion was entrancing and started doing things to his groin area. He made himself stare into her face.

"Looking for more of those pearl onions," he replied benignly. "You look like you could use another gibson."

"Nah, no more drinks. Wanna do kinky. Now." She made a clumsy grab for him and managed to latch onto his belt. She tugged at it, as one might on the bridle of an unwilling burro.

"OK, OK," said Guma, detaching her hand. "Kinky coming right up. Hey, Rhoda, whyn't you head for the bedroom and I'll, uh, get some supplies from here."

"Wha'? Wha' splies?"

"Foodstuffs, Rhoda baby. You can't go kinky without all kinds of foodstuffs. Now run along and make yourself, you know, ready." He reached out and gave her left nipple a friendly honk.

She giggled and arched her back, ran a thick tongue across her lips. "Oh, yeah. OK, a'right. I got all the stuff inna room." She staggered out. It's working, she thought dully. I got him nailed.

Her bedroom was dominated by a huge brass bed dressed with black satin and set in the middle of a round white shag rug. It was lit dimly by wall sconces. On a side table were arranged a bottle of massage oil and a large white plastic vibrator with numerous rub-ber attachments. Sophisticated.

Rhoda plunged into the lowest drawer of her bureau, dragged out a large brown paper bag, and dumped its contents on the bed. Thin chains, a pair of knee-length leather boots with five-inch heels, chrome-studded black leather garments, and various other accessories fell in a tangle. She crumpled up the bag and shoved it under the bed. It would be tacky if he knew she had bought all this stuff yesterday.

Rhoda shucked off her pajama outfit and underpants. Clumsily she tried to sort out the tangle. She extracted a leather bra with shiny needle spikes around the cut-out nipple holes and heaved herself into it. It closed in the back with a miniature lock and key. Next, the boots. They were tight, and she had to struggle to pull them on. She felt sweat running down her sides and matting her hair to her forehead. Wobbling to her feet, she stood up and sagged toward her full-length mirror to take a look at the effect. Immediately she crashed face forward to the ground. The tops of the boots were still wired together. She cursed viciously and tried to roll over, but found that her bra spikes were tangled inextricably in the shag rug. She lay there humping and thrashing like a tied hog.

Entering the bedroom with the tray he had loaded from the refrigerator and pantry, Guma observed this spectacle for some time, fascinated by the bounce and quiver of her generous but-tocks. Chivalrously he suppressed a guffaw. Instead he said, "That's a new one, Rhoda, baby. You getting all hot there by yourself?"

She heard this as from afar. Yes, it made sense. That was indeed what she was doing. She produced a quasi-sensual moan to suit. He put down the tray and quickly sorted things out. He unlocked the bra so she could get up and cut the boot wire with a nail scissors he found on her vanity table. She collapsed back on the bed and watched the ceiling rotate.

"What have we got here?" she heard him say. "Chains? OK, let's check it out."

She felt him fumbling at her wrists and sat bolt upright. Some-thing was wrong here. "No, no, you're spose to be tied up," she complained. In fact, she had looked forward to having him helpless on her bed, but the idea of being chained up herself had never occurred to her. She began to panic through her stupor. "No, don' wanna," she cried, and tried to get on her feet.

He gently pushed her back and massaged her neck. "Sure, I'll do it, baby, but you know the routine. You been around, right? I mean, Rhoda, would I waste my time with somebody who didn't know the score?" And more of this, in such a smooth, knowing, insistent tone, that she came to think that this is what she had planned all along. In short order she was tied by her wrists and ankles to the four corners of the brass bed.

She felt his weight on the bed and soon after something cold was placed on her eyes, blotting out her vision. She felt him leave the bed. She rattled her chains and waited for the kinky stuff to start. From time to time he would return to the bed and touch her body. He was putting substances on her flesh, cool, viscous, dripping. Strange odors arose from her body. Maddening at first, these sensations soon become intensely sensual. Now he was doing something between her thighs. Waves of heat erupted from her loins. She gasped and writhed her hips. She began to murmur the obscenities she had learned from her extensive readings in softcore pornography.

Guma looked up from his handiwork. Rhoda's eyes were covered with two beef patties. In the center of each one was a raw egg garnished with a maraschino cherry. He had decorated her breasts with catsup and Cool-Whip in a barber-pole pattern, and elaborately covered her hips and belly with a melange of oyster sauce, chocolate syrup, and a mass of lo mein he had found in a take-out container. Her crotch was heavily slathered with Louis Sherry grape jam. "Be right back, baby," he murmured and proceeded to toss the room in a professional manner, except that from time to time he had to pass by the bed and stir the grape jam a bit to keep Rhoda amused.

Still, it took him barely five minutes to find them, about twenty keys in all shapes on a heavy ring with an "I love New York" brass tag on it. He turned to go.

"Hey Rhoda, I just forgot something I had to do at the office. I'll be right back."

This did not register in the slightest. "Uhnng, uhh, I want it. Give it to me. I'm burning up!" she sighed.

"Rhoda," he said severely, "real people don't say shit like that."

"Ooh, I want that big passion pole," she cried, flapping and spreading her thighs to the limits imposed by the thin chains. His gaze was drawn involuntarily to the center of this movement, to the little slivers of tender pink visible amid the dark purplish glop. He felt a familiar, if unexpected, stirring.

"Ah, what the hell," he said, undoing his belt, "as long as I'm here."

The second morning of his captivity Karp felt well enough to get out of bed. The previous day had passed in fitful bouts of sleep and dull awakenings. He knew he ought to have made a fuss, railed at Leventhal, tried to get away to a phone, but he simply didn't have the energy.

"Being shot," observed Devra Blok as she helped him to his feet and into a blue terrycloth robe, "is not like anything else. It knocks the stuffings out, isn't it so?"

"Yo," Karp answered shakily, concentrating on keeping his feet. He leaned heavily against her and was conscious of her strength and the heat of her body under the thin shirt. "You sound like you've been shot yourself."

She shook her head. "Not me. But I have taken care of casualties. So, let us go get you feed."

"Fed," said Karp. "Bacon and eggs? Or is this a kosher kidnap? How about bagels and lox?"

A faint smile. "What you like."

She brought him into a sunny breakfast nook that smelled of toast and coffee and frying onions. Karp felt the saliva flow; he hadn't eaten any serious food since before he had been shot. He sat gingerly down at a round white table, and Devra sat next to him. Across the counter in the kitchen a lean man in a dark T-shirt stirred something at the range.

Devra poured coffee, and in a few moments the man came in from the kitchen holding a frying pan full of scrambled eggs made with minced lox and onions and a plate of toasted rye. The man nodded to Karp and sat down. Devra said, "Natan likes to cook breakfast, don't you, Natan?" Natan grinned shyly and dug into the meal. Karp did the same, wondering what Natan did when he wasn't cooking breakfast. The man was well built in a wiry way. He had a thick head of dirty blond curls and a wide mouth loaded with big white teeth. He had the air of a college student, but Karp figured he was four or five years into his twenties.

A door slammed somewhere in the back of the house. A few seconds later, Yaacov the weightlifter strode into the room, rubbing his hands. He had traded his track suit for a puffy red down parka, jeans, and hiking boots. He said "good morning" all around, unzipped his parka, and sat at the table.

Karp remarked lightly, "Yaacov, hang onto that parka. If the commando business ever goes bad, you can get a job with Michelin."

"Pardon?" Yaacov asked politely.

"You know, Michelin, the tire company. Their little man?" Karp mimicked the great girth of *l'homme Michelin* and got blank looks. It must be the language barrier, he thought.

After breakfast they adjourned to the living room. This was furnished in an anonymous suburban style, vaguely early American. Floor-length drapes in a pale green silky material covered one wall. There were pictures on the walls and hook rugs on the floors, but no knickknacks or personal photographs to be seen. Karp wondered who lived here, or if anybody did. He presumed it was what the spy stories called a safe house. He spotted a phone sitting on a corner table and thought about what they would do if he just walked up to it and tried to call.

Yaacov turned on a TV and sat on a couch to watch it. Soaps. He seemed interested. Devra sat in a ladderback rocker and took out her knitting. Natan disappeared somewhere. There was a grandfather clock that ticked loudly. After half an hour of this, Karp felt his mind softening. He wanted to know what these people wanted from him. He wanted to know what Leventhal was up to. And most of all, he wanted to know what he had meant about Karavitch not being Karavitch, but somebody else instead, who had killed the real Karavitch.

The hours dragged by. They had lunch—tuna fish sandwiches and Pepsi—and then returned to their original places. Karp studied his captors. The three of them seemed curiously flat in their personalities. No little jokes. No byplay. Very solemn. Of course, he reflected, maybe this is what kidnappers learn in kidnapping school: don't flash anything at the victim, be cool. Maybe he could get a rise out of them.

"This is fun," he said, "I always wanted to sit around for days on end and watch daytime TV. The problem is, I didn't bring my ironing." He stood up, walked over to the phone, and picked up the receiver. It was dead. Then he noticed that someone had removed the wire connecting it to the wall jack.

"Damn, I really could have gone for a pizza," he remarked. Devra looked up from her knitting. "We can get. Do you like it?"

"No, Devra. It was sort of a joke. Kind of an incongruity that in many people would produce the sensation of humor, perhaps leading to a laugh." She looked at him blankly.

Karp walked over to the floor-length drapes, pulled them back, and looked out through the huge picture window they concealed. A cleared gravel driveway and hedge-lined road, a snowy lawn, a row of black trees. A figure, a large man, was hurrying up the road. Leventhal? Before he could decide, Yaacov was by his side, closing the drapes.

"Please. You shouldn't do."

"Huh? Why shouldn't I? You're afraid I'll make signals? Help, I'm a prisoner in a matzoh-ball factory?"

Yaacov looked uncomfortable. He exchanged a quick look with Devra. "No," he said, "these men who shot you. They are outside."

239

"What? Oh, for crying out loud! What is this shit, guys? Why the hell don't you just call the goddamn cops?"

"I'm afraid we can't do that yet, Mr. Karp," said Leventhal.

Karp spun around. Leventhal was standing in the doorway of the living room, taking off his gloves. He was wearing a double-breasted tan car-coat, to which he gave a decidedly military air. His face was reddened, either with cold or exertion.

"Why not? When are you going to tell me what's going on?"

Leventhal smiled. "Now, if you like." He spoke to the two others in clipped phrases in guttural Hebrew, orders. They vanished. Leventhal removed his coat and threw it on the couch, then sat and gestured Karp cordially into an armchair opposite him.

"Now," he said when Karp had seated himself, "we can have our talk. You are being well treated?"

"Sure. First class. Best kidnapping I ever had. Look, Leventhal, when are you going to let me get out of here? And what was all that about those guys that shot me hanging around outside? And what was all the stuff about Karavitch being somebody else?"

Leventhal, still smiling, held up his hands in mock defense. "Please, one question at a time. First, let me deal with your personal danger. It is true we have observed a van on the local roads that appears to be the one that carried the would-be assassins. There is also a Cadillac sedan that travels with it. These two vehicles are now parked about a quarter of a mile from the main entrance to this property, and Natan is observing them. They have automatic weapons and shotguns. We think it is possible they will attempt to assault this house, perhaps this evening. It will be quite dark by six."

"How many guys do they have?"

"Natan says ten."

"Ten! For chrissakes, Leventhal, how you going to hold off ten guys with machine guns? You got three people and a girl."

Leventhal smiled and shrugged. "They're Cuban gangsters, Mr. Karp, and we're Israeli soldiers. You remember the Bay of Pigs? You remember Entebbe? I think we will do all right. Besides, we don't intend to hold them off. We will attack."

"Now I know you're crazy," Karp snapped. Leventhal's beaming confidence was beginning to get on his nerves. "OK, before you get killed, just tell me, why not bring in the cops? Just let me make a couple of calls, I guarantee you, you won't have to be involved."

"Well, I'm afraid we are involved, and the presence of the police at this time would complicate matters in a way that would be inconvenient to our mission."

"What are you talking, inconvenient? Stop these riddles, Leventhal. Tell me who you are, what you're doing here, and most of all, what the fuck you want with me."

Leventhal gave him a long look. His smile faded and was replaced by an expression that was both sad and angry. "All right, fine. You want information, I give you information. I notice there's no 'Thank you, Ben, you saved my life, you're risking your lives to keep on saving it.'"

"You could just call the cops; nobody's asking you—"

"The cops? Don't you know anything yet? What cops? The New York police? The FBI? Don't you know when you've been set up? How do you think those gentlemen out there in those cars found us so fast? Believe me, Mr. Karp, you want me to bring cops, I'll give you a gun first, you could blow your own brains out."

Karp looked at the floor and said nothing. He felt an odd shame about how plausible this was to him, that he could so easily credit the corruption of his country's and his city's police forces. After a moment Leventhal went on.

"Now, you are correct in thinking that I have a proposition for you. Simply, it is this. I am determined to capture and bring to justice in Israel an infamous war criminal whom you have in custody. I wish your help and cooperation in doing this."

"You mean Karavitch?"

"The man you know as Karavitch, the man you are holding now on a kidnap and murder charge, is not Djordje Karavitch. He is Josef Karl Dreb, Hauptsturmfuehrer Dreb of the Prinz Eugen Division of the Waffen-SS and before that a junior officer in the Reichssicherheitshauptamt, Eichmann's organization. Dreb was among the most promising officers in Amt IV B4, the organization responsible for the final solution to the Jewish problem. Accordingly, he was given a sensitive and important mission, which was mobilizing the forces of the Croatian puppet state and helping them round up all the forty thousand Jews in that country and dispose of them. Now, you understand that this was no easy task—"

"Wait a minute, Leventhal. How do you know Karavitch is what's-his-name, Dreb? He looks like Karavitch, he talks like Karavitch, also the Croatians accept him as Karavitch, and he entered the country as Karavitch. On top of that, if there was a Nazi who wanted to cover his tracks, why would he use Karavitch as a cover? Apparently Karavitch wasn't any sweetheart in the war either. It's like Jesse James trying to pass as Billy the Kid."

"No, it is not. Karavitch was a typical Croat fascist. He backed the wrong side in the war, maybe he shot the odd Jew, the odd

241

Serb, but what's a massacre or two or three against a good anticommunist Catholic background? No, Mr. Karp, Karavitch is small beer compared to Dreb. A Karavitch could get into the Croatian nationalist escape routes, could enter the United States, a poor refugee, everybody very sympathetic, you understand? Start a new life, bygones are bygones, no?

"But not Dreb. Mr. Karp, do you know what an *einsatzgruppe* was?"

"Yeah, as a matter of fact, I do. They were SS murder squads that followed the army and killed people the Nazis didn't like."

Leventhal raised his eyebrows. "Very good. Very interesting that you should have such knowledge. You have a special interest in the Holocaust perhaps?"

"No. But I was born Jewish in New York in 1943. Eat your soup, children are starving in Europe—that generation. My mother was a big-time Zionist, regional Hadassah officer for years, and for two hours every Sunday for six years I had Jewish history and culture pounded into my head, along with a load of Zionist propaganda. Mostly by Israelis, as a matter of fact. They had a lot of cachet in Brooklyn at that time. For years we had this book on our coffee table. Other people had, I don't know, horses of the world, flowers, Picasso; we had Auschwitz snaps—piles of human hair, the guys, the skeletons in striped pajamas, the room with a hundred thousand eyeglasses on the floor.

"Which is how come I know what *einsatzgruppen* are. I also know the names of all the concentration camps, their years of operation, and approximately how many people died in each one. Also their commandants, and the particular or unusual atrocities associated with particular camps: the human skin lampshades at Bergen-Belsen, the rock quarry at Majdenek, the medical experiments at Ravensbrucke. I remember there was one guy who liked to kill little children one by one with a hammer, in front of their parents—"

"Scharfuehrer Schmidt."

"Right, Sergeant Schmidt. They caught him and gave him eight years in the slammer. Apparently slept like a baby every night. Funny how that kind of stuff sticks in your head. Anyway, I'm just telling you this so you don't think that raising my Jewish guilt or conscience with a bunch of Holocaust stories will make me help you move Karavitch illegally out of the jurisdiction of the County of New York. Sorry."

Leventhal looked at Karp for several long minutes without saying anything. He was no longer smiling. Instead his large, liquid eyes glowed in their dark pouches with sadness, disappointment, a hint of contempt. It was high-intensity Jewish guilt-generating radiation, and Karp knew it well from countless cringing moments of his childhood. Despite himself he began to feel generalized shame and discomfort.

"It's not going to work, Leventhal," said Karp, feigning more confidence than he felt at that moment. "Get my grandmother in here, maybe you got a shot, but otherwise I can't help you."

"Yes, I see that," said the other man. "And I'm sorry too. For you. It must be sad to be so cut off from your own people. Funny, we don't learn. United we stand." He clenched his fist. "Divided we fall." He wiggled his fingers.

"I'm an American, Leventhal. We invented that."

"Yes, and they thought they were Germans and French and Poles, but in the end, all that counted was, they were Jews."

"True, but it turns out the Nazis aren't on the ballot this year. Not in New York anyway. If they ever come to power again, I'm going to go with the Remington autoloader twelve-gauge, modified with the drum magazine. I ought to be able to take out most of a *sturmbann* before they get me."

Leventhal looked sad again and cluck-clucked like an old lady. "What a shame we should be having a conversation like this, two Jews. A shame and a disgrace. Forgive me, Mr. Karp, if I must bore you with one more little tale from that time. You can add it to your coffee table collection, heh?

"In Zagreb in 1941, there were many Jews, refugees from Austria and Germany. The Yugoslavs were generous with visas at that time; perhaps they wanted Croatia salted with people who had some reason to be grateful to the Belgrade regime. And we were, we were.

"In April the Nazis came in. The war lasted ten days. Yugoslavia was broken up and Croatia became a German puppet, run by Pavelic and the *ustashi*. The pogroms started very soon. Of course, with so many Serbs to kill, it was hard for the *ustashi* to make room for the Jews, but they tried. These were, you understand, old-fashioned pogroms, with priests. The Jews were being beaten and killed because they weren't goyim.

"But this was too sluggish for the Final Solution. So in March 1942 an *einsatzkommando* was detailed from *Einsatzgruppe C* and sent to Zagreb to inspire the multitudes by a special action, as they called it. Now, there was in Zagreb at that time a large kosher slaughterhouse, because of the big Jewish community there. In 1942, of course, it had been shut down for some time. There was no meat for anyone by then, much less for Jews.

"This particular *sonderaktion* began with a riot, which started in the evening of Good Friday, an Eastern European specialty, as I'm sure you know. The torches came out and soon virtually the whole of the Jewish quarter was engulfed. By dawn there were perhaps ten thousand homeless people on the street, and slowly they began to gravitate for shelter to the old slaughterhouse, which anyone could see was a good choice: it was large, strongly built, dry, and it had, of course, adequate water and sewage.

"Therefore, when the *einsatzkommando* and its Croat allies set out on its task, the remnants of the Jewish community of Zagreb were conveniently at hand in, of all places, a kosher slaughterhouse. Naturally, the humor of this did not escape the SS. The Jews were herded into the pens formerly used for the animals, the children and the good-looking women were separated out, and the remainder were divided by sex and stripped. Then the machinery, the hoists and sluices and so forth, was started up, and the Jews were, literally, slaughtered. They were knocked on the head, a hook was driven through their heels, they were jerked upside down by the moving hoist, and their throats were slashed.

"The children were killed in different ways according to the whim of the murderers and the availability of equipment. Some were beheaded like chickens. They had skinning equipment, of course, so some were skinned, alive, dead, who knows? Some were flung into the boiling vats used to remove feathers from fowl. The little corpses were hung neatly on hooks, twenty-three hundred and fifty-two of them, aged four months through twelve years.

"Of course, in the main room there was a great deal more fun, because the SS and the *ustashi* were pretending to observe the rituals involved in kosher butchering: the draining of the blood, the salt rubbed into the flesh, and so on. There was a catwalk in the koshering room so that the supervising rabbi and his assistants could have a good view that the rituals were being followed. Now this catwalk was occupied by the leader of the *einsatzkommando*. He had there with him, bound and watching in the most extreme horror, the religious leaders of the Jewish community, with whom he would mockingly consult from time to time about fine points of slaughtering ritual. Every victim was marked with a red-hot electric brand that said 'kosher meat.' We can imagine what was going on in their minds. This commander, I don't need to tell you, was SS-Hauptsturmfuehrer Josef Karl Dreb.

"As you would expect, this event made his reputation. He was promoted and given the post of liaison officer between the SS and the Croatian police authorities. Did I tell you he was a native of Zagreb? Yes, indeed, a local boy, the son of an Austro-Hungarian imperial official and a Croat mother. In 1918, of course, they had to go back to Austria in disgrace.

"Not to psychologize, Mr. Karp, but you couldn't ask for a better breeding ground for a Nazi. The ruined authoritarian father, impotent, enraged; the mother, a fanatic Catholic, tyrannized by the man, both of them anti-Semites and Slav haters. Of course, the mother *is* a Slav, but that just spices the pot, you see. And of course, in their intimate moments together, Momma teaches her first-born son perfect idiomatic Serbo-Croat, even with the Zagreb dialect. Of course, it is only German in public: the father insists.

"Well, Karl does well in school, mechanical engineering, joins the Nazis in 1934, and after Anschluss is admitted into the SS, very squeaky that is, because the Momma is not perfectly Aryan. However, he gets in, has a good record, a brave fighter and imaginative murderer, not like Eichmann, afraid to get dirty hands, not a paper pusher at all, a head breaker instead. Ideal for *sonderaktionen*. We see him in 1943, at the height of his powers, a very important young Sturmbannfuehrer now, working closely with the Croat allies to crush the partisans and the Serbs and other underpeople.

"Of course, he had an opposite number on the Croat side, with whom he liaisoned, didn't he? And how marvelously he got on with this other young man! They were the same age, they shared the same ideals, they had similar backgrounds. Also, strange to say, they even resembled each other, both tall, sturdy, blue eyes, long skull, straight blond hair, and the rest. Now, Mr. Karp, you are a clever man. What do you suppose the name of this other fellow was?"

Karp had to clear his throat. "Djordje Karavitch," he answered hoarsely.

Leventhal seemed delighted with the reply. "Yes! Yes, Djordje Karavitch, a Croat patriot, reviving an ancient nation in the glow of the New Order. Well, they were thick as thieves for the next year or so, until things started to go badly for the Germans. The Russians were coming, the partisans were getting stronger. Dreb was detailed to a Waffen-SS division, the Prinz Eugen, where he was one of those responsible for reprisals against villages that were supposed to have helped the partisans. Dreb was able to get his good friend Karavitch the command of a company of *ustashi* attached to the German unit. Thus they were together when in the winter of 1945, their small column was ambushed by a reinforced battalion of partisans. From this attack only three men escaped alive. One was Dreb, one was Karavitch, and the other was, can you guess? No? It was Macek, whom I think you know, and who was then little more than a boy. They were scraping the barrel in 1945.

"So they escape and have many merry adventures, and at last in 1946 they find themselves in the city of Trieste. Karavitch and Macek are making contact with an organization that arranges the transportation of Croat fascists—I'm sorry, now it is Catholic nationalist anticommunists—to the United States.

"But Dreb? No, he is in much deeper trouble. He has to hide while his good friends bring him food. Because, you see, Dreb has made in the war a serious error. Oh, not the atrocities. People who were worse even than Dreb were at that moment being recruited by your government, Mr. Karp, to spy against the Russians. But in 1944 the American air force was conducting heavy raids from Foggia airbase against the industries of Central Europe. Many of these aircraft were forced down in Yugoslavia, and of course the partisans wished to help the crews escape as much as the Germans wished to capture them.

"To this game, Dreb brought his peculiar imagination. When he was able to capture an American crew he would send the healthy crew members to the stalags, to keep Luftwaffe intelligence off his back, but the wounded ones, these he would use as bait to catch partisans. His favorite trick was to stick a bunch of them in a barn or house and then have the partisans tipped off. The place would be heavily booby-trapped with the delayed-action devices he loved to use. He liked to observe the 'rescue' at long distance through his field glasses. Smiles, relief, cheers, then boom! Interesting, don't you think?"

"Fascinating. So if that was known, nobody would have him, not even our intelligence guys. What happened then?"

"Ah, yes, the denouement. On August 14, 1946, a corpse was found in a cheap lodging house in Trieste. The throat had been cut. This was not an unusual occurrence at the time, of course, but what attracted attention to this particular corpse was that it had an SS identification number tattooed in the armpit. On checking, it was found to be the number of Josef Karl Dreb, SS-Sturmbannfuehrer. Imagine that! Shortly thereafter, Djordje Karavitch and Pavle Macek entered the employment of the U.S. Army's Counterintelligence Corps, and a year later, that of the Central Intelligence Agency."

"And you think this was really Dreb?"

"We know it."

"What's your proof?"

"We have informants."

"Yeah? Who?"

Leventhal smiled. "They are reliable. It is the man."

"If you say so. But there's something funny about this operation, boss. I mean, you're not making a public fuss, not going through DOJ in Washington. Shit, they got a whole unit there does nothing but kick old Nazis out of the country. We got an election year here, you think maybe Begin could shake out a war criminal or two for the Jewish vote? Are you joking? President Ford goes, 'Hey, Betty, guy says he saw you chalking swastikas in Bucharest in '43. Sorry, kid, write when you get to Jerusalem.'

"Especially, you got a mutt who aced a bunch of our wounded guys in the war, hey, piece of cake. So why the hanky-panky, Leventhal? Maybe this isn't an official operation, huh? Where you from, Leventhal? I don't mean Tel Aviv, I mean before. Maybe Yugoslavia? Maybe Zagreb? You got a special interest in this one, a personal interest? Maybe your boy isn't heading for a glass cage in Jerusalem. Maybe someplace a lot closer, like a car trunk in LaGuardia, how about that?"

"How about justice?" shouted Leventhal, his face darkening. He rose to his feet and glared down at Karp. "Justice is what's at stake here, not somebody's bureaucratic skirts getting dirty. He's protected, as you well know. And you know why, too. Because the CIA people who hired him knew very well who he was, and that he had murdered American airmen in cold blood. So do you think we will be allowed to just take him away, thank you very much, so he can tell all that to the world?"

"Right," Karp said wearily. "You got justice mixed up with revenge, Leventhal. Not the same thing at all."

It had grown dark in the room. Light was no longer coming in through the drapes, and no one had turned on any lights. There was a scuffling noise in the hallway and a shadowy form entered the living room. Karp saw that it was Natan, his face blackened, dressed in baggy coveralls and a wool watchcap. He wore a belt from which hung various items of equipment and a large knife. Slung on his shoulder was an Uzi submachine gun. He conversed briefly with Leventhal and left.

Leventhal turned to Karp. "We are about to begin our operation. You must return to the bedroom, where Devra will look after you. If we are unsuccessful, she will help you get to safety. But under no circumstances are you to attempt to leave here by yourself. Is that clear?"

Karp started to object, then shrugged and went back to the bedroom. The curtains had been drawn over the glass door and the blinds on the window were closed. The only real light came from a tiny nightlamp plugged into the baseboard. By its glow Karp could make out Devra sitting in the armchair, her knitting in her lap.

Karp lay on the bed. Outside, it grew darker. The woman stopped knitting. They were silent, waiting.

The noises started, a string of pops far off, shouts, once a shrill cry like that of a tropical bird. Karp wiped the sweat off his palms and concentrated on breathing.

Something exploded outside the room and a red glare shone through the glass of the sliding doors. Then the doors exploded inward, and a man leaped into the room amid a shower of glass and curtain rags.

He really does look just like a snake, was Karp's first thought. The man was small and lithe and dressed in army fatigues. The face was so narrow and the yellow-brown eyes were so close together as to be almost a deformity. The mouth was a nearly lipless *V*, the nose two pits in a flat bump, and Sergio Ruiz had skin trouble too; his pale ochre face was covered with shiny bumps and excavations, adding to the reptilian effect.

On leaping into the room, he had crouched, sighting down the barrel of his Armalite automatic rifle into the four corners of the room in approved infantry-school fashion. He was angry and upset. He couldn't understand why he was having all these problems with shooting one man, nor did he understand why his people were being shot down in the dark outside by hidden strangers. He wanted to do the job as quickly as possible and get out of this crazy place.

Ruiz saw the woman first, sitting wide-eyed in her armchair. A woman was no danger, another piece of the furniture; he would deal with her later. Turning a quarter turn, he spotted Karp sitting up in his bed. Even in the dim light the target was unmistakable. He raised his rifle, sighted on Karp's chest, and touched the trigger. Karp had at that instant begun to roll off the bed in the direction of the nightlight. His hand reached out to swat it from its wall socket.

As soon as Ruiz's eyes were no longer on her, Devra Blok reached into her knitting bag and drew out one of the little alloy .22-caliber automatic pistols the Mossad issues to its agents when they are in foreign parts and need to kill people. In one long-practiced motion she yanked the slide back to chamber a round, pointed, and fired twice into the back of Sergio Ruiz's head. The assassin's hand tightened reflexively on the trigger as the slugs tore into his brain and the Armalite erupted.

Karp landed on his bad knee and grunted in pain. He was down in the narrow space between the bed and the wall, trying to make himself small and reaching for the nightlight with a shaking hand. Above him, Ruiz's assault rifle roared and bits of plaster, wood, and pillow feathers fell down on him. He waited for the pain of the bullets and worried fleetingly about wetting his pants. Then the firing stopped and he felt the bed jerk with the impact of a weight falling upon it.

He stuck his head up cautiously. Ruiz was facedown on the bed, his head in the center of a spreading red stain. One of his legs was twitching rhythmically. He was still breathing, a hoarse rasp, but Karp could see, and smell, that he had lost control of his bowels and bladder. Karp saw Devra Blok bend over Ruiz, as if to examine him. He saw the little dark gun in her hand and saw what she was about to do. He said, "Hey . . ."

She pressed the muzzle of the pistol against the base of Ruiz's skull and pulled the trigger twice. The shots made almost no sound: *bnff! bnff!* Ruiz stopped breathing. Karp looked at the expression on the woman's face. It was neutral, somewhat fatigued, like a suburban housewife who has just brought a load of garbage to the curb.

Their eyes met. She said, "Are you all right?"

Karp nodded. He stood up unsteadily, shaking, and felt an urgent need to visit the bathroom. He looked at the stinking corpse, then at Devra. She was sliding a fresh clip into her gun. "No more Anne Frank, right, Devra?" he said. She looked at him blankly, her brown eyes as innocent as a seal's.

19

KARP STOOD IN the living room window, watching them stack the bodies of the Cubans in their own white van. The Israelis had killed six of them, including Ruiz, and the others had escaped in the Cadillac. Natan and Yaacov tossed the corpses in with an easy, swinging motion, as if they had done it all many times before. The entire battle had taken no more than half an hour. It was now nine-thirty on a chill and cloudy night. The men worked by the glare of the floodlights that illuminated the driveway.

"Does this disturb you, Mr. Karp?" Karp turned to see Ben Leventhal standing by the doorway, wearing his own gray coverall assassin suit.

Karp shrugged. "No. Not unless you're going to put me in the van. Are you?"

Leventhal smiled and shook his head. "I can't understand you, Mr. Karp. We are the good guys. We're on your side. How many times do we have to save your life before you understand that?"

Karp tried to summon up gratitude, but it curdled in the horror he felt in the presence of these decent, clean-cut, efficient killers, his people. *Landsman'*.

Natan and Yaacov finished their work and slammed the doors of the van. Yaacov got in and drove off, rattling gravel. In a moment Karp saw the blue van follow down the drive. He let the curtain fall.

"Where are they going?" he asked Leventhal.

"The river is close by. They will be back shortly."

"Good thing we're not in New York County. We're not, are we?"

"No, Mr. Karp, we are not," Leventhal said with a chuckle. "Why? Would you arrest us if we were in your jurisdiction? I confess, I have never been able to understand the legal mind. People studying words scratched on paper while the world falls apart around them."

"Well, that certainly shitcans two thousand years of Talmudic history, doesn't it? I thought we were supposed to be the People of the Book."

"Oh, yes, and we know where all that ended up. In the slaughterhouse! On the ashheap! At least we know what justice is, believe me! Did you want us to leave Eichmann in his little house in South America to plan another escape while we waited for extradition papers? Let me tell you, Mr. Karp, nobody is ever going to murder Jews again and get away with it. Never! Not while we are strong."

"Of course," Karp said mildly. "Agreed. The problem is where you draw the line. Snatch Eichmann? Sure. Pop a couple of Arab terrorists? OK. How about some guys who might be thinking about terrorism? Why not? It gets easier, Leventhal, and the problem becomes how to stop. It's hard, once you've got a government committed to going around killing people and a bunch of guys who're good at it on hand. Those guys out there stacked in the van: *we* hired them to fight commies, and then we hired them to break up a terrorist organization in Miami. More killing people in a good cause. It's not surprising they start using their one marketable skill in a cause that's not so good. I mean, we didn't hire them because of their ability to make fine moral discriminations, did we?

"Your boy Dreb, same thing. He escaped because somebody thought spying on the Reds was more important than nailing him for all those murders he did in the war—"

Leventhal broke in angrily. "That is not the same thing at all. Israel is fighting for its life."

"Right. Of course, a lot of people thought that the U.S. was fighting for its life against the red menace back then. Also, I think we both know that this particular caper has very little to do with Israeli national security and a lot to do with your personal desire for revenge."

"Justice, Mr. Karp. It is not the same thing. You are a good talker. Very logical. I am not so. Perhaps if I had you with me, I could have convinced those idiots in Jerusalem of what I know to be true about this man. But it's hard to be logical when the voices of these murdered children are always in your head, crying for justice. I see you think I am being over-dramatic, no?"

"No. I think I can understand what you're feeling, though. I spend a lot of time with innocent victims, and sometimes I have to explain to them why the people who hurt them can't be touched, or can't be hurt the way they've hurt their victims. It's hard to make the law serve justice, but I guess I think it's better to keep trying."

"And while you are trying, the monsters eat you alive."

Karp sighed. He had heard this argument from a hundred cops, a thousand victims. "Not all the time. We win a few. The point is, when you get down to it, the only difference between us and the bad guys is that we have rules and they don't. They get to do what suits them and we tie ourselves up. I think that's what makes us good guys. I'm not a bleeding heart, Leventhal. If the laws of the State of New York required me, after proper adjudication, to take Josef Dreb apart with a nail scissors, believe me, I would do it. Meanwhile . . ." Karp shrugged.

"Yes. You will not help us. I hoped, I really did, that you would come to your senses and act as a Jew. But no. Fortunately, I have taken precautions. Come with me. I want to show you something."

Leventhal took him to a room he hadn't seen before, a small bedroom upstairs. The room contained two wooden folding chairs and a plywood trestle table covered with a litter of tools and wires and, ranged along one wall, a steel rack loaded with electronic equipment.

Leventhal sat in one of the chairs and flipped some switches on a large reel-to-reel tape recorder. As the spools turned, he said, "This was made several hours ago. I understand that tape recordings do not make good evidence in court. I can see why. You see, whatever else I am, I really am the Stereo King."

Out of a small speaker on the table Karp heard the ringing of a phone, then a click as someone answered. Then he heard his own voice say, "This is Roger Gimmel Karp."

"Karp?" said the man on the phone, surprise in his voice. "Are you OK? I heard somebody snatched you."

"I'm fine," said the Karp voice. "Yamada, right?"

"Yeah. What happened? Where the hell are you?"

"I'm safe. Look, I need to see Karavitch. Tonight. At my office."

"Tonight? Why tonight?"

"It's an emergency. A lineup. I'd like him there in two hours. Can you?"

There was a moment of hesitation, and then Yamada said, "Yeah, sure, they're your prisoners. Two hours. Say twelve."

"Right," said Karp's voice, and the connection was broken.

"It was the stereo," Karp said. "You bugged my place." He felt an involuntary surge of anger mixed with intense embarrassment. If they had taped this, then they had taped his argument with Marlene and its passionate and noisy resolution.

"Yes," Leventhal replied, "your phone too, but the tone is better if you take it from a room. Then you cut up the raw tape and reassemble it into useful phrases and put them on tape loops in these cassette players. Naturally, if the person on the other end decides to launch into a conversation on the theory of relativity, or demands some specific word we don't have, then we could have a problem, but otherwise we can handle it with loops we have made for all the little conversational sounds, the 'uh-huhs' and the 'yeahs.' The fake conversation is played through this mixing board, like an organ. It sounded quite natural, didn't you think?"

"Leventhal, if you had this, why did you go through that song and dance to get me to help you?"

"Oh, that. Well, first of all, I would not have taken you if it had not become necessary to save your life. And it would have been less risky if you had cooperated. That policeman could have become suspicious. As I said, perhaps he would start a conversation we could not follow on the tapes. So it would have been better. And perhaps I wanted to give you the opportunity to help Israel."

"Oh, helping Israel. Is that what you're doing? Well, thanks, but I hung up coats for Hadassah ladies for five years, I figure I paid my dues in that area."

Leventhal gave him a look of undisguised contempt. "You really are disgusting, Mr. Karp. I almost believe you are anti-Semitic."

Karp said nothing as he followed Leventhal out of the room. The man had touched one of his secret bruises. It was true, and a source of shame. He was tired of it all: Israel, the Holocaust, the whole us-and-them of it. None of his close friends were Jewish. His girlfriend was Italian. He certainly didn't like any of his relatives. And the three young Israelis repelled him in a way he didn't quite understand.

"Hey, Leventhal, tell me something. Just out of curiosity, what's wrong with your troops?"

Leventhal stopped. "Wrong? How do you mean?"

"You got them on drugs or something? No talking, no sense of humor—they're weird. I mean, it probably doesn't mean much coming from an old Nazi like me, but they don't seem very, um, Jewish."

Leventhal favored him with a chill smile. "They are kibbutzniks. They all three come from a very old-fashioned kibbutz in northern Galilee, near the Golan. They still practice communal rearing there. It makes for certain . . . differences in the personality. But they make the best soldiers. More than you would expect of the officers in the Israeli armed forces and in this line of work here are kibbutzniks."

"Like janissaries."

Leventhal looked pained. "No, not like janissaries, Mr. Karp. Janissaries were taken from their parents by force and raised to be soldiers of an empire. It's not the same thing at all."

I rest my case, thought Karp, but said nothing.

* * *

They left for the city in the blue van. Karp sat in the rear seat between Leventhal and Yaacov. He was wearing his suit trousers and a pajama top with the sleeve cut away from his wounded arm. His overcoat was draped around his shoulders the way Italian movie stars wore them. The van was warm, but he felt cold clear through his vitals.

Natan was driving. Devra had stayed behind in the house, to watch the store, Karp supposed. They blindfolded him on the drive to the city, taking the scarf from his eyes only when they hit Seventh Avenue at midtown. It was nearly midnight when they got to the courthouse, which was still open. Justice never sleeps. The guard at the desk at the main entrance was dozing, however, and Karp had no difficulty in talking his way through.

He unlocked the door to the Criminal Courts Bureau outer office and turned on the overhead lights. The three Israelis followed. Leventhal sat Karp on the battered leather couch next to the outer door and placed himself in a swivel chair a few yards away. Natan stood at the inner side of the door, and Yaacov hid himself behind a filing cabinet on the opposite side, both in good ambush position. They waited. Karp looked longingly at the telephone on the secretary's desk. There was no hope that he could get to it now, but perhaps there would be a struggle when they jumped the cops who were bringing in Karavitch and he could get free. The need to do something, anything, was as frustrating as the itching of his arm under its plaster cast.

A door clicked open, but it wasn't the outer door. It was an inner door, the door to the bureau chief's office. Two blond men came out fast, jumping into the center of the room. Both were carrying heavy automatic pistols in a way that showed they were not unfamiliar with their use. Natan glanced at Leventhal, who gave a tiny shrug. There was obviously no point in resisting, not yet at any rate, and in Leventhal's extensive experience people who pointed guns at you and did not immediately kill were not particularly fearsome.

The two frisked and disarmed the Israelis and herded them and Karp into the center of the room. Leventhal said dryly, "Very good, Mr. Karp, I give you credit. However did you arrange this reception?"

"Give me a break, Leventhal. I never saw these guys before—" Then he had to take a deep breath, because through the same door now walked two people he did know. One of them was the Yugoslav translator, Stefan Terzich, with a gun. The other was Marlene Ciampi, unarmed but for a smile.

"Butch, what are *you* doing here?" she said.

"Yeah, right," said Karp, looking closely at her. Her face was tense. She was frightened under her cockiness. He gestured to Terzich. "But also, what's he doing here?"

Terzich said, "We do not have time for lengthy explanations, Mr. Karp. I am here for the same reason you and your friends are here: to take charge of Djordje Karavitch." He said something in Serbo-Croat to the two blonds, who ushered Marlene, Karp, and the Israelis into the bureau chief's office. The big blond hauled out a huge clasp knife and opened it. Karp tensed and looked around for throwable weapons, but all the man wanted was to cut the wires on the desk phone. Then he reversed his pistol and knocked the twist handle off the inside door latch. He smiled unpleasantly and left, taking the phone and his partner with him.

The door closed behind them and the bolt lock was turned; the office was now a cell. Karp immediately flung his arms around Marlene and they embraced like orphans in the storm, but with more mouth action. When she could breathe again, she said, "What happened to you? I heard you were shot. Is this it?" She touched his cast gingerly. "Does it hurt?"

"No," he lied, suddenly aware again of the three others locked in with them. The two younger men were exploring the room like recently caged leopards, looking for a way out or for some weapon they could use. Natan was fingering an ornamental letter opener; Yaacov was examining the sill outside the window. Leventhal was observing Karp and Marlene, a faint smile on his broad face.

"What are you smiling about? You're in deep shit." Karp snarled.

"It always gives me pleasure to see lovers reunited," said Leventhal blandly. "And as for being in, as you put it, 'deep shit,' we will have to see. But tell me, Miss Ciampi, however did you inveigle the New York *rezident* of Yugoslav Military Intelligence into helping you in this way?"

"What's he talking about, Marlene?" asked Karp. "That guy is a college professor. He's the translator that Flanagan got that tainted lead on the typewriter from."

"So it now seems," Marlene replied. "Terzich and Dushan are the same guy, which I didn't realize because I hadn't really seen the translator's face and I only saw Dushan for the first time tonight. It makes sense, though. He tried to screw up the case with Flanagan, and when that didn't work, he decided to try a little direct action."

That at least made sense to Karp, but everything else was

confusion. "Yeah, but Marlene, why did you get involved with him? I don't understand—"

"Because he wanted Karavitch, Butch. I figured whoever snatched you wanted Karavitch too. I made a deal with Dushan: I'd help him get Karavitch if he helped me get you away from these guys. I figured you'd call to set it up, so I told Yamada that I was second seating you on the case and if you brought Karavitch in anyplace he should call me. And you did, and he did. So it all worked out." She smiled brightly. "Who are these guys, by the way—Croats?"

"No, Israelis. But, Marlene, for shit's sake—"

"Israelis? What the hell are Israelis doing in this?"

"Marlene, it's too complicated to explain. But, but, Marlene, why did you go with this guy? Why didn't you bring the cops in?"

"The cops? Well, things sort of got out of hand. I was just going to Dushan for some information, and he said he knew who had you, they were Croats, and they were going to kill you, and he could stop it if I gave him Karavitch, because one of his guys had infiltrated this Croat terrorist group. You think I should have called the cops in?"

Karp flung his hands up in despair. "Of course! God, Marlene, we got nothing going for us now. What makes you think this sweetheart, Dushan, is going to let us go after he's got Karavitch? We've blown his cover, one, and another we're witnesses to a damn kidnapping. He lets us go and the fucking FBI will be over him like flies on shit."

"Maybe he'll just go away, like back to Yugoslavia."

"Yeah, maybe. You better start praying, baby, because that's all we got left. Shit!"

"You're mad at me?" she said in a small voice. "I thought I was doing OK. Why are you getting all mean?"

"Mean?! Mean? We're dead and you're worried about mean? I can't believe I'm having this conversation." Karp slapped himself on the head and walked across the room to the window. There Yaacov and Natan were doing what looked like a crafts project with strips they had torn off the heavy blue drapes. Karp watched them dully while minutes passed. Then Leventhal cleared his throat heavily and said, "I'm afraid Mr. Karp is right, Miss Ciampi. We are all in grave danger."

Marlene looked at him closely for the first time. "Hey, I know you. You're the guy in the rain, the stereo guy."

"Yeah, and he's also an Israeli agent," said Karp nastily, "and he used that stereo you bought to bug my place. That call to Yamada was a phony he rigged up out of different recordings."

Marlene frowned. "You set that whole scene with the car up,

right? Just so you could get a mike into Karp's place. And you had the nerve to charge me for the damn stereo?"

Leventhal smiled and shrugged. "Don't complain, lady, believe me, you got it *below* wholesale. What d'you think, we're the CIA, we can throw money out the window? Meanwhile, look here—we still have a chance to get out of this. You see the boys have got a little rope together. Yaacov will hold it and Natan will slide down to the floor below and get out. We have weapons in the van. Then he will come back and ambush our Yugoslav friends."

Yaacov had the window open and Natan, with a rope made of torn curtain slung over his shoulder and between his legs, was perched on the sill, preparing to rappel down to the floor below. He lowered himself out and disappeared.

A minute later there was a hoarse shout from below and Yaacov hauled Natan up flopping across the window sill like a landed cod. A burst of Hebrew from Natan, and Leventhal, his eyebrows elevated almost to the hairline, turned to Karp and Marlene. "He says men are coming down from the roof on ladders and going into the offices next to this one. Have you perhaps an idea who they might be?"

"Yeah," said Karp, "it's the KGB and the Mafia. They couldn't stand to miss any of this action. I don't know, Leventhal! Maybe it's the Vienna Boys Choir."

Leventhal put on his pained expression. "Mr. Karp, you don't seem to understand that this might be a serious development—"

Any speculation about the identity of the new players was resolved at that instant by several loud crashes, the sound of a shot, a yell of pain from the adjoining office, and a huge voice bellowing, "I said freeze, assholes!" the characteristic greeting of the New York City Police Department.

"It's the cops," Karp shouted gleefully. He pounded on the door and shouted. Then he stopped, frowned, and looked at Marlene, who was examining the ceiling and trying to keep a straight face. "You set this up, didn't you?" he said.

"Yup."

"You told me you didn't call the cops."

"No, actually, you assumed that. But in fact, I didn't. I got Goddy Taylor to set it up after I met Dushan. I figured Dushan would have me followed and I was right. That little blondie out there was on my ass from the minute I left Dushan's office."

Karp waggled his head in admiration. "Amazing. You don't see a triple-cross like this every day. Tell me, since you brought the cops in anyway, why did you keep Terzich on a string?"

"Oh, when Goddy told me that he knew Dushan maintained a

cover as a college professor and translator, I knew he had to be the guy that set up the tainted evidence. So I figured it would be good if we had something on him, like maybe he would talk about where the idea for that scam came from."

"Yeah, good thinking, Marlene. But you could of told me, you know."

"Yeah, I could of. But I guess I figured you would trust me not to fuck up, at this late date."

"A little test, huh?"

"Yep."

"I failed, huh?"

"Yep. Hey, we're being rescued."

Somebody was turning a key in the lock. It clicked and the door was flung violently open, revealing two crouching SWAT cops equipped with black coveralls, flak vests, reversed baseball hats, and big, nasty-looking assault rifles. Karp was getting tired of having guns pointed at him. He said, "Don't point that thing at me, officer, we're the good guys. I'm Karp, DA's office. I need to talk to Chief Denton like right now."

The cops stopped crouching and lowered their weapons. One of them gestured like a maître d' and said, "The Chief's right out there. Who are all these people?"

"Friends and enemies, but they're not sorted out yet. Could you keep an eye on these three guys? Don't cuff 'em, but don't let them leave either."

At this, Leventhal strode forward and interjected, "Wait, Mr. Karp, I would like to know why we are being detained."

Karp stared at him openmouthed. "Are you joking? Where have you been the last three days?"

"Attending to my business, Mr. Karp. And keeping an eye out for you. Are you intending to charge me with some crime?"

"You bet your sweet ass I am."

"Really? What would that be?"

"Oh, homicide, kidnapping, obstruction of justice, and that's just off the top of my head."

Leventhal sadly shook his head. "You have been through a severe trial, Mr. Karp, and it is not surprising that you may not be thinking clearly. What evidence is there for these crimes?"

"Evidence? Leventhal, I was *there*. You shot a bunch of Cubans, you kept me in captivity, you phonyed up a phone call so you could kidnap a person in state custody. As soon as I'm through here, I'm going to get a squad into that house of yours and take it apart."

Leventhal smiled sweetly as he asked, "What house is that, Mr.

258

Karp? I think you will find the house I live in very different from what you may remember. You have been delirious. You only came to your senses this evening, and asked to be brought to this office, which I did. I confess to being amazed at your attitude. My bodyguard, Yaacov Tsvi, happened upon the scene while you were being attacked and was fortunate enough to drive off your attackers—at grave personal risk, I might add. Then you were taken to my home and nursed back to health by my niece, who is a registered nurse. A difficult task, since you fell into a paranoid delirium and had to be restrained.

"Cubans? Phony calls? You made one telephone call yourself, a perfectly normal one, it seemed to me, from my New Rochelle number. I'm sure it can be checked."

"And you didn't report any of this Good Samaritan shit to the police?"

Leventhal's smile broadened. "Guilty, Mr. Karp. I was busy, and in the confusion it slipped my mind. Also, I am a refugee from Nazi persecution. Many of us do not like dealing with police."

"Son of a bitch," said Karp, half in admiration. "You know, Leventhal, I never really understood the meaning of chutzpah until this moment. You really set it up right. I don't know where the house is. It probably doesn't matter, since it's probably clean as a whistle by now. We probably weren't in New Rochelle either, but I can't prove that. I'm sure you played that tape over your own phone, and I'm sure you've probably got the bed I was in set up there in your guest room by now, and I'm positive your people will back you up in every detail. And most of all, you know I can't afford to bust my hump over something that didn't even happen on my turf. Did you forget to remove the bug from my stereo and phone?"

"I have no idea what you're referring to, Mr. Karp," said Leventhal blandly.

"That means you didn't. You're a menace, you know that, Leventhal? I tell you what, I'm going to keep you here on a weapons charge, until we check out whether the pieces we took off you and whatever you've got in the van are kosher—"

"Strictly kosher, Mr. Karp, it goes without saying."

"We'll see," Karp said lamely. "Come on, Marlene."

Denton was standing in the middle of the outer office, observing the work of his minions. Dushan and the big blond man were parked on the couch with their hands cuffed behind their backs, looking nervous. The small blond man was lying on the floor, covered by a blanket, his face pale. A police officer was tending to him.

Denton's face brightened when he saw Karp and Marlene. "I'm glad to see you. That Taylor said you'd be here when we rousted these guys, but I wasn't sure about it. We've been tearing the place up looking for you for the past three days. Where were you?"

"I have no idea. A house somewhere. Out of town."

"Who snatched you? Ruiz?"

"No, Ruiz was the one trying to shoot me. By the way, he's dead, also a bunch of his guys. I saw the whole thing." Denton raised an eyebrow at that, but Karp did not explain further. Instead he said, pointing to Terzich, "Look, I need to talk to that guy right away. Could you stick him in my office?"

Denton nodded. "There's one guy needs a hospital, but what about the others?"

"Oh, stick them in a pen for now. We'll straighten out what we want to do with them later."

Terzich sat erect in the straight chair in Karp's office as Karp read him his rights. A thin gloss of sweat covered his bony face, but otherwise he seemed calm. Karp sat across the desk from him, and Marlene was curled up in the corner in a secretary's chair she had rolled in. "I don't need a lawyer," Terzich said. "What will the charges be?"

"We have considerable discretion in that, Mr., ah, Terzich. Kidnapping, resisting arrest, assault with a deadly weapon, obstruction of justice, for starters, and we haven't even begun an investigation. But what charges we actually bring, or if we bring any charges, may be influenced by the kind of cooperation we get from you. Now, I have no authority to make any binding promises to you in that regard, but do I make myself clear?" The familiar words felt strange in his mouth, as if his recent immersion in untrammeled violence had somehow unsuited him for the cloaked violence of the law.

Terzich grimaced. "I understand I am in your power. What do you wish to know?"

"Mr. Terzich, I don't know what it's like in your country, but in this country there is a very strong division between ordinary criminal justice and the national security apparatus. That is, there's supposed to be. People tell me you're a spy. Whether you are or not is irrelevant to me. Spying for Yugoslavia is not a violation of the New York State criminal code. Ever since this damn case started, people have been trying to get me interested in cloak-and-dagger stuff, but let me tell you that I could care less about anything that happens off the island of Manhattan, unless it's connected with criminal violations in New York County.

"My only interest is in bringing the perpetrators of a particular murder, the murder of a policeman, to justice. So whatever you tell me that's not so related will stay right here in this room. If you feel there's something that you can't tell me because it relates to your country's security, then tell me, and I'll see if it's essential to me or not. And we can take it from there.

"I hope you believe that, but if not, let me tell you something else. This affair has lots of threads—some you know about, and others you don't, but I think I have just about all of them in my head. If you try lying to me, I'll know, and then this conversation ends and I call the cops out there to take you out, and I prepare the strongest case I can possibly make against you for the grand jury, no screwing around and no second chances. You follow me?"

Terzich nodded and a humorless smile flickered across his mouth. He said softly, "I understand. Please do not take offense, Mr. Karp, but it is difficult for me to believe that you are as naive as you pretend. No connection between the national security apparatus and your office? If you wish to pretend this, I will indulge you. As for your questions, please go on. As you point out so well, I do not have a choice in the matter."

"OK." Karp began, "First, I want to know how you came to supply information about the location of Milo Rukovina's typewriter to Sergeant Paul Flanagan."

A look of faint surprise appeared on Terzich's face. "Oh, that." He took a pack of cigarettes out of his jacket pocket. "May I?" Karp nodded and he lit up and took a deep drag. "Well, of course, when Karavitch was captured with Raditch and Rukovina, it became essential that we get our hands on him at once, so—"

"Why was it essential?"

"Because we knew that Rukovina and Raditch had been the conduit for money and arms from the U.S. to Croatian terrorists in Europe. Now, Rukovina is a rabbit and the other one is a moron. They had to be very closely directed by someone. What we did not know was who, although we had other evidence that it was a Croat living in this country, with former ties to the CIA. There are many such, and we did not have the resources to track him down."

He smiled. "You understand, Yugoslavia is still a poor country. In any event, when Karavitch was captured with the other two, it became most probable that he was the one. We wished to talk with him because he, of course, would have the names of Croat sympathizers both in Yugoslavia and in other places. Also we wished to know what further mischief they were planning. But how could we get to him? We have no resources. As you say, we are on one shoestring here.

261

"So, while I am pondering this, I receive a telephone call from a man I know, a Croat, and an officer in an organization called Association for European Freedom. This organization is of course funded by the CIA, but this man and I have reached an understanding. He knows what I am, I know what he is, but we have an understanding, and sometimes money changes hands."

"A double agent?" asked Marlene.

Terzich inclined his head a few inches. "Double agent is perhaps too dramatic. In any case, this man informs me that some people in the CIA are extremely upset about what Karavitch has done and do not wish him to remain in custody. They wish the case against him, the local murder case, that is, dismissed."

Karp said, "Did he say that? The local case?"

"Yes, he was very definite."

Marlene said, "Sure. The skyjacking's a federal rap. Once he's in federal custody he's a puff of smoke."

"Right," Karp replied. "OK, Mr. Terzich, go on."

"So I asked him how this was to be done, and he said that if I was willing, arrangements would be made with the local authorities to retain me as a translator for the court, and that once this was done some means would be found to destroy the legal case. Naturally, I was suspicious, for I do not wish to expose myself in this affair. But he was firm. His people want me to do this, and no one else. So I agree. Why shouldn't a professor work as a court translator? I think that if it is too dangerous, I can always remove myself, and perhaps I can learn something by this, or find some way to get to Karavitch alone.

"In a few days, a Mr. Wharton calls me and asks me to be the translator, and I agree. For a while, nothing. I am very frustrated because never do they leave me alone with Karavitch. Then, one day, in a conversation between this Rukovina and his lawyer, John Evans, Evans asks him where is the typewriter that types the note and the message found with the bomb. Rukovina tells him, and Evans says he hopes the police do not find it, because it would be very good evidence against us. Later Evans mentions to me, as a joke it seemed then, how strange it is that the rules of evidence say that if the police find the typewriter it would hurt the client, but if he or I should tell the police about it, the case would be ruined and the client would go free."

"Evans said that? Christ! What did you do?"

"Nothing. I waited for what I knew must come. Then this policeman, this Flanagan called me and said that he heard I might have some information that would be useful to the police. And I thought of the typewriter and about what Evans had said. This must be why I am hired. So I agreed to meet him, but anonymously, and I took him to the machine.

"Now perhaps the case would be destroyed. But this is no great help to me. I must get to Karavitch before he is transferred to federal custody. Then my Croat friend calls me again. He says that Croatian nationalists have kidnapped the prosecutor in the case, you, Mr. Karp, and they plan to exchange him for Karavitch. Naturally, I must try to prevent this.

"Then Miss Ciampi comes to see me. She has the information I am lacking about Karavitch's location and movements. This confuses me because naturally I believe that the district attorney is working with the CIA. But perhaps, I think, there is a personal involvement. Perhaps she is more interested in Karp than in Karavitch. This is why I tell her that I have an agent with the terrorists, which is a lie, but I see by her face that she fears for your life. So I believe she is operating privately. Of course, I believe the police are involved, and that therefore she will not go to them. Obviously I have been mistaken in this. But all in all, I still believe it was a chance I had to take."

Karp glanced at Marlene. She said, "It jibes."

"Yeah, it does," he answered. "Look, Mr. Terzich, I think that's all we need from you tonight. I'll come by with a stenographer tomorrow and take a formal statement. We're going to have to hold you and your people for a while, but I want you to know we appreciate your cooperation."

He got up and called one of the cops Denton had left on duty. As Terzich stood to go, Karp said, "Wait a second, Mr. Terzich. Let me ask you one more thing: does the name Josef Dreb mean anything to you?"

Terzich nodded slowly, his expression neutral. "Yes, he was an SS officer based in Zagreb during the war and then later with the Prinz Eugen Division. A war criminal. Why do you ask that?"

"His name came up in connection with the case. What happened to him, do you know?"

"He escaped Yugoslavia after the war, but I recall he died shortly thereafter. Murdered in Italy, I think, by one of his companions."

"I see. OK, that's it. Oh, one more thing. Have you got any idea why Karavitch would have wanted to hijack an airliner and plant a bomb at this particular time?"

Terzich appeared to consider this question for a long moment. Then he said, "You mean that it was irrational for an elderly man, who was secure in his situation, and besides an important link in a terrorist organization, to risk all for so futile a gesture. I have considered this as well, and I have come up with no rational answer. But perhaps there are irrational answers. You and I once had a pleasant conversation about the history of my country. You know that if a child is tormented and deprived enough, there is a good chance that he will grow up to be a madman. In the same way, some nations have a history so dreadful that their politics can become a kind of insanity. Often I think it is like that with Yugoslavia. In that view, for Karavitch to end his career in a demented fashion is perhaps understandable, even natural.

"There is a little story about this. A viper waits on the banks of the Drina. He wishes to cross, but he cannot swim. Soon an ox comes by and the viper asks it if he can ride across on its back. The ox says, 'Of course not! You are a viper and you will bite me.' So the viper says, 'Don't be foolish. If I bite you, we will both drown. Why would I bite you?' So the ox sees that this is true and he allows the viper to climb up on his back. Halfway across, the ox feels the sting of the viper's fangs. As he sinks he cries out, 'Why have you bitten me, viper? Now we are both doomed.' And the viper says, 'You forgot, ox. We are in the Balkans.' Perhaps you will get a better answer than this from Karavitch, Mr. Karp, but I doubt it."

"God, I'm tired," Karp said. "What time is it?"

"Almost three," said Marlene. "Want to go home?"

They were sitting on the couch in the outer office. The cops and their prisoners had gone, leaving nothing but a wastebasket full of broken glass and plaster shards, and the dried bloodstains where the injured Yugoslavian had lain.

He let out a short, exhausted chuckle. "Yeah, can you carry me over your back? I can't believe I'm going through this shit. I'm a lawyer, it's supposed to be indoor work with no heavy lifting." He paused and pulled her close. "I didn't say I was sorry yet for bitching at you. You rescued me, all right, just like in that song."

"Tam Lin. But from Israelis, another layer of weirdness. What's the story on that? You were going to tell me."

He filled her in on what had happened since the attempted assassination in front of the courthouse. She took it all in, and then said, "So what do you think? Karavitch is Karavitch? Or Karavitch is this Nazi, Dreb?"

"I don't know. It seems kind of academic at this point, except to Leventhal and company. Who gives a rat's ass what his real name is. He killed Terry Doyle and he's going down for it. It's funny, though. This case started with a million questions. I wrote them down on a Chinese menu—who was doing what to whom and why.

They're almost all answered now. The Church was screwing up the investigation because they didn't want one of their heroes exposed as a fascist killer. Pillman was screwing it up because of the connection between a couple of the Croats and a gang of Cubans the Bureau had been using for dirty tricks down south. The CIA? Because of the same Cubans, but mainly to protect whoever knowingly recruited a Nazi war criminal who had murdered American troops.

"The CIA involved Terzich because they needed a stooge to trash the case. And since it couldn't be any of Roberts's white shoe lawyers and it certainly couldn't be our glorious leader the DA, who better than a commie agent? They protect their people in Europe and knock out a senior agent in one shot, not to mention keeping the cover pulled up over World War fucking Two."

"And Bloom went for it because . . . ?"

"He's a schmuck. Somebody called him from Washington and enlisted him in the service of this great nation. Somebody with major party connections, no doubt, who got him dreaming about Albany or the Senate, provided he did the right thing. And also, I hope I'm not flattering myself, it was a chance to get rid of the kid here. So, that fills in all the boxes, except for the big one, which could be the stopper if we don't get a good answer."

"You mean the ox's question—why did he do it?"

"Yeah. It's time to go back and talk to the bad guys a little. And I think we can do it with more cooperation from their distinguished counsel than we have had heretofore. If we could just get some kind of total crusher on Karavitch or—who the hell is that?"

Somebody was walking down the hall singing an upbeat version of "I Love New York," pausing to tap out the rhythm on the glass doors of the offices with something metallic and jingling as he passed them. At the door of the Criminal Courts office he beat a particularly loud crescendo as he finished the song and flung open the door.

"Guma! What are you doing here?" Karp asked in amazement.

Guma was equally amazed. "Butch, you got rescued! What happened? Marlene! What's going on?"

"Don't ask," she replied. "Butch is safe and the bad guys are out of action. Hey, Guma, what's that funny smell?"

"Like aftershave, you mean?"

"No, sweeter, like candy." She sniffed closer. "Smells like grape jelly."

"Oh, yeah, I got a bite to eat on the way down. I must of spilled some on me. But look, what'd you mean they're out of action? What about Ruiz?"

"He sleeps with the fishes," Karp answered.

Guma whistled. "Damn. Way to go. Who got him?"

"Later, Goom, I can't go through this whole thing again. But what are you doing here?"

"Oh, tonight was my big date with the divine Rhoda. I just thought I'd come by and clear up some details."

"How'd it go?" Marlene asked.

"Great. I'm in love. By the way, I got to talk to you, Marlene, about these rumors you're spreading about my style in the rack. This shit gets around, it's gonna scare off all the cocktail waitresses."

"Yeah, but Mad Dog," Karp asked, "how'd it go? Did you get the keys?"

Guma grinned and held up the object he had been using to tap out the time: Klepp's key ring. "I just came by to pick up some blank tape. Then I was going to raid the DA's office, pull the originals, make copies, and get the originals back before morning."

"Mad Dog, I love you! Hey, many hands make light work. Let's me and Marlene help."

"I thought you were wiped out," she said.

"I am, but this is too good to miss. Look, we should do the taping over at my place. I got this great stereo Marlene bought me."

Guma said, "Sounds good. We'll go up, steal Bloom's shit, I'll drive you down to your joint, and while you do the copy, I'll go find somebody to slip Rhoda's keys back to her before she gets up."

"Goom," Marlene said, "it's past three in the morning. Who you going to get to run an errand like that?"

"Hey, babe, the city never sleeps. I'll find somebody suitable. OK, now give with the story, Butch. I'm on fucking hooks here."

Rhoda Klepp groaned and tried to force her scrambled brains into order. It was a mistake. With consciousness came sensation, none of it pleasant. Her head hurt, a sharp, white-hot bar between her eyes. Eyes? She couldn't see. She tried to remove whatever was blocking her vision, and found that her hands wouldn't go to her face. She shook her head violently and chunks of something cool and slimy fell down past the side of her head. Then she got the smell, a sour garbagey odor, with something sweet added that seemed to be emanating from her own body. Then nausea hit her, and both ends of her digestive system demanded a visit to the bathroom at the earliest opportunity.

Rhoda heaved herself up, came to the end of her chains, and collapsed back on the bed. Memory returned in a hideous rush.

"Guma!" she howled. "You bastard! Get me out of this right now!" Nothing. She knew the apartment was empty. She shrieked and cursed for a minute or two, and tears of rage poured down her greasy cheeks. Then she stopped short. Somebody was opening the door to her apartment.

"Guma, get in here, you son of a bitch! I'll murder you!"

Silence. The knob on the bedroom door turned. The door slowly opened.

"Guma?" she said, the first shivers of fear beginning to rise through her. "Guma, is that you?"

The door opened wide and he came into the room. Rhoda put back her head and screamed. She closed her eyes tight and screamed her head off, but she could not close her nostrils.

"Ahhrnk'oon'od uh ennk'y." said the Walking Booger, coming closer.

20

As Conrad Wharton tied his yellow tie in front of the mirror, he wondered fleetingly, but not for the first time, whether he could wear a bow tie. A bow tie was distinctive and bespoke confidence. More important, you could wear it forever without fear of getting food stains on it, something that eventually happened with a four-in-hand tie no matter how careful one was, and then it was shot to hell. You might as well throw it away, because the cleaners never got the stains out right. Wharton spent a lot of money on his ties. This one was a Countess Mara, thirty-two fifty, but he felt it was worth it, especially when he removed his jacket and you could see the little monogram on the bottom. His shirts were monogrammed too, on the cuffs, a *W* inside a *C*. He had designed it himself, and approved the memos emanating from his office with the same mark. He called it his chop mark.

He studied his face, wishing for length and cragginess, then sighed. No, a bow tie would make him look even more like a cheap doll, one with a ribbon around its neck. He attached his tie tack, a pair of miniature silver handcuffs, and donned the jacket of his dark gray suit. He buttoned it, then let it hang open, revealing the tie tack and the Countess Mara monogram. He loved this effect, the combination of class and a touch of violence—handcuffs. It wiped the chicks out in the singles bars, where he found it an unfailing conversation starter. Women loved a crime fighter.

Unfortunately, when he stood up to give his speech this afternoon at the Waldorf, he would have to keep his jacket buttoned. As he thought of the speech, butterflies jumped from little perches in his belly and started to flutter about. It was an important speech, one that would make his reputation in the wider world represented by the International Association of Prosecuting Attorneys, at whose winter meeting he was speaking. It was an important step for him; Bloom, he well knew, had wider ambitions—the governorship for starters—and in a year or so would leave a convenient hole for somebody with the right political connections, reputation, and skills.

Wharton collected his wallet, keys, and briefcase, slipped into a camel-hair overcoat, and left his apartment. It was shaping up very well, he thought. The missing ingredient was serious money, because if Bloom decided to run for higher office, there would be a real race for the job and plenty of money would be required to make a real stab at the DA's slot. And he thought he would make a start on getting close to serious money this afternoon, because he was having lunch with V.T. Newbury.

Wharton had been sucking around Newbury ever since he found out that his father was Edwin Brace Newbury, senior partner at Vernon Cornwell Gibbs, and among the half dozen wealthiest and most influential lawyers in New York. Until now, unaccountably, and despite the offer of numerous favors, he had met with no luck. Newbury always seemed to be busy for lunch and never showed up at the evenings Wharton arranged in his apartment for selected pols and presentable attorneys from the office. Two days ago, however, Newbury had called him up and actually invited him to lunch. They had arranged to eat at what Newbury had described as the best little Northern Italian restaurant in New York. The speech was at two. He had time for a leisurely meal and then an unhurried cab ride uptown to the Waldorf. As he walked out onto the chilly street, the butterflies vanished. It was all working out. He was golden.

His good mood dissipated abruptly when he got to the office and found that Rhoda Klepp had not reported for work that morning. Wharton made it a point never to appear at any official function without at least one special assistant to carry things and dance attendance. Rhoda was scheduled to meet him at the hotel, and more important, she had written the speech itself and was supposed to have left it on his desk. Yet it was not to be found.

"What do you mean you can't find her," Wharton shrieked at his secretary. "Just find her!"

"I called her ten times," the secretary responded. "She doesn't answer her phone. Maybe she's real sick."

"Oh don't be stupid, Rhoda's never sick," he snapped. "What am I supposed to do now? I've got to give a speech this afternoon. Do you think you could find that maybe?"

He stomped into his office and slammed the door. While he sulked, all other administrative work stopped as half a dozen public employees examined every stack of exposed paper in the office and thumbed through every file drawer. Eventually a carbon of the speech was found in one of Rhoda Klepp's desk drawers. It had to be retyped, naturally, since Wharton could not be expected to give a speech from a carbon copy.

After that, peace reigned in the Bureau of Administration, and Wharton left for his luncheon appointment at eleven-fifty with a jaunty wave. Everybody in the outer office smiled and waved back, and wished him good luck on his speech. Wharton liked what he called a happy ship. In fact, he demanded it.

Karp stood up, stretched, and went to his bedroom window. He twitched the cord on the venetian blinds and pale morning sunlight streamed in. On the bed, Marlene groaned and covered her eyes. "It can't be morning already," she wailed. "I reject that entire concept."

"I'm afraid it is, cutie. We danced the night away and now it's time to go to work."

"Oh, let's bag work. I can't believe we just spent six hours listening to that moron schmoozing on the phone." She groaned again and rolled facedown. Then she popped her head back up. "No, Christ, we can't bag work, can we? Today's the big day."

"Yeah, lots to do. God, this fucking case! I can't believe we're going to wrap up Karavitch today. And Bloom. You think it'll really go down like we figured?"

"No question. We're the two greatest prosecutors in the galaxy and we're on a roll. Why are you worried about Bloom? Shit, he's dead meat with what we got on those tapes." She giggled. "I still can't believe it. Arthur Bingham Roberts and Sanford Bloom, two of the great legal minds of the century, dancing around each other to see how they can get this case thrown out with tainted evidence without actually coming out and saying it—'I'm a scumbag, Sandy, and so are you, so get the fucking typewriter admitted, and it's a wrap.' Oh, no, too indelicate. How did it go? I got it here somewhere."

She rummaged through the sheets and pads of yellow legal paper that were scattered around the bed and the floor, found what she was looking for, put on her glasses, and read.

"OK, this is the part I love. Roberts says, 'Yes, I quite understand. It's unfortunate that the victim should have been a policeman.' And Bloom says, 'Yes, there's no question of simply dropping the case. The publicity, ah, and of course the evidence is heavily against them, the bomb and the note. I mean, Arthur, they did plant the thing.' Roberts says, 'Yes, unless some technicality should intrude that would taint the evidence.' Bloom: 'Technicality?' Duhhhh! It's like the Three Stooges. Then Roberts: 'Yes. That young man you have on the case, Karp. He seems like a hard charger. Perhaps he could be induced to charge a bit too hard.' Bloom says, 'Umm, naturally, the integrity of my office can't be

270

compromised in any way.' He means, how am I going to cover my personal tushie. Roberts gives him the zinger: 'Naturally. And of course we feel the same way. But you'll recall that there is a translator involved here, a Professor Terzich. Now our man Evans has regrettably let slip to this Terzich the consequences of the defense providing the prosecution with evidence obtained during constitutionally protected conversation between the defense counsel and the defendant. We have reason to believe that Terzich would not be adverse to a dismissal in this case, and can be counted on to cooperate. Now, if somehow the police were to contact Terzich and obtain this evidence—do you follow?' Does he follow? Does the pope have indoor plumbing? Bloom says, 'Umm, what sort of evidence are we talking about here?' And Roberts says, 'The typewriter that typed the note with the bomb, Sandy. Rukovina's typewriter. Tempting, wouldn't you say?' And Bloom gives this little conspiratorial chuckle, and he says, 'Oh, yeah, tempting as hell. OK, Arthur, I think I can handle things at this end, all right. This could just about solve our little problem here.' And Roberts says, 'I thought it might. I trust that this Karp is not indispensable to your organization?' And our leader says, 'Oh, he's dispensable, is he ever dispensable! He's a piece of Kleenex, the son of a bitch.' Bango! Go directly to jail, Mr. Bloom. Shit, they'll burn his license to practice law in Foley Square at high noon. And Roberts's too. I love it!''

Karp nodded, his face grim. The naked confirmation of his suspicions about Bloom gave him no pleasure. "It's still hard for me to believe. Even hearing it I can hardly believe it. Throwing away the integrity of the district attorney's office, Garrahy's office. And for what? To do some national security shitheads in Washington a favor? Yeah, we got Bloom and Roberts. It's Karavitch I'm still worried about. If we just had something solid that he was really Dreb, it'd be such a shot from left field that he'd crumple. Which reminds me."

He sat on the bed and dialed John Evans's number. The conversation was brief. When he had hung up, Marlene asked, "How did it go?"

"How could it go? I got him by the balls. I told him we're interviewing Cindy Karavitch, Macek, and the old man starting at four-thirty today. I also told him we were hip to the typewriter scam and about the statements we've got from Flanagan and Terzich."

"And about the tapes?"

"I think I'll save that for Bloom. As it was, he was practically blubbering. Let him make some panicky phone calls, stir up the pot a little."

271

"Sounds good. By the way, what are we doing about the Israelis?"

"If they're clean on the weapons charge, all I intend to do is write a note to Elmer Pillman describing what happened. Let him take it from there. Foreign agents are an FBI matter."

"He'll probably give them a kiss. They solved his problem with the Cubanos."

"Frankly, Scarlet, I don't give a damn. Speaking of kisses—"

"Get away from me. We both smell like bread mold. I'm taking a shower. Want to join?"

"Love to, but I got this cast. You'll have to bathe me all over with your tiny pink tongue."

"Make an appointment. You going to go to the Prosecuting Attorney's meeting with me later?"

"If I can figure out how to get dressed with this thing on my arm, I wouldn't miss it for the world."

The Villa Cella on Mulberry Street was not what Wharton had expected. It was small—just ten tables—and dark, with a low brown tin ceiling and white tiles on the floor, like a public restroom. The rickety tables were done with paper placemats printed with maps of Italy, folded paper napkins, thick glass tumblers, and vases of plastic flowers. The walls were yellow stucco and covered with framed oil paintings of mountains, vineyards, and ruins.

The headwaiter had greeted V.T. effusively and ushered them to a table in the rear of the room. When they were seated, Wharton looked around him dubiously. The clientele seemed to be mostly prune-faced old men with napkins tucked into their necks, slurping soup. "You say the food here is good?" he ventured.

"Good? The best. They keep rather a low profile because they're Piedmontese, and this is a southern Italian neighborhood. I've wanted to bring you here for some time, Conrad—"

"Please, Chip."

"Yes, Chip, of course. As I say, you struck me as someone who had the capacity to appreciate the finer things. Ah, Giusseppe, *mille grazie*." The waiter had brought their menus. Wharton was dismayed to find it handwritten entirely in Italian.

"Ah, marvelous," V.T. exclaimed, "they have *bollito misto*. And I think cold spinach pancakes to start. What looks good to you, Con—ah, Chip?"

"Oh, I'll have the same. I haven't had any *bollito misto* in years."

"You'll love the way they do it here. They use the whole calf's head. What about wine? The house red is Barbera D'Asti. Let's split a carafe."

"Well, actually, I have to give this speech today, I'd like to keep my head clear."

"Oh, nonsense. If you don't take any wine with your meal, they'll know you're a barbarian." The waiter returned and V.T. ordered. Wharton was thinking about how he could avoid eating the disgusting food in this trashy place, and how he could avoid drinking more than a token amount of wine. Wharton would have liked a martini, but he didn't suppose they knew how to make a decent one in this place. He was also thinking about how he could bring the conversation around so as to wangle an invitation to meet Edwin Brace Newbury.

"So, V.T., how's your father?" he began.

"My father? Fine, so far as I know. How's yours?"

"Umm, I meant, he must be a fascinating man."

"Father fascinating? Yes, I suppose so, if you're mad about the half dozen sailing anecdotes that make up the bulk of his conversation, or if you're interested in trusts, but otherwise not. Now his brother, my Uncle Preston, he's fascinating. Ran away from Choate at sixteen and hopped a freighter to New Zealand. Married a Maori princess, I understand and—oh, good, here's our wine."

A busboy balancing a large tin tray on his shoulder was hovering over the table. On the tray were twelve one-liter carafes of the house red. The busboy plucked one of them off and set it in front of V.T. Then, as he walked away, he seemed to stumble. The tray wobbled, broke loose from his grip, and deposited most of the eleven liters of dark purplish Barbera D'Asti on Conrad Wharton.

After the pandemonium had died down, after the prune-faced old men had been treated to the spectacle of Wharton leaping about like a purple jack-in-the-box, shrieking about lawsuits, pursued by the restaurant's entire staff lavishing apologies, after the busboy had been ostentatiously fired, only then did V.T. manage to get Wharton seated and concentrated on his immediate problem.

"Look, Chip, I can't tell you how sorry I am about this, but all is not lost. There's a place I know on Grand Street, does dry cleaning while you wait. It's quarter of one now. If I take your suit, shirt, and tie up there, they can do them and I can be back here by twenty past. It's only two blocks away. You can sit in the can and read the paper. I'll be back before you know it."

Wharton grumpily agreed. Not only did he have no choice, not if he still wanted to make that speech, but he began to realize that what was, after all, a fairly minor inconvenience could be parlayed into something far more important, a hook into V.T. Newbury. They went to the men's room; Wharton stripped down to his shoes, socks, and underwear and made himself as comfortable as he could in the single booth. The privacy lock in the door had been removed, leaving a small round hole so he wadded up some toilet paper and wedged it shut.

As he sat, he thought about the best way to handle payment for this obligation. Maybe a game of squash at the old man's club. Tennis in the country. Sailing? Not until next year, but it was a good thought. Alone for hours on a yacht, he would be able to . . . These pleasant thoughts jolted to a stop and Wharton let out a short yowl of alarm. There was a brown eye staring at him through the round hole in the door.

"Hi, sugar," said a low voice. "Are you waitin' for me?"

Wharton shot to his feet as the door was pulled open. He tried to keep it closed, but could get no purchase on the smooth metal. "Excuse me, I'm using this toilet," he shouted.

"If you are, you shittin' through your damn underpants, man," said the person who opened the door. She was very tall, and dressed in a canary yellow turtleneck sweater dress cut above the knee and tight as skin. She had strong features, heavily made up, and a huge mane of elaborately curled dyed blond hair. She came toward him, smiling with a wide mouth of glossy violet.

Wharton backed up. "What are you doing here?" he cried, "This is a men's room." He could back up no farther. The toilet handle was pressing into his buttock and his legs were straddled on either side of the bowl.

"Sugar playing hard to get?" she said. "Well, some like to bust the door down, some like to be coaxed. Come to Momma, son. I ain't got all day." With that, her hand shot out like a striking cobra, pulled down the waistband of his Jockey shorts, and grabbed a handful. Wharton yelped and threw a clumsy punch at her head, which she easily batted aside with her other hand.

"Oh, rough trade, huh? Listen, fat boy, you mess my hair I'm gonna dance on your head. Now settle down and get your blow job." She sank to her knees in one practiced motion, and began to haul Wharton by his penis toward her mouth.

"OK, Jerome, that's enough." The speaker was an immense, hachet-faced, balding man of about fifty. There was a shorter, heavier man behind him. The big man said, "Stand up, Jerome! You," to Wharton, "put it away, the party's over. Let's go."

The blond let go of Wharton and stood up. "Goddamn it, Sharkey, what the fuck you doin' this side a town? Vice never come by Little Italy."

Sharkey grinned. "That would be telling, sweetheart." To Wharton he snapped, "Hey, Tubby, get your clothes on. Move it!"

Things were moving too fast for Wharton. He decided to exert some control, forgetting for the moment how difficult it is to exert control when one is clad in wine-soaked skivvies. "Just one moment," he said in a commanding tone. "Are you men police officers?"

Sharkey's eyes widened. "Who the fuck you think we are, Alice?"

"Let me see your identification!" Wharton ordered in the same peremptory tone.

Ed Sharkey had been a vice cop in New York for almost twenty years. Unlike other kinds of police officers, vice cops almost never have to deal with innocent victims of crime. All those with whom they come into contact on the job are involved willingly in some nasty illegal act; all of them are, to use the technical criminal justice term, scumbags. That many vice cops (and Sharkey was no exception) derive a substantial portion of their personal income from shaking down these scumbags does not help their attitude. Thus vice cops do not easily learn patience and forbearance. They are very often angry and disgusted people, and their anger and disgust are directed not so much at the professionals in the vice trade—the pushers and whores—as at the users and johns, the solid citizens whose lust and hypocrisy make it necessary for vice cops to earn their living in such a degrading fashion.

This explains why, when Wharton asked to see some identification in the commanding tone that worked so well with his frightened subordinates, Ed Sharkey reached out, grabbed Wharton by the front of his T-shirt, yanked him out of the booth, and clouted him across the face twice with a hand having the general dimension and texture of a first-baseman's mitt. Then he punched Wharton in the center of his pot belly. The T-shirt ripped away from the cop's fist and Wharton collapsed to the floor, wheezing and bleeding heavily from the nose.

Sharkey moved in for a few kicks, but his partner put a firm hand on his arm. "Ed, enough," he said. The big cop's shoulders relaxed and the deep flush passed out of his face. He became all business again.

"Jerome, what'd you do with the john's clothes?" he asked the blond.

"Me? I didn't do shit! He was just like you see when I got in here. Hey, dude is fuckin' crazy anyway. You ever hear of a guy want to run away from a blow job? And it was a house call, like. Dude drives by my walk last night, he says here's twenty, you be such and such place, such and such time, give me good head, you get another twenty. So I come here and the little fucker freaks. And I get busted. Hey, Sharkey, this some kind of entrapment shit?"

Sharkey ignored her and helped his partner heave Wharton up

on his wobbly legs. People who graduate from law school usually miss the experience of being hit in the face by a big cop, although there are those who would like it to be made part of the bar examination. It certainly made Conrad Wharton forget about issuing any orders. Instead he whimpered, "Please, I didn't . . . it was that woman's fault. She attacked me."

Sharkey laughed. "Woman? I don't see any woman here. How about you, Jerome? You see any woman?"

The blond sniffed haughtily. "You're a pig, Sharkey, you know that? You don't let a girl have any secrets."

The panel on "The Systems Approach to Criminal Justice" was meeting in the Imperial Ballroom, and by ten of two the ornate chamber was nearly filled with prosecuting attorneys and affiliated crime fighters from across the nation. Among them were Butch Karp and Marlene Ciampi. A stage at one end of the room was furnished with a cloth-covered table and a podium with microphones. To the left of the stage an easel sign displayed the title of the session, and the panel members had little cards in front of their places with their names on them. Three panel members and a moderator had already taken their seats, which left one empty, the one marked "CONRAD T. WHARTON."

Karp looked around at the crowd. "Big turnout for this bullshit."

"Yeah, I haven't see so many white males in one room since I graduated from Yale Law. I hope our main speaker isn't late."

"You nervous?"

"Only about that enormous chandelier suspended over our heads. I hate having shit like that over me. Do you think there's any chance it'll fall?"

"I hope not. Wipe out all these guys it'd set criminal justice back two weeks. Hey, V.T., how's it going?"

Newbury, slightly out of breath, slid himself into the empty seat beside them. He was carrying a white paper dry-cleaner's bag and hangers. "I didn't miss anything yet, I see. You know, I just had the most peculiar experience. I was lunching with Chip Wharton, and he had an unfortunate accident with some wine—"

"How sad!" Marlene exclaimed. "And did you place him in a booth in the men's room and go to get his clothes dry-cleaned?"

"As a matter of fact, I did. But imagine! When I returned, he was gone. I wonder what could have happened to him?"

Karp said, "Maybe he got tired of waiting and came here to speak in his undies, like in a bad dream."

V.T. said, "Possible, but . . . look, I do believe that's him now, taking his place behind his little name card."

"Gosh, V.T., are you sure?" Marlene asked. "It doesn't look much like Wharton to me."

"I'm prepared to swear to it. Look, he's even wearing the little name tag with the blue speaker's ribbon on it."

"Oh, *well*, then, I guess you're right. Hey, they're starting."

At the podium, the moderator, a chubby, balding person wearing a serious suit and a little mustache, made greeting noises, a little joke, and then introduced the first speaker, the distinguished lawyer and administrator, and a great pioneer in criminal-justice-systems development, Conrad T. Wharton. Consulting an index card, he then described Wharton's career in glowing terms. There was a brief round of applause, the moderator sat down, and the speaker marched up to the podium. He adjusted the microphone and put a thin sheaf of paper on the podium. He smiled and began to read his speech. "Ladies and gentlemen," he said, "it is a great honor to be able to speakable shit you here buggy today. For years the crimanix whorehouse rat turds butt fucker justice system has been plagued by the simple inabilititty cunt face asshole to evaluate its suckass cocksucker in prickassing cases."

Since it was an after-lunch meeting, perhaps the audience was a little slow on the uptake. But a few minutes into the speech there were murmurs and nervous laughter. A few minutes later the murmurs grew angry and the shouts began. People started to walk out.

"Hey, where's Guma?" Marlene asked. "He should be here to see this."

"No," V.T. said. "Like all great directors he never attends opening night. Actually, I think he's paying off the troops. And he's got to spring Jerome."

The place was emptying fast. The panelists and the moderator were standing about, flapping jaws and wondering what to do.

"Want to go?" Karp asked.

"I don't know," said Marlene. "Dirty Warren is really wailing. Maybe I'll stay and see what happens. You?"

"Got to go see Bloom."

"Oh-ho! Give him one from me too."

"I will. You coming, V.T.?"

"No, I think I'll stay for the peroration. I never realized the systems approach was so interesting."

Sanford Bloom's day had started off quite well and had gone precipitously downhill from there. At nine that morning he had met with the New York State Attorney General and some important people from Justice in Washington. He had managed to let

277

them know he was available for higher office, and they had appeared to consider this seriously. At noon he had given the welcome and keynote address to an appreciative audience of IAPA members at the Waldorf, which had been received, he had noted, with much more than perfunctory applause.

In the afternoon, however, things had started to come unglued. First there was an hysterical call from Wharton, in which he claimed to have been assaulted by a transvestite prostitute while dressed in his underwear in the men's room of an Italian restaurant, and then to have been beaten and arrested by the police. He was calling from the precinct cells.

Saying he would arrange for a lawyer, Bloom had cut the conversation short. He found it very disturbing to think that Wharton was anything but completely in charge. The man knew all the secrets. Then the courthouse reporter from the *Post* called, asking questions about some disturbance during a session down at the Waldorf. Wharton had apparently gone crazy and started shouting obscenities at the audience. Bloom had put the reporter off until later, but could not do the same with the president of the IAPA, who had called in a fury to denounce Wharton as a disgrace to the profession. Bloom was confused. How could Wharton deliver an obscene speech when he was being arrested on a sex offense? He got rid of the president by promising a full investigation and a meeting the next afternoon. Then he took two aspirins and a Gelusel.

But the worst call was from Arthur Bingham Roberts. John Evans had called Roberts that morning in a blind panic, with a story about how Karp knew all about the typewriter and the translator, and what should he do, what should he do? Roberts had told him to stonewall, and he was advising Bloom to do the same. There was no direct evidence proving collusion between defense and prosecution to obstruct justice by throwing the case. As long as they kept that in mind, and kept their heads, Karp could do nothing.

Good advice, but still hard for Bloom to take, since he knew there was direct evidence. He had just accumulated a few more feet of it while Roberts was talking. By the time Roberts had said good-bye, Bloom's forehead was covered by a thin sheen of sweat. The first thing he did after hanging up the phone was to remove the tapes for the last two months from the locked cabinet where he kept them, shove them in his briefcase, and lock the briefcase. The next thing was to pick up the phone.

He needed somebody to fix this, and he was not a fixer. He preferred to stay above the messy fray, at what he called "the policy level." When his secretary came on, he snapped, "Get me Wharton's private line." The phone rang twice before he realized

278

what he was doing. Wharton wasn't there, of course. Wharton was in jail on a sex charge. He slammed the receiver down. I'm losing my mind, he thought. This can't be happening.

Rhoda Klepp. Rhoda was in on the whole thing. He remembered the three of them laughing about it over drinks—'We just fucked Karp in the ass'—it must have been just last week. In fact, it had been her idea to bring Floyd in on it. They needed a dependable cop, as she put it, and she had gone to Floyd herself. Rhoda would know what to do.

He buzzed his secretary and told her to get Rhoda Klepp. While he waited, he played with a desk toy, a clear plastic box holding a substance that mimicked breaking surf when you rocked it. It was supposed to soothe. It hadn't worked by the time the secretary rang back. Bloom dropped it like a hot iron and grabbed the phone. The secretary said, "I'm sorry, Mr. Bloom. Ms. Klepp is on sick leave today."

"Sick leave? Call her at home. I need to talk to her."

"I did that, Mr. Bloom. Her mother is there with her. Apparently Ms. Klepp has had a, she said a kind of temporary breakdown. She's, ah, heavily sedated."

"Oh. Well, leave word I want to see her as soon as she's back."

"Yes, sir. Oh, while I have you on: Mr. Karp is here and wants a few minutes. He says it's urgent."

"No! Absolutely not. I can't see him at all today. I'm booked solid."

"Yes, sir, I told him that, but he was very insistent. He said if you couldn't see him now, then you should be sure to watch ABC at seven tonight because they were going to break the, um, Yugoslavian typewriter story."

"Oh. He said that? Well, OK, but just for five minutes."

When Karp entered the big office, Bloom came around the desk with his hand out and his famous charming smile pumping out wattage.

"Butch! So glad to see you're up and around. My God, were we worried when we heard! How are you feeling? Have a seat."

Bloom ushered Karp to one of a set of comfortable leather club chairs arranged around a glass coffee table, and sat down in another.

"Coffee? No? Too early for a drink, ha-ha. Well, what can we do for you?"

Karp peered at him as at a museum specimen: genus Politician, species empty suit. He thought, how can a man be so phony and still process real food and air? At length he said, "It's a legal problem—evidentiary law. I thought I'd consult with you before I did anything."

"Sure. Glad to help. That's what I'm here for, hah-hah. What is it?"

"Last week a police officer tried to palm off on me some evidence in the Karavitch case, evidence that was the result of unlawful collusion between the defense, in the person of the translator, Stefan Terzich, and the police. If I had accepted this tainted evidence, of course, it would have compromised our entire case. Luckily I did not. I have written statements from both the officer, Flanagan, and the translator, that confirms that the presentation of this evidence was part of a conscious plot to destroy our case and, incidentally, to ruin me."

"Come now! Isn't that a bit extreme?"

The tone of this remark was hearty, as usual, but Karp could see the tightness around Bloom's eyes and the pearls of sweat on his upper lip. The man was frightened half to death.

"Yes, it did seem hard to believe. Who would want to do that? It was a real mystery, until last night, when someone placed on my desk additional evidence that established beyond doubt the identity of the person responsible for the collusion."

"It did?"

"Yes."

"Who was it?"

"You."

"Me?"

"Yes, you and Arthur Bingham Roberts conspired to concoct the taint and palm it off on me. Here's the evidence." Karp reached into his suit pocket, pulled out four cassette tapes, and placed them in front of Bloom on the coffee table. Bloom bent forward rigidly at the waist, his hands gripping the ends of the armrests, white-fingered, the smile freezing into a rictus of terror.

"These are tapes of telephone conversations you had and recorded during the past two months. One of them has a conversation between you and Roberts that outlines the entire plot. Other conversations between you and some of your staff confirm it. They're copies, of course. I suppose you still have the originals."

Bloom darted a glance at his briefcase, then looked up at Karp. He cleared his throat, but his voice still croaked. "This was illegally obtained. You can't use this in court."

"Yes, I agree. Of course, given the statements I've taken down alluding to the involvement of your office and Roberts in this thing, there's certainly probable cause to subpoena the originals."

"It was Wharton's idea."

"Oh?"

"Yes, he worked it all out with Roberts. You don't understand the kind of pressure we were under. You have no idea in the world. Important people are involved. Issues of national security."

280

Bloom stammered and flung his hands up in the air, as if to illustrate the futility of explaining how important it all was. "That man, Karavitch, he knows too much. It's absolutely impossible for him to be allowed to go to open trial. Impossible. So we had to . . . so Wharton had to set it up. I knew it was wrong."

"What did he know?"

"Who?"

"Karavitch. What did he know that was so important? Did they tell you?"

Bloom looked shocked. "No, God, no. It's top secret. They said national security, I told you."

"But *I* know."

"You do?"

"Yes. Karavitch is actually a man named Josef Dreb, a Nazi war criminal, who murdered the real Karavitch and took his identity. During the war, not only did he kill Jews and other civilians, but he also murdered a number of Allied flyers. Despite that, he was recruited into the U.S. intelligence services by men that knew who he really was and most likely what he had done. It didn't matter to them because it was, as you keep saying, national security. There's other stuff, but that's the nut of it. This whole thing has been about protecting those men. Your part was springing a Nazi mass murderer. That's the national security angle. That's why you compromised the integrity of the District Attorney's office."

"My God!" Bloom collapsed back in his chair and stared into space. He seemed to be deflating as Karp watched, like a rubber raft with a hole in it. Karp stood up. Bloom shook himself and said, "What! Where are you going?"

"Back to my office."

"But—but, what are you going to do?"

"Do? Well, I'm going to continue to prosecute the Karavitch case, for one thing."

"No, not that shit! About me—these tapes."

"I don't know. What do you suggest?"

"What do you want?" said Bloom, his eyes darting like frightened roaches.

"Want? I don't understand." Karp stared at Bloom in silence, watching the expressions flicker over his sweaty face.

"I mean," Bloom said at last, "I just thought that while you're here, hah, we could discuss your career. Now that business about the bureau chief job, that was all Wharton's doing. There's no reason why we couldn't put you right back there."

"In the bureau chief slot?"

"I meant the assistant bureau chief slot. No, no, of course, the bureau chief. Needs some new blood in there, absolutely."

"I agree. Well, that's a pleasant surprise. And ah, speaking of Wharton, he's been very resistant to getting Marlene Ciampi's appeal for compensation approved. Maybe you could—"

"Of course, anything I can do—oh, no!" Bloom seemed genuinely stricken.

"What's wrong?"

"We denied the appeal already. It's out of our hands. I'll have to go to Albany on that."

"Well, whatever you can do. I have to go back down now. I have some interrogations scheduled."

"Is that it?"

"Sure."

"But . . . these tapes. What about the . . . you know."

"What about them?" Karp said mildly. "I uncovered evidence of a serious crime and I turned it over to you. You're the district attorney."

"Christ on a crutch!" Marlene said. "I would've given anything to have seen his face when you said that—'You're the district attorney.' He must of messed his pants."

They were in Karp's office, waiting for the cops to bring in the hijackers. Karp was in his swivel chair and Marlene was perched on the edge of the desk, smoking.

"I'm surprised you were so calm. You must have wanted to ream him up one side and down the other."

"Yeah, but the game's over and I won by twenty. It's an old jock habit. Also, I'm pretty sure he bugs his office too. So I wanted to get on the record that there was no quid pro quo."

"You think he understood that we kept another copy of the tapes?"

"God, yes! He's not that stupid. He's finished and he knows it. Next case."

"Yeah. Want to go over our game plan one more time?"

"Sure." He was looking at the poster of the young Karavitch still pinned to the wall. He continued to do so as Marlene went over the line of questioning she intended to pursue with Cindy Karavitch. There was something wrong with the poster. He had felt it every time he looked at the blank photo of the young man, the real Djordje Karavitch, dead these thirty years. Maybe.

"Hey, are you listening? I just asked you a question," Marlene said peevishly. "Why are you staring at that poster?"

Karp turned around, his face lit with a grin of pure delight. "I just figured it out. Our shot from left field."

21

A MONTH OR SO in captivity had not done Cindy Wilson Karavitch any harm, Marlene thought, at least not physically. She had gained some weight, which had softened her features and given her a lush sensuality. You could get it, but not on the first date. Her body made even the dull jail uniform look good, and her shoulder-length blond hair was bright and pulled neatly back into a ponytail that made her look much younger than her thirty-five years.

She also seemed more relaxed than she had been when first captured. Jail agrees with some people, Marlene thought, or maybe it was just getting away from her husband and her boyfriend, a furlough from the sexual wars.

And she was a lot more relaxed than John Evans, who sat by her side across the broad table from Marlene, stiff, drawn, and twitching around the eyes. Marlene looked him in the eye. He did not meet her gaze for more than a second. A broken reed, she thought. If she brought out the thumb screws he might demur, but otherwise she was being given a free ride with this witness.

Marlene introduced herself and the stenographer at the far end of the table. Then she said, "Mrs. Karavitch, although I'm sure your lawyer has told you that you are not obliged to say anything to us, nothing prevents you from telling us anything you please. Also, you should know that in sentencing, the court may take into account the extent to which the defendant has cooperated in the interest of justice. This does not constitute a promise of leniency in exchange for information. I would also remind you that you cannot testify against your husband with respect to confidential, personal conversations had between the two of you. Is all that clear?"

The woman nodded, and Marlene continued. "Good. Now, Mrs. Karavitch—can I call you Cindy?—thank you. Cindy, I need to establish some background. You are now thirty-five years old and are employed as a clerk at Transistor Master, a TV and electronics repair shop owned by Pavle Macek?"

Cindy Karavitch had a low voice, only a little louder than a whisper. "Yes. Assistant manager really."

"And you are a college graduate?"

"Yes. University of Montana. I majored in art. And cheerleading." A nervous laugh.

"And you are originally from . . . ?"

"Montana. Near Helena. My dad ran a car wash near the university."

"I see. Could you tell me briefly how you came to meet and marry Djordje Karavitch?"

"I met him in New York. I made a trip here after graduation to see the museums. There aren't too many Impressionists in Montana, or anything else. We met in the Museum of Modern Art. I was looking at a Kandinsky, and he came up and asked me would I like to know where that picture came from. When I said yes, he began talking about the depths of the Slavic soul. I never heard anybody talk like that before. He took me for lunch to the members' dining room on the top floor. I remember how impressed I was—a member!"

As Cindy talked she became more animated, as if in talking about her youth she was rekindling it. Marlene put in, "And this was when, please?"

"Twelve years ago. I was twenty-three. God, was I green!"

"And that would make him, what? Fifty-four?"

"Yes, but he didn't look it. He looked fifteen years younger. Anyway, I was thrilled. Here was this sophisticated European man talking to me about art and literature, and about stuff I never heard of—history, politics, and Croatia. And he was taking me seriously. He would listen and nod when I talked, not that I talked very much. I just wanted to hear that voice roll over me. We stayed up half the night at this little café he took me to. All these people would come by and talk to him in foreign languages. You could see all the respect they had for him.

"I was knocked out, you know? My experience with men was limited to frat parties and drives in the pickup out to the rock quarry. He took me back to my hotel that night and kissed my hand. I about fell over. Not much hand kissing goes on in Helena.

"I saw him every day, all day, during my stay in the city. We went to museums, concerts, restaurants, everything. He bought me clothes and flowers. But most of all, I remember the talk. About the war, and Croatia, always Croatia, and his mission to liberate it, to make it great again, and all. I guess it, his mission, just thrilled me. It was like being in a movie—dramatic, like that."

Marlene thought, the woman is gushing like a pump. It must be years since anybody's let her get out two sentences in a row. She nodded amiably and made sympathetic noises as Cindy went on.

"Anyway, I went back to Helena, promising to write, but I didn't think I'd ever see or hear from him again. Was I wrong! As soon as I got home, these letters started to arrive—long, beautiful letters. Also flowers and gifts. Well, my dad was really mad when he found out Djordje was near as old as him. Then he took a heart attack and died. He was only fifty-eight. After that there didn't seem any point in staying around. I mean, my ma and I never got along. So Djordje sent me a ticket and I went back to New York, and we got married."

"I see. That sounds really romantic. So did it work out? Has it been a happy marriage?"

Cindy frowned and looked hard at Marlene. "How come you want to know this stuff?"

"Just background, like I said. I'd like to know how a cheerleader from Montana ended up helping a group of Croat terrorists hijack an airliner and kill a policeman."

A flush appeared on Cindy's face, and she looked toward Evans, who shrugged and mumbled something in her ear. She turned back to Marlene and said, "I don't know anything about any policeman and we're not terrorists."

"Oh, no? What are you, then?"

"Freedom fighters. And my husband is a great national hero of Croatia. He was a hero in the war. He lives and breathes the struggle to liberate the Croatian people from the slavery of godless communism. And he's been honored by the Catholic Church. And I'm proud to be a part of the struggle."

"I see. So you're proud of what you did, what your husband does?"

"Yes, I am. I'm completely committed to the armed struggle for a free Croatia under the leadership of Djordje Karavitch."

Marlene noted that the woman had entirely changed during the past minute. The almost childish woman gushing about her youthful romance was gone. In her place was someone trying hard to be a tough revolutionary, a clone of Djordje Karavitch.

"Right. Cindy, does your husband have any scars on his body?"

"Scars. Yes. From war wounds. He was a hero in the war."

"Does he have any tattoos?"

"No."

"Does he have a scar under his right armpit, between two and three inches long?"

"Yes, he does. How did you know?"

285

"We'll talk about that later. Let's talk about your relationship. You obviously care about him very much."

"Yes, I do."

"Uh-huh. Even though he bats you around?"

"I beg your pardon?"

"When did he start beating you up? He does beat you, doesn't he?"

"Certainly not. Who told you that?"

Marlene sighed. "Nobody had to tell me, sister. I spend half my life with victims of domestic violence. You've got the look. But I guess I could find out easy enough—neighbors see a lot and they love to talk about stuff like that."

Another transformation. Cindy's face grew hard, her fine jaw tightened, and her blue eyes popped with anger. Her voice grew loud, strident. "What do they know? They don't know anything about it. You don't know anything. It was discipline. A fighter has to be perfect. I did everything for him. I became a Catholic. I learned the language, the history, hours and hours, listening to him talking. And then I had to give the right answers, perfectly. Sometimes I couldn't, I was still too soft, a soft, materialistic American baby-girl. But I deserved it. He did it where it wouldn't show. You can't understand what it was like—he was making me a perfect hard tool of the struggle. And I was, I was perfect."

"I see. And your affair with Pavle Macek, was that part of the struggle, too?"

A shadow of fear crossed her face. "I never did! How did you . . . I mean, what are you talking about?"

"Come on, sister, you haven't been exactly discreet. That little expedition to the john on the airplane? Does your husband know?"

"No! It's nothing with Macek. It's just something that happened. Macek is a tool of the struggle, also. And he was a hero in the war, with Djordje."

"OK, now it seems to me that despite this perfect discipline, the tools of the struggle are a little blunt. You screwed up the hijack, you blew up a cop, and now you're in jail. Did Karavitch plan this mess?"

Cindy shook her head and a pitying smile appeared on her lips. "You think we failed? You have no idea, no idea at all. We are martyrs. We lit a torch for the Croatian people that will never go out. In Croatia they sing ballads about heroes who fell against the Turks five hundred years ago. They'll sing the same kind of songs about Karavitch five hundred years from now, and about all of us. You think they'll sing any songs about you, Miss Ciampi?"

"I never gave it much thought. Who had the idea of rigging the bomb with a booby trap? Was that Karavitch, too?"

She became wary. "You said I didn't have to say anything against my husband."

"No, you don't. But Macek, the things were made in his shop. He must have done the actual work."

"We all did. We all did it together," she declared proudly.

That's a lie, Marlene thought, everybody in your little cell was playing a different game. She closed her notepad and said casually, "Well, Cindy, thank you for your cooperation. I think that will be all for now. Oh, by the way, has it ever been suggested to you that your husband is someone other than Djordje Karavitch, the Croatian hero? That he might be a German SS officer named Josef Dreb?"

The reaction was explosive. Cindy Karavitch came out of her chair like a parting steel cable, her face white with rage. "That's bullshit!" she cried. "Bullshit! Why are you fucking with my mind?" She turned to the startled Evans. "I'm tired of this. Get me the fuck out of here!"

Then her face went bright red and she brought her hand up over her mouth. "Oh, my God, my language. Oh, God, he hates me to use bad language." She looked pleadingly at Marlene. "You won't tell him, will you?"

"No, dear," Marlene said gently, "your secret is safe with me."

"So what do you think?" Karp asked after Marlene had given him a quick briefing on her interrogation of Cindy Karavitch. The two of them were huddled in the hallway outside the interrogation room, waiting for the guards to bring in Pavle Macek.

"What do I think? A nut case, is what I think. Christ, Butchie, it was like Three Faces of Eve in there. She's got her whole life built around this sado-maz relationship with the old man. He tortures her and she takes it, because it's for the struggle. She went batshit when I suggested that Georgie the K. might not be Mr. Croatia. I don't think she knows, and if she suspects, she's buried it deep, about two feet under Rosebud. Another thing—she might rat out Macek, but she's tied to the old man solid."

"Yeah, as long as he's who she thinks he is. Does he have the scar?"

"She says yes."

"OK, that's great, I can use all that. See you later."

When Karp came into the interrogation room, Evans was whispering in Macek's ear. Whatever he was saying was not making Macek any happier. He looked like a caged wolf with an ingrown fang. Karp went through the usual preliminaries, then said, "Mr. Macek, just for background, could you tell me how you first met Djordje Karavitch?"

Macek glanced nervously at Evans, who nodded. When he spoke, his voice was a slow growl. "It was during the war, in 1943. I was a schoolboy. This was in a little town outside Glina, in Croatia. My father was an important man, a leader of the Croat Peasant Party. One night there was an attack by the partisans, the communists. They took over the town and sent squads to the homes of prominent people, those who supported the Pavelic regime. I woke up to hear voices from the parlor downstairs, shouts. I heard my mother screaming. There were shots, explosions all around. I was frightened and hid under the bed. When I came downstairs I found my mother dead in the doorway. My father had been shot against the wall and thrown into the farmyard. Our pig was eating him.

"The *ustashi* troops came and drove the partisans away. I went to the town square to find someone to bury my parents. The *ustashi* had captured some communists. They were beating and kicking them around the square and stabbing them with their knives. Then they started to cut their throats. I went up to one of the *ustashi* officers who were watching this, and I said who I was and what had happened in my house, and could they help me with my parents. One officer said he would send some men. Then I asked if I could kill one of the communists. The officer laughed and said if I had the balls for it I could, and gave me his knife. That was Karavitch.

"I took the knife and cut the communist's throat. I felt nothing for him, I just thought, here might be the one who killed my mother. Afterward, Karavitch put his arm around me and said I was now a child of the Croatian nation, and he would take care of me. From that day to this day, we have been together."

"Uh-huh. OK, let's bring it a little closer to the present. Who was responsible for planning the hijacking of Flight 501?"

A slight hesitation. "We all were equally."

"Including Raditch? I think he would have a hard time planning which shoe to put on first."

"No, not Raditch, but the rest, all of us were equal."

"Really? I thought Karavitch was the leader."

"Of course. Yes, he is the leader."

"So it was his idea."

"He led and we all contributed our parts."

"And your part was manufacturing the bombs?"

"No."

"The fake bomb on the plane and the real one that was booby-trapped to kill a policeman?"

"I don't wish to answer this question."

"OK, let's try something else. You must really admire Mr. Karavitch, isn't that true?"

"Yes, he is the greatest man I have ever known."

"How about Mrs. Karavitch? Do you admire her too?"

"She is a fine woman."

"I'm sure she is. Does the great man know you are sleeping with her?"

"That is a lie!"

"I'm afraid it isn't, Mr. Macek. There are witnesses to your carrying-on while aboard Flight 501, and the relationship has been confirmed by Mrs. Karavitch herself not ten minutes ago. Mrs. Karavitch was, in fact, quite forthcoming with my colleague. She said that you, and you alone, manufactured the bomb that killed the police officer."

"That is a lie! It was—" He stopped and pressed his mouth tightly into a white line under his fierce mustache.

"It was who, Mr. Macek?"

"I do not wish to answer this question."

"That's all right, Mr. Macek. We know you built the bomb, and we know where, and what with. You were with Karavitch during the war. You were a bright kid, it shouldn't have been hard to learn how to rig a RDO1Z booby trap. It would have been nothing for you to attach it to the pot bomb you made with the Soviet hand grenade you got from the Cubans at Tel-Air. No, we know all that. What we don't know is why. Why would a guy like Karavitch with a nice little terrorist network of his own, surrounded by worshipful supporters, pull a stunt like hijacking a jetliner and killing a cop? Got any ideas on that, Mr. Macek?"

As Karp spoke, Macek's jaw had been dropping by millimeters, until his mouth was nearly wide open. Karp could see his large yellow teeth. His amber eyes were wide and his forehead was slick with sweat. "You know all this? How do you know all this?"

"How? No problem, Mr. Macek. Your girlfriend and her husband decided that you were the disposable side of the triangle. They're singing like birds and you're being set up to take the fall on this. Now, you understand that all parties to a felony murder are equally culpable, but in practice we usually single out the trigger man for special treatment. And that's you. No, don't look at Mr. Evans, Mr. Macek! He can't help you. There're only two people in this room who can help you: me and yourself."

Evans cleared his throat. "Mr. Macek, you are under no compulsion to answer any questions."

Way to go, Evans, Karp thought. Just getting on the record to eliminate the possibility of a legal malpractice suit. "Shut up" is always good advice. Now let's see if your client takes it.

"Mr. Evans is correct, Mr. Macek," he said. "How about it? You want to let things stand as they are? Or would you like to straighten out my impression?"

Macek licked his lips and shook his head, as if to rattle his thoughts into order. "It was her," he said, grinding the words out like hard grain. "It started . . . she came to me in the shop. She knew I wanted her, I wanted her from the first time he brought her around. He would beat her with a strap, and later she would show me the marks he made. On her thighs, her back, and lower down. She would let me touch the marks. I would sympathize. I would say, you should leave him, but always she would go back. He was like God to her. So we started together."

"Did he know?"

"Did he know? Of course, he knew. He knows everything. He came to me, he grabbed my throat, he would have killed me, but then he remembered. If I should die like that, they would find papers that I have hidden with someone. A secret that would destroy him, the great Croatian national hero."

"You mean that Karavitch is really Josef Dreb?"

"My God! You know this?"

"It's all over town. The question is, how come he let you live so long knowing that secret? Why didn't he kill you back in Trieste? Come to that, why did you hang out with him so long?"

Macek said, "Please, I must have a cigarette." He lit one with trembling fingers, sucked the smoke deep, and blew out twin plumes from flared nostrils. "First, you must understand, as I was to Karavitch, so was Karavitch to Dreb. Dreb was a Croatian with the power of the Germans behind him. They used to talk for hours about the world after the war. Over maps they would talk about a Greater Croatia, from the Adriatic to Bulgaria and up to the Danube. Karavitch was a big frog in a small pond, but Dreb was the biggest frog any of us had ever seen. He knew Heydrich, he had talked with Himmler, he dealt with Pavelic as an equal.

"When it started to collapse, Karavitch could not bear it. He was a dreamer, and only that. Dreb had great dreams, but at the root he was a survivor. Karavitch wanted to die in Zagreb, fighting the partisans. But when the partisans broke through the Srem front, Dreb made him escape with the SS. He began to drink. He was useless. When our column was ambushed by the partisans, I had to drag him into the truck. Of all the *ustashi* in the column, only we two escaped. Dreb made the contacts with church groups, using Karavitch's name. They knew him, you see. We had travel papers, Karavitch and I. We parted in Hungary and we thought we would never see Dreb again.

"Karavitch and I wound up in Trieste. We had a tiny room, a little bigger than a closet, and we were lucky to get it. He would lie in bed all day ranting and drunk. I would try to find food for us and grappa for him. Steal it, usually. I found out I was a survivor, too. One day I come back to the room. Dreb is there and Karavitch is lying on the bed with his throat cut. Dreb tells me he found him like this. I believe him. People in those days would kill you for a pair of shoes, a half kilo of cheese. Also, if I don't believe him, if I believe he killed Karavitch himself, then he will know it, and he will kill me too. I was sixteen and I wanted to live.

"So, he says he will take Karavitch's papers and we will escape together. They look very much alike, did I mention that? They could have been brothers. He says he has a contact with the U.S. Army. We will go away and work for them and have lots of food and clothes and not have to run any more. But first he must tattoo numbers under Karavitch's arm, where all the SS have them. Then they will think the body is Dreb. He has the equipment. I don't know where he got it, but he has it, and he does the job. Underneath his own arm there is a bandage. He has taken off his own number.

"So then I realize, he is not going to kill me. He needs me. Who can vouch for Djordje Karavitch better than his little shadow, Pavle Macek? I tell him everything about Karavitch, so he can pass better, and I know a lot about Karavitch: his mother, his father, his schools, he is allergic to milk, everything. Karavitch likes to talk about himself, and I am always there, like a dog at his feet. But with such a man as Dreb, it is a good thing not to be too trusting. So when we come to America I write a paper, and I give it to someone I know, someone important to Croatian affairs here in New York, and say if I die, to open it and tell everyone what is inside."

"That's interesting. Is this just a letter, or is there documentary proof that he isn't Karavitch?"

"There are no documents, only my word, but that is good enough."

Yeah, thought Karp, it was before you started balling his old lady. Now your word isn't worth shit. "OK, go on," he said. "How come you're still with him?"

"As for that, you should also understand that what I have felt for

Karavitch, so now I feel for Dreb. But Dreb is no longer Dreb—he becomes Karavitch. He does all the things Karavitch would do, among the Croatians here in New York, but better even than the real Karavitch would have done. He is stronger, more powerful. And I follow him, and things go well, until her.

"Now he is getting old and she is so young and beautiful, an American, a girl from the West. But he cannot bear such a free creature always around him. So he must break her to his will. And how does he do this? As he learned in Keinschlag, in the SS school there. Discipline. Political lectures. History. We are going back to Croatia, we will crush the reds, the people will rise to welcome us, and so on, year after year.

"And he succeeds. She is on fire to liberate Croatia. To strike a blow. She is tamed, but she is no lapdog. He has made a wolf. He beats her—she loves it, she laughs in his face—'Make me hard,' she says, 'to fight for Croatia.' I am a Croatian, and he is half Croatian, and she never saw Croatia, but she is more Croatian than the two of us together.

"Now she starts to taunt him. You know how emigrés are all the time talking, talking about what they will do, how to make the revolt, how it will be when they are in power. Especially Rukovina, chatter, chatter. She is at all the meetings. Afterward, she mocks us, Karavitch and me. Of course, she speaks Serbo-Croatian, so it's even worse. She says we are not men, that we are chattering grandmothers. We are too fat and comfortable, she says, to really do anything. We are afraid of a little blood. She says this to us, we who have walked to our knees in blood.

"I see it working on him. The Croatian people, the honor, the glory, all he taught her. You see, now he has forgotten he is Dreb. He is really Karavitch. And this plane, this bomb, this is what Karavitch would do, the mad gesture."

"And he got you to make the bomb?"

"Me?" Macek laughed, an unlikely high cackle. "*He* built it. In my shop, as she looked on. She handed him the tools. He had saved this timer switch from the war, and his skill was still what it was. I wished many times as I watched him that he would slip, and we would all be blown to Hell."

"So who did it? Macek or Karavitch?" Marlene asked as they waited in the hallway for Karavitch to be brought up from the pens.

"Damned if I know. Not that it matters. We got the story now and we got our shocker. He's dead meat."

"Get 'em, tiger."

*   *   *

The man who called himself Djordje Karavitch smiled broadly
after Karp had laid out, point by point, the case against him.
"Come, now, Mr. Karp, you must try something better than that. I
have also interrogated prisoners in my time, and of course, the
game is to convince one that the others have betrayed him, so that
he will in turn betray them. I compliment you; you have learned a
good deal about the construction of this bomb you claim has killed
a policeman, and you may have convinced my wife and Macek to
say that I made it. But what is that good for? Do you believe a
man in my position would risk all to construct a booby trap with
the sole purpose of killing a policeman? And you say it was to
impress my wife?

"And yet you know my wife has betrayed me with this man. Will
anyone accept the evidence of these two lovebirds against me? I
would not need the services of so distinguished a law firm as the one
Mr. Evans represents to make a fool of you in court."

"Yes, but it's not likely that you will have the services of Arthur
Bingham Roberts much longer."

"Oh?" Karavitch looked toward Evans, who shrugged.

"Uh-huh. Because the Church put up the money to pay for
defending Djordje Karavitch, who is a kind of hero in its eyes.
And you're not Djordje Karavitch."

The old man barked a laugh. "That is insane. Has someone been
filling your head with nonsense about me?"

"Nope. I figured it out all by myself. With some help from the
Mossad. You know about the Mossad, don't you? You've probably
felt their breath on you from time to time." Karp reached into his
briefcase and pulled out the Yugoslav poster with the young
Karavitch's picture on it. "Would you examine that, please?"

Karavitch took the poster, put on a pair of thick reading glasses,
and looked at it. "So?" he said. "The communists wanted me after
the war. They wanted thousands. What of it?"

"That is you, then?"

"Of course, it is me. It looks like me, it has my name on it. Of
course it is me. What nonsense are you talking?"

"Bear with me a moment, Mr. Karavitch. Would you sign your
name on this paper?" Karp pushed a yellow pad and a pen across
the table.

The old man smiled and signed his "Djordje Karavitch" with a
flourish. "You know, Mr. Karp, in case you have any other old
papers you wish to compare with this, sometimes signatures change
over the years."

"I'm aware of that. But some things never change. I notice you signed with your left hand and took the poster I gave you with your left hand. You are left-handed, are you not?"

"Of course."

"Of course, but you know it's amazing about handedness. It pervades our own lives, but it's one of the last things we remember about others. I bet you couldn't recall the handedness of a single one of your friends or acquaintances. It's not something that ever comes up, except on athletic teams. Now in this poster here, for example, you're writing, and of course, you're using your left hand."

"Of course. What are you driving at, Mr. Karp?"

"Wait, I'm almost there. That's what I thought too. Then I began studying this poster. It's very interesting because it's really a poster within a poster. The subject is photographed in his office, and there's a poster on the wall behind him. Are you familiar with that poster?"

The old man peered at the paper. "Yes, it's a propaganda poster, against the communists."

"Uh-huh. Can you read the writing on it?"

"No, I cannot. It is too blurred. What is the point of this? It's just an old poster."

Karp reached into his briefcase again and took out a hemispherical glass paperweight, a common object on nearly every desk in the building. They made fairly good magnifiers.

"My eyes are better than yours, but I can't read it, either, because it's in Cyrillic script, or so I thought. It looks that way at first glance. But just now I thought to myself, why would a poster on the wall of a Croat nationalist be in Cyrillic script? The Croats use Latin script, don't they?"

The old man did not answer. Karp slammed the paperweight down on the poster. The sound echoed in the room, startling the stenographer. "Now you can read it and so can I. I don't know what it says, but I can read it, because it's not Cyrillic script at all. Those are Latin letters, but they're reversed. The negative was reversed when it was printed. It must have been a rush job during the war. Djordje Karavitch is writing with his right hand, isn't he, Hauptsturmfuehrer Josef Karl Dreb?"

The old man waved his hand weakly in front of his face, as if waving away flies. "I don't know what you are talking about. I am Djordje Karavitch."

"No, you're not. This photograph proves you're not. And it would be child's play to get the records, school records, dental records, medical records, to demonstrate it beyond a shadow of a doubt. The Yugoslavs would love to help and so would the Israelis.

Especially the Israelis. No, your scam is based on nobody looking very closely, on the fact that you fixed it so that everyone thought that Dreb was dead, on the acceptance of the man who knew Karavitch best, Pavle Macek."

"I am Karavitch," the old man intoned.

"Yes. And you're going to Attica for life as Karavitch. Because, you Nazi fucker, you are going to plead guilty to the top count of the indictment, and you're going to rat out your friends too, because if you don't, this—who you really are, Dreb—will be all over town. The Croatians will spit on you. The Church will wash its hands. Your wife will know she married a goddamn fake. You'll stand in a glass cage in Jerusalem and whine that you vas only following orderz, and the Jews will hang your filthy ass."

"I am Karavitch. *I am Karavitch!*" screamed the old man. His face was turning red and flecks of spittle flew through the air and fell to the tabletop.

"Calm down your client, counselor," said Karp to the white-faced Evans. "He needs some legal advice."

As Karp left the room, the old man began to shout once again his identity to the world, his voice high and cracking.

"My hero," said Marlene.

"Yeah, who was that masked man? Christ, Marlene, I'm dead. When was the last time I got a night's sleep?"

"I think a week after this past Shevuos. I might even give up my chance to possess your fine young body for eight straight."

"I'm not that tired."

"Oh, you thing! So, that's it. One down, only six hundred and twelve homicides to go. It all worked out."

"Yeah. Except for one detail. Your compensation. I don't trust Bloom worth a shit to muscle the state. In fact, he could fuck it up so bad that we'd never see daylight and never prove that it was him that screwed us."

"Oh, that. Well, you did your best—"

"Bullshit. I haven't started. Here, sit on my lap so your ear's next to the phone. I want you to hear this."

She did so, squirming nicely, while Karp dialed a long-distance number. "This is his private number. I screwed it out of Evans. Only presidents and above get this one."

The phone rang for two rings and someone picked it up.

"Hello?" said the golden voice of Arthur Bingham Roberts.

"Roberts? Karp here, of the New York DA."

The voice lost forty degrees of warmth. "Yes? What do you want?"

"Well, Roberts, I want a favor."

"A favor?"

"Yeah, a legal favor. I want to retain you as counsel in a compensation case. I want you to sue the State of New York for a friend of mine."

"You can't be serious."

"Oh, I'm dead serious, Roberts. It won't be hard to win, because justice is on our side, and justice is something I know you dote on. You and our fine district attorney. Come on, say you'll take the case. For me." A pause.

"Very well. One of my associates will contact you."

"Uh-uh, Roberts, no associates. I want you up there in Albany personally. After all, it *is* the most important case of your career, because if you lose it, I guarantee you won't have a career." A longer pause.

"I see. I should warn you that my fees are quite high in cases like this."

"Oh, get real, Roberts. Your fee is zero on this one. *Nada*. We get *all* the money, and it better be a whole shitload of it. Am I making myself clear?" The longest pause of all.

"Perfectly clear. Is that all?"

Marlene put her soft lips to Karp's ear and whispered, "Ask him if he does divorce work."